YOU WERE WARNED

BOOK 2 OF
THE CONVENTION OF FIENDS

by

Benjamin Gorman

Trigger Warning for
The Convention of Fiends
Series

As a school teacher, I learned that just about anything can be a trigger for an anxiety/PTSD attack for someone out there. I was once showing the most innocuous of films, and a student had a PTSD attack because, she realized during the movie, it was the exact one which had been playing when she experienced a traumatic event. So no list like this is ever complete.

That being said, I do think trigger warnings identifying some common triggers are valuable in case you, Dear Reader, are aware of some content which could threaten your mental health. Your health is more important than my story, and I want to give you this list for the entire series so you don't get invested and then find you shouldn't have taken these books on right now.

But some of you may read this list and think, "That sounds right up my alley." And that's fine. Warnings are also invitations to mischief.

Some of these triggers take the form of comments by the antagonists, so they are obviously things I oppose, but you should be aware they exist in the text:

- references racism, sexism, religious bigotry
- a description of an attempted sexual assault
- trolls waggling their naughty bits non-consensually

Most of the sexuality is loving and consensual, but if you are not in a mental place to read about it, this series does contain:

- lesbian sex
- sexual encounters between a human woman and vampire (arguably bestiality)
- a sexual encounter between a human woman and a dragon (bestiality)

And, though I didn't set out to write a story with so much violence, it turns out, when monsters are involved, one ends up with:

- vampires killing people
- werewolves killing people
- werewolves and vampires killing one another
- people killing a vampire
- merfolk killing people
- people killing merfolk

- a minotaur killing a person
- lots of other monsters attempting to kill people
- trolls attempting to kill monsters by flinging flaming feces
- vampires being tortured by trolls
- a dragon killing lots of other monsters
- panicked trolls stampeding upon, and almost certainly killing, one another
- gun violence
- sword violence
- hand-to-hand violence
- biting
- a warlock seducing people while glamoured (which is, technically, a form of sexual assault)
- a giant tentacle monster killing and consuming like … tons of people (and merfolk)
- a golem punching a Nazi to death

Perhaps most challenging, our protagonist struggles with

- depression
- suicidal ideation

Oh, and characters use "bad words." (There's no such thing. But they do use words some people find offensive.)

Take care of yourself. You were warned!

Novels by Benjamin Gorman

The Sum of Our Gods

Corporate High School

The Digital Storm:
A Science Fiction Reimagining of
William Shakespeare's The Tempest

Don't Read This Book
Book 1 of The Convention of Fiends

You People Are Monsters
Book 3 of The Convention of Fiends

Poetry Collections

When She Leaves Me:
A Story Told In Poems

This Uneven Universe

Non-Fiction

Dear America: A Breakup Letter

YOU WERE WARNED

BOOK 2 OF

THE CONVENTION OF FIENDS

Dedication

*For those who wonder
if it's all worthwhile: Hold on.
Remain. Uncertain.*

"Thou and my bosom henceforth shall be twain."

-*William Shakespeare*
Romeo and Juliet

Prologue

"Stupid fucking humans. I am not going to be killed by a bunch of humans. Not today. Not ever."

Nathaniel kept muttering curses against the lower species as he stumbled through the last of the trees. Guided mostly by his sense of smell and the direction of the light, he made his way through the edge of the forest toward the salt air and the faint glow of the approaching dawn. Instinct screamed to hide from the light, but he still had enough of his wits about him to override that animal impulse and strategize toward the deeper drive to survive. Nathaniel's vision, normally much more sensitive than any human's, had begun to fail him shortly after the first dart hit. His long black hair was pulled back into its usual ponytail, so his hair wasn't obscuring his sight, but the vampire perceived the dark forest like a human looking through a veil. The forest was filled with larch trees, those conifers with branches of different lengths which made them look less like triangular pines and more like their distant deciduous cousins, and their silhouetted branches merged into interlocking tentacles, their depths mysterious. They made him hesitant. The humans were still hunting him, but he didn't know that. He hoped he'd lost them, but he couldn't be sure. He didn't want to run into the branches and make too much noise or cause obvious motion. The humans couldn't match his speed under normal circumstances, but he doubted himself. At one stutter step, he even looked back over his shoulder, then chided himself. *If I can't see the trees, how am I going to see the humans? Stupid. I'd hear them first anyway. Wouldn't I? Do my ears still work? Fucking humans!* He waggled his head to fling out some of the pain and confusion, then leaned into his run through the forest. The cold wind on his face told him he was moving faster than any human could. "I'm going to make it," he whispered.

Deceiving oneself is often the worst betrayal.

Nathaniel ducked under the last of the waving fuzzy shapes and took in the horizon as best he could, mostly just a line of faint light in the midst of gray and gray and gray. He knew the darkness below was the beach, the darkness above a receding night sky. If he could make it across the sand and snow, then wade and crawl and swim and plunge, he could get far enough beneath the surface to avoid the light. And then, he convinced himself, he'd hold his breath and swim far enough away to escape the humans before returning to shore to bury himself and heal. It would hurt. He couldn't hold his breath all day, a few hours maybe, and then he'd have to surface and endure the light long enough to bury himself. But he thought he could do it.

The water would be cold, and that would be a comfort. Every part of him felt like it was on fire. The darts had been syringes, and the liquid inside contained silver, so every vein and artery was melting and then doing its best to heal as it pumped the poison along. These humans, Nathaniel admitted, were clearly professionals. He reluctantly afforded them a tiny dollop of respect. Sure, humans in general had adopted an almost completely inverted value system, desiring most those baubles with the least survival value and assigning the most important labor the least compensation, but these particular humans were at least working on eliminating the apex predators who fed on their species. That showed some forethought and species-level self preservation most individual humans lacked. But the vampire remained confident in his ability to escape them.

The silver was melting his soft tissue. The jelly in his eyes had proven too fragile. He tried to hear the waves and realized his tympanic membranes hadn't held up, either. Only that constant horizon line, like a pilot's turn-and-slip indicator, kept him from leaning too much one way or the other. His sense of balance was shot. The sea water would be barely above freezing here, north of Vladivostok, Russia, in the Sea of Japan, and that would be just fine. His heart would slow, the blood would thicken, and he'd be able to push the silver out of his system. It would hurt, but he couldn't imagine the pain being any greater than the agony he was currently experiencing.

The cliff was not part of his plan. Just beyond the last of the trees, Nathaniel's ankles twisted as he made his way over increasingly rocky ground, but he kept going. And then the ground was gone.

He had a momentary flash of memory from two hundred years earlier, before he was a vampire. Back then they'd called someone his age a young man. It was before teenagers were invented. He'd been messing around with friends after dark, drinking and throwing rocks at the whale oil lanterns the city had put up. If you hit them just right, they would break, spill oil onto the cobblestones, and then light it on fire in a whoosh which told all the boys you'd succeeded. Marvelous fun magnified by the threat of getting caught and the danger of starting a fire, it was a mischievous boy's dream, but it took a man's skill, and Nathaniel was young enough to be right in the sweet spot in between. After a success and a whoosh and the attendant cries, someone claimed to have heard the constable coming, and they all ran for home before verifying for themselves. Unharmed and uncaught, he'd run into the door of his family's cottage with a shoulder, quietly poked the key home, turned it, and slipped inside, then closed the door as softly as he could. He knew his mother would box his ears if she discovered him coming home so late, and that would be better than what he'd get if she woke his father. His parents slept in a room on the ground floor, and he shared a room with his three younger brothers upstairs. He crept past his parents' door and into the kitchen, using his hands to find his way in the darkness, until one bumped into the banister. Then he made his way around to the stairs. The house shared a wall with the one next door, and the pitched roofs connected between them, so the space at the top of the staircase was the highest point in the house; he didn't have to duck and worry about hitting his head on the rafters like he did on the side of the room where his bed and his sleeping brothers' beds lay. Leaning on the banister in the darkness, he carefully removed his boots and hugged them to his chest with one arm. Excited to be past his parents' room and emboldened by the silence of his stocking feet, he ran up the stairs.

Too fast. He'd lived in the house all his life, but Nathaniel had grown so much over the last year, his native sense of the space was compromised. In the light of day (never particularly bright in the dim house, but bright enough), he'd started taking the stairs two and then three at a time, just to enjoy the new length of his legs. Now, in the darkness, he carefully planted his toes on each one, but somehow he'd lost count of the number of stairs. When he got to the top, he thought he still had a few more to go. One moment he was ascending quickly, and the next he was falling even faster, but in between, before his gangly body crashed to the floor, before his brothers woke up laughing, before his mother cried out and his father stomped up the stairs and kicked at him in the darkness until he crawled to his bed and got a few lashes from his father's belt as a final goodnight, in that tiny moment in between, he'd been weightless at the top of the parabola, floating in the perfect darkness of his room, a dust mote in the night sky, a solitary star.

He'd remembered the experience a hundred and fifty years later when he first saw images of men in blocky suits floating in space. Then he'd forgotten his memory. Vampires do not dwell on their human lives. They don't carry regrets or nostalgia. The hunger takes care of that. Humans are their food. Who wants to reminisce about the days when one was food?

He remembered now. Though the silver melting his insides slowed him considerably from his normal super-human speed, he was still running as fast as a human track star when the ground disappeared. He barely had time to flail, his once perfect vampire body reverted to that gangly teenage awkwardness in midair, and then he crashed into the rocks. Bones which should have been able to shrug off such an impact, weakened by the silver, cracked when he landed on his right shoulder, his hip, his shin, and the side of his face. The material in his right eye gave up the fight and splashed out onto the rocks like a water balloon. His clavicle broke completely, so when he hauled himself up to his feet, one shoulder hung forward and threw him off balance. He tried to see the glow of the horizon line to regulate himself, but he overcompensated and fell onto his left side, this time into a more forgiving mixture of snow, ice, and sand.

Dazed and unsure if he was completely blind or just had his only remaining eye buried in the icy loam, he tried to remember the plan. He knew he had to get to the water, but he wasn't sure why. His body was on fire, he was sure of it. *Do I just need to put the fire out? Maybe my brain has also burned up because I think I was running towards the sunrise. Why would I do that?*

That's when the first arrow hit him. It embedded itself in his butt cheek and had a powerful restorative effect on his memory. *Fucking humans!*

He clambered to his feet and shuffled toward the sound of the waves. Blinking, he found he could still make out a bit of a hazy line of light. *Good. I still have some of one eye.* Though he knew it was a risk to his balance, he made an effort to reach back with his right arm, hoping to grab the arrow. But that arm, connected to that floppy shoulder wobbling on that broken clavicle, wouldn't cooperate. He stopped completely so he wouldn't fall, reached back with his left, and swiped at the arrow on the far side of his backside. *It's too embarrassing,* he thought. *I'm not dying with an arrow sticking out of my ass.* And then he hissed aloud, "Fucking humans." He grabbed the arrow and pulled it free without much pain, not enough to register compared to what was happening inside him. He recognized the arrow was too light to be wood, some kind of carbon fiber, and it didn't even have a silver tip. *What are the humans trying to do?*

He dropped it and took another step. The next arrow passed through his leg, between his Achilles tendon and his ankle, and stuck into the ground. "The fuck?" Were the humans too far away to hit him? he wondered.

The third arrow hit the top of his foot, rudely shoved the bones apart, and embedded itself in the sand as well. "Oh." He recognized two things at once. Before the fourth, fifth, sixth, and seventh arrows struck his feet and ankles, he figured out the motivation. He also realized the archers were not just chasing him through the forest. They were ahead of him on the beach, too. They were all around him. He was dying, he was pinned like a butterfly on a spreading board, and the sun was coming up. He decided to remain standing rather than give them a reason to add some more arrows. He was fucked.

"So, you're pretty well fucked, aren't you?" a voice said. It was low and gravelly, and the vampire could tell the human was shouting a bit to compensate for his diminished hearing. The voice came from further down the beach and off to his right. This was the man who'd stood between him and the water, the one who had fired the arrow into his foot.

"Sure seems that way," the vampire said.

"It does. It does." The man had some kind of drawl the vampire couldn't quite place. American, but not Southern. Midwest, but not too far north. He sounded like a farmer. "So, a little test to see how far gone you are. You know those arrows don't have any silver in 'em, right?"

The vampire decided to make fun of the man's accent. He could mimic accents in lots of languages, so it came easily. "Yep. Yessiree, partner."

"Good. And you know you got a healthy dose of silver in that dart back in town, right?"

Contemplating this fact took some of the joy out of the accent. "Yep."

"So when I tell you the bullets in my gun are silver, you still have enough of your brain left to figure out we could have put you down already, and your only chance to buy yourself some last minutes of life is to hold really still, right?"

The vampire didn't move. "What do you want?"

"I would like to know whatever you can tell me about The Convention of Fiends. The location of the annual meeting would be a good start."

The vampire did his best to continue not moving. "You're that monster hunter, aren't you?"

"One of 'em, yeah. Name's Esau."

"That's a stupid name," the vampire said.

"I like it. Glad my parents didn't ask your opinion."

"Ah. Your parents. Is that what this is about? Did I kill them? If so, please know I seduce my victims before I kill them. So, your mother? She loved it. Then I killed her. Or was it some other monster, and you're just using me to get to The Convention for your revenge?"

There was a silence. The vampire thought he might have goaded the hunter a bit. But when Esau spoke, the vampire could hear the smile in his voice. "My dad made it to the ripe ol' human age of 82 before he fell off a ladder putting up Christmas lights on the house. Mom is still with us, living in a nice facility. Seems content though she's not always sure what year it is."

Now it was the vampire's turn to smile. "So I still have a chance with her, then."

Esau laughed. "Much as she might appreciate more visitors in the nursing home, I don't think you have the time in your schedule."

The vampire heard other voices laughing, some male, some female, one woman's particularly loud. They were all around him.

"So," Esau continued, "here's the deal. Pretty simple. You tell me everything I want to know, and I'll shoot you. You don't, we'll stand around until the sun comes up and burns you to charcoal. I know that's not like the movies. At this latitude and overcast as it is, it will start like a bad sunburn and take all goddamned day. Would be a boring movie. But you'll find I am a very patient man."

A woman's voice, the loud laugher, broke in. "Plus, we have supplies!" Then there was a repetitive sound the vampire couldn't quite make out. She was patting something in a plastic bag, but Nathaniel wasn't capable of identifying the marshmallows by sound or smell anymore.

"I'm not going to tell you humans anything," the vampire said. Nathaniel wanted to sound tough, or at least certain, but Esau could hear the fear in his voice.

Esau was tall enough that when he flopped his head forward in mock disappointment and shook it back and forth slowly, his short-cropped gray beard scratching against the front of his winter coat, he was still taller than his first lieutenant. "Torreblanca," he said, butchering her name as always with his flat Nebraska accent, "you might as well break 'em out. Men, cook your marshmallows however you like 'em. But please remember to use long sticks, and none of you try setting a graham cracker on a rock near him. He can still move faster than you think. It would be a stupid way to go."

Nathaniel heard some rueful chuckles and decided that moment was his best chance. He could also hear the change in Esau's voice and knew the man's head was lowered. Nathaniel twisted at the waist, his feet yanking at the arrows, ripping up the frozen beach but also tearing his flesh and cracking a few bones. Because of his incredible speed, he managed to make it an entire step toward Esau before all the new arrows hit him and he went down. He'd been lunging with his left hand out, fingers close together and flat, his sharp nails aimed like an axe head. When the new arrows caught his feet and legs, he sprawled and fell onto his useless right shoulder and discovered the broken clavicle could jab into his body cavity in a new way.

Then, to add insult to insult to insult to injury after injury, someone put an arrow through his outstretched hand. For the first time in two hundred years, he found he didn't have the strength to move. And with one useless arm beneath him, he was stuck facing the impending dawn. The horizon, such a dim glow minutes before, suddenly lit up a solid white as the sun inched over the edge of the world. The vampire wrinkled his face and shut his eyes, instinctively trying to preserve the bit of one remaining. Nathaniel felt a brief coolness and saw the shadow pass over his face even through his closed eyelid. But Esau didn't stop where his shadow could do Nathaniel the most help. Esau twisted on the balls of his feet, creating a grating noise the vampire could hear, and he addressed his soldiers.

"See, men?" Esau said to the men and women, "I told you he could still move fast. But don't be fooled. He knew he wouldn't kill me. He wanted me to shoot him, to end it, to put him down like that dog with rabies in *To Kill a Mockingbird*." He addressed the vampire. "Isn't that right? Your best chance at dignity was to die like a rabid dog in the street on a hot day in Alabama. And you fucked that up, too, because we saw it coming. We planned for that shit, didn't we, men?"

More sounds, voices calling out agreement.

Esau crouched down and bounced on the balls of his feet in front of the vampire, just a bit more than an arm's length away, and just too far to one side to cast a shadow blocking the sun's rays. "You thought you'd get some mercy out of me, but you're wrong. Mercy is for humans."

Torreblanca looked over the fire at Esau's back. He

stood close enough to warm himself, but he faced the ocean. The tide had come in during the day, but not this far, and, now that the sun had set, it was far back out, the sound of the waves a pleasant, distant rumble of pebbles on ice.

She wondered what Esau was looking at. She knew it wasn't the moon because that was back over the treeline, so bright in the clear, cold night it cast her shadow in front of her, fighting with the firelight. She desperately wanted to know what was going on in Esau's head, and not just because of the bet.

She looked at the new guy. "Hey," she hissed, conspiratorial. "Thomas, c'mere."

The new guy, in his mid-thirties, just out of a career with a mercenary outfit after a couple of tours as a Ranger in Afghanistan, walked over to where she sat by the fire. The way he sat made her suspect he expected her to hit on him. And maybe she would later. She wasn't much older, and the night was cold, and there were monsters in the world that didn't leave you time to put things off for another moonlit night.

But first, she had to get this done. "Hey, Thomas, have you heard Esau's story?"

Thomas looked up at their leader. "Nope. He seems to know his shit, though." He pointed at the fire. They'd had to add wood to keep it going, but the vampire's ashes were down there somewhere. And a melted-down silver bullet, too. But he'd mostly burned up before he talked and Esau shot him. Torreblanca had been surprised by how long the vampire had held out.

"Oh, yeah, he knows his shit. But I mean, do you know what drives him? Has anyone told you why he does this work? We've all got stories, man. They don't just hire people and say, 'Oh, by the way, there are real, honest-to-fucking-God monsters in the world, and we want you to go kill some.' Either they know we've had some contact with monsters, and the company reach out to us, or we have contact with a monster and then start looking for the company. But we all have stories before we get recruited. Has anyone told you Esau's?"

When Torreblanca said "the company," she meant the people who cut the checks, arranged the flights, the suits who showed up and brought her in, but she didn't really know much about who was in charge. Some part of her suspected it might actually be Esau himself. Her military background voted against that theory; a general who goes into battle isn't a very smart general, and Esau was plenty smart. If he wasn't following orders, he was a fool to put himself at risk the way he did, and she didn't take him for a fool. *But,* she thought, *maybe he has some reason to make it personal.*

Thomas shook his head. "He never told me. And I haven't asked anybody. People usually tell the stories they need to tell and keep the secrets they need to keep. You were in what branch?"

"Marines," Torreblanca said. She only used one word, but it also held, "and damned proud of it."

"Action?"

"Plenty," she said. She knew they weren't flirting now, but she wasn't unaware of the double meaning.

"Then you know what I mean."

"Yeah, well, I think you ought to know his story."

Thomas shrugged. "Fire away."

"So you can tell he was a soldier, of course."

"Sure," Thomas said.

"Yeah, well here's the crazy thing. It wasn't while he was in action. It was back home. Esau had these two cute daughters. Loved them like crazy. While he was back home, living in base housing, a vamp sneaks onto the base and kills his kids. Right in his house. While he's asleep. Probably would have gotten away with it, but Esau had one of those nanny cams in a teddy bear in his daughters' room to make sure the babysitter was treating them right, and it recorded the whole thing. So he watched it. Over and over. Like, solid proof vamps exist, and he's got it, and he can't turn it over to the MPs or the government or anybody because they wouldn't believe him. And also, he wants to get the vamp himself, right? So he learns everything he can. Studies for years. Hunts them all over the world. Not just vampires. Werewolves. Witches. Fuckin' mermaids and shit. All kinds. He learns they are even organized as part of this big thing called The Convention of Fiends. That's how they cover up their existence; they're all working together to keep their existence on the DL. So now he's hunting them, and he's going to find them and totally wreck their shit, all so he can find this one vampire who killed his kids."

She paused. "That's some big time, heavy shit, right?"

Thomas nodded. "Sure. Pretty fucked up."

"So you believe me? You see why it's a big deal?"

"Yeah," Thomas said. Then he caught himself. "I mean, no. I mean, I believe you but I don't get why-"

"You all heard him!" she shouted. "He said he believed me!"

A chorus of groans rose up.

"Pay up, pay up," she said.

The men and women reached into their wallets and started looking for bills.

Esau heard the grumbles, turned, and walked around the fire. He looked at Thomas and smiled. "Torreblanca get you?"

Thomas scowled and shook his head. "I guess. What the hell?"

"It's her game," Esau explained. "She's got these two pools going. One is all about seeing if she can trick the new people into believing whatever story about me she makes up. And she makes up a new one each time. Torreblanca, what was the story this time?"

The crowd of men and women suddenly fell silent. Some leaned forward. All were listening hard.

Torreblanca looked up at Esau. "Two daughters? Killed on base back home by a vamp?"

Esau shook his head.

"One daughter? Off base?"

He chuckled. "You're way off base. Not even close."

"Dammit!"

More laughter. "Put your money in the pool, Torreblanca," someone shouted.

"I know, I know," she said, and took one of the bills out of her new stack, then started rummaging through her pack for the other envelope.

"What's that?" Thomas asked.

With her back to him, still searching through her pack, Torreblanca spoke at her gear and the envelope at the bottom of it all. "The second pool goes to the person who guesses it right. Esau won't tell. And you can't just ask. You can only guess a story you make someone else believe. If nobody guesses it by the time he retires, Esau gets the money. Ah, here it is." She pulled the envelope out, a medium-sized brown envelope with bubble wrap lining. The sides were bent in because the wad of cash inside was two inches thick.

"Holy shit!" Thomas said.

"Yeah, we get a lot of newbies in this work. Don't let it freak you out. Just learn to be careful and do exactly what Esau and I say, and we'll keep you alive. It's the people who go off-script who get replaced."

"Wow," Thomas said. Then he stared at the fire, wide-eyed. "Wow. That's ... Okay, well ... Wait. One thing. If no one knows the story, how would you all know if Esau isn't just lying? You could tell him the right story, and he could just say it's not it, and then he'd get to keep the money."

Torreblanca put the tip of her index finger to the end of her small nose and tapped it twice. "That's the point of the game. It reminds us all to trust Esau. You gotta' learn to believe him. He's going to order you to do crazy-sounding stuff. Like letting the vampire lunge at him. Hell, letting the vampire live long enough to talk is pretty crazy. Somebody could have killed the vamp in the woods, or felt sorry for him while he was screaming and shot him. But no one did. And it worked. We got the information we were looking for. When somebody gets it, Esau will tell the truth. And if you don't believe that, it won't matter, because you'll be dead before he ever tells a lie."

Thomas looked up at Esau, trying to understand this reverence. The leader had turned his back again and taken a few steps away from the group, toward the waves and out of the fire's warmth. Esau didn't seem to react to the cold. When Esau stood still looking out over the ocean, he wasn't a statue of ice, but one carved in stone.

Esau watched the waves come in, stubby, humble ones on this part of the beach. Their white, foamy edges picked up the moonlight and firelight, and the water beyond was obsidian, reflective blackness. Now they had the location of the annual convention. Learning it was in rural Canada was a bit of a surprise. Esau had suspected the meeting would be held in a city. Better transportation options for the monsters, and lots of human victims for them to consume. But Esau now considered the possibility the monsters felt a remote location was more fitting for a meeting focused on keeping their existence a secret. Esau was sure the vampire had been in too much pain to lie when Nathaniel had finally described the camp in Saskatchewan. Now Esau's calculations mirrored the waves. Thanks to the vampire's information, they would do this. And then that would happen. And then this. And then that. Contingencies washed in. If this, that. If that, this. His planning was never rushed. Rhythmic. Meticulous. Consistent. Waves.

Esau was a man who could see the waves. He could focus on the steps. He could build a tide. But he was a human being. He couldn't stand still long enough to contemplate the miniscule distance each wave hid in its ebb and flow. Some waves came up higher than others. Some tides came up higher. Less than an inch a year, it made its uneven advance. If Esau survived to his father's age and fell off his own ladder at 82, the sea would only have climbed five and a half feet. He could lie down on that frozen, icy sand and cover more ground than the ocean's slow march. How could he, how could any human, possibly care about some distant doom when there were monsters in the world, creatures who could fall upon them and consume them in seconds?

Esau hunted monsters. Never too fast, never too slow. He achieved the perfect monster hunter speed.

And the ocean climbed the beach.

Stupid fucking humans.

Chapter 1

Matt watched from a perch in a tree just beyond the wall around her backyard. Lena sat on the back porch in a cushioned, outdoor chair under a matching gazebo awning. The midday sunlight hammered down on everything it could oppress, carving dark hiding places like his. The stiff canvas of the gazebo did its best to give Lena equal protection, but the light bounced off the glass door of the house, off the water in the pool, off the waxy surfaces of the leaves of the jungle plants, leaving her in a glow she couldn't escape. She was staring off into the distance so intently, Matt once tried to track her line of sight, expecting to find something there, anything, perhaps one of the iguanas that actually enjoyed basking in the Costa Rican sun. Nothing. Lena stared at nothing. Very slowly, she'd raise her hand, take a long drag on one of the Viceroy cigarettes the locals enjoyed, smooth but too empty so they burned fast, and then she'd tap the ash into the little tray on the table, a black plastic one, too cheap and inelegant for the luxury home. Lena did this without looking down, her face aimed at the spot Matt couldn't identify, her eyes unmoving but alive with a sobriety and intelligence clashing with their stillness.

When she suddenly looked down, stubbed out the cigarette, and stood, he tensed in surprise and almost revealed his hiding place. Lena didn't react to his slight movement, though. She picked up the half-full pack of cigarettes and slipped it into the pocket of her green cargo shorts which she wore over her white one-piece bathing suit. She didn't know if she'd have another cigarette on her walk, but she wanted to be prepared. Her sunglasses were holding back her curly hair, a loose collection of carefully smoothed ringlets which always wanted to frizz into an afro in the tropical humidity. When she pulled the glasses down over her eyes, the ringlets in front were set free to provide a bit of shade to her forehead as she stepped out from under the gazebo. The sunlight hit her brown skin, darker now than it had ever been when she lived in Oregon, and she felt the radiating warmth immediately, like approaching a hearth in a cold home. She set off at a deceptive pace, walking like a person who had somewhere she needed to go. After circumnavigating the pool, she pulled her phone out of her other pocket, tapped on the screen a couple times to disable the alarms, and opened the gate in the high wall.

Matt had to crane his neck to peer around leaves hanging between his hiding place and his moving target. He watched her walk down the zig-zag path toward the beach. She'd put on weight since he'd seen her in Ireland, returning to her healthier figure. When she walked, as she stepped over jutting rocks and slippery patches, she would bend her arms at the elbows and hold out her hands to steady herself. Her whole body would bounce with a buoyancy creating the impression she was carefree, even joyous. Her walk was a lie. Lena had contemplated the pointlessness of a human life in a way no other human being had ever managed without giving up entirely. After the events of last year, when she'd been captured and forced to write a manuscript for a necromancer who was trying to end human civilization and possibly wipe out the human race, she'd chosen to read the book herself. She'd endured it and had chosen to go on, containing a knowledge that could never be shared. Matt knew, if he'd read her book, the one designed to take away all hope, the one the necromancer had titled *Don't Read This Book*, in spite of his powers and superhuman age, he would not have survived. He was too fragile. He would have succumbed. Lena was stronger, in that way, than perhaps anyone on Earth. But her trial had taken its toll. She was not happy, not hopeful. She was beyond hope in a way Matt couldn't understand.

When she reached the beach, her hands went up in that loose, bouncy way again, and she half-jogged to the firm sand where the edges of the waves made each approach. There, she kicked off her flip-flops, her hands fell, and she began walking down the beach to the south, letting the edges of the waves come up over the tops of her feet as she went. She reached into her pocket without conscious choice, pulled out the box of Viceroy's, removed a cigarette, held it in her lips, and shoved the box back. She forgot to light the cigarette, just held it in her lips as she walked.

She flickered in Matt's vision, disappearing and reappearing on the other side of the first trees, then flashing more and more infrequently until she was completely hidden by the jungle between them.

Very carefully, he stuck one leg out of its position in the crook of the branches, extending it out like a ballet dancer to stretch the stiff muscles. Despite the fact he had the body of a twenty-year-old man in excellent physical shape, a body which could have been mistaken for a ballet dancer's, the single straight leg looked inhuman, almost insectile. He lifted his torso with both arms, pulled the first leg back into its perch on the branch, and extended the other in that same alien way. Then he thrust himself from the tree and fell to the hard ground just outside the walled-in backyard. He landed in a superhero crouch producing very little noise, held still, and looked around to make sure he hadn't disturbed anything. A nearby iguana eyed him but wasn't frightened enough by his sudden relocation to make a move from its sunny perch on a tree trunk.

Matt stood slowly. He was a hundred and forty-seven years old, and sometimes he moved that way, though he could decide to move with the vigor of youth by whispering a few simple words. Extending his life, altering his appearance, and changing his physical movement were all distinct kinds of spells he'd learned early in his training. These spells' effects were related and necessary to maintain his human disguise, but they came from different schools of magic, and he'd honed them with different teachers. The life extension was a particularly decisive step in losing his humanity. Blood magic involved killing humans in specific, ritualistic ways. The murdering itself hadn't altered Matt's humanity much. Humans kill one another all the time. The ritual drinking and injection of the blood had side effects which left the warlock altered permanently, not just younger but crippled psychologically. Yet, compared to some of the spells he'd tried since, those effects were minor. Matteo Bernasconi had seen things in his life that would leave any human a gibbering vegetable. He had looked into dimensions a human's mind could not comprehend. Only his magic had protected him from complete insanity, and even then he was scarred. But he knew those horrific experiences didn't compare to the despair Lena had confronted.

She knew what he could not.

And he needed her help.

Rounding the stone wall, he used a variation on one of the spells hiding his age, now employed to deceive the cameras and laser sensors connecting the back gate to the alarm system. The house's security was elaborate, excessive for any realistic threat from the friendly and peaceful people of Costa Rica. Sure, the country had its burglars and even home invasion robbers. It wasn't a nation composed entirely of saints. But this security system was designed to detect a band of highly trained and well-armed werewolves or vampires.

Matt was only able to trick the security system by pushing out a spell to deceive the devices before he even detected them. No matter how advanced her technology, gears and microchips were no match for magic. By the time he reached the gate, the lasers were convincing themselves they saw unbroken beams, and the cameras were sending back footage of the warlock's absence. Even the gate's lock strained to disengage as he approached, but Matt made the metal bars of the gate take a brief vacation to an extradimensional tunnel connecting The Shadowlands of the Sidhe, Jotunheim of the Norse giants, and Bogalusa, Louisiana. Then he allowed the metal gate to reappear behind him as he trespassed around the pool toward the back patio door. That was how a lot of magic worked; he pushed something out of place for a time using the right pressure point and the force of his will, and then he allowed it to revert to its normal place. Objects in the universe had such a strong impulse to return to their proper places, Matt couldn't help but anthropomorphize them. He imagined the steel of the gate *wanted* to be back in this universe, in this nation, on this hillside, in this wall. He pushed it into that space between dimensions for a brief time, then let it return to the place it wanted to be.

Similarly, he bent the light in front of the cameras to make them see an undisturbed image, but once he was past, the light wanted to come back, and he allowed it. He allowed the laser sensors to return to the work they wanted to do.

Next he considered how he would push the sliding

glass patio door out of his way. Glass was tricky. If he tried to send it to another dimension, like the gate, but he missed some of the pane, it would shatter when the rest returned. Instead, he thought he might turn it to a liquid, then a gas. It would float out of his way, and then, when he was standing inside her house, it would return to the solid state it preferred in this universe. That, he decided, would be the most elegant solution, though pushing a solid into a liquid and then a gas was difficult, delicate work. First, he summoned the words to the spell. Then he held out a hand, his index finger pointed at the glass, his eyelids fluttering shut while he focused on repeating the words in his mind.

"You know what?" a voice asked.

Matt's eyes popped open at the sound, and he tried to spin around to stare at the speaker, but he found he could only pivot at the waist and look at her over his shoulder. His feet were firmly trapped in the concrete of the patio floor.

Lena rested her elbows on the top of the newly reappeared gate. "I'll bet you didn't know this," she continued. "It turns out, a person can be overwhelmed by despair and also be paranoid. It's okay if you didn't expect that. Most people don't. They see somebody like me staring off into the middle distance, and they think, 'She's barely even here. She's sleepwalking. I could quote her the wrong fare for the cab ride. I could take her wallet right now. I could drop this pill in her drink. I could sit very quietly in this tree until she goes out for a walk, then break into her house.' People think these things. They really do. I suspect they can't imagine both depression and a manic hypervigilance could coexist in the same brain, let alone my levels of cosmic hopelessness and any kind of awareness of what is going on around me. Yet here we are. You've been spying on me. I've been spying on you spying on me. And you thought you could just use magic to sneak into my house. Josef doesn't think much of your plan there, Mister Wizard. Might be a good time for you to come clean before I ask my friend to do some permanent no-trespass enforcement."

Matt turned back toward Lena's sliding door to see it was now blocked by a huge figure made of what appeared to be sandstone. The creature's chest was as high as Matt's eyes and only a few inches away. The shifting rock flexed as the creature breathed. Yet when Matt looked up at Josef's face, there were no nostrils or mouth through which the golem could take in a breath. Nor did Josef have eyes, yet it tilted its head toward Matt in a way that made it quite clear the creature was looking at him. Matt scanned down the creature's body, a slow elevator glance taking in the hulking form, and then admired the way the behemoth had abandoned the shape of human feet to instead take on something like the bottom of a tree trunk with the roots encasing Matt's feet up to his shins.

"Ah, yes," Matt said. He sounded calm, considering, but he made sure his voice carried back in Lena's direction, so it also sounded theatrical. "This is the mighty golem, Josef. Your reputation precedes you, sir."

"It doesn't identify as male or female. It doesn't like they/them pronouns, either. Too human for its taste." Then she called over Matt's shoulder. "Josef, this motherfucker still hasn't told us why he was breaking into my house, has he? Maybe you should dislocate his arm or twist one of his feet off just to let him know we don't have all day to wait."

Matt raised his hands in surrender. "Hold on. First, we've established we have both been watching each other. Second, you want me to be truthful. So we should all be honest with one another, right?" He twisted and looked over his shoulder at Lena. "You *do* have all day. You have no plans. I am the most interesting thing that has happened here in weeks."

Lena smiled just enough to make the edges of her eyes crinkle and to feel a tightening in her apple cheeks. She hadn't smiled much since she'd moved to Costa Rica, and the sensation in her face was a letter from a nearly forgotten friend. "That's fair. Josef, want to just rip one of his toes off to let him know we're getting impatient?"

Matt flashed the empty hands again. "Hold on. Hold on." He didn't sound particularly frightened, just annoyed. "Mr., um, Ms., uh, Honored Golem Josef, I will explain myself as completely as Ms. Wallace will allow and more quickly than she expects, and when I'm done, you can rip off as many of my toes as she thinks best, but if you could just set my feet free temporarily, I would like to be able to walk around while I explain myself. Pacing is a bit of a habit of mine, and you, Sir, er, Josef, you make me a bit nervous, and that just exacerbates my desire to pace. You understand, don't you?"

Josef crossed its arms over its broad chest, leaned its head sideways to look around the man it held captive, and aimed its blank face at Lena, then shrugged quickly, just a shoulder bounce as punctuation.

"Sure, let him go I guess," Lena said. "He tries anything, grab him."

Josef nodded. Then the mass of dirt and pebbles encasing Matt's feet retreated into Josef until his own legs and feet resolved into more humanoid shapes.

Matt wiggled his toes in his hiking boots, took some tentative steps to make sure his feet were unharmed, and then began to pace. Very intentionally, he chose to walk back and forth on the side of the pool furthest from Lena and closest to Josef, just to make it clear he was no threat to the human.

Suddenly he stopped, pivoted on the balls of his feet, and looked at Lena. The turn made a dramatic grinding sound as his boots scraped loose sand over the cement by the side of the pool. He held one of his elbows with one hand and held up the other hand in a foppish, lecturing gesture. "First, allow me to introduce myself. My name is Matteo Bern. Spelled like the city in Switzerland. I'm called Matteo Bernusconi in some places. Sometimes I'm Matt Bern. I'm a warlock. I like long walks on the beach and feeding on human emotions, so you know I didn't seek *you* out for a meal. I'm going to explain all of Western philosophy to you in about ten minutes, and by the end you'll understand why I need you to leave here with me, today, and go save the world."

Chapter 2

Bel stared out the window into the forest. The light was fading though it never really achieved complete darkness in mid-summer this far north in Saskatchewan. Because of her heightened senses, Bel could make out every pine needle on the trees even in the deepening gloom. But there wasn't much to see out there. And she wasn't really looking.

She thought about a single night with a particular woman far, far away. It wasn't just the sex. That had been exceptional because of Bel's growing emotional connection. It was the conversation. The walk through the streets of Llangollen in Wales. The laughter. The growing mutual respect and even admiration. Had Lena really held Bel in the same kind of esteem Bel held Lena? Now she doubted it. Lena had probably shifted from terror to a kind of Stockholm syndrome; Bel had rescued her from torturous captivity and kept her alive while they ran from creatures Lena could only have imagined before. But Lena must have detested her, Bel was sure. An indiscriminate murderer of humans. A monster. Yet there had been that one magical night.

"So, where do you stand on the name change, Bel?"

Bel spun around so fast it startled Lucia into dropping a plate back into the soapy water.

Nando, who stood next to his girlfriend, was rinsing and drying the dishes in the other half of the sink before setting them in the rack. Bel's superhuman speed didn't surprise him anymore. "She does that when you surprise her. Vampires move even faster than we do. She was probably thinking of Lena."

Lucia gave Nando a quick, sharp look, then turned back to Bel. "Does he always do that?"

"He's gotten better, believe it or not. He used to try to mansplain everything."

Nando kept looking at the plate he was drying. "Sorry," he muttered.

"See? Progress," Bel said. "Once upon a time, if I called him out on it, he would mansplain why he mansplains."

Lucia quickly wiped one hand on her shirt, then ran her half-dried fingers through the back of Nando's hair. It was growing out, the thick black hair curling in every direction. Lucia liked it that way. "Lemme guess: a joke about old dogs and new tricks?"

Bel shook her head. "He's better than that. He'd explain he was a product of the patriarchy and had to be reconditioned."

Nando looked over at his oldest friend and smiled sheepishly.

Bel looked at Lucia and tilted her head. "And he'd say it like I didn't know it."

Nando intended to move away from this topic of his obtuse male-ness and get back to the issue at hand, but when he looked into Lucia's eyes, he became momentarily distracted. He was unaware of the lost time, but Bel grew impatient with the love-sick puppies. She gently cleared her throat.

Nando remembered his question. "So, about the name change."

Bel frowned, not because she was deeply pondering the question, but because she was trying to decide if it mattered at all.

Their new home in Saskatchewan was called "Camp Bigfoot." Back in the fifties, when the WWII parents had crapped out the baby-boomer generation and needed to one-up the neighbors who had an identical white picket fence, the same model Chrysler, and the same vacuum cleaner, one way to show one's devotion to their nuclear family and also get a few weeks of blessed grown-up time was to send your kids off to an expensive camp far away. While the factory workers had to settle for the local church camp or YMCA day camp, some of the country-club set who managed the factories could send their kids all the way to northern Saskatchewan. To be clear, the top four fifths of Saskatchewan is "Northern Saskatchewan," and Camp Bigfoot was still in the lower half of the province, but that's far away from civilization. Kids had to be brought in on a pontoon plane which landed on the lake at the camp. Once there, they learned archery and rowed canoes and flirted with lifeguards and told ghost stories around a bonfire. The camp's location didn't make it so different from the local camps kids could have attended outside of Milwaukee or Chicago or Vancouver or Denver or a dozen other cities enjoying the postwar boom. But the isolation and cost-prohibitive nature of the campers' arrival ensured they were doing their bonding and flirting and kumbaya-ing with the sort of kids their parents approved of.

Tradition kept the camp alive for a while. The product of the marriages between former campers were sent to the aging camp their parents remembered fondly. But Camp Bigfoot didn't have the same cachet as some of the fancier summer camps in New England, and the world moved on to the point where the sorts of parents who might once have sent their kids there now hired nannies to keep an eye on the kids during a family trip to Dubai or a couple weeks on a cruise to one of the resorts in the Caribbean that do a good job of keeping out the riff raff. So Camp Bigfoot fell into decline, a death spiral for a place which depended on status.

As a last-ditch marketing ploy, the camp leaned into

the Bigfoot mythology. The Bigfoot name, present since the camp's creation, became a new kind of draw. Sasquatch decorations were hung everywhere. Wooden cut-outs were placed in the woods to create Bigfoot silhouettes at dawn and dusk to startle campers. By day they were chintzy. Caught in a flashlight at night, they were fake to the point of groan-inducing. But during the gloaming hours, they could elicit teenage screams that became a camp session's gossip and lore, especially if those screams came from one of the boys.

The wooden cut-outs and other branding and genuine, happy memories couldn't justify the camp's high price tag, and eventually it closed and was sold. The owners probably thought the buyers would be West Fraser Timber, the largest logging company in Canada. Instead, it went to an overseas firm owned by a larger conglomerate owned by a private partnership held by two anonymous investors. The names Jezebel Shipwright and Fernando de Castille couldn't be found on any of the official paperwork. The numbers of the Swiss bank accounts paid out, though, and that was all the humans cared about.

"Do you really care what the sasquatches think of the name?" Bel asked.

"I'm just trying to be sensitive. They're a very secretive bunch, so they will appreciate it's a cover and not an insult. But using their likeness as a front for the community? It just seems like … " Nando shrugged. "It's like cultural appropriation. Species appropriation?"

Bel looked up diagonally, a quarter of an eye-roll. "So, what? 'Camp Werewolf?'"

Lucia guffawed. She'd only known Bel for a few months, and Bel's wry sense of humor still took her by surprise. Nando completed the other three quarters of Bel's eye-roll.

"We were thinking of doing something like the Convention," he said. "Something that will sound possible but also off-putting to the humans."

When The Convention of Fiends, the representatives of all the various kinds of monsters in the world, held their annual meeting in Las Vegas, they used to be up-front about it. The mob bosses who ran the city were firmly in power back then and had kept the whole thing on the down-low. But as Vegas became its modern, slightly more family-friendly tourist-attraction self, The Convention decided they needed a cover story to keep any curious humans from stumbling into a room full of sirens and trolls. Everyone knew the cover would be designed to make the meeting sound like a boring conference, but then the gremlins gave input on the draft of the policy change, and before anyone could think of something better, they were all attending the annual Colorectal Obstruction Federation Conference. It worked well, and Bel hated it.

"So, like, 'Camp Shits-In-The-Woods'?"

Lucia laughed again.

Nando shook his head. "No. All summer camps sound a little too homey. Too welcoming."

"Except the one with Jason Vorhees," Lucia said.

Nando smiled. "Right, but 'Camp Jason Vorhees' would be an even bigger draw. And probably get us involved in some estupid lawsuit." Even after learning five different languages and spending most of his life outside of Spanish speaking countries, Nando still added a hint of an "eh" sound before some words beginning in "st," especially "stupid," one of his favorite descriptors. "I was thinking we could make it sound like there is something slightly dangerous going on up here. Not so dangerous it brings in government regulator types. Just ominous."

Bel liked the way Nando's accent improved the word "ominous." It became "ohm-ee-noose," like a yogi's mantra interrupted by a mild surprise ending in a hanging.

"How about 'labs,'?" Lucia asked. "Laboratories are boring and also ominous."

Despite her Latin name, Lucia had no Spanish or Italian roots. She'd come by her Canadian accent the old fashioned way. Bel thought her pronunciation of "ominous" sounded like she'd set the word down on the counter and flattened it with a meat tenderizer. Despite Lucia's boring accent, Bel could understand what Nando saw in his new girlfriend. She was smart, funny, and very sexy. If she'd swung Bel's way, Bel may have made a pass at her herself, even though Lucia wasn't her normal type. A little too muscular, a little too tall, and smelling faintly of a dog in heat. Vampires generally didn't go for werewolves due to the smell, but Bel would have made an exception for Lucia because of her full lips and vibrant, dark eyes. She had lips and eyes which reminded Bel of someone far away.

"'Labs' is good," Nando said. "Oh, and 'biological.' That could even give us a cover story if someone sees one of the pups roaming too far from home."

Lucia and Nando didn't have any children, of course. They'd only been together for a few months. The community they were building had grown quickly since Nando had killed his old pack leader, Apocalumus, and scattered his pack to the winds. Some of the wolves from Apo's pack, the ones who had been exiled or who had fled for their lives when that maniac took power, heard rumors about Nando's new pack or received direct invitations, and they'd moved into the camp's dorms. Some even had children, so the little community now rang with the sounds of giggles and shouts in the lake and yips and squeals of little wolves wrestling and nipping at each other on the shore. But when Nando made reference to the pups, Lucia dipped a plate in the soapy water, and Bel noticed Lucia's dark eyes flash away from the work she was doing and in his direction.

Bel drew a deep breath in through her nose, slowly enough she made no sound. No, Lucia wasn't pregnant yet. But Bel could smell Lucia was ovulating and hopeful. Bel casually wondered why this smelled sexy to her. Did it trace back to some pre-vampire human desire to propagate the species? No, she thought cynically. She'd evolved too much for that. It must be a vampire need. The ability to detect a woman who should be spared long enough to provide a second meal.

Bel could go months between meals, but it sapped her strength, and she hadn't fed since she'd picked up that hitchhiker outside of Murray Point. And it had been a lucky break. This far north, the pickings were sparse, and the people tended to live in communities where an abrupt disappearance would be noticeable. She watched Lucia and Nando trying not to look at one another and decided to borrow Nando's truck and give them some alone time.

"I gotta go," she said. "Gimme the keys, willya?"

Nando reached for the towel and dried one hand before fishing for the keys in his jeans pocket. "How long will you be gone for?"

She considered saying, "Longer than it will take you to knock her up," but decided against it. Her jealousy didn't have to spoil their evening. "I'll try to be back by dawn. Just going to feed, not travel."

Nando tossed the keys across the island. Bel was sitting when they left his hand, but she rose and plucked them out of the air faster than the werewolves could track her, just for fun. Still moving at her full vampire speed, she curved around the kitchen island, gave Lucia a meaty spank, and then continued until she reached the kitchen's doorway. There she slowed to a human's pace so she could give a parting shot over her shoulder. "Don't waste time while I'm gone. I'll do the rest of the dishes when I get home."

She heard them laugh as she zipped out the front door, across the semi-circular clearing made by the turn-around and sporting the flagpole in its center. Saskatchewan's summer nights weren't quite dark enough for her to fully enjoy them, but the glow over the horizon didn't burn her. The red maple leaf on the flag would have been clear to her on the darkest winter night, but, in the liminal summer dusk, the white space around it almost glowed. She decided she would look for

Canadians that night. And not some lonely hitchhiker. A young, happy pair of Canadian humans who could be talked into a ménage à trois by a beautiful stranger with a hard-to-pin-down foreign accent. She'd even try to make it painless for them afterwards. She'd taken to doing that since Paris, out of guilt. But she would still end their love affair. Because fuck love.

The camp's satellite cable was connected to a powerful Wi-Fi router. She would not have received the call even a couple minutes later, but she was just out on the highway when her phone vibrated because it was still picking up the signal. She pulled it out of her pocket, looked at the glowing screen (always brighter than she wanted it to be) and read the number.

She slammed on the brakes, and the car slid on the dirt road.

Using the same super-human speed with which she'd crossed the kitchen, Bel poked at the green circle on the screen and slid it to accept the call. Then she took a deep breath like a human, cursing herself internally for needing to do so. But she wanted to calm herself, to sound nonchalant.

"Hey," she said. But she couldn't bring herself to wait. "Did you find her?"

"Like the pecking order in a chicken yard, insensate cruelty to those you can whip and groveling submission to those you can't. Once having set up her idols and built altars to them, it was inevitable that she would worship there. It was inevitable that she should accept any inconsistency and cruelty from her deity, as all good worshipers do from theirs. All gods who receive homage are cruel. All gods dispense suffering without reason. Otherwise, they would not be worshipped. Through indiscriminate suffering, men know fear, and fear is the most divine emotion. It is the stones for altars and the beginning of wisdom. Half-gods are worshiped in wine and flowers. Real gods require blood."

-Zora Neale Hurston
Their Eyes Were Watching God

Chapter 3

Cassius turned in his chair just enough to put his feet up on the corner of his desk. He sighed. "No, Bel, we still haven't found her. I'm sorry I keep having to say this, but she probably isn't alive. And if she is, she's doing a damned good job of hiding." Though his heels had only rested there for eight seconds, he dropped his feet back to the floor and leaned over the desk, propping his head up on an elbow and holding it in place by yanking on his thick, dark brown hair in a way that would have caused a human a great deal of pain, but which was just a dramatic affectation for the vampire.

"Bel, you and I both know … again, I'm sorry, but … there's just not much time. She's human. She's got, what, 50 years left to live, right? That's only if she didn't read the book, and she told you she was going to read it. But if she didn't read it, she's been hiding for, what, more than a year now? If she can hide that long, she can hide for a human lifetime. And be honest: You aren't going to want her when she's 80 anyway."

He listened for Bel's reply and heard only silence. She was holding her breath. Cassius would have heard breathing even under the mechanical waves of the car's engine and the fuzzy blanket of the static of the satellite connection. "Bel?" he asked. His voice carried just enough of a sharpness to make it clear he was not asking if he'd lost the connection but was demanding a reply.

"No. You're right. I don't want to find her when she's 80."

"Okay. I'll let you know if we discover her whereabouts. But I need you to come back, Bel. Bring Nando if you can. You two were the best team I had. But if not, come back yourself. There's work to be done, my dear. CimBim went out of its way to navigate that whole bloody business in London and keep your record clear, but if they get cross with you and decide to reopen that file… Well, you know it was a judgment call which could have gone either way. Were you bringing in Apocalumus and he resisted arrest, so he was dispatched, or were you thwarting his lawful work and violating The Convention? Kind of depends on where one stands, doesn't it? And it matters. You really want The Convention standing on your side on this one."

The silence was brief this time. By mentioning CimBim, The Convention's enforcement body which maintained the agreement between different kinds of monsters using lethal force, Cassius was sending one clear hint, but there was another message beneath that threat. Bel had worked (with her partner, Nando) as a freelancer for CimBim for decades, so Cassius was reminding her of all she was sacrificing for this single human.

Finally Bel replied. "Cassius, can you just buy me some more time? Tell them I'm working on an extended mission for you? Investigating a rumor of some wayward monsters who might need to be brought in?"

He leaned back again. "Perhaps. Tell me, Bel, where would I say these wayward monsters are located?"

She didn't hesitate. "I'm in southern Chile, on the southern coast near Cape Horn, but next I'm going to head up into the Andes. Lena talked about coming down here, maybe traveling on one of those Antarctic expeditions, maybe just staying in the mountains, so I've been asking around. No luck, though."

"Yes. We have our ears open, but we haven't heard anything since she moved all the money she got from the Archduke into numbered accounts while she was at sea on her way to Argentina. We've been keeping tabs on her family in Oregon, and we've even watched her distant relations in Argentina. Nothing. Bel, honey, it's time to come home."

"I can't quite yet. But I will. Soon. I just need a little more time."

"I'm sorry, Bel," Cassius said. "This is not a request. Now it's an order. An order from someone who cares about you and knows what's best for you. Better than you know it for yourself. Come home. As soon as you can. Is that understood?"

This time the silence lingered, but Cassius could hear her breathing, a single slow sigh, then a quick inhalation. "I hear you. And I'm not saying, 'No.' But I'm saying, 'Not yet.' I understand if you take that as a violation of a direct order. I know you think you know what's best. I'm sorry, Cassius. I need this."

Now it was his turn to sigh. "I can't say I'm happy to hear that, but I understand you're trying to do what you need to do, and of course I will support you with CimBim if I can. Please reconsider. I will call you if I hear anything about your human. Contact me with your location if you move or need a pick-up or money or just want someone to talk to, okay, Bel?"

"Thank you, Cassius. And I'm sorry."

The line clicked faintly, and the sound of the car's engine and the soft satellite static and the distance disappeared.

With a similar gentleness, Cassius pressed the "End Call" button on his satellite phone, then carefully set the receiver face down on his desk, just long enough for the plastic to kiss the clean mahogany surface. Then he changed his mind, lifted the phone, and smashed it on the desk. Once. Twice. It shattered, pieces of plastic spinning across the room, bouncing off the unflinching faces of the two men sitting across from him. Before bringing it down a third time, he caught himself and gently dropped the phone's remains, just a single piece of circuit board and a three-inch piece of black plastic that had been the device's back.

"I'm going to need a new one of those," he said. He kept his voice eerily calm. Frozen. Deadly calm.

Thaddeus nodded. "So, she's in Chile?"

Cassius shook his head, a tight little motion. "No. She was lying about that. She tried to cover the lie, but I could hear it. Also, the car wasn't right. A big, older model Chevy Blazer running on synthetic oil and 89 octane gasoline. In rural Chile? Doubtful. I'm guessing somewhere in North America, but that's not specific enough to be actionable. But I'll need a new sat phone to communicate with your team because you're headed to Costa Rica. The human is there."

The other man, Nicabar, managed to frown and lift the middle of his eyebrows at the same time, creasing the center of his forehead in a way Cassius found simultaneously amusing and slightly repellent. "How'd you find her there?"

"Her gardener was trying to put together a crew to rob the house of the rich American woman he was working for. Spreading the word in some criminal circles. One of our listeners heard the rumors and pressed him for more details. We got enough to verify her identity, and we're fairly certain the gardener is still interested in cooperating with deactivating the security system and helping us rob his rich, Black, American boss who is very generous and lives all alone in a house overlooking the Pacific. Seems this human spends all day looking out at the ocean and being '*deprimida al punto de estar paralizada con su tristesa.*'"

Nicabar nodded, but Thaddeus looked sideways, so Cassius translated. "She's depressed to the point of being paralyzed by her own sadness. Sounds to me like she read the book. We might even be doing her a favor."

"So that's the plan?" Thaddeus said. "We go down and take her out?"

"Not quite. Nicabar will take a team and bring her back here, alive if possible. And the book. I need the book. While he does that, Thaddeus, you are going to go hire me a warlock. I need to be able to make her write the book again if it's been destroyed, maybe write me something more effective. A screenplay I can get turned into a movie that kills humans? A deadly leaflet I can pass out on street corners? I don't know yet. But I need that to have leverage over The Convention."

"And Bel? What do you want us to do about her?" Thaddeus asked.

Cassius did not like the way Thaddeus organized those questions. It could have been an honest coincidence. Or maybe his lieutenant suspected Cassius wanted leverage over Bel rather than The Convention. Some warlocks were more difficult to contact than others. Cassius decided to send Thaddeus down a rabbit hole where he might get a little singed while acquiring the contact information.

He shrugged. "Maybe she'll call. Maybe she won't. I'm not too worried about her. The book is a higher priority. And the warlock who can get me more books. But to find him, I'm going to need to send you to talk with the Troll King."

Thaddeus slumped in his chair but was wise enough to say nothing.

"Okay, go start making your arrangements. Nicabar, you're going to need to put a team together. This Lena is human, but she's managed to survive encounters with werewolves, witches, a necromancer, a skeleton army, and a bunch of those Fomorians in Ireland. She should have been dead a long time ago. So be cautious. And choose your team carefully. I want her alive and in good enough shape to write me more books."

He turned to Thaddeus. "I'll get you more information about who I'm looking for while you're in the air. Be sure not to get even a little bit of their shit on you. It burns."

The two vampires stood and bowed to Cassius. It was a gesture he'd come to appreciate when he'd lived in Jakarta in the 1700s. He made all his employees adopt the custom when entering or leaving his presence. It showed deference and produced literal vulnerability or a warning if they didn't want to make themselves vulnerable, and Cassius liked knowing he could kill his employees or get a heads-up if they were planning anything. Thaddeus bowed as low as ever despite his unsavory mission. That impressed Cassius. A little burning for the boss without complaint was a sign of a good employee.

As they filed out, Cassius leaned back in his chair and put his feet up to try to convince himself he felt relaxed. He brushed his hands together roughly, extricating the last bits of plastic embedded in his palm and healing the little cuts almost instantly.

"'Not saying, 'No,'" he muttered. "'But I'm saying, 'Not yet.'" He shook his head slowly, exasperated. "'Not yet.' 'Not yet'? How the fuck does she think this is going to go?" He imagined Bel in silver chains, burning in the sunlight, calling out the name of a human. Every time she screamed out Lena's name, his anger would swell. And then, when she fell silent and just burned, he'd feel some satisfaction. He breathed to this rhythm, an act almost optional for a two-thousand, two-hundred and eighty-six year-old vampire. He meditated through his breathing. Rage at her betrayal. Satisfaction at her pain. Rage. Satisfaction. And a growing sense of peace at the knowledge he was still capable of such strong feeling after all the centuries. It was a gift to be reminded how to feel such passion and bitterness. It made him feel young. And hungry.

He pulled his intact cell phone out of his pocket and tapped a couple times to reach his assistant.

"Mildred, I'm a bit peckish. What do we have on tap?"

He heard her clicking the button on her mouse, pulling up a spreadsheet on her computer. She was very organized. "Let's see here," she said. "I have a homeless

Vietnam vet, a homeless prostitute, ooo, this one is fresh and a perfect start to your night's work, sir: A Starbucks barista. He agreed to come home with Alba after his shift ended. You remember Alba from shipping and receiving? Doing some overtime acquisition work, I guess. Real go-getter. She brought the barista directly to the holding cell without knocking him out. Guess she told him it was some kind of dungeon sex-play thing. So he's fully conscious and very scared. Fresh brewed, we might say. Shall I have him brought up?"

"Tell me about the prostitute."

"Twenty-something. Parents kicked her out of the house for being gay. She's been on the streets for a while and has been doing some sex work and some self-medicating with dirty needles, so her blood won't be too clean and will have that Hep B aftertaste. Heroin and meth, so she's pretty scabby. I recommend the barista, sir. Clean and fresh."

"No, send me the girl. I'm in a sour mood."

"Oh, I'm sorry to hear that, sir. Yes, I'll have the girl brought to your office right away."

"Thank you, Mildred."

He pulled up the Tetris app on his phone and played while he waited for his breakfast to arrive. Cassius liked Tetris. He might not always get the pieces he wanted, but they always did exactly what they were told to do.

Chapter 4

Esau watched Homer's rosy fingers of dawn on the eastern horizon. He marveled the old poet's description still applied after three millennia and on the other side of the world, but there they were, those pink rays of light inching through mists on the endless Pacific. Though he found it irritating, he understood why a platoon of 32 men and women carrying a lot of odd but clearly fearsome weaponry couldn't board non-military aircraft. The fact they could so easily book passage on a container ship carrying McDonald's toys and Walmart tube socks from China through Vladivostok to Vancouver, British Columbia and on to Oakland, California was almost as shocking as a 2800 year-old bit of poetry describing his current experience. On a ship.

"I hate boats," he said, only half to himself.

"What was that, sir?"

He'd heard the boots clomping on the stairs, then scratching on the roughened, textured surface of the top deck. He turned and smiled briefly at her when she handed him one of the mugs of coffee she carried. Torreblanca could move quietly when she wanted to. Maybe she'd just wanted to warn him she was approaching, but he suspected her heavy footfalls were a product of a sense of safety and a bit of a victory dance; she'd successfully seduced Thomas, the new guy they'd picked up in Okinawa. Good for her, he thought.

"Nothing. Just hate traveling by sea."

"Not me," she said. "When I was still in, we traveled on Navy ships smaller than this. And on waters that were a lot rougher. Never got seasick." She balled a fist and pounded on her abs. "Steel, sir. Stomach of steel."

"Not my stomach that bothers me. Just so damned slow. I feel trapped out here. Can't even plan until we do some recon once we arrive, so beyond the travel logistics, I feel useless and restless."

"Some of the guys are playing a lot of cards. There's an old sailor down there who seems to be some kind of gambling addict and keeps losing his money, so the guys are raking it in. His name is either Long or Lung. Chinese, and every time I try to say it, he says I'm saying it wrong."

"Mandarin," Esau said.

"Sir?"

"Madarin is the language. Chinese is the people. He doesn't speak Chinese just like you don't speak American."

Torreblanca gave one quick, business-like nod. "Yessir. If cards aren't your thing, there are other diversions, sir. I know you don't fraternize with your subordinates, but I noticed a couple of the ship's crew are women. It is a pleasant way to pass the time, sir."

Esau smiled. "I'll take that under advisement, Lieutenant."

He turned back and rested his forearms on the wooden railing on top of the deck fence that lined the gunwale. The air was still, but the ship's movement created a steady breeze that sent the steam from the coffee towards their wake, and he let this cool his coffee for him while the mug warmed his hands against the chill. "So, besides trying to find me a date, anything to report about the ship's crew?"

"All seem to be human. We did as many of the tests as we could without taking blood samples. It seems they all piss and all produce human piss, so I think we're safe. No monsters for a thousand miles and counting."

That did not increase Esau's comfort. Instead, it flicked some switch deep inside him. "How many men do you have on watch?"

"Six. One fore. One aft. One starboard. One port. Two keeping an eye on the crew down below."

"Good. Gimme another two starboard and port looking out over the water."

"Got a twitchy feeling, sir?"

"Might be nothing."

"No problem, sir." Torreblanca pulled out her cellphone. It was connected to a sat relay in her duffel bag that encoded and linked it to all the cellphones in the platoon. The encoding wasn't perfect, of course, but it was good enough for field operations, and the ability to use standard cell phones helped the soldiers look less conspicuous than walkies. For one thing, she could send texts rather than speak into a device, and those were much easier to check surreptitiously.

Torreblanca typed:

Switching to an 8 man dogged watch. Current six are on Squad A with Jones and Li joining them now. Jones: Starboard. Li: Port. Space evenly around ship, watch the water. Rest of you have until 0800 to divide into Squad B and C. Squad B gets forenoon watch, and so on.

She held her phone out to Esau. "Look right?"

"Send," he said.

As she did so, she noticed Esau unzipping his heavy coat down to his belly and reaching one hand inside to touch the grip of the pistol in his shoulder holster. She clicked send, then popped the buttons on the cargo pockets of her pants that hid the Ruger LC9S Compact 9mms she kept on each leg. *What's making the old man so goddamned twitchy?* she thought. But she didn't doubt the seriousness of the situation for a second.

Her phone buzzed, squad leaders reporting in, Jones and Li letting her know they were on their way to their new posts, no grumbling or jokes yet. They would get where they needed to go before sending those.

"Sir?"

"If it's gonna' come, the smartest time would be when they realize we're about to increase the watch but before it arrives. Have your six report in."

She clicked on the second-to-last group in her messenger app, the six men who'd made up the original morning watch.

Report.

The messages came back quickly.

Brighton: Clear
Estevez: Clear
Morris: Clear
White: Clear
McLaughlin: Clear
Kirsch: Clear

She looked up at Esau. "All clear." Then her phone buzzed again. She read and relayed. "Li is in position on the port side."

"Has Jones reported in?"

"Not yet. Needs to get his fat ass in gear."

Esau tapped the grip of his pistol with the pad of his index finger, counting time. "Who else is starboard? Have 'em report again."

She found Morris' name in the list of the contacts for the most recent conversation, clicked on his name, and typed.

Report.

Nothing. Esau was tapping his pistol again, so softly Torreblanca couldn't hear the sound, but she could see the slight motion of the movement of his coat. She didn't breathe. When her phone buzzed, it was enough to make her clench her abs.

It wasn't a text. It was a phone call from Morris. She swiped to answer. Instead of a voice, she heard the sounds of gunfire through a silencer. He'd called her, then pocketed the phone. Her head snapped up. "Fire. Starboard."

Esau started to run around the ship. They were near the prow on the port side. As they passed Brighton at his post near the prow, he raised his eyebrows, asking for orders without slowing them down.

"Stay at your post," Esau said, his voice commanding but without any more volume than necessary.

Torreblanca was trying to keep up while also tapping a few times on her phone. "Orders?" she shouted ahead of her.

"Watch hold their posts. Everybody else get starboard with ears on. Ears on! Could be sirens."

And she saw he was digging in his coat's glove pockets and finding his special earplugs. They were bigger than standard earbuds, too large to be inconspicuous, but small enough to wrap over each ear and molded to the wearer. They produced a white noise that blocked out sound while functioning as walkies so the men could hear one another.

Torreblanca spoke the message into her phone, the call going out to all the men at once. She repeated the message as they ran so the soldiers who hadn't picked up fast enough heard the whole thing. Then she disconnected so she could use both hands to put on her own ears. Once those were on, she grabbed the pistols out of her pockets. They were double action, so she didn't need to cock them, just pull the trigger harder the first time. With a pistol in each hand, she sprinted and caught up to Esau who had drawn his own pistol. His gun had a silencer, and her pair would be loud, so she'd have to decide if he wanted her to fire and alert the ship's crew or let him do the shooting and keep things quiet.

When they got near enough, he answered her question by dropping down to one knee before taking aim so she could fire over his head. Less than twenty feet ahead of him, a writhing pile of green limbs reacted to their appearance. The creatures were tall, each over seven feet, and thin. Their sexes were easy to distinguish; the men had thin torsos and hips and a dorsal fin running down the middle of their bald heads, while the women had slightly wider hips, obvious small breasts, and long, wavy hair that hid their head fins. From the waist down, they had the tentacles of octopuses. These tentacles were wrapped around the arms, legs, and neck of Morris, suspending him two feet off the ground and pulling him in every direction like a man being quartered. All the skin on his face was already gone, and they'd begun ripping through his clothing to get at the skin underneath. Because the creatures were soaking wet and violent in their movements, Morris' blood was splattered all over the gunwale, the fence, and the wall.

Esau opened fire. After his first two shots, he began to speak, his voice clipped but not loud or panicked. The earplugs blocked out most of the sound of his pistol, and even when Torreblanca opened fire, the sound of her much louder guns was masked, creating a surreal auditory experience where the clarity of Esau's voice seemed to be coming in from a different universe than the one she inhabited.

"Not sirens. Some kind of merpeople. They can be injured by conventional weapons … killed. They can be killed by conventional weapons. Weapons free. Two men down. We don't know how many are coming up the side. Watch the other sides of the ship." He stopped speaking while he reloaded. "Watch out for friendly fire. Choose your targets carefully. Head and torso shots both seem equally effective."

As he spoke, Torreblanca helped him in his work. They carefully picked off the seven creatures who had killed Morris. They couldn't hear the merpeople screaming as they dropped Morris' body and tried to cover the distance to their new attackers. They were fast on those tentacle legs, but not vampire-fast. They would have been far quicker in the water. Each tentacle seemed to have a mind of its own, allowing the creatures to grab onto one another and wrestle their way towards their new prey, the claws on their human-shaped hands pointed forwards, fanged mouths open, not slowing one another down. It was a wall of dark green tentacles and pale, sickly white flesh. Torreblanca could imagine why sailors who had been at sea for too long found these women beautiful, though to her they all had the pallor of someone about to puke. Plus the fangs and tentacles didn't really do it for her. And the blood in their hair was a turn off, though it barely stuck to their wet skin. Maybe they were covered in a layer of oily hair like otters, or feathers like ducks, she speculated.

Once they'd shot the last one twice in the face and three times in the chest, Torrebalnca stopped firing, and Esau stood and started making his way down the gunwale toward the next pile of tentacles, reloading as he went. Torreblanca had a chance to see their skin up close as she stepped between their bodies. Very small, shiny scales. Even their tentacles had scales on the rougher sides, so while the suction cup sides looked like those of cephalopods, the backs looked like snakes. And the tentacles kept moving after the merfolk were dead, though they lacked any clear sense of what to do besides twisting and grasping. She stomped on one nearing her ankle as she passed, and the attached corpse didn't react.

The group attacking Jones was smaller because he'd killed a few before they got to him. Esau dropped to a knee and started firing again. It took the creatures a second to realize they were under attack, and then there were only three coming at them. Because Torreblanca was standing and had two pistols, Esau left the headshots for her and worked on torso shots, trying to hit the ones who were furthest back by aiming in between the first two and through the writing cloud of tentacles. When the creatures really got going, the tentacles almost turned into wheels, spinning in large arcs and slapping down on the gunwale, the sounds of those suction cups smacking the deck completely eliminated by the earplugs he wore. The two in front got much closer than Esau expected, their tentacles coming to rest just inches from his extended boot. He realized Torreblanca had been missing. That was when he felt the kick in the middle of his back.

He spun and saw Torreblanca hanging above him. Her feet were three feet off the ground. Both her guns were still in her hands, but one wrist had a tentacle around it, and she was trying desperately to aim her other pistol at the tentacle wrapped around her neck. The monster was coming up from the side of the deck. Torreblanca managed to put a bullet through its tentacle, but it didn't let go.

Esau leaned over the side of the ship and fired at the creature holding Torreblanca. His first shot would have gone through the merman's forehead, but when Esau leaned over the railing and the creature spotted him, it opened its mouth and lunged forward, so the bullet went through the roof of its mouth and exited through the back of its head. The creature suddenly released its grip on the side of the ship and started to fall the hundred feet from the deck to the water. The creature didn't immediately release his grip on Torreblanca's neck, however. Knowing she would be smashed against the railing, then strangled until her neck snapped under the creature's weight, or worse, would have her head torn off completely, Esau jumped towards her like a lineman, wrapping his arms around her and pushing against the railing with his feet. The impact was terrible. He thought his back would break, and he was sure her neck would snap despite his efforts, but he managed to serve as just enough of a shock absorber to strain the tentacle. She'd already perforated it with three gunshots, and it tore free. She fell hard to the deck, landing on her hands and knees, wearing a snake-and-suction-cup boa.

Esau couldn't wait for her to recover, though, because when he'd looked over the side, he'd seen at least a dozen other merfolk climbing up the side of the ship. "Lots of hostiles coming up the starboard side," he said. "Report. Are the other sides of the boat clear?"

"Port is clear."

"Fore is clear.

"Aft is clear."

Esau hauled himself up by grabbing onto the cables that made up the lower railings of the fence, and he swung his pistol over, prepared to dangle it there and do his best to aim despite his exhaustion. He pulled the trigger once, and all fourteen of the creatures fell off the side of the ship like snow cleared off a windshield by a single wiper. It took him a split second to identify what had happened, but he allowed himself an extra moment to enjoy the serendipity, turning his pistol sideways and looking at the seemingly magical weapon as the bodies of the merfolk splashed into the water below it.

"Well, that was pretty cool," he said aloud. Then, still half dangling over the railing, he turned his head to the right and left slowly, nodding at the men. He hadn't heard their automatic rifles open up on the monsters thanks to the earplugs, but he was certainly grateful for their timing.

He recovered himself. "Okay, I want two extra men

fore, two aft, and four port. They may keep coming. And I need four men to clean up here." He looked around. "Make that six. Bring a couple mops and buckets. And I need four of you to keep the crew away from this starboard deck until it's spotless. I'm going to go talk to the captain. Tell him we were attacked by pirates but we held them off and sank their ship. Lost two men in the process." He stood slowly and looked over at Morris' body, then back at Jones'. "We're going to have to throw all the bodies overboard. I hate that, but they're too chewed up to explain. Make sure you get their tags for their families, watches, wallets, anything else that's intact before you do it. No ceremony for the monsters, though. Toss them first and do it fast. They're heavy. Just ask Torreblanca."

He reached out a hand and helped her to her feet. She started to speak but he raised a stiff hand. "Don't try to talk yet. You'll just strain your voice. It's going to take a while to heal. Good news, everybody: Torreblanca has taken a vow of silence for the rest of the trip."

Chuckles and a whoop trickled in through the earplugs.

"Careful," Esau said. "Her ears work just fine, and she has a long memory."

He smiled at her and expected to see her return the expression. Instead, she pulled absently at the piece of tentacle still hanging like a disgusting necklace, and she frowned and looked up into the lightening sky. Curious, Esau tried to follow her gaze, saw nothing, then looked back. She pointed, and he stepped toward her to look down the ray of her arm.

And there, some thirty feet off the side of the boat and ten feet higher than the deck, a soap bubble floated through the air. It was six inches across and looked like clear glass, the way all soap bubbles seem to defy the laws of physics that make them possible. But this one was defying common sense because it floated there, over a hundred feet above the blue topsheet of the Pacific, a thousand miles from any child with a plastic bubble wand on a beach.

"Oh, that mother fucker," Esau said. He lifted his pistol despite his arm weighing a thousand pounds, aimed carefully, and fired once.

The bubble did a little dance in the air, circling on some invisible eddy in the breeze, and then it returned to its lazy path to nowhere.

Esau holstered his pistol.

"Add that to your bet," he told Torreblanca. He pointed angrily at the bubble. "It's not the fucking monsters. That, that right there? That's why I hate boats."

Then he stomped away to find the captain, leaving the voiceless Torreblanca to wonder what in the hell he meant.

"I do not know what I may appear to the world, but to myself I seem to have been only like a boy playing on the seashore, and diverting myself in now and then finding a smoother pebble or a prettier shell than ordinary, whilst the great ocean of truth lay all undiscovered before me."

-Sir Isaac Newton

Chapter 5

He did it. In under ten minutes. Nine minutes and 36 seconds, to be exact.

That's how long it took Matt to summarize all of Western philosophy and convince Lena to come with him to save the world.

He had to skip some things for the sake of brevity, of course. The pre-Socratics, for example. He started with an uncharitably brief summary of Socrates, a grossly unfair account of Plato's entire oeuvre, and an insulting pair of sentences for Aristotle. Then he glossed over 1,952 years that didn't really serve his purposes, found she knew enough about Descartes to rely on her prior understanding, and basically patted Hobbes and Locke on their heads.

"Slowly, philosophy turns more and more into science, or at least it keeps giving ground to science, until it becomes this little God-of-the-gaps field of study. Then this Scottish philosopher, David Hume comes along and wrecks it all. He points out ideas like causality, gravity, even notions of our own existence, are really just habits of our minds. We think about things that way because we have to, but it doesn't make those ideas objectively true. So he says we should just grab some beers and play some pool because philosophy is dead."

"And when was this?" Lena asked.

"The 1730s and 40s. But the philosophers didn't just throw in the towel, quit their university jobs, and become professional pool players. They had a vested interest in showing there was still a point to figuring out how things really are. But after Hume, they did a pretty shit job. Then this guy named Immanuel Kant comes along, and he sort of solves the problem. He says, sure, there is this world out there which we can't really know. We just know how we think about it. You might be a brain in a jar receiving electrical impulses creating the illusion of all your sense experience, and you wouldn't know."

"We're in the Matrix."

"Right. But Kant came up with it way before the Wachowskis made Keanu Reeves into computer-Jesus. Kant was writing about this in the 1780s."

"But with less Kung Fu, I'm guessing." Lena smiled, a complete smile, and she didn't even feel guilty that her amusement came from her own joke.

"Not nearly enough, no." Matt shrugged. "But it was important. Kant not only essentially invented psychology, but he made this space where philosophers could keep doing their work, no longer studying the way reality really is, but studying the way we experience reality and what that experience means."

"Okay," Lena said. She drew the word out and twisted it up at the end just enough to let the intruder know she wanted him to explain a little faster.

"Right, so then things get split up. And then split again." Matt explained how the the Brits and Americans mostly focused on logic and they fell into the certainty trap for almost two hundred years. Meanwhile, on the Continent, philosophers split into a couple camps, the phenomenologists and the existentialists. The first group wanted to study the lived experience with some remove, to step back and see if examining the relationship between consciousness and the world illuminated something about either one. Meanwhile, the existentialists were concerned with how humans should live when the objective reality of God was now out of the picture. "They weren't all atheists, mind you," Matt footnoted aloud. "There were Christian existentialists and Muslim existentialists and Jewish existentialists as well as atheists and agnostics. But they recognized even interaction with the Divine, if there is such a thing, is still an experience of the conscious mind. Instead of worrying about whether there is a God, they were big on ethics.

They wanted to figure out how people should behave now that they couldn't just plod along in the certainty that the universe is real and organized by sensible rules or a bearded old white man dictating right and wrong."

He put his hands together, palm to palm, then veered them away from one another. "These projects don't really end, but they fall out of fashion and are replaced by new camps, the philologists and the post-modernists." The philologists, Matt explained, took the tools of literary criticism and applied them to human experience, turning everything into an infinite series of overlapping texts which could be read carefully and plumbed for meaning. The post-modernists came out of other disciplines like studies of gender, race, and economics, and recognized that human experience can be understood and described as interlocking systems of power relationships.

"And then, quite by accident, all of this comes together when a necromancer asks three witches to find him the world's best writer so he can have a weapon of mass destruction in the form of a book. He has you kidnapped, you write the book, and, without even trying, you bring all these schools of thought together. Or, at least, you push them to a place none of them are fully ready to attend."

Lena raised an eyebrow. "Okay, you win. I'm curious now. Explain."

"Well, you wrote a book that pushed out beyond what these philosophers were willing to consider. The existentialists wanted to figure out how people should act without some entity out there telling them what to do, and they struggled to articulate various kinds of humanism rooted in free will, but when really pressed, they couldn't say why. Kind of arbitrary, actually. But they were all pretty fixated on the consequences of a world without God (or an objective certainty of God), not focused on wrestling with the objective certainty of *death*. That, they conceded, would lead to nihilism, and they were afraid to be called nihilists.

"Similarly, the phenomenologists wanted to examine experiences as though our consciousness made those experiences real. They didn't want to consider that death makes any product of the consciousness vanish, and that this might mean all the experiences were not 'real' or meaningful in some cosmic sense. They knew admitting this would have opened them up for criticism as nihilists, too.

"The philologists and post-modernists have similar limits. The philologists read texts in a certain way, presuming intentionality and meaning, not because they are assured those things exist, but because they know texts aren't worth examining if one concludes in advance that texts have no meaning.

"Meanwhile, the post-modernists acknowledge all the systems of power they examine are social constructs, but they keep reminding themselves these social constructs have a lot of import for, and impact on, the lives of the people affected by these beliefs. Post-modernists might be able to concede these socially constructed beliefs won't matter once the believers die, but the post-modernists focus on the systems, not the individual believers, because focusing on the believer and the meaninglessness of that one person's beliefs in isolation, both in life and oblivion afterwards, would open up the post-modernists up to the charge that irritates them most; they are relativists who make everything permissible."

Matt stopped his pacing and tilted his head towards Lena. "This isn't accurate, of course, but the post-modernists' fear of being called relativists (or at least irritation at having to knock the charge down over and over) keeps them from pushing beyond the false charge to a more damning real one."

Then Matt's face brightened, and he held out both hands in Lena's direction, palms up, like he was lifting her face. "And that's where you come in, Lena! You, or at least your book, asks all these thinkers to join you in a room." He waggled his hand, swirling invisible philosophers together. "And then your book asks them to take their most precious idols out of the boxes made out of their defensiveness. And all these philosophers pull their most sacred conclusions out of the protection of their insecurities. And you light them all on fire. The idols *and* the insecurities. You burn them all up."

Lena set her chin on her forearms on the top of the gate, and when she spoke, the pressure on her bottom jaw made her speak through her teeth. "I thought about the existentialists when I came up with the idea for the book, long before the necromancer and the witches. I thought of Albert Camus, and thought I could maybe outclass him a tiny bit. Ridiculously arrogant, I know…"

"Not at all," Matt said. "You outdid Camus and the others, too. You convinced readers to consider nihilism and relativism and the meaninglessness of texts and the meaninglessness of systems of power, and then you went even further. You made them feel it! All of it. You didn't say, 'Death makes everything that comes after it meaningless.' You said, 'Death makes everything that comes *before* it a vain effort to create false meaning. And now you have felt that and have to deal with it.' And, of course, the people who believed their lives were the most meaningful of all, those who, by virtue of life experience, felt the most entitled to make a difference in the world … they couldn't handle it. They just said, 'Well, fuck it all, I guess.' Some went catatonic, some became homicidal hedonists, and some decided to kill themselves rather than wasting time carrying that feeling around."

He paused and tilted his head, staring into her eyes so deeply, Lena had to fight an urge to take a step backwards. "But not you. You are different. And you know why?"

Lena nodded. "Sure. I never expected to make a difference. I'm a queer Afro-Latina woman. Everything in my life experience told me I wouldn't be allowed to make a difference. So I could choose to go on or not, and it was up to me, because I always had to make the choice to go on without expectations."

"Right!" Matt shouted. "Aren't systems of oppression wonderful?"

Lena scowled. "You want Josef to explain what it thinks of systems of oppression?"

The former golem of Prague leaned closer to Matt.

Matt held up his hands. "I was kidding. Kidding! And I should not have been. Not something to kid about. I see that. My sincerest apologies, my handsome homuncular friend."

"Okay, so I wrote this book that's a perfect argument for nihilism, and I decided to live with it. Now what do you need me for?"

"Because the book may be completely nihilistic, but your story isn't." He pointed a finger at her. "You have chosen to value things." He pointed a thumb back towards her house. "For example, you didn't decide to turn it over to the werewolves or the necromancer. That would have been easier. Maybe you hadn't felt that complete nihilism before you read the book, but once you had read it? Why not call them up and say, 'Come get it. It's right here. Who cares?' But you've gone to all this trouble to hide. You care about the world and the people in it. You know that's an arbitrary choice, that they will all die and won't matter eventually, and that just about everything they do is this gigantic waste of time and effort to trick themselves into believing it will matter, so everything they do while they're still alive is pointless, too. Yet you have prevented the monsters from destroying the human race and accidentally destroying themselves in the process. Why?"

"I don't know." Lena hooked her chin over her arms and stared down at the ground inside the gate. "I really don't. That's the question I ask myself every day. Why do I do this? This existing? Why should I?"

Matt raised his finger. "And that is the answer I'm here to provide, and it's why you'll come with me! Here's my theory. Ready for it? Here it is: Love." As he said it, he looked up into the sky and waved a hand slowly in an arc like he was doing bad musical theater. "I know. Total bullshit, right? Just some hippy-dippy karma-crystal answer to the most complicated question of human existence. Only it's not. You recognize that everything you've ever experienced is, on some level, a meaningless social construction to ward off the inescapable fact of your own death. But one of those meaningless social constructions is particularly pure and beautiful. Sure, it might just be this evolutionary habit that keeps humans from letting their aging parents die and keeps them from eating their babies, but even so, you value that thing evolution or God or society gave you which pressures two humans to form a bond upon which all of your civilization is built. You don't want those bonds to come to an end. You love love. You hate that it sounds so corny, but, on some level, you know it's true."

Lena rolled her eyes. "Yeah, maybe. It's corny, but maybe you're right. So that whole long-ass mansplanation was just to point out I am philosophically inconsistent? What does that have to do with me going with you?"

"In a few days, some monsters will come to this house. They will try to capture you or the book or both. They don't intend to use them right away. They plan to bring you and the book back to The Convention. Then the monsters will have a huge fight to see who gets to keep the book or make the writer create a new one. The book will go one way, and you will go the other. It will be The Convention's version of the Missouri Compromise."

"Sounds a little more like a 3/5ths compromise to the person who will be shackled up and forced to work for her captors."

"Yes, well, that probably is a more apt analogy, it's true. I was just trying to avoid it because, you know…"

"Because I'm Black. I'm aware."

"Sure, of course. Anyway, the side with the book will eventually decide they have to deploy it before the other side can get their own copy. Or the side with you will get a book and decide it's not very powerful leverage unless they deploy it and prove they have it. Both still think it will only reduce the population of humans dramatically. They're chaos muppets; they rely on their belief others will reinstitute order after they get their kicks. They can't believe they could really bring it all to an end, then starve to death. It's beyond their comprehension. So one side or the other will distribute the book. And by the time the humans figure out they can't read the book to understand why it keeps killing people, it will be too late.

"Now, if I'd just showed up and told you that, you may have said, 'So what. I'm tired of running. It doesn't matter.' That's what the book says. But it's not what you say, what your life says. You do want love to continue to exist. Specifically, you want to be with the one you love. Bel. And she loves you. And I know where she is and can take you to her. And she can keep you safe.

"So you see, all of Western philosophy comes down to one woman knowingly embracing a possibly artificial bond with no great cosmic meaning, and it will save the whole world. Pretty cool, eh?"

"Seems like a bit of a stretch when you could have said, 'Some monsters are coming to kill or enslave you.

Let's GTFO.'"

"And what would you have said?"

"Same thing I'm saying now: How do you know?"

"Ah, that's the place where I can go beyond what is dreamt of in your philosophy, dear Horatio. You see, I have…" Matt did another of those absurd slow rainbow hand waves. When the arc reached its nadir, he vanished. No cloud of smoke. No sound. He was just gone.

"Magic!" he called down from the roof.

Lena just had time to raise her hand to shield her eyes from the oppressive Costa Rican sun, and then he disappeared again.

…and reappeared standing on the water in the middle of the pool. "Or 'miracles' if you don't mind a bit of blasphemy. Want to see what it would look like if Jesus tap danced?" And then he started to dance, his toes and heels slapping gently on the surface of the water, occasionally leaping or spinning. Lena recognized the dance just before he started to sing in a very pleasant baritone,

"I'm singin' on your pool
Just singin' on your pool
What a glorious feeling
I look like a fool
I'm laughin' at sun
So bright up above
Your golem's in my heart
And I'm ready for love
It may not have gender
But I'll kiss its…"

He stopped suddenly. "What rhymes with 'gender'?"

Then he plunged into the water feet first like he'd been standing on thin ice.

Lena laughed, and when he rose back up, straight as a rod, and stood on the water's surface once again, then took a dramatic bow, she couldn't stop herself from clapping.

Matt turned to face Josef who remained next to the sliding glass door, its legs merged with the concrete. Matt bowed deeply in the golem's direction, and Josef clapped also.

That really made Lena laugh.

Lena believed Matt's demonstrated magic ability also allowed him to peer into the future and see the monsters who would be invading her home, and Matt did not disabuse her of this mistake. He couldn't see the future at all, but he didn't want to tell her how he'd been warned about the very real threat headed her way.

Instead, Matt beamed at her joy. "See? You haven't laughed in quite some time, have you? Let's go save the world. It will be a hoot!"

"[We] live in a deranged age, more deranged than usual, because in spite of great scientific and technological advances, man has not the faintest idea of who he is or what he is doing."

-Walker Percy

Chapter 6

Just after dusk, the limousine pulled up to the curb at 1211 Avenue of the Americas (that's Sixth Avenue to people who know better), and Thaddeus stepped out. His clean-shaven, chiseled features, the slight hint of fake tanner, and his blond hair perfectly slicked back made him look like the exact type they would love to have upstairs in their building. The executives of that particular company wouldn't have cared about his need to drink human blood to survive any more than they would care about his personal political ideology as long as he was good at looking the part while telling retirees to be afraid of immigrants and people of color (but really only immigrants who were also people of color) and outraged by a looming communist take-over. But Thaddeus wasn't there to apply for a job reading propaganda off of a teleprompter. Though he was fairly certain he would make it out alive, Thaddeus felt dread about the impending meeting, an emotion he hadn't experienced in at least a century.

The man who crossed the lobby to meet him didn't look too happy to be there, either. Frankly, Chaz Prince looked like hell. The last time he'd been given the assignment to take a special VIP down to the super-secret basement, it had felt like a major steppingstone in his career. That was back when everything seemed to be going right. Ratings were up. Their guy was in office. The heartland loved them. His aunt was the Secretary of Education, for fuck's sake. What could go wrong?

Unfortunately for Chaz, he didn't live in the heartland. Since that last meeting, ratings were still up, the people in the heartland still loved them, and he'd been celibate for a year. No one would date him in New York. Women wouldn't even give him the time of day. He could afford to hire prostitutes, of course, but there was always the risk that someone would snap a picture of the woman arriving or departing, or of Chaz entering some seedy massage parlor, and he'd spend the next few years screaming, "Fake News" and only fooling half the people in the country into believing he'd never slept with anyone for money while convincing the half who didn't mind sex work as much that he was a liar, so he just whacked off more and more angrily to increasingly violent Nazi porn on his computer before praying for forgiveness and begging Jesus to make sure that if his browser history was hacked, God would give him the strength to convince everyone he'd downloaded a virus sent by socialists affiliated with the Black Panther Party. Oh, and his hair was falling out despite the Rogaine, and he was starting to suspect one of the sores on his penis wasn't caused by chaffing but by some kind of cancerous growth ... which he also blamed on socialists and the Black Panther Party. And when he traced it all back, he couldn't escape the suspicion the previous trip down to the super-secret elevator had been the start of it all.

"Hello Mr. Felix. My name is Chaz Prince. A pleasure to meet you. They sent me down to escort you." His voice carried far less enthusiasm than he used to be able to muster, and it hit its sourest note on his own name. Perhaps, it said, it would be better if you forgot all about me the moment I leave you down there.

Thaddeus barely looked at the production assistant. "Thanks," was all he said.

Chaz flashed his ID badge at the security guard operating the metal detector, allowing Thaddeus to pass through without stopping. Next, Chaz raised his ID at another group of receptionists at a desk, letting it flop back down like it weighed a hundred pounds, before lifting it again to plug it into a scanner for one of the eight elevators. After a moment, someone flipped a switch to the furthest one. The pair took that elevator down four flights. They stepped out into a small, dimly lit room with a single desk where a burly man sat wearing a security guard outfit. Behind him were the smooth doors of another elevator. Chaz used to wish he could go into that one. Now he just wished he could go back to the fraternity at Yale and live there forever.

"Okay, um, there you go," he said.

"Thanks," the vampire repeated.

When Chaz was on his way back to his pathetic life of wealth, privilege, and victimhood, Thaddeus nodded to the guard.

The guard looked him up and down. "You look ugly as fuck. You dead or something?

"I look better than that ugly glamour." He knew trolls preferred to relate through insults. "Does it feel like polyester? Looks cheap."

"Yeah. And itchy." The troll shivered, and as he did so, he seemed to stand. But as he climbed out of the glamor, he revealed he had been standing before, his huge arms and shoulders on the table, his tiny legs on the chair. Now he was just lifting himself up onto the desk so his nudity would make Thaddeus uncomfortable.

The vampire looked at the troll's green, scaly skin with the coarse purple hairs poking out. Claws like purple bird's talons scratched the surface of the desk. His tongue dangled from his mouth, bright pink like his waggling penis. Saliva dripped down his chin, and snot rang from his long, bulbous, crooked nose. His shiny, black eyes lacking any white sclera peeked out from under a single protruding, scaly brow. His ears, the size of dinner plates but with lobes that hung lower than his chin, rested against his chest. "Shit," Thaddeus said, "you're ugly but you look ridiculous. Like a cartoon of a monster on an off-brand box of kids' cereal."

That might have actually hurt the troll's feelings. "Scarier than you, you baby-powdered fuck-boi necrophiliac cocksucker."

Thaddeus smiled. And then his smile kept going. His lips parted just as his human teeth retracted into his gums, and the tunnel of hollow, curved syringe teeth, layer upon layer curving in towards darkness, wriggled in his mouth as he hissed a wordless threat.

The troll shrugged. "Fine, you're scarier, too. Go fuck yourself. I'm half-tempted to tell you to push B45. They would teach you a thing or two about fear down there. But I'm a lot more afraid of the King than I am of you, and he said to tell you to push B44, so now I did. So push whichever one you want, sphincter-face."

The troll pushed a button on the back side of the desk. The elevator doors opened. Thaddeus stepped inside, pushed B44, and flipped off the troll as the doors closed.

And then he let himself admit he was really nervous. What if he'd made the troll too angry and the thing had been ordered to tell him to hit B45, but he'd lied and said B44? What would Thaddeus find on the other side of that door?

His relief almost exceeded his amazement. The doors opened to a metal catwalk wrapping around a room the size of multiple football fields. Massive columns held the ceiling up, and stalactites dripped water from the Hudson and spoke to the age of the cave. Trolls crawled up and down the columns, delivering messages and Cheetos and cans of Red Bull. And below, on the cavern floor, the messages and Cheetos and Red Bulls were consumed by an army of trolls sitting at row after row of computers.

When the elevator doors closed, a soft bell dinged, and that was enough to alert some of the trolls below. One stood on his chair, hooted, and made a strange growling sound as he forced out a handful of flaming fecal material. Handful. Literally. Into his hand. And then he cocked that hand back and launched the flaming turd at Thaddeus.

The vampire could move fast enough to dodge bullets, so the incoming projectile didn't worry him too much. It splattered on the wall, tossing off fiery little chunks, and was followed by a volley from the other trolls who'd noticed his arrival. Dodging became more challenging. Thaddeus heard a booming voice shouting, "Knock it off back there. Get back to work! If I have to come back there, I'm going to bite your arms off, chew em up, shit 'em out, and set you on fire with your own digested arms. You know I'll do it. I've done it before!"

Though he'd never heard those exact words in that exact order, Thaddeus recognized the voice of authority. With a vampire's unique speed, he raced around the catwalk, down a stairwell at the far end near the front of the room, and across and up onto a raised platform where the King of Trolls sat on a throne carved out of a block of obsidian. Thaddeus ran up onto the stage and stopped right in front of the King so any troll who decided to throw more flaming shit would have to risk hitting the boss. The combination of speed and the sudden stop made it seem like Thaddeus simply appeared, and that startled the King.

The giant troll roared, "Gerald Ford tittyfucking Richard Nixon, you nearly gave me a heart attack, you bloodsucking welfare queen! God dammit!" The twelve silver rings in his ears, the one in his nose, and the ones in his eyebrows shook. His silver diadem nearly fell off his head. But the King caught it, straightened it, and calmed himself. "And I even knew you were coming, you lamprey-faced blood Hoover. That was … that was pretty fucking cool, to be honest. Haven't been startled like that in a while. Gets the old blood flowing." He pointed down. "Check it out. Gave me a woody. It's been a while."

"Very impressive, Your Highness."

"Ha! Thanks, you many-fanged cocksucker, but you aren't my type. So, what did your boss tell you to ask me for while you were licking his asshole?"

"He said you could put me in touch with a certain warlock, sir."

"That Erdogan Ueda, the Pictish warlock who was working for the necromancer Nigel Marion? He got stabbed with a knife dipped in basilisk blood. He's deader than you are. About as dead as Marion himself, though the Brothers of Saint Quentin of Amiens, those necrophiliac skeleton-humping monks in England, may have brought Marion back as one of their skeleton servants for all I know. Maybe he's plowing a field or getting plowed by a fat old monk right this very minute. Who knows? But the warlock, Erdogan? He's super-dead."

Thaddeus nodded. "They used Erdogan to try to capture the golem, but he's not the one we're looking for. We've found the human named Magdalena Wallace. We have her in custody now. We want the warlock who actually forced Magdalena Wallace to write her book. His name is Matteo Bern. Or Matt Bernusconi. Or Matt Bern. He was the one who enchanted the writer. We've been putting out feelers, trying to track him down. We'll need him in case we need her to write another. After all, we have an obligation to fulfill the New Business Item you helped push on the floor of The Convention. My employer would very much like to stay in your good graces, Your Highness."

"Don't try to blow smoke up a troll's ass, son," the King said. "We'll take a flaming dump on your face. You want the book for yourselves, and now you've got it, and you want me to know you've got it, and now I do."

"Well, I'm not privy to those kinds of machinations, Your Highness. I'm just here to find out how to contact the warlock."

"He's not an easy guy to reach."

"We'll pay whatever you ask."

"You think I need money?"

Thaddeus looked over his shoulder. "You must have a very high internet bill."

"We're trolls. We own the internet. But I do have a price for your boss. You say he's got the writer? Fine. You tell him to put two buckets of clean water under the writer's bed. She'll sleep over them for a night. Then next morning, there will be two flowers, one growing in each bucket. One will be pretty, a water lily. The other will be ugly as fuck. It's called a spatulate-leaved sundew, technically a *Drossera intermedia*. They're plants that eat bugs, and about the ugliest ones you can think of. I want that plant. Not just any sundew your jackhole boss bought online either. The one that grew in the bucket under her bed. Both of the plants. You bring me those flowers, I'll get you in touch with the warlock. Should be a pretty quick turn-around time. A night to grow the flowers, a day to fly it here to me. Think you can do that?"

"I'll certainly relay the message, and I can't speak for my employer, but I suspect he'll abide by your wishes, Your Highness."

The giant troll sat back in his throne. "Well that's just great to hear, ass-face. It's so nice doing business with you."

Thaddeus bowed curtly but deeply at the waist, just as Cassius had taught him, and then took off running back to the elevator. He only had to dodge a few flaming projectiles while he waited for the doors to open. It wasn't until he was safely inside that he breathed a sigh of relief and reflected on the conversation. *Dammit*, he thought. *'So nice doing business with you'? 'So nice'? Shit. He knows we don't really have her yet. He knows, and he wants Cassius to know he knows.*

Below, the King of Trolls called to some of the messengers. "Bring me my computer for Skype calling, you little failed abortions!"

Two small trolls brought out a huge monitor with a small webcam attached to the top, and they did their best to hold it still while a third troll carried a computer tower half his size and rolled out a blue line of ethernet cable behind him. Once the little techie troll was positioned behind the monitor, he set down the tower and busied himself plugging the cord from the tower to the monitor. A fourth troll ran an orange extension cord up onto the stage, plugged both the monitor and the tower into a surge protector connected to the cord, and then made a wise retreat. The troll who had carried the computer tower up onto the stage now stood idle next to it, watching the fourth go. His eyes widened at the realization that he should have escaped as well, but it was too late.

"That doesn't seem fair," the King said. "They have to hold that big hunk of shit, and you get to just stand there like some kind of fucking middle-manager? C'mere. I need a mouse pad."

The messenger troll positioned himself at the end of the king's throne. He'd seen this done before. He turned his face up toward the cavern's vaulted ceiling and stood still. The king reached behind his throne and grabbed a fancy remote keyboard, which he set in his lap, and a matching gaming mouse. He set this on the messenger's cheek, the tiny red laser reflecting off the small troll's skin. Then the king began sliding the mouse around on the messenger's face. Just when the gesture might have seemed pleasant, almost affectionate, the king would reach some point where his desired location on the screen didn't match nicely with the contours of the messenger's face, and then he'd lift the mouse and smack it down in a more convenient location, taking out his mild irritation at the mouse's lack of accuracy on the messenger. At other times he'd linger on the messenger's eye, letting the laser burn the small troll's retina as he read the screen. Eventually the king found the icon for the video conferencing program, clicked through the menu, and launched the call with one final raising and slamming of the mouse, producing a wet slapping sound on the minion's cheek and starting the program dialing.

"This is going to be a fucking weird conversation," the king muttered beneath the sound of an old fashioned phone ringing. "I'm irritated by all this royal ass-kissing horseshit already."

The program connected the call, activating a clicking sound just as artificial as the ring-tone had been. A small window opened, off center on the massive TV wobbling in the thin arms of the two small trolls. The king clicked hard on the mouse button to enlarge the image to full screen, but he didn't raise the mouse and slap it down because he was already trying to be on his best behavior.

The monster on the screen did not look dangerous, but the King knew better. Tisina, Queen of the Sirens, Lord over all the Merfolk, Rider of the Leviathan, Ruler of the Depths and Heights of the Sea floated in the water on the screen, and almost everything about her outward appearance was a lie. She appeared to be a human woman, short and thin, with long, straight, dark hair (mostly black but with purple and turquoise highlights) that flowed around her head in the gentle current. She seemed to be wearing a decorative gown, precariously strapless on top and formal with a bodice-style waist and a ballooning skirt, all made out of some shimmery, dark green material with gauzy white skirts rippling in the water beneath. The King of the Trolls had never seen Tisina as she truly was, but he could tell everything about her outward appearance was designed to both deceive and entice. He knew this because, as a troll, he fed on chaos, and even through the computer screen and the vast distance, he could smell the perfume of his favorite meal. Deception was the fertilizer of chaos. It grew in bullshit. And Tisina reeked of bullshit in a way only monsters could truly appreciate.

"Your Highness," the king drawled. "Would it be offensive to say you look as eminently fuckable as ever?"

Tisina smiled slightly and said nothing for just long enough the King thought she might not respond. He inhaled to speak, and she made the breath catch, timed in such a way it almost made him cough.

"Thank you for trying to be polite, Your Highness."

Her voice was soft. She wasn't using a phone to speak for her as she would have been required to do at a meeting of The Convention. Sirens were not allowed to speak because of their mind control powers, but no one would dare tell Tisina she could not speak as she saw fit. It was possible she was manipulating him with those powers, the King knew. He hoped his nose would alert him to such a dangerous deception, but he recognized the powers might obscure his ability to identify their use. He'd calculated the risk and decided the payoff was worthwhile.

"Um, sure. So, here's the situation. The vampire I told you about is trying to pull a fast one. He sent one of his little butt boys just now to tell me they have this writer girl, the one Nigel was using to make that book for him. But the vampire was lying. They don't have her. They're playing for time. They think they can make excuses and get our support at the next meeting of The Convention, then not deliver. We need to make it clear we need the magical ingredients *before* they get our support. So I told him how to make the ingredients you asked for, and I ordered him to deliver them tomorrow. Which they can't do because they don't have the girl yet. So that's gonna light a fire under their asses to get the writer and get the flowers for you."

Tisina stared at the King intently, seeming to listen. But then, when he finished, her gaze didn't waver at all, and she didn't respond.

Another pause drew out until he drew breath.

She interrupted his next words at the last moment

once again. "Good."

The King blinked. "Good? Which part?"

"All of it. Good. Pressure them. Get me what I want." She said this so lightly, almost childishly, as though she barely cared. "I will convey that my support will be withheld until I have the ingredients. He will deliver the magic plants to you. You will deliver them to me. And then I will have my revenge on the humans as I have planned. So this is all good."

"Alright then," the King said. "Fuckin' A. You let them know they've got to get their shit together. I'll ride 'em hard when they don't deliver tomorrow. They'll get you what you need. And you know how the spell works. You put the flowers under the bed, fuck your consort or whoever, and then eat the pretty plant and plant the ugly one under the moonlight. You do that, and you'll get pregnant with the child you want, the beautiful hero who will avenge your people. That's what the warlock said, and he knows his shit. But he also said you gotta follow the directions perfectly or you'll fuck it all up real bad. He was very clear on that, too. Don't, under any circumstances, eat the ugly plant. If you do, you'll have twins, and one of them will be … well, he said it would be a bad scene. Rivers of blood and the oceans boiling and the sky filled with sulfur and all that apocalyptic stuff you and I know all too well. I got you the plan, and I'll get you the flowers, and you'll have your revenge on the humans. A deal is a deal, right?"

Another of those painful pauses. "Good," she said.

"Um, right. So we're agreed. I'll get you those as soon

as I have 'em. I guess we'll talk again, then, right?"

Pause. "Mm-hmm."

And then her end of the connection was cut.

The king saw himself clearly in the bright, small box on the screen displaying the image he was sending, and he also saw the dark reflection of his face bouncing off the larger black box where her image had been. Twins, one much darker and larger than the other. He smiled and examined his yellowed fangs in both images, but the mirth drained out of the grin before he closed his lips.

The messenger troll serving as a mousepad felt the computer mouse hovering above his head, not making contact, and he dared to turn, very slowly, to see his king. "Um, Your Highness? Is she going to keep her side of the bargain? I couldn't even tell if …?"

The king raised the mouse as though he was going to smash it down on the mousepad. The little troll quailed but tried to stay upright, knowing he'd get a more severe thrashing if the mousepad wasn't within arm's reach when the king needed it. But at the last second, the king demurred. "What couldn't you tell, you little shit-stain?"

"I … I … I couldn't tell if she even understood what you were telling her."

"What's your name, you little bag of piss?"

"It's Egg, Your Highness. Because of the shape of my head. And the twitter insult."

"Right." The king sounded contemplative, his voice aimed somewhere far off. Then he suddenly threw the mouse at one of the two trolls holding the monitor. "You two fuck off with that. Don't break it, or I'll rip your spines out and use your coccyges for toothpicks." Then he looked down at Egg. "But you stay here. You're just the right amount of stupid to talk to. Smart enough to help me process some ideas. Stupid enough to dare to make me mad. I'll most likely kill you in the morning."

"Oh, thank you, Your Highness."

"Shut the fuck up."

The two trolls holding the monitor carefully lowered it so one could scoop up the mouse that had just hit him. The other reached out in the king's direction and waited.

"What? Oh, yea," the king said, then tossed the wireless keyboard like a frisbee, smacking the troll with the outstretched hand directly in the face. The struck troll nodded in appreciation, then picked up the keyboard. The monitor in his other hand swayed dangerously, and the king scowled, but the two trolls righted it and scuttled off the stage.

The king looked down at Egg. "So, you noticed that? Yes, that's what is scariest about Tisina. Maybe she's this brilliant strategist who works very hard to keep from revealing her secret plans. Or maybe she's a fucking moron who doesn't have any plan at all. It's extra hard to tell with royalty; not like she had to earn her position. Just born a princess and became queen, right? Did she have to outmaneuver her siblings? Maybe. But maybe they were morons, too. Can't tell. Lotta inbreeding with royal families. So maybe she's clever, and maybe she's an idiot." The king watched Egg carefully. The small troll registered the irony of a royal making this critique of royals, then recognized the king was aware of the irony, then considered laughing at the king's clever joke, then decided against it all in a flash the king admired.

"So," the little troll said, and then he brightened. "You're making a double bet, aren't you? You have a strategy if she's clever, and another if she's stupid!"

The king smiled slowly, a leering and revolting expression that would have repulsed anyone who wasn't a troll. "Ah, there's something to you, Egg. But you're not quite there, yet. Double bets aren't enough anymore. I had one of those when I was dealing with that necromancer, Nigel. If he got the writer and nearly destroyed the world, I had a plan to turn that to my advantage. And when he fucked it up and got himself and a bunch of his allies killed in the process, I had a plan for that, too. Used it to split the vampires into factions. Got one of them to work for me in exchange for my support. Worked out just fine. This time, I have three bets. Maybe the vampires I've been supporting fuck this up and fail to get the queen of the merfolk what she wants. If that happens, I have a plan. Or maybe they do get it, and I get it to her. If I do, she'll either do her thing, create her hero successor, and set him loose to lead the merfolk army in their attack on the humans. Or she'll screw it up and cause the apocalypse the warlock told me about. And I have a plan for that, too. In fact, the upside for me might be even better if she does. So I keep telling her to be careful and follow the instructions. If she's smart, she will make her messiah baby, and I win. But I'm skeptical. I suspect if I keep telling her what to do, she'll be even more inclined to screw it up out of a combination of confusion and spite. And then the shit will hit the fan, and we'll come out of that as the stronger survivors."

"Survivors? All of us?"

"Oh, probably not. If she fucks it up, it's gonna be really bad. Hell-on-Earth kinda' bad. Lots of trolls will die. Our whole online trolling game will probably be worthless because there will be no more internet and not very many humans left to rebuild it. It will be back to the days of eating the occasional Viking. But we'll make it, and lots of our competition will be eliminated. And that Nigel, for all his stupidity, convinced me, in the long run, the humans are a bigger danger than any of the groups of monsters we deal with. They really could end all life on this planet, and those of us who are magic have our needs. I can't eat chaos when there's no one left to produce chaos. I'd starve, too. So we'll send the humans back to the stone age to save them, not because we care about them, but because we need to maintain our food supply."

He sat back in his throne. His massive shoulders rolled to either side of the chair's thin back. His elbows stuck out behind the chair while his huge hands squeezed the chair's arms. His legs, meanwhile, were short enough his clawed feet kicked above the ground when he was excited, and clearly this idea of outmaneuvering Tisina pleased him. Not only were those claws flashing as the feet swung, but his crotch was right at Egg's eye level, and his erection had returned.

"Yeah, Tisina may or may not turn out to be the key

to the biggest chaos buffet we've ever seen and our salvation from the human danger. Who knows? But I have a feeling she's going to make a mess, whether she means to or not." Then his legs stopped kicking. "Know what, Egg? In times like this, when I'm feeling really good about my plans, know what makes me a good king?"

Egg considered guessing, ran through a couple answers, and decided the safest was: "What, Your Highness?"

"I stop and consider the possibility I might be wrong. I'm worried I may have underestimated Tisina."

"Her intelligence?" Egg asked.

"No." The king of the trolls shook his head in a way that made his jowls waggle. "No, her obliviousness. Maybe she's faking, but if she is as flighty and capricious as she seems, that kind of complete ignorance, when mixed with power, is a far more dangerous combination than cleverness and malice and power. Those are at least predictable. They have identifiable, selfish goals. You can follow the money. Even selfless religious zealotry, though often more dangerous than selfishness, is more predictable than obliviousness mixed with power. Obliviousness and power is the worst combination. Who knows how much damage a person can do when they are willing to destroy everything on a whim?"

Egg frowned quizzically. "But if obliviousness mixed with power can cause the most chaos, and we trolls need chaos, shouldn't we be rooting for Tisina to be as dense as she seems?"

The King of Trolls reached down and patted Egg on the head almost gently. "Ah, Egg, there are some good scrambled brains in that misshapen skull of yours. You've identified the supreme irony of my job. See, all you little bastards like Cheetos and RedBull, right? So I'm a good king because I give you those things, right?"

Egg nodded enthusiastically. Just the thought of RedBull gave him the jitters.

"But if I poured too much of that shit in here and drowned you all, you wouldn't like it anymore, would you? It's my job to feed you chaos, too. Enough to keep us all fat and happy." He patted his potbelly. "But chaos is harder to manage than Redbull and Cheetos. This is a lesson those fuckwits are learning the hard way." He pointed straight up, though whether he was pointing at the people who worked for Fox News or at the entire human species was unclear. "It's very difficult to create chaos and stay in control of it."

"Woe to him who doesn't know how to wear his mask, be he king or pope!"

-Luigi Pirandello

Chapter 7

It wasn't exactly a limousine, but Matt had rented the nicest car he could order on the west coast of Costa Rica to come pick them up at Lena's house. It was some fancy sedan she couldn't identify, far more practical than a limo for the rough, twisty streets making all those tight turns through the hills, but far too clean and black for the dust and dirt of those unpaved roads. The driver was a member of Matt's crew. When Matt described her as such, Lena thought it odd he'd use slang to describe a friend or an employee. She didn't understand he meant "crew" in the most traditional sense. The woman, Sara Summerfield, wore a white polo shirt and khaki slacks that could have been a uniform but may also have been her summer vacation clothing. She had olive skin and flashed a bright smile when Matt introduced her, then turned her eyes to the road and ignored her passengers. Her dark hair and Mediterranean features didn't match the name "Summerfield," and she didn't speak on the entire drive, behavior Lena didn't consider particularly summer-y.

Matt couldn't quite understand Lena's mood. He could sense her curiosity about their journey, but it didn't rise to the level of either enthusiasm or anxiety he expected of someone leaving her home for the first time in a year.

After some jostling on the uneven roads, as the asphalt smoothed and told them they were nearing a larger population center, Matt broke the silence. "You don't seem particularly excited about our trip. How are you feeling?" He knew exactly how she was feeling. He wanted to know if she understood why she was feeling that way.

"I don't know," she said, not wistful but matter-of-fact. "My life used to make sense to me, you know? It was boring, just routine on top of a layer of background disappointment, but it was also comfortable. Like, it may not have been what I wanted, but it was predictable. I worked at a bank. I had brief relationships that always failed. I wrote short stories but didn't have the guts to send them to anyone for publication. Then there was this brief little explosion of craziness." She shrugged and cocked her head to the side, smiling quickly. "Met some monsters. Saved the human race. NBD." Her shoulders slumped. "And since then I've been trying to get back to something resembling normal. And I just can't find my way there."

"Here's my guess," Matt said, "and this is coming from a sorcerer who is not really human anymore, so how's that for a grain of salt? But, also, I'm quite a bit older than you are, so maybe I've acquired a bit of wisdom. Your life was predictable and disappointing, right? You are trying to get back to predictable, but you can't, so you are following the only path you know, and it's the one back to disappointment. Maybe, instead of trying to go back, you should just embrace the madness. Sure, you'll miss out on the comfort, but..." He raised an eyebrow and drew out the last word, looking at her sideways.

"I suppose you're right. I'm starting to suspect the comfort was just a product of a lot of lies I told myself."

"Oh, don't be unfair. It was also a product of a lot of lies told to you. Conspiracies and glamours and monsters hiding in the shadows. How could you be expected to know about all of that?"

"I don't feel bad I didn't know about vampires and werewolves, Matt. I feel bad I didn't want to know about myself."

Matt couldn't think of a clever riposte, so they rode on in silence.

When the car arrived at the dock, Matt's use of the

term "crew" suddenly made sense. The car stopped in a thin lot lining the western side of the street. Across a short strip of sand running along the bay, an aluminum dock stretched out toward the horizon and then made a T shape. A handful of small fishing boats and tourist water taxis bobbed on the wakes of the ones leaving or approaching, but one stood out. It was a small, rubber craft, but clearly far more expensive than the others.

"That's your ship?" Lena asked.

"That's my tender, but I will not be offended if you refer to her as a dinghy. It will take us to that." Matt pointed out into the open water beyond the little bay. "That's my yacht. I give you the S.S. Exclamation."

Lena turned to Summerfield who was holding her door to close behind her. "Wow. The Exclamation, huh? Compensate much? Does he also have a truck with giant tires?"

Summerfield shook her head and deadpanned: "I cannot speak to that, ma'am. Not onboard, ma'am." Then she flashed a tiny smile at the sound of Lena's big laugh.

Matt ignored the exchange. "Ms. Wallace, I must ask. Your large friend. Will he retain his current form? I'm concerned he may present a structural problem. How much does our earthen companion weigh? Is he going to fall through the ship's hull like a cartoon cannonball?"

Josef, who had followed the car in the form of a dust devil, swirled around Lena's feet playfully. Lena smiled. "Its pronouns are it/its," she reminded him. "It sailed here with me. It can take on more mass or reduce it at will. There may be a little less Josef when we get to our destination than when it came aboard. Or it may absorb some of the hull if it needs it." She nodded toward the S.S. Exclamation. "But when it comes aboard, if it thinks I'm threatened or finds some Nazis to punch..." She shrugged. "Well, how flimsy is your boat?"

"Boat!" Matt scoffed. "Ms. Summerfield, when we get to the ship, please remind me to tell Captain Emory she has my permission to make Ms. Wallace here walk the plank if she continues to insult The Exclamation."

"Yessir."

They made their way past the concrete portion of the dock and stepped onto the system of aluminum bridges connecting the boats in the marina. Lena had read about the crocodiles that sunned themselves on some Costa Rican beaches, terrifying and thrilling tourists. She looked through the metal slats at the rippling shadows and tried to reach inside herself and discover if she was scared of crocodiles. She'd seen werewolves and vampires. She'd been captured by an army of reanimated skeletons. Crocodiles just didn't thrill her anymore.

The little rubber tender had an outboard motor, and Ms. Summerfield steered her three passengers across the bay. Matt reclined in the middle of the boat, bouncing along on the wakes of the bay's other crafts, his face more placid than the water. And up at the prow, Lena sat looking ahead like a mermaid sculpture hewn from an ancient mast, her curly hair barely moving in the wind. Ms. Summerfield couldn't see Josef, though she was aware of the golem's presence. Matt hadn't tried to hide Josef's existence from her any more than he tried to hide his magic powers. The humans could only see what the monsters let them see, and they could understand and believe far less. Josef was mostly an invisible bulk sitting protectively between Lena and Matt, but some of it was also sand in Lena's backpack, and even this had barely any weight, certainly nothing the woman at the tiller could detect from the way the little craft behaved in the water.

Lena watched the yacht grow until she could make out the shapes of the five women waiting on the top deck, waving to the oncoming craft. One of the women jumped up and down as she waved, exuberant and childish. Another made broad, consistent waves from the elbow, either holding onto her dignity or constrained by it. Between the big wavers, the other three made small finger flicking gestures, tickling the air but mostly focused on leaning over the railing to present themselves to Matt in the most lascivious ways they could manage. They clearly weren't professionals, so their poses were awkward mash-ups of come-hithers from Instagram and Vogue and a lifetime of mass media telling them how men were to be seduced, while reality had shaped their bodies into the un-airbrushed forms of working moms who didn't feel comfortable in their bikinis until after the second margarita. Because the women couldn't tell quite how far their voices would carry over the sound of the skiff's motor and the waves slapping the side of the yacht, and because they wanted to distinguish themselves from their peers while not embarrassing themselves, their chorus of "Ma-att!" sounded like the early, uncertain beginnings of a spontaneous chant that doesn't coalesce.

Matt looked up from his position in the middle of the boat and waved at the women, his gesture stiff enough to be distant, his smile just bright enough to be warm, finding the sweet spot of coolness which had to seem effortless to be successful. Lena could imagine the women swooning, and she rolled her eyes. "Who are they?"

"Oh, just some new friends I picked up for a little ride a few days ago. They were the perfect mixture for me. Judy, the woman on the end, is single and desperate to find the love of her life. On the other end, Tina is newly divorced and eager to prove to herself she isn't past her prime. Next to Tina is Allison. She's happily married and trying to convince the others she's not boring. In the middle, that's..." He looked to Ms. Summerfield. "What's her name?"

"Madge, I think?"

He shook his head. "It's something like that. She's not really sure what she wants out of this girl's trip or her life or much of anything. Kind of forgettable, obviously. Next to her is Eleanor. She is also happily married but is looking to cheat to convince herself she can."

Lena shook her head. "So that's how you think of them. Not their jobs. Not their relationships to one another. Just whether they are available for you?"

"Oh, no, their relationships to one another are of paramount importance." He made a visible show of pointing at them all as he spoke about them, going down the line. "Tina and Allison are best friends, and Tina is very worried Allison won't like her anymore now that she's divorced and living the single life. Allison is very worried Tina will love the single life and leave her behind. The middle one thinks none of the others like her very much because she's quiet, and her discomfort makes her even more quiet, but when she remembers this it compels her to say transparently cheesy things to earn their approval, so they don't really like her very much. She's basically as deep as a Hallmark card. Eleanor is whip-smart and wants to believe the others don't bore the shit out of her because she feels guilty for feeling superior. Also, they bore the shit out of her and she feels superior. And Judy is the most committed to the idea this is a group and can't bear it when there's even the slightest hint of a sidelong glance among them. So I make them shoot a lot of sidelong glances in her presence."

"So this is how you entertain yourself? You pick up groups of women and bring them on your yacht to fuck them?"

Matt shook his head violently. "No, Ma'am." Then he smiled. "To fuck with them."

"You're a monster." But she sounded unimpressed, even bored.

"Exactly."

"So it's trolling?"

"Not quite. Trolling is what trolls do. Trolls feed on chaos. A troll would want the ship to turn into Lord of the Flies with these women ultimately going after one another with machetes or forks or homemade spears or hairspray-and-cigarette-lighter blowtorches-"

"Got it. But not you?"

"No, I'm a warlock. I feed on passions. The stronger the feeling, the more I can convert that energy into power for my spells. You, my dear, are … not helpful. You barely have any feelings left." He looked at her bag and spoke to the sand swirling around her feet. "Most of her useful feelings are love for you, my homuncular friend."

Lena rested a hand on the top of the bag. "Josef is one of the best, kindest, most gentle people I've ever known."

Matt raised an eyebrow. "Even when it's putting a fist through a Nazi's skull?"

Lena gave a slow, somber nod. "Especially then."

The small boat curved out and arced back in so it ran parallel to the hull near the back of the yacht, and the three of them ducked as Ms. Summerfield steered it into a rope contraption which then raised it up to the level of the main deck. Two additional crewmembers, both women dressed in the same khakis-and-polo-shirt uniform of Ms. Summerfield, assisted them out of the tender, then lifted the whole boat up onto its side and into a space where it was unobtrusive.

A new crewmember walked over and stood stiffly next to Matt. "Lena," Matt said, "this is the captain of the S.S. Exclamation, Meili Emory. Captain Emory, this is Magdalena Wallace, the greatest writer in the world."

Captain Emory wore the same uniform of khaki shorts and a white polo, but she had a white captain's hat resting on a tightly pulled black ponytail. Her features, like her name, spoke to some interesting ethnic mix which made Lena feel an immediate affinity, some Asian, some European, but Lena couldn't guess more specifically. Meili herself only knew her ancestors were Chinese, Nordic, and Portuguese, but she knew the math hinted at a more complicated story. Even the name Meili could have come from the Chinese or the Norse. The mix gave her striking features, traditional Asiatic eyes, an aquiline nose, plump Mediterranean lips. She was shorter than Lena's 5'8 by a couple inches and a bit wider in the shoulders and hips, and Lena found her attractive, but mostly because of the way she carried herself with an authority Lena envied and admired. Though the women looked completely different, that air of confidence reminded Lena of Bel, and a pang of longing constricted her chest.

Captain Emory held out a hand and shook Lena's firmly. "Welcome aboard The Exclamation. It's our honor. If you'll forgive me, I don't think I've read any of your work."

Lena looked at the deck, bashful. "Oh, Matt is being too kind. I'm unpublished."

Matt nodded. "Being the most talented and being unpublished; these are not mutually exclusive states of being. I must agree with Captain Emory: It's our honor to have you aboard. Now, Captain, will you have someone escort Ms. Wallace to her quarters, and will you prepare us to disembark?" He turned and started walking off, then remembered. "Oh, and we need to deposit our previous guests on land here. Have someone zip them back to shore and arrange for their transportation back to their resort. I'll be sure to see them off before they go."

"Yessir," Captain Emory said to his back. Then she turned to Lena. "Ms. Wallace, we have excellent quarters all prepared for you. Right this way."

As Lena followed her around to the stairway in the front of the ship which led down into the hallway on the second deck with the sleeping quarters, Lena examined the members of the crew as they went about their work preparing the yacht. Before they stepped inside, Lena stopped. "Um, Captain Emory, can I ask you something?"

"Of course."

"I notice everyone on the crew…"

"Yes?"

"They're - you're all women."

"Correct." Captain Emory smiled and waited.

"It's just, I was wondering if that's because of Matt's whole … thing?"

"Being a warlock?"

"Oh, you know about that?"

"I do. I know I'm not supposed to. I know speaking about it to a fellow human could get him killed. But I also know you've brought a golem onto my ship, so you're clearly in on the secret nature of our supernatural companions."

"Yeah. It's fucking weird, isn't it?"

"You'll be surprised by how much you get used to it. But yes, I found it disconcerting at first. I've worked for

Mr. Bernusconi for twenty years. I'm very used to it."

"Twenty years? So, this?" Lena made an elevator gesture in Captain Emory's direction, her wrist waggling her hand up and down. "Is this a glamour, too?"

Captain Emory smiled again, more deeply, and closed her eyes slowly, nodding slightly. "Thank you very much, but no. I just look young for my age. I'm 46. Mr. Bernusconi recruited me right out of the Navy when I was twenty-six. I was a promising officer, served for four years after college, and he convinced me not to re-up. And I've never looked back."

"So, why all women? Is it his whole eating-passions thing? Like, women are more emotional?"

Emory tilted her head slightly and frowned. "You know that's not true, don't you?"

"Sure, but does Matt know? People hold onto bullshit stereotypes as long as they are convenient."

Emory shook her head. "No, he can't lie to himself about that. Reality undermines stereotypes. He needs feelings; not assumptions about feelings. But he doesn't want them from his crew. He hires us to be dispassionate people who can do our jobs in the midst of the passions he creates. His ability to detect passions makes him good at hiring dispassionate people. You'll find the crew is the most chill, competent group of sailors you could ask for."

"So why all women?"

"It makes humans, both men and women, think he's cooler. And that, in turn, helps him attract the kinds of people he wants to bring aboard. Men and women. They all admire him. He constructs his persona very carefully."

"I believe you. But does it bother you at all, working for a guy who is … well … a monster?"

"Best boss I ever had."

"But you know he'd sacrifice you to save his own skin, right?"

"So would every human boss I ever worked for before, and they were a lot more fragile than a magical warlock."

"True. True," Lena intoned.

"I won't pretend he's a good person. What he does to people … Well, it isn't nice, but it's not like he's killing anybody. And he really is a good boss. He takes good care of me and my crew, and that's what I worry about. It's a living."

Lena didn't know enough to judge this particular moral compromise, so she could only shrug and follow the captain into the ship, down the stairs, through the narrow hall, to the door to her cabin. Through the door with the rounded corners, Lena stepped into a room that looked like the most cramped room in a luxury hotel. Everything was brilliant white walls or marble counters, the surface of the desk matching the counter in the kitchenette and the one in the bathroom, but everything pinched around the queen-sized bed with the fancy duvet and the decorative pillows arranged just so. The room even smelled fancy thanks to a bowl on the counter in the kitchenette where rose petals, bright red and blinding white, floated in scented water. Lena turned back to the captain who remained in the hallway. "It's beautiful."

"Like I said, Mr. Bernusconi cares a lot about the little details. Please make yourself comfortable. We'll have lunch prepared for you and Mr. Bernusconi shortly. I can send someone for you here, or you can drop your things and explore the ship if you like. I do hope you'll enjoy your trip with us."

Lena thanked her, and Captain Emory left. Lena closed the cabin door, pulled her backpack off, and set it on the bed. "Well, Josef? What do you think?"

Lena felt a swirl of air push against her curls, and then Josef was there, towering over her, hunched down against the low ceiling. It made an exaggerated shrug, and its shoulders scraped the walls.

She nodded. "I feel the same way. Would you mind staying here and guarding my backpack? And if anything happens to me, just punch a hole in the hull and sink the ship, okay? I would feel bad for the sailors, but if this is some trap, it's better to sink this whole giant prosthetic penis than let Matt get what's in my pack."

The golem nodded. Lena pushed her backpack under the bed, gave herself a quick glance in the mirror, decided she didn't care what she looked like, and started toward the door. Josef made itself into a permeable cloud so Lena could pass, but when her hand was on the doorknob, she changed her mind. The vision in the mirror had caught up with her, and she decided she was too ashy to be seen in public, so she went back to the bed, fished her lotion out of the backpack underneath, sat on the edge of the bed and carefully massaged the cocoa butter into all her exposed skin. It felt like a religious rite, a transition from the world of the undead to this world of social interaction. She knew she hadn't recovered from reading the book, but the layer of lotion was like a cosplay costume of a character who cared about life, and that was progress.

When she got up to the main deck, she found Matt with his guests. "I'm so sorry, ladies, but work calls, and I'm going to have to say goodbye to you all. I've sent for a car to take you back to your resort." He looked at the women one at a time with a rakish grin that was almost a secret wink for each one. "I'm sure we could have had so much fun if we had more time, but Lena and I have some business to attend to."

Lena wished she could turn on her heel and go right back to her cabin, but it was too late.

"Aw, Matt, that sucks," Judy whined.

"Yeah, we could have had a lot of fun," Tina said.

"Frankly, this is bullshit," Eleanor said.

"Yeah, I agree," Allison said. "Tina, it's his loss."

"Right," Judy said, but she gave Lena a hard stare.

Eleanor sent Lena an eyeroll.

Tina gave her an elevator glance followed by a harrumph.

Allison nodded at that, then glared at Lena.

Madge looked at her friends, confused, then at Lena, confused, then back at her friends, still confused.

"I'll tell you what," Matt said, gesturing them towards the waiting skiff which already held their bags. "Tonight, go to the club at your resort, and all the drinks you want are on me. My treat. And then, the next time I'm in Cleveland, I'll look you all up."

Eleanor wheeled on him. "It's an all-inclusive resort, asshole. And we're from Cincinnati."

"Of course you are. Go Steelers."

"Bengals!" Madge shouted, happy to contribute.

"Yes, that's right. Next time I'm there, we'll all go together and catch some Bengals baseball."

"Football," Tina said without much conviction.

"He knows," Eleanor said. "He's making fun of you." She stomped into the skiff.

The others followed, and one of the members of the crew lowered the skiff into the water, started the engine, and steered the skiff towards the harbor. Judy and Madge looked forwards, but Tina, Eleanor, and Allison looked back as Matt waved. Eleanor flipped him off, but mostly the three looked at Lena.

She turned to Matt. "That was … unpleasant. Why were they angry with me? What did I do to them?"

"I showed up with a prettier woman and kicked them all off my ship. I was hoping for a longer meal, but the jealousy was a nice dessert."

"Prettier?" Lena asked. She wasn't fishing but genuinely skeptical.

"Believe it or not, every one of you thinks the others are prettier," Matt said. "Except Eleanor. She thinks she's prettier and thinks she's a bitch for having that opinion." He raised a fist halfheartedly and intoned dryly, "Yea, patriarchy."

They watched as the skiff deposited the women and

their bags at the dock, then came zipping back.

Matt clapped his hands. "Alright, well, I'm going to head up to the pilothouse and give the order to raise the anchor and depart. They don't need me to do that, mind you. The crew is entirely capable. But I do so enjoy 'giving the order.'"

Lena matched his fist and tone. "Yea, patriarchy."

He smiled. "Touché."

Alone, she looked out over the rail, felt the yacht's gentle lurch into motion, and watched the little harbor town begin to slide away. In minutes, there were only sharp rocks and lush jungle moving past.

Lena hummed a few notes, then sang quietly:

"Don't cry for me, Costa Rica,

The truth is, I never knew you

Not in my brightest days

My blind existence

You kept your promise

I kept my ..."

She tried to think of a rhyme other than "distance." Her new comprehension of existence had prevented her from fully embracing Costa Rica, and if there was one thing she'd learned in her 11 months there, it was that "existence" does not rhyme with "existence."

"Damn," she muttered. "That's a good line." She patted her pockets, looking for the pen and notepad which were in her backpack under her bed. Lena, like most writers, harbored a fear any idea not immediately jotted down would disappear and never make it into her writing. And she was correct; as soon as the first bubble caught her eye, she forgot the line, so those words would never make it onto paper.

It looked like a soap bubble floating on the wind, but her subconscious recognized the wrongness of it before her conscious mind deduced its unusual flightpath. The gentle breeze flowed in off the Pacific toward the shore east of her, but most of that was lost in the artificial wind of the ship's movement. Since the ship was heading north, the wind seemed to be moving southeast. But the bubble floated faster than the ship, moving to the north, about five feet from the railing in her hands. Then the bubble zigged in towards the ship, directly against the wind, on a trajectory which seemed to be aimed at her. As it got closer, she could see it more clearly. It did have the rainbow oily sheen of a soap bubble, but it looked thicker, and the rainbow stains didn't move the way they should have, sliding down toward the bottom and making the bubble turn over and redistribute the weight. Instead, these colors moved around the bubble in argyle swirls. It was around ten inches in diameter, an impressive bubble if blown out of a normal plastic wand, but not ridiculously large. Almost normal. Almost. As it neared her, Lena felt the childish compulsion to reach out and pop it. Then she hesitated. She decided to pop it because of its wrongness. Only, when she stretched out her arm, the bubble suddenly swirled, spiraling around her wrist, then rising up into the air. She watched it gain altitude, then change direction again, floating up over the boat and directly into the Pacific wind, headed out over open water towards that mind-boggling Pacific horizon.

"The fuck?" she whispered. Turning back to its source, she saw three more bubbles, each about the same size and five or six feet apart, moving in her direction, but they didn't come so close. Instead, they bobbed along, six feet off the starboard side, between Lena and the jungle, then made that same slow leap over the ship and headed out to sea on the port side.

Curious, she walked back along their path to the stern of the ship. Matt stood there, looking out to the west. As she watched, he held up a hand and slowly closed his eyes. The next bubble didn't grow there. It just appeared, fully formed, an inch above his fingertips. Then Matt waved his hand, and the bubble was set free. It flew behind his back with the wind, then made that impossible northward turn. This time, with no steep drop between them, Lena felt more confident indulging her impulse to pop Matt's bubble. She leapt at it and flailed her arms, but it dodged, swooping in a spiral that kept it on track to wherever it was headed.

Matt turned and looked at her. "You won't be able to catch them," he said.

"Why? What are they? Just … why?"

"I think of them as 'permanent ephemera,'" he said. "An excretion of an emulsion of excess emotion. Basically, they're feeling poop. I make passions into magic fuel. These are the parts of that converted fuel I can't use. They are made of low-grade feelings. Pleasantness. Mild irritation. Trifling despondency. Nothing strong enough to make a lasting glamour or move matter beyond displacing a few air molecules by a few nanometers."

"Where are they going?" she asked, trying, in vain, to see them once they'd become too small to make out as they floated toward the horizon.

"I don't know, to be quite honest. You'd think, after all these years, I might have found out what they're after. Clearly they defy the wind, so they have some kind of intentionality. I have a theory. I think they want to want. That's all. They wish they could be stronger feelings. So they push against the wind and try to go somewhere because they want to defy something, they want to matter more. But I might just be romanticizing."

"They're beautiful," Lena almost whispered.

Matt pursed his lips and looked at the deck, then frowned at Lena. "You aren't the woman you were before you read that book, are you?"

She continued staring out over the ocean and shook her head.

"You weren't supposed to survive. It was meant to destroy you. Tell me: How did it change you?"

"I know what you're doing, Matt. You're trying to get me to feel something."

"Just tell me what you've learned. If it doesn't make you feel anything, then it doesn't."

Lena frowned, then nodded. "It changed me in a lot of ways, I guess. For one thing, I don't fight to win anymore. There is no winning. We struggle, and then we die, and all the struggling doesn't make a damned bit of difference for us once we're gone. I engage in the struggle in order to be the kind of person who engages in the struggle. I'm a meaningless bubble of a person, I guess."

"What struggle? Not for peace. Not justice. Not love. You were just hiding out in a house and taking walks on the beach."

"The struggle looks different every second of every day for each person on the planet from the dawn of time until the end. For me, for the last year, sometimes the struggle is finding the strength to take the next breath."

"Well..." Matt rolled his eyes a little. "I'm glad to hear you're still trying to succeed at that one."

"No, I'm not trying. That's another way I've changed. I've stopped giving people credit for their efforts, for their good intentions. I'm not trying. I don't do that anymore. And I've stopped making excuses for people. I did that my whole life. It made me a pleasant person. Very forgiving. I wrote the stories of their efforts in my mind. Sure, they were fucking things up, but they had good intentions, right? But I'm done with all that. I'm not trying to live my best life or seize the day or YOLO or count how few fucks I have to give. I am an obelisk of stone standing in a desert of stinging wind and piercing sand. I'm not trying to be more or less than what I am today, all the while knowing I will be nothing eventually."

"But can an obelisk feel happiness? Can an obelisk love?"

At that word, Lena pictured Bel's face, so pale it nearly glowed in the scant moonlight piercing into the hotel room in Wales, looking down on her from just a few inches away, hovering up and down, back and forth like ocean waves, floating on the sensation of their coupling. "I don't know," she said. "I know the obelisk cannot try to love. It loves or it doesn't. It will love, or it won't." And then she pictured Bel in a different hotel room, on that first night after her rescue in Ireland, when she saw Bel open her mouth, unhinge her jaw, and reveal ring after ring of spiny, hollow, curved teeth, wriggling in the air, grasping for human flesh to drain. "I will love, or I won't."

"You can't just float there, Lena," Matt said. "I know a bit about passion. You will have to try in order to love."

"Seems like someone will just show up and put me on a ship and literally float me there, Matt. All I have to do is stand here."

"It will not always be this easy."

"What makes you think this is easy?"

Matt nodded and turned his gaze to follow hers out to sea. Then he made a strange sound, a hitch in his breath like choking on a burp.

"What?" she asked.

"Nothing. Let's go to the pilothouse. I'll let you steer. Have you ever steered a yacht before? It's far less interesting than you'd think. You mostly-"

"Matt?" she interrupted.

"Yes?"

"For a guy whose whole thing is glamours, you are a bad liar."

"What are you talking about?"

"What did you see?" She scanned the horizon as she asked. And then she spotted something so small, she had to squint. She put a hand on Matt's shoulder and stepped toward the rail. "What is it?"

"Um …" Matt struggled. He couldn't even think of the lie to cover what he was seeing. "What are you seeing that I'm not seeing?"

Lena assumed he was being coy. He wasn't. He was being perfectly direct in order to hide the fact he needed to know what he should or should not say.

"I think it's …" She stared in silence for a moment. It was moving toward them, resolving into something. "It's a little boat. Like your lifeboat. Yellow. And there's a man standing up in it. Waving! He's waving, Matt. We have to rescue him."

"Let's decide that when we get a bit closer."

Getting closer was no small feat. Up in the pilot house, while Matt gave directions to the crew just out of Lena's earshot, Lena steered the ship as he'd promised. Making the most dramatic turn of the wheel the ship would see on its entire journey still managed to be boring; apparently very rich people liked sports cars that could turn on a dime and boats that were the exact opposite. Eventually the ship made a large half circle and came up right next to the yellow lifeboat, and then Lena relinquished the wheel to a member of the crew and ran out with Matt to see the man she wanted to save.

He was standing up in the boat. He wore a sleeveless white undershirt, the kind Lena thought of as wife-beaters, under a dingy orange life jacket. He'd tied some other, indistinguishable kind of shirt around his head in a rough way that told Lena he was not an experienced turban-wearer but was protecting himself from the sun. Below the waist, he wore blue boxer shorts she thought of as old man boxers, simple, inexpensive, thin cotton, certainly not to be mistaken for public apparel.

Though he was more than twenty feet below her, he noticed where she was looking. "I apologize about the lack of pants," he said. "I used my jeans to collect rainwater to drink."

The man's voice took Lena off guard. For one thing, he was obviously Asian, so she hadn't predicted English with a strong British accent. Also, he looked like he was in his seventies, but his voice sounded younger and stronger than she expected. "We came to rescue you," Lena said. "You do need a rescue, right?"

He tilted his head to the side, thought about it, and started nodding slowly as he spoke. "You know what? A rescue, you say? I hadn't considered that possibility, but it could be fun."

Lena shot Matt a confused frown. She couldn't tell if the man was being sarcastic or not.

Matt leaned against the rail and called down. "Um, good sir, if you don't mind me asking, what's your name?"

"Xìngyún Lóng," the man said. "But just call me Lóng."

"Lung?" Lena asked.

"Close enough," Long said.

Matt shook his head. "Well, that's a little-"

Long shook his head. It was a tight shake, but Matt couldn't miss it. His head was eight feet wide.

"...uh, coincidental," Matt continued. "I knew someone who was … maybe related to you? Who knows. Regardless, you're welcome aboard The S. S. Exclamation. I'll just have some of my crew bring the tender around to tow your boat in."

"Why thank you," Long said. "It's a pleasant surprise to meet you both. Yes, jolly good."

Lena whispered to Matt, "Do you think he's crazy?"

Matt looked down at Xìngyún Lóng. Not the man, Long, who Lena saw. The real Xìngyún Lóng. He worried about his yacht's structural integrity again. But the way Long stood in the middle of the small boat, rocking gently on the balls of his feet despite a slightly bent posture that accentuated his little beer belly, made Matt suspect he wouldn't damage the ship any more than the golem down in Lena's cabin below.

"Maybe the sun and the days at sea have affected his mind," Matt told Lena. "But let's take a gamble on him."

*"A man always has two reasons for what he does
– a good one and the real one."*

-John Pierpont Morgan

Chapter 8

Cassius knew a bit about collecting strays, too.

It's common for humans to anchor their conception of the world around major historical events. Personal moments which define their lives — weddings, graduations, the births of children, funerals — are contextualized among these seemingly more significant occurrences; the rises and falls of heads of state, the beginnings and ending of wars, the occasional global plague. Cassius thought himself beyond such human concerns, but the truth was he was just as formed by one as the humans he disdained. While they thought about their world in relation to events like the 9/11 attacks, he was shaped by the fall of Constantinople in 1453.

Just as most humans were not in New York or Washington D.C. or rural Pennsylvania when their world changed on the 11th of September of 2001, Cassius was not in the city of Constantinople on the 23rd of March of 1453, nor was he inside it during any of the 53 day siege. In fact, by then, he was a few hundred years old and living in Paris with a small family of vampires of his own creation, but the news shook him to the core and changed his whole conception of the way the world functioned.

When Cassius had been human, he'd served as one of the *Droungarios* of the Watch, the elite force that protected the Byzantine emperor and the city of Constantinople, his childhood home. He'd joined the military as soon as he could, mostly to get away from his father's house. He'd traveled more extensively than most people, as far west as Otranto in the Byzantine portion of Italy before that fell to the Normans, and as far east as Manzikert (which is now Malazgirt in modern Turkey), years before that fell to the Seljuk Empire of the Turks, but he'd spent most of his life inside the city of Constantinople, proudly guarding the Theodosian Walls, the system of defenses built hundreds of years before he was born. He'd been taught they were impregnable, and this was one of his most fundamental beliefs, more than his devotion to a single emperor or to the Eastern Orthodox Church or even Jesus Christ Himself. Cassius loved his city and its walls, and he believed those walls would keep the city safe forever. And if he was inside those walls (and a man with a sword), he knew he was safe in a way he'd never been as a boy in his father's grip.

In 1053, Emperor Constantine IX disbanded the Drungary of the Watch. Even this did not come as a huge shock to Cassius. For decades there had been rumblings that maintaining a standing army was impractical. Mercenaries could be hired at times of war but didn't need to be fed and kept during times of peace, and a large army was, itself, a threat to the power of the emperor. More than one emperor had been killed by his own army. So when the Watch was disbanded, Cassius employed his greatest skill; he rolled with it, sliding nimbly from a position very clearly defined within a strict military hierarchy into a job in a mercenary corp where promotion was easier, loyalty was more of a performance, and ambition was the unspoken expectation. His tagma of 200 cavalry and infantry formed a private company, the Bastard Sons of Occasus. That was a dangerous time in his life, but also an entertaining one. At every turn, someone was stabbing someone in the back to take over, and Cassius learned to make the right friends, to be valuable to the people who might not be friendly enough to promote him but who might let him sleep through a coup, and to kill the friends who couldn't keep him alive. He rose up the ranks faster than he would have in the Drungary, and most of his coin still came from the same Emperor Constantine IX who'd fired him. His furloughs were still inside the city of his birth, and the revelry during those years as a mercenary, the drinking and whoring and backstabbing within the Theodosian Walls, remained some of his happiest memories for centuries to come.

Then, on his way to a mercenary job in Antioch on the Orontes, his company was attacked. The Bastard Sons of Occasus were much smaller than the full army he'd marched with back when he was a droungarios. Those could be groups of 40,000 men; they didn't have worry about attacks by roadside thieves when traveling. But Cassius' whole company of mercenaries was smaller than a tagma of 200. Cassius rode on horseback, as he'd been promoted from a *Noumeroi* of the Watch to an *Exkoubitoi* of their little company, not the highest ranking *Scholai*, but a mid-level officer and mounted cavalryman. The journey to the front should have been uneventful. They weren't on their guard as far as they were from the edge of the empire. While the Normans to the west often made smaller incursions, out on the eastern side, the movements of the sultanates tended to be massive, huge armies attacking cities. The Sultans were building fortifications further and further into the shrinking Byzantine Empire. The large, predictable pushes back sometimes succeeded but left the Empire shrinking and fracturing. The Bastard Sons of Occasus had been hired to participate in one of those retaliatory pushes, to take back a fortification built by the Byzantines and recently captured by the Seljuk Turks, but that was days off.

The Scholai had ordered they should march into the night, a risky decision, since men were more likely to roll ankles and, even worse, horses were more likely to break legs, when the company was marching by torchlight. But there were bonuses in the contract if they could arrive more quickly, so the company's leaders at the front of the line (under orders from those safely in their beds in Constantinople) were continuing the march for a couple hours after sunset before ordering the making of camp, then setting off at dawn, cutting the travel time to arrive a full day early. Cassius' attention was on keeping the infantry moving, keeping the torch bearers evenly spaced to provide enough light for the other marchers, and watching for drooping eyes and bobbing heads that might hint one of his men was going to fall asleep while walking, collapse, and cause a tangle of bodies in the darkness. They'd descended into a broad, shallow valley, barely an indentation in the earth but just deep enough Cassius could see the full line of the company's torches ahead and behind him. The road was particularly straight, and there were few trees in the rocky soil. Though he resented the choice to continue the march in the dark after such a long day, he enjoyed the sight of the serpent of fire slowly climbing out of the valley of perfect shadow under the moonless but bright sea of stars.

The head of the serpent hadn't yet crested the hill beyond, so Cassius was shocked when the sound of an attack came from the head of the line. Why, he wondered, were the Seljuk Turks so far into Byzantine territory? What were they doing, just waiting there in the darkness on the side of the road? And why were they attacking at night? How large of a force dared to attack hundreds of armed soldiers? Should he charge to the front? Hold his place until some foolish little band of thieves were quickly dispatched? And then, as the sounds of swords on shields and screams began to ring in his ears from both the front and rear of the line, he began to wonder if all of Anatolia had fallen and the Bastard Sons of Occasus had stumbled into the middle of a huge force of Turkish warriors. Even from his position on horseback, he couldn't see much beyond the line of torches heading east towards their destination, and the line heading west back to the rear of the company. These flickered through the branches of the few, short, scraggly olive trees which lined the roadway.

But the sound of the battle was off, somehow. The screams of pain were not paired with the normal shouts of triumph. The sounds of swords ripping through shields were not accompanied by the ringing of swords on swords, that unique bell chime made when the stiff Byzantine gladius parried the Turkish scimitar. This group of enemies, attacking in the darkness at both ends of the company, were screaming and dying in near silence. And yet, the sound seemed to be growing, getting closer, creeping towards him.

"Torches!" Cassius shouted. "We need more light!"

Most of the men around him were too confused to react quickly, but the torch bearers, feeling called upon, scrambled to rouse the other infantryman and even a few of the mounted cavalry to sheathe their swords and light torches of their own.

"Closer together," Cassius cried. "To the sound of my voice. To me, men! To me!"

His voice carried, and even his fellow *Exkoubitoi* obeyed, bringing their men and torches into a tight bunch. The horses couldn't keep still, but Cassius could feel his mount, normally eager to charge ahead, wanted to flee.

"Cassius?" one of the other *Exkoubitoi* shouted. "What in the hell is going on? Turks?"

"I don't know. Everyone, torches and swords. Lay your shields down close, ready to build a shield wall at my command, but I want torches and swords in hand. I want more light, damn you all! More light!"

The men obeyed, circling into a tighter oval in the road and the field around it, first a bulge in the serpent of fire, like a large rat dinner, then a ball of fifty frightened men as the serpent's head and tail were cut off and disappeared into the darkness.

"Cassius, can you see them?" the same *Exkoubitoi* asked.

"Nothing," Cassius said. He didn't need to shout anymore, and he knew if he tried, his voice would betray his uncertainty.

The first one he spotted was a man-shaped shadow which darted forward to stomp on the head of a torch and disappear again. But Cassius knew it was not a man. No man could move that fast.

And then a dozen shapes appeared at the edge of the light of the company's remaining torches. The creatures, which looked like men, did not step into the light. They ran faster than any horse could run, then stopped as though they'd hit the Theodosian Walls. They weren't dressed like Turks at all, more like the Normans he'd seen in his journeys to the western side of the empire, but they clearly weren't Normans, either. They wore heavy, dark cloaks, fur pelts wrapped around their shoulders, and no mail, just jerkins and pants beneath. A few, he realized, were women, one in a long dress but the other obscenely standing there in pants, feet shoulder width apart so her legs were just as visible and splayed as the men's. And yet, even this horror could not distract him from their faces. The hoods were all thrown back, and the creatures' mouths were open, their jaws hanging lower than any man's should have been able to open, like asp's, only instead of a pair of venomous fangs, the spaces inside those gaping holes were filled with ring after ring of tiny teeth. Cassius squinted against the flickering of the torches. Yes, it seemed the teeth were moving!

The men of The Bastard Sons of Occasus had fallen silent. Cassius knew many wanted to scream; he did himself. But why? The creatures had stopped and were standing in the road. No one was moving. Nothing was moving. Except their teeth. Why should he scream when he wouldn't know how to stop?

One of the men broke. Cassius couldn't tell if the mercenary intended to charge at the creatures or try to run past them and all the way back to Constantinople. The creatures were standing in the road between the men and the safety of their beds, after all. When the man ran towards them, they launched themselves forward, briefly disappearing. Then the man's sword was taken from his hand and shoved through his body, pierced in from the base of his neck just above his mail shirt and driven downwards into his belly. He dropped his torch as he fell, and one of the other creatures appeared and stomped on it just as it landed. But as he stomped, he looked up at the rest of the company, his mouth filled with those wriggling teeth, and he smiled.

While all human eyes were on that smile, another of the creatures, the woman in pants, seemed to appear in the hole in the front line left by the mercenary who had run. She grabbed the wrist of the nearest man and shoved his sword through the head of his comrade standing next to him. While he tried to comprehend this, examining his hand holding the hilt in his friend's face, honestly unsure if he'd done it himself, another of the creatures grabbed the bottom of his mail shirt, lifted it up, and ran a clawed hand across his belly. His intestines spilled out like he was giving birth to yards of rope on the deck of a ship sailing through a storm of red rain.

Another man was so confused he leapt back from the guts as though they were the real danger, and he bumped into another of the creatures who'd appeared behind him. This creature tilted the man's head to the side like a doctor examining a compliant patient's ear, then wrapped that distended mouth around the man's neck. The man had time to scream, a high-pitched dog-whine of pain that bubbled and gurgled as it was drowned. Then the creature ripped back, those wriggling teeth taking most of the man's neck.

For the first time, one of the soldiers took action, bringing his sword down in a large arc into the meaty section just above the creature's shoulder, a blow that should have removed the monster's arm. When the sword stopped in the beast's clavicle, the mercenary was too shocked to pull it back and try again. The creature turned back to him, the sword still embedded in his shoulder, and cut the man's throat open with a swipe

Cassius thought of as dismissive. Then the monster hissed, and one of his compatriots grabbed the hilt of the sword, yanked, and used it to split the head of the next man in the circle.

But the moment had served to remind the mercenaries they held swords for a reason. As swords began to flash, Cassius woke up, too. He spurred his horse and charged at the creatures. He mowed down some of his own soldiers as he made his way from the middle of the pack toward this battle. Vaguely, his ear registered cries from the other side of the ring of mercenaries, and he knew his brave charge was also a retreat from the other front. He swung his gladius at the head of one of the creatures who dodged easily, but with his other hand Cassius swung his lit torch like a club. This caught another of the monsters in the side of the face while it was biting into the neck of a screaming mercenary. The flames didn't seem to be quenched by any of the spraying blood flying in all directions. Instead, the creature's flesh caught like kindling. The monster dashed out of the fight so quickly Cassius almost couldn't track the movement, but the trail of light from the flaming face painted a glow into the field beside the road, and Cassius watched as the creature stopped, slapped at its own face, its hissing mingling with the sound of the burning. Then, to Cassius' surprise, the creature crouched down on all fours, pressed its burning face to the ground, and began using both hands to bury its head in the dirt. The flames went out, and the creature vanished.

"Burn them!" Cassius shouted. "They burn! Burn the demons!" He hauled on the reins, aimed his horse back into the most active part of the fray, and spurred. The horse leapt forward, and this time Cassius pointed his torch straight back, then crossed his body with the hand holding his sword. As he charged in, he swiped backhanded at one of the creatures who saw him coming. Again, the monster dodged the sword easily, but its eyes followed the sword as it flashed by. It didn't expect the torch to follow. Cassius caught it squarely in the head with enough force to crush a man's skull. The impact nearly broke Cassius' wrist, but the monster's skull didn't crunch as he'd expected. Instead, the flesh and hair caught just like the last creature's, and, again, the monster ran off into the darkness.

Cassius didn't follow it but immediately started looking for another. He charged and was preparing the same trick, meaning he was twisted sideways on the horse's back, when something hit him in the chest with enough force to send him flying. If he'd been lucky, he might have been caught by the last of his men still huddled in a circle in the midst of all the gore. Some had dropped their swords and were employing their most desperate weapon, the power of prayer. If Cassius had landed on them, it wouldn't have made those soldiers any more or less effective. If he'd been unlucky, he might have flown into the swordpoints of the last mercenaries still trying to fight. Prayer may or may not be effective; it rarely accidentally kills one's compatriots. But Cassius missed both those wielding steel and those wielding the shield of the love of Christ. He landed on his back, and any air in his lungs not driven out by the first punch departed with the second. Choking and gaping at the stars, he held onto the object that had driven him from his horse's back until, at last, his throat rediscovered the value of oxygen. Only then, as he gulped like a beached fish, did he realize he was hugging a helmeted, severed head.

An experienced soldier, Cassius batted it aside without much disgust, then scrambled on his hands and knees until he found two torches. On foot, he didn't expect to surprise any of the creatures with speed, but he swung the torches in wide arcs as he turned around, trying to find them in the darkness. The torches of the fallen Bastard Sons of Occasus littered the ground among their corpses, but the creatures were stomping them out, the valley descending into deeper and deeper darkness.

"Torches!" Cassius shouted at the last mercenaries remaining. "Take up torches!"

He watched as one man nodded, scanned the ground, reached forward and bent down for a torch, and then stood up straight, dumbfounded, to examine the stump where his hand had been. Then, when the creature grabbed him and pulled his head to the side, it also dragged him away from Cassius into the darkness. Cassius spun to find more of his comrades just in time to see their boots sliding out of the light.

And then he was alone.

In the tiny fortress of his torches' light, he examined the roadway. Dismembered limbs were difficult to distinguish from the discarded weapons of his comrades, but he found a few smoldering torches among the litter, and he risked lighting them by pointing one of his own while swinging the other in the opposite direction.

Slowly, he built a bigger ring of light. Amidst the sound of the flames, he heard groans from men who were fallen but still alive, clutching at wounds, mumbling the names of loved ones in Constantinople or Heaven or other lands all equally distant now. And on the periphery, in the darkness, the sounds of predators chewing on meat.

There was a hiss from the darkness, and the slurping and crunching stopped suddenly. Cassius pirouetted with his torches outstretched, trying to find a location in the silence. Then he heard new speech, a human language but not a wounded man's last mutterings in his Byzantine Latin. The voice seemed to be giving orders of some kind. Then there were replies in other voices, other directions. They were all around him. Cassius spun at each new voice, aiming his torches. There seemed to be some disagreement among his attackers. He hoped they would turn on one another, a constant possibility among his own Bastard Sons of Occasus, but the creatures didn't seem nearly angry enough. He could hear smiles on their lips as they spoke. It was a friendly disagreement, complete with some name calling and, once, laughter. It dwindled to tones of resignation and acquiescence. Then silence again.

Suddenly the creatures were in a ring around him. He saw their shadows against the slate blue night sky before they stepped into the light of his torches. They'd changed in two ways. Their hoods were all on, so the light of his torches pierced into their faces like it was exploring caves. And inside those tunnels, Cassius saw their mouths were closed, their jaws retracted back into the shape of men's.

"Back!" he shouted, swinging the torches around. "I'll burn you all, if I can. Back, I say!"

One of them spoke. His voice was soft, soothing even, though Cassius did not understand the language. Was he asking to parlay? Offering some kind of truce?

Then the creature in the guise of a man pointed to Cassius' left and spoke to one of the man-shaped demons there. Cassius looked where he was directed. The man did not move. But he smiled benignly. There must have been a joke, but a very small one.

Then something hit Cassius in the back of the head, and he lost consciousness.

When Cassius awoke, before he even opened his eyes, he noted he felt far better than he should have. Not only had he escaped the battle without a wound, but his head didn't hurt from the last blow, and even the aches and pains of a normal life were gone. That toothache he'd had for years? Gone. The pain in his knee which used to bother him back when he'd been unmounted infantry? Gone. In fact, the painlessness was so complete, he could only compare it to the numb euphoria of drunkenness. But he was alert, more aware than he could ever remember being. He opened his eyes in a room with no distinguishable source of light, yet he could identify everything in the gloom.

He was tied to a chair in the center of a small room with a dirt floor. The walls were stone, but there was no mortar. His eyes could see the grains of dirt dribbling between the stones. So, it was a poor man's cellar. But instead of casks of wine or stores of food, the floor was packed with bodies of two kinds, so many they were lying on top of each other, sometimes three deep. Wrapped in their heavy, long cloaks and animal skins, the creatures slept comfortably on the floor. And strewn between them, members of his own company. He counted the bodies. 23 monsters. 27 Bastard Sons of Occasus.

He sniffed. The air was thick with terrible smells, but not in the order he'd expected. The urine and shit were less objectionable than the sweat and fetid breath. And he could even tell who was breathing by the smells. His comrades at arms stank of rot. They were barely alive, their breath ragged and uneven. Some were quite dead, and he found their smell the most offensive. The breath of his attackers smelled coppery and sweet and delicious. It smelled like the blood seeping out of every one of his fellow mercenaries. It smelled like his own breath. And his attackers smelled like him in some other way, like every part of their body was clean and healthy and throbbing with life despite their incredibly shallow breathing and slow heartbeats. Somehow, he knew they were not quite alive or dead in any way he could understand. They were a third thing; they were digesting life.

And then he felt something new. It was not a pain he'd ever known before. It was not a hunger that cries out from an empty stomach. It was some hybrid of needs, as many parts jealousy and sexual longing as a desire for food. He wanted to have what the other monsters had. He wanted to fill himself with the life they contained. He wanted to sleep the way they slept. He wanted to take from his former comrades, to rip them apart and own them and destroy them. He wanted. He wanted.

Without deciding to do so, Cassius snapped the ropes around his wrists and dove towards one of the bodies in front of him. His ankles were tied to the chair legs, but he merely brought the chair along, breaking it apart as he kicked backwards, like an over-eager lover trying to remove his socks with his feet while the rest of his body is otherwise occupied. The body he found belonged to a man whose name he'd known, but in that moment he couldn't remember it. He could remember the man had possessed two working hands and now had only one. He placed his lips around the stump and dragged on it, not like a person trying to consume meat, but like a person who wants to drink a whole lake through a reed. There wasn't enough blood; the stump had mostly stopped bleeding and had begun to rot. Still moving like that overeager lover, Cassius pawed at the man's body and hauled himself on top of it. He tore the man's jerkin free like it was made of paper, then ran his hands over the cold flesh underneath. The heart was still beating, if faintly, and Cassius considered ripping through the ribcage to get to it, but while he did so, his hand felt the pulse elsewhere. His lips found the place in the man's armpit. It was within that concave hollow. How would he get to it?

And then he felt his jaw change. It didn't hurt, but Cassius felt a thrill of energy run through the bone, like he'd hit an elbow in just the wrong place, only starting from within his skull and running down to his chin. He could feel his teeth sliding up into his gums, a gentle retreat no more unpleasant than running his tongue over the roof of his mouth. Only his tongue was also retracting down into his throat and pressing forward to create an opening to that yawning core. He could not feel the other teeth, the ones moving on their own, until he dove into the man's armpit and felt them sink in around the flesh, then poke through, then pull. In three quick bites, he'd pierced the tough tendons and shredded the softer skin, grinding his way into the man's body like a rooting boar. And then he found the vein and drank until the last of his humanity was gone forever.

Cassius' first family of vampires had carefully chosen the time and place to convert him. They knew adding to the family was something requiring patience and provisions. They'd come down to Asia Minor because the warring between the Byzantines and the Turks offered them a constant supply of food while the relative peace in their region of Banat meant they were more likely to be discovered. They'd basically followed the wars south along the edge of the Byzantine Empire. In

Asia Minor they could wait for Cassius to grow from a baby vampire to a fully functional adult. There was a lot to learn, and he had to acquire a whole new set of skills simultaneously. After Cassius discovered their language had some Greek roots, he was able to learn their dialect, though it took years until he was fluent. Meanwhile, he was taught to hunt, to find places where he could sleep safely, and how best to hide himself among their prey. A lot of the latter involved learning to control his appetite. If he didn't feed enough, he'd grow weak, but if his diet was too immoderate, he'd call attention to the group. Feasts of companies of mercenaries were rare, but lots of small caravans of traders went missing, as did just enough roving bands of thieves. (The disappearances of the traders could be blamed on the thieves, and the reduced number of thieves kept the number of missing traders less suspicious.) After a few decades, the group came to think of Cassius as a part of the family, and ultimately, they bestowed upon him their greatest secret, the ceremony by which he could convert another human into a vampire. Under their tutelage, he made his first, Thaddeus, a crusader escorting a retinue of monks to the Holy Land in the early 1200s.

With the addition of Thaddeus and a few others, the group had grown too large. It was getting increasingly challenging to hide their effects on the local population or to move without bringing attention. Disputes about where to go next fractured the group. Some decided to maintain the strategy of following conflicts, and they headed into the Holy Lands. Those members of his family, Cassius would later learn, were discovered by a group of wizards working on behalf of a Caliph, were found during the day, and dragged out into the sun. Another faction of the family chose to return to Banat where plenty of warfare had returned. Cassius and Thaddeus had no connection to that land, so they decided to travel west. After a sojourn in Rome, they made their way as far west as they were interested in traveling, all the way to the lands of the *Brythoniaid*, which had only recently come under the power of the Prince of Wales. There, they added a woman to their group. Her name was not Jezebel when they found her, but she didn't like the way foreigners pronounced her name, so she changed it to Jezebel when she learned the very mention of the Phoenecian princess' name made men's hearts race. Sometimes it was longing, and sometimes it was rage at the thought of an empowered woman who mocked her holier-than-thou adversaries and died on her own terms. Bel didn't care why the men's blood pressure increased as long as it made them easier to drink.

The trio traveled back to the continent and then up into Scandinavia, seeking shorter days and longer nights, but they found the population too scattered to justify the longer days half the year, so they turned back and ended up in Paris, the most populous city in Europe at the time. There, they thrived on city life and the anonymity it could afford them.

And that's where they were when Cassius got the news Constantinople had fallen. The shock of the news changed him. Despite all he'd seen over the centuries, some part of him clung to his unshakable faith in the

Theodosian Walls' ability to protect the city from invasion. Even when the city had been sacked in 1204 as part of the Fourth Crusade, it hadn't bothered him too much. It felt more like an inside job, coming as it did at the hands of other Christians just as the previous coups against Byzantine emperors had throughout the city's history. But when it was conquered by Turks, this shook his sense of the world order. (He assured Bel and Thaddeus this wasn't because of any religious bias against the Muslim conquerors, since he no longer considered himself any more Christian than any of them, but Thaddeus and Bel knew he was half-lying to himself.) If the Theodosian Walls couldn't protect Constantinople, Cassius couldn't predict the world of men anymore, and he found that deeply unsettling.

So he did what many humans also do when they find themselves frightened by the world; he sought to build systems to increase predictability. He reached out to other families of vampires. He started creating more of his own children. And though Bel would remain with him, on and off, for more than 600 years, this was the beginning of their rift. Because Bel recognized she was a creature who lived within the tension between chaos and order. She could work for CimBim and protect the secrecy of The Convention while simultaneously feeding on random humans with little eye for the social consequences of their disappearance. She wanted to shake things up, and she wanted them to remain stable. She could want both, fearlessly and unapologetically.

But Cassius couldn't. He demanded the strict loyalty exhibited by his top lieutenants, vampires like Thaddeus and Nicabar and Gunnar and Blake. He still thought of them as *Exkoubitoi* and considered himself the *Scholai* of all that remained of The Bastard Sons of Occasus. And he'd made his mercenary company too powerful to ever stop and feel safe. He needed to complete the work of the Necromancer, to decimate the human population, but that was just a stepping stone. A billion human deaths felt insignificant to Cassius. He had a longer term goal. If he could get Tisina and the Merfolk, the Trolls, and a half dozen other groups of monsters on his side, he could overthrow the Archduke and rule the vampires and probably the whole Convention. Then he would not be the man spinning in the road with two torches, or the *Droungarios* of the Watch who could be dismissed by the Emperor, or the human boy who had to join the Watch to escape his father's fists.

If he had all the power, he would remember how the Theodosian Walls had made him feel. He would be safe.

Chapter 9

About as far away as possible from the Pacific coast of Costa Rica, on a chilly, wet hill, the darkness pressed down on the three Wyrd Sisters McElroy just as oppressively as the midday sun weighed on Magdalena Wallace' shoulders on the other side of the world. The witches' cauldron didn't sit over a fire, and it produced no heat, but they stood closely around it as though for warmth because the brightness of that sun glowing out of the surface of the water in the big pot created' the illusion of heat. The witches didn't mind this illusion, especially since the show they were watching in their cauldron was moving away from Lena's current location into her future, and a bunch of their misconceptions were being knocked down like dominoes.

"Oooo," Garifinia cooed. "It gets sexy here in a minute. I like this part. I may need some time to myself later, ladies. If you know what I mean. Down on Main Street. Me time."

Taravissa rolled her eyes. At present, her left one was blue and her right one was green. "We have no idea." Then she looked into the cauldron again as the scene changed, still in that Costa Rican glow, but now to a walled house on a hill. "I like the explosions. Action, you know?"

"I like a different kind of action," Garifinia said. Her left eye was brown and her right was blue, and both flashed as she bobbed her eyebrows up and down. "Sexy action."

"We get it, alright?" Justinia, the eldest, growled. She was haggard and wrinkled and clearly balding, and she leaned on an aluminum cane with four legs at the base, each with a sliced tennis ball pinching the feet and sinking into the muddy Scottish loam. "The bone zone. You want to see more fuckin'. Well, we see what we see, okay? This is what's going to happen, not what we want to happen. It's not all going to be sex and explosions, dinglebrains. Now pay attention."

Taravissa nodded sagely. "That's right." She was the middle-est of the three sisters, with a giant quiff of hair like Sean Young's Rachel in Blade Runner, and a high-necked, dark red dress, accented with white lace at the collar and white petticoats underneath the hem around her boots, like she'd picked out her clothes in an old-timey photo booth at a carnival. Ironically, she hadn't dressed this way in the mid-1800s. She was just into steampunk. "Thanks for keeping us focused, Justinia." Then she leaned over to Garifinia. "I was actually with you on that," she whispered loudly. "That's why you're my favorite."

"I'm standing right next to you!" Justinia shouted.

Taravissa leaned over toward her older sister and stage-whispered, "Yes, but I'm trying to boost her ego because she's the baby. I know you'll be able to take it. That's why you're my real favorite."

Justinia matched her whisper. "You're not doing this right."

Taravissa stood up straighter and flipped the umbrella in her hands onto her shoulder. It advertised for the Loch Ness Centre and Exhibition in Drumnadrochit, blue with the white logo of Nessy mostly hidden since it was collapsed. Her voice returned to its normal, slightly loud and glottal fullness. "I think I'm doing just fine, thank you."

Garifinia nodded. "You're crushing it, Sis." Her umbrella was a Japanese parasol decorated with white lotus blossoms, red maple leaves, and black kanji mixed to make it look pink when collapsed, and she held it straight up behind her, its handle in her hands at the small of her back, its middle bouncing softly between her shoulder blades as she rocked back and forth on the balls of her feet. She looked like she was in her twenties, and she'd recently taken to doing her blond hair into a pixie cut with very close-cropped sides and some gel to point the top straight up, inspired by a vampire she met briefly in Edinburgh and then London about a year ago. But unlike that vampire whose sexiness spoke of danger and confidence, Garifinia's body seemed to want to dance and bob from subject to subject just as her mind did. "So, to get very, very real for a hot second, it looks like shit is about to go down in a bad way."

They all continued staring into the cauldron. Without sound coming from the images, they had to imagine the cracks of the guns, the splattering of blood on walls, the crunching of bones, and all that violence didn't bother them too much, but one particular gunshot made them all flinch. "Um, not to be a buzzkill," Taravissa said, "but have y'all considered the possibility this is all our fault? I mean, we did play a role in this. We told that twat necromancer where to find the writer just so he'd leave us alone-"

"-and get himself killed." Garifinia added. "That was important. We wanted him to get himself killed."

"And fail in his whole plot to destroy the humans," Justinia said. "Don't forget that part. We did that. And we intervened a little and made it possible. I mean, we're kind of heroes if you think about it."

"Right, right. No doubt. But..." Taravissa took a deep

breath. "...also our interventions have caused all this, and it looks like it's going to be a whole lot worse than just killing off most of the humans."

They watched in silence some more.

"Yeah, okay, you're right," Justinia said. "It's worse."

"And it's on us, right?" Taravissa asked.

Justinia shook her head tightly, her thin wisps of gray floating over the liver spots on her scalp. "Oh, I wouldn't go that far. Heroes, remember? Our intentions were good."

"Not to get all philosophical," Taravissa said, "and I absolutely agree on the whole heroes thing, but I'm starting to come to the conclusion our intentions don't matter a whole lot."

Justinia shot her younger sister a glare. Her left eye was green and her right was brown, and both gave a warning. "I just don't think blame is very constructive in a time like this. That's what I'm saying."

Garifinia shrugged. "I think we can all agree the queen is the one to blame. I mean, c'mon!"

Justinia nodded once, slowly. "That's what I'm saying. She's the one who is going to cause all..." She waved her hand over the cauldron, pointing at the whole mess. "...that. All that."

"Right, and I'm not making excuses for her," Taravissa said. "It's funny we thought the danger would come from intentional malice. From that malignant narcissist corpse-fucker. What he wanted to do on purpose. But it turns out the greatest danger of all is what will come about because of negligence and inattentiveness and just … stupidity. Thoughtlessness."

"Criminal negligence if you ask me," Justinia muttered.

"Sure, she should know better."

Garifinia tapped her umbrella against the back of her head. "She should have started using her noggin a long time ago. It's amazing she got as far as she did."

"But ladies, that's why I'm talking about blame. She's going to get her own kind of punishment. We've seen it. And it's bad."

Justinia breathed her words. "So, so bad."

Garafinia bounced. "And really fucking gross!"

"Right. Agreed," Taravissa said. "But that won't really make things any better for the rest of us, will it?"

Justinia shrugged. "I'll feel a tiny bit better."

"Same," Garafinia said.

"Fine, but then the whole world is still the poops, right? So maybe, and hear me out here, maybe we should intervene again."

"I'm listening," Justinia said.

Taravissa cocked her head to the side. "What?"

"I'm listening."

"To what?"

"You said, 'and hear me out here.' So, what's your plan? I'm hearing you out."

"Oh, I don't have a plan yet. I just mean we should consider intervening again."

It was Garifinia's turn to nod sagely. "This plan is …

not very good?"

Justinia pointed at her youngest sister. "It is a bit incomplete, isn't it." She made a show of looking into the cauldron and away from Taravissa. "Stupid," she muttered. "So stupid."

Garifinia looked at Taravissa. "Not to get all Alan-Moore-*Watchmen* on you, Travvy, but the last time we intervened, we clearly made things worse."

Taravissa pointed at Garifinia. "What happened to us being heroes, Griffy? We saved most of the human race, remember?"

Garifinia pointed into the cauldron. "And that led to this big giant pile of flaming radioactive shit, now didn't it Travvy?"

Taravissa's shoulders slumped, and her voice sank into her chest. "I mean, there's sex as well as explosions before the flaming radioactive shit, so it's not all bad, but, yeah, I get that."

They continued to watch the scene in the cauldron. The bright light of the Pacific sun had been replaced by a dimmer glow as the characters moved about the globe, but now the sun was tropical and augmented by the flashes of explosions in increasing speed and size until the horrorshow in the cauldron created a club vibe on the faces of the three women standing on a lonely hill in the Scottish highlands, but the silence became more oppressive than the darkness or the night's damp chill. It was the world's worst rave.

Justinia's voice was low and unusually sad. "Gals, I

think we just have to sit this one out. And yes, it's going to be really bad. I can't even fully wrap my mind around how bad it's going to be. But I just don't think there's anything we can do."

"It's beyond us," Garifinia agreed. "We observe. We know shit. We give excellent advice. Like, the best advice. But that's all we can do. And no one is asking because this just has to play itself out."

"Exactly," Justinia said. "We're just witches. Just three dumb witches with a cauldron. There's nothing we can do."

Suddenly Taravissa stood up straighter, her bouffant bouncing once and then remembering it wasn't Garifinia and standing still like Justinia. "You're right. We're just three dumb witches with a cauldron, and there's nothing we can do. Unless…"

"Unless?" Justinia asked.

"Unless" Garifinia asked.

"Okay, hear me out for realsies this time." And she proceeded to tell them a different ending to the cauldron's story.

"Evil deeds do not prosper; the slow man catches up with the swift."

-Homer
The Odyssey

Chapter 10

Nicobar sweltered inside the motorcycle helmet and heavy leather clothes. On some level, he knew the blazing sun couldn't reach his skin, but he couldn't help but suspect he was cooking anyway.

"It's too bright," he muttered.

"Word," Gunnar said.

"Agreed," Blake said. "So why couldn't we wait to do this at night?"

They were walking up the gravel road toward the

house, boots crunching and echoing off trees which provided far less shade than Nicobar had expected from a tropical rainforest. "Two reasons. One: Thaddeus called and told me Cassius wants this done right now. Like yesterday. If we were going to wait until nightfall, he'd hire somebody else to do it and probably never hire us again. Or maybe worse. Like, he's freaked out about this. Enough to make Thaddeus sound worried, and that guy is cold as a witch's titty in Antarctica." He chuckled at his own joke. "Antarctica," he repeated under his breath.

The other guys laughed, too.

"And two, we got to meet the contact, and he works there during the day. We're trying not to scare him off. He doesn't know we're coming. If he gets too worried, he might not show. And he gets us in undetected."

"What's the security system?" Blake asked.

"All kinds, apparently. Cameras. Tripwires. Laser tripwires. Magical wards. And a mother-fucking security golem."

Blake stopped. "How do we fight a golem?"

Gunnar tapped the butt of the gun in his holster, then jiggled the strap of the backpack where he carried a small arsenal of other weapons. The backpack prominently sported a patch of the Gadsden flag. "Same way I fight everything. Every way. I'll shoot it. I'll cut its head off. I'll shove a grenade up its ass. I can move a lot faster than some big dumb golem."

Nicobar thought about pointing out Gunnar, himself,

was big and very, very dumb, and then made the same calculation everyone did. Gunnar was also fast as lightning and a terrible judge of what fights to get in. Better not to piss him off. Easier to aim him and pull the trigger.

"That's basically the plan. The contact gets us past the security system. Blake, you go after the girl. Just grab her and run. I'll go for the book. Gunnar, you look around and find the golem, and then keep him busy until I give the word that we've got the girl and the book, and then we book it." He'd amused himself again. "Book it."

"This is kind of a stupid plan," Blake said. "We should recon the place and know what we're getting into."

"No time," Nicobar said. "We gotta get the girl and the book and get to Vegas right away. We're going to be late as is. This has to be a smash and grab job." He thought about that. "Book it," he mumbled again, chuckling. Then he saw the car parked on the side of the road up ahead. "There he is. He'll take us the rest of the way. Now remember, he's already spooked about this, so we can't let him run away. When I say 'go' we're just gonna appear next to his car doors, me in front and you two in the back, but then stay real calm so he thinks he just dozed off and we startled him. I'm sick of being out in the sun."

"Word," Gunnar said.

"Agreed," Blake said.

"Okay ... go!"

The three men broke into a sprint that made them

nearly invisible. Then they opened the car's doors and slid inside at human speeds, all nonchalance.

"*Madre de Dios*," the driver said, and he clutched his chest, made a sign of the cross, and then clutched his chest again. "You guys give me attack of the heart. I did no see you on the … the road."

The driver was human, probably in his early forties but looked like he was in his sixties, a weather-beaten, short, portly man with a thin mustache and an even thinner beard just on his chin.

Nicobar noted the angle of the sun and risked it. "You must have dozed off," he said, opening the visor of his motorcycle helmet to reveal the clean-shaven face of a human in his early thirties, though he was neither human nor in his early thirties.

"What?" the man said.

"Sleep," Gunnar said from the back seat. "You sleeped. You no hear us cuz you sleeped." He turned to Blake. "Mexicans need to learn American."

Nicobar shot a glance over his shoulder. "He's not Mexican, and he speaks two languages better than you speak one." Then he looked back at the driver. "Sorry about my friend. He's … Gunnar."

"What?" Gunnar asked.

"Nothing. Shut up and let me handle this part." He looked back at the driver. "Sorry. So, you know the deal. You already got half. You get the other half when you get us through the security system."

"Yes. I feel bad. She's a nice lady. But it's a lot of

money for gardener." He raised his hands as if to say, "I have no choice."

"We're not going to hurt her. But she hasn't always been so nice. It's our job to take her back with us."

"You *policia*?"

Nicobar pointed at his own chest. "*Policia especial,*" he said in an accent that didn't occur anywhere in the world.

"Okay, I take you to her and no security." Then he started the little Chevy and drove up the hill to Lena's house.

The gardener parked where he always did, next to the driveway but out of sight of the road. Lena had never told him to park there, but Gerardo understood part of his job was to be inconspicuous. He came weekly to care for the garden, and the house's owner had never had guests while he'd been present, but other wealthy foreign mansion dwellers had made it clear he was not to allow his car to mar the view of the homes they wanted to show off to their vacationing friends. And just as he learned the security systems of those other mansion dwellers and sold the information on the black market, he'd learned as much as he could about Lena's. He was completely unaware of the magical wards and of Josef who stayed invisible during all his shifts, but Gerardo knew the locations of the cameras and sensors, and the passcode for the box just inside the door. When he'd advertised his knowledge of this information, every group of thieves he knew passed on the job for reasons he couldn't comprehend. A single woman in a mansion by herself? It seemed like an easy score to him. But there hadn't been any takers. For some reason, no one wanted to come anywhere near the house except Imelda, the cleaning lady, and himself, and they both felt completely fine about it.

So he'd spread the word of his knowledge a bit more broadly than usual, and one day he received a call from a man in the United States. The man lived in Las Vegas. His voice was always pleasant, but something about him gave Gerardo the heebie-jeebies. He sounded cold, as dispassionate as a man who encounters a harmless fly on his arm. And if such a man is fast, woe to the fly. The scary man had put Gerardo in contact with this Nicobar. Gerardo was fairly certain neither were affiliated with any police force of any kind. He suspected some kind of crime, though. A woman as beautiful as the lady who owned the house? His mind went immediately to diamond smuggling. That explained the safe. He would tell them about that once they were inside. He wanted to make sure they didn't kill the woman. He wasn't particularly attached to her, but she had been kind to him, and she seemed sad, tragically so, in a way that aroused his sympathy. But the money! So much more than usual. Sure, he had to show up and be involved, and he was very uncomfortable with that part, but this was more than ten years' salary. And he got half in advance, so even if they didn't pay him the second half, he would be able to relax, maybe buy a new house or a boat, give enough to his parents to get his mom off his back for a while and make his dad very proud. Gerardo was a man whose price had been found.

The four men climbed out of the car, and Gerardo grabbed Nicobar by the arm. "The first camera," he said. He hooked his finger, pointing toward the driveway. "I will go in and turn off the cameras. And put in the code for to turn off security." He fished in his pocket, then dangled the keys. "I have a key. Then I will come back for you, okay?"

Nicobar had dropped the helmet's visor, but he nodded, and Gerardo went to work.

When they heard the front door close, Blake said, "We're going to kill him, too, right?"

"Of course," Nicobar said.

"Good," Blake said.

"Yeah, good. I don't like that little fucker," Gunnar said.

Blake shrugged. "Seems fine to me. I'm just being professional. And I'm hungry. It's too bright."

"Agreed," Nicobar said.

"Word," Gunnar said.

They fell silent when they heard the front door open. Then Gerardo crossed the driveway and came back around the corner.

"The lady is no home. I no see her. But the cameras I turned off. The lady, she go down to the beach I think."

"Okay, well, come with us," Nicobar said.

Gerardo shook his head. "I tell you other things about

the house. But I no go in."

"You were just in there," Gunnar said.

"In yes. But just gardener. I no…" he searched for the word. "…arrest the lady."

"Oh, c'mon," Nicobar said, irritated, and then he grabbed a big ball of the short man's shirt and nearly lifted him as they walked across the driveway, into the gate, past the pool, and up to the front door. "You sure all the alarms are off?"

"*Si*. Yes. All off."

"Open it."

Gerardo reached forward and turned the knob. He'd left it unlocked and hadn't imagined any danger the man was nervous about, but now he pictured a trap or a person with a gun on the other side, so as he opened the door he peered through the slit nervously. It was exactly as he'd left it.

"Okay, get inside," Nicobar said. He pushed Gerardo over the threshold. Gerardo stumbled, then turned to see Nicobar still standing outside, his hands on his hips, silhouetted against the bright sun. "Okay, now you have to invite us in."

"What?" Gerardo asked.

"I'm just fuckin' with you. Old joke," and he strode into the house, stepping past the little man and looking around the foyer.

Blake and Gunnar followed, checking the corners. Gunnar made a point to shoulder Gerardo hard as he passed.

While Gerardo rubbed his shoulder, Nicobar walked back behind him and closed the front door. Then he looked at Blake. "She's got covers for the skylights. And heavy curtains. I think she was expecting our kind of company, maybe." He looked at Gerardo. "Sensors on the windows?"

"I turn them all off."

"Good." Nicobar looked back at Blake. "Close it up."

"Will she know we're here when she comes back and sees the curtains closed?"

"Maybe. Or maybe she'll think her guest arrived. Either way, we'll see her better in the dark than she'll see us."

"Word," Gunnar said.

"Agreed," Blake said.

As Blake found the remote for the skylights over the living room and kitchen, Gunnar set his backpack on a little half-table in the foyer, then started pulling out weapons. Gerardo watched the big man set out different guns, large knives, and hand grenades.

"I should go to the car," Gerardo said.

"No," Nicobar said simply. "Now, have you seen the golem?"

"Go- golem? What is this?" Gerardo asked.

"He probably never saw it," Gunnar said without looking up from his task of arranging his toys.

"And where are her valuables?" Nicobar asked Gerardo.

Gerardo shook his head. "I can no turn off security on

the box. Need the lady first."

"Show it to me."

"I will show it to you. But no touch. Security."

"Fine. Show me."

Gerardo led Nicobar through the living room and down a hall to Lena's study, feeling ahead of himself and running his hands along the wall in the new darkness Blake had created. He pointed at the floor. He was surprised to see Nicobar following his gesture in the darkness with such ease. Then Gerardo folded back an area rug and revealed the face of a safe, three feet long on each square side, a handprint scanner in the center and a simple system of lights above it, the green one turned off, one red steady, and another blinking.

Nicobar looked at Gerardo. "You know a lot for a gardener."

Gerardo shrugged. "I come inside when she go to the beach. I look and find."

"So what did you find out about this security system?"

"Different. Made by different ..." he struggled for the word "...negotiation?"

"Company?"

"Yes. Different company of mens."

"Fine," Nicobar said, but not to Gerardo. He walked back to the foyer, the gardener following behind. "Okay," Nicobar muttered, "we need her and the book. She's not here. Book in the safe. No golem. Where's the fuckin' golem?" He rounded the corner and barked at

Gunnar. "Where's the golem? Find him. Maybe outside. Search the perimeter. Keep an eye out for the girl, too."

Gunnar sighed, flipped the visor of his helmet down, and started stuffing his toys back in his backpack.

"Faster!" Nicobar shouted.

"I'm going!" Gunnar said.

Gerardo's eyes widened as Gunnar's arm became a blur. And then the big man was barely present, there was a whoosh of air, and the front door clicked two times like a computer mouse. The darkness returned, and Gerardo found it far more ominous than when the big dumb one had been in the room.

"Blake," Nicobar said, "I don't want to wait. Let's get the book so we can grab her and go as soon as she gets back. We'll have to crack the safe. I don't know how Gunnar thinks he's going to fight a golem anyway. But I'd rather be halfway to the airport when that fight ends."

"Agreed," Blake said.

Gerardo shook his head. "You cannot break the box." He pointed towards the hallway to the study. "The underhouse."

"The basement?"

Gerardo shook his head. "No, not basement. But under house."

"I saw it. It's in the floor. Under the carpet."

"But the light."

"Look, we'll figure it out. There's no time for this. We can break it."

"No," Gerardo said. He shook his head violently. He

didn't know how to say *trampa* in English, and he didn't know the nature of the booby trap, so he couldn't have explained it even if he had the words at his disposal. "I go to the car."

"Uh-uh. First things first. Your pay."

Gerardo slumped. "Okay. I take money to the car?"

"Fine. But c'mere. I'll lay it out in the kitchen so you can count it. Blake, come with us. Axillary artery okay?"

"Agreed," Blake said.

Nicobar pulled his helmet off and set it on the thin table Gunnar had been using as a workbench. Blake did the same. Gerardo looked at the two men, trying to make out their features at this, his first real opportunity, but the tiny amount of light peeking over the curtains and around the covers of the skylights left the house in nearly complete darkness. Nicobar put a hand gently on Gerardo's back and escorted him into the kitchen. They walked around the island, Gerardo feeling his way with his hands, then stopped when Gerardo was standing next to the sink. Nicobar grabbed the rubber plug by the handle and inserted it into the drain.

"What?" Gerardo said.

And then Nicobar's fingers were in his thick hair, yanking his head up and to one side, while Blake grabbed his wrist and stretched his arm upwards so hard and fast he pulled Gerardo's shoulder out of the socket. In the darkness, Gerado couldn't see the men's mouths open, their lower jaws unhinging like snakes' but also extending like no natural thing on Earth. He couldn't see the rows of teeth descend into place, circles of thin, pointy, curved spines, each hollow, each sucking. He felt it when more than a hundred needles sank into his neck and his armpit. He felt the fiery pain, then the throbbing in his head caused by his own screaming and the blood leaving his brain, a pain like drowning, and he stopped screaming, hitched, gasped, kept gasping like a beached fish, his most primal self still screaming, screaming for oxygen for his starving brain. And then he couldn't even think about that.

Nicobar tapped on Blake's shoulder, and both vampires pulled away in unison. The force ripped away the chunks of flesh in their mouths, leaving gaping holes, and the timing, while the heart still beat the last few times, pushed the blood out of the wounds. Nicobar bent the little man over the sink so the blood, unable to spurt but still strong enough to drain, would run into the sink. Then he spit the flesh in his mouth onto the floor, and Blake did the same.

"Okay, not much time to hold him here for Gunnar's dinner. We have work to do."

"He's not draining much anymore anyway," Blake said. "And also, fuck Gunnar. He's an idiot."

Nicobar's teeth flashed in the darkness. "Word," he said, and laughed. He tried to prop Gerardo's body over the sink, but as soon as he let go of the short man, the corpse slid sideways and fell to the kitchen floor. "Oh well. Okay, let's crack that safe and be ready to grab the girl and high tail it as soon as she gets back."

"Book it," Blake said.

They laughed as they made their way back to the study. The carpet was still turned up, but Nicobar yanked it away entirely.

"So how do we crack it without her hand?"" Blake asked. "There's nothing to grip on it. No handle or anything."

"No time. I'm just going to punch it. Or stomp on it? Should we stomp on it?"

"Sure," Blake said. "Same time, or take turns?"

"I'll go first. Then you. Then both."

"Agreed," Blake said.

Nicobar stood above the safe, took a breath, reared up, and brought down one heel with inhuman speed. The impact broke the concrete floor beneath the hardwood and left the safe about two inches lower than it had been, the face badly dented but still sealed. The lights had changed, though. The glass on top of the little bulbs was shattered, but the bulbs still glowed. The green one was still dead, but now the red solid light blinked slowly, and the blinking red one flashed on and off at a furious pace.

"What do you think that means?" Blakes asked.

"It means I almost broke this fucker. Want to try to finish it off?"

"Let's do it at the same time," Blake said.

"You sure?"

"It's not a contest," Blake said. "What, you want to make it a contest? I'm just trying to be professional."

"Fine." Nicobar said. "Okay, I'll count down. Ready,

pussy?"

Blake laughed. "Agreed."

"Three. Two. O-"

But the time expired before they stomped.

The house was built with vampires in mind. The explosion probably would have done the trick, but Lena hadn't been satisfied with "probably." After reading the book she'd been forced to write, she'd decided to spend each day and night in a house that had a layer cake foundation; concrete under the house, then six inches of plastique, then six inches of phosphorus and titanium and magnesium powder, and another layer of concrete, then some thin padding, then expensive hardwood, then her bed, and then her body on a mattress resting more easily knowing before any monster, including the notoriously hard-to-kill vampires, got their hands on that book, they would all be consumed by a blast so bright it would eclipse the sun.

That was how Lena had been able to sleep for the last year. On top of a bomb.

"The trick is to love somebody ... If you love one person, you see everybody else differently."

-James Baldwin

Chapter 11

The Exclamation had docked in Vancouver, British Columbia. From there, a party consisting of Lena, Matt, Captain Emory, Joseph hidden in Lena's bag, and, for reasons Lena did not understand, Xìngyún Lóng the castaway, boarded a very expensive rented corporate jet. It turned out Captain Emory could not only pilot a massive yacht, but she could also fly a plane.

"Of course you can fly a plane, too," Lena had said, rolling her eyes but smiling. "Of course you can. But are you a good pilot?"

"Good enough. I mean, we'll see, I guess," Meili had said. She didn't smile much, but Lena caught it.

They'd flown to an airport so remote it was actually named "Kilometer 176 Airport." There, they boarded a van Matt had rented (well, Meili had rented and paid for with Matt's money) from an Enterprise in Saskatoon. Lena didn't want to imagine the cost, and Matt didn't seem to care. He also didn't seem upset by the quality of the van.

"But you ride around in a yacht and fly in extra-fancy rented airplanes," Lena said. "Isn't this slumming it for you?"

"My dear," he'd said, "you have to remember, I once rode around in the most luxurious car in the world which, in 1886, was also the only car in the world. The Benz Patent-Motorwagen could only go 10 miles per hour, but it had no shock absorbers or front windshield, and it turned out even at 10 miles per hour one could develop a sore ass and get bugs in one's teeth. So, while this is no Rolls Royce Sweptail, to me it's just fine." He'd leaned closer. "I don't own a Rolls Royce Sweptail, in case you were wondering. It's the second most expensive car in the world and classier, I think, than the most expensive, but even I find that kind of ostentatious spending to be gauche."

By the fourth hour of the five hour drive, Lena's backside was telling her she would not have been altogether upset if Matt had been a little more gauche.

The group didn't speak much during the whole of the trip. They did listen to some music, and at one point Long led them in a sing-along to a song with a copyrighted title by a band which was appropriately named for such a journey. The song encouraged them to continue believing in something, a notion Lena found disquietingly tragic even though she thoroughly enjoyed Long's delivery.

And then Meili said, "We're here."

Only they weren't anywhere as far as Lena could tell. They'd been bumping along a gravel road that was more mud than gravel for twenty minutes, passed into a clearing, and it seemed the road continued into the woods ahead.

"Why are we stopping?" Lena asked.

Matt patted her hand condescendingly. "For security reasons. It would be unwise to go on without a guide.

"I don't see anyone here to guide us."

"They don't want to be seen yet. But if we kept going, I promise you would see people coming to kill us. Waiting until they come to guide us is a wiser course of action."

And then, about twenty feet ahead of the van, off to the side of the road just enough to still be clearly illuminated by the headlights, a man stood up out of the tall grass. He was completely naked, and the tall grass was not tall enough.

Lena made a single word out of "Holyshit" as she bounced in her seat from fright, then averted her eyes, then looked back. He was not her type, mostly on account of the appendage that dangled above the grass, but also because of the chest hair and scraggly beard, two other characteristics she wouldn't have liked any of her romantic interests to possess. She didn't even like armpit hair, though she felt like a bad feminist for admitting that to herself. But chest hair and beards? Yuck. Still, the man was obviously quite confident, always an attractive feature. Or he was completely crazy, standing naked in the dark in the middle of Saskatchewan. Or he was…

"Oh," she said out loud.

"Get outta here," the man shouted. "This is private property. We're nudists, but not the friendly kind, so unless you want to get punched in the dicks, turn around and go back on down the road."

Matt rolled the passenger side window down (Meili was driving, of course), and leaned his head out. "We're here to see a Mr. Fernando DeCastille. And a Ms. Jezebel Shipwright. They are not expecting us, but they will be very pleased to see us. Tell them Magdalena Wallace is here."

"Never heard of her." The man sniffed. "What all you got in that van?"

Matt looked back at the passengers who shrugged.

"Cheetos," Lena said.

"Corn nuts," Long said.

"I've had four Diet Cokes," Meili said, "so if he doesn't let us in soon, he's going to be smelling something else."

Matt leaned out the window. "Junk food, mostly. No weapons, if that's what you me-"

"I mean what kind of monsters are in the van, dumbass."

"Ah. Yes. Well, I'm a warlock."

"Your smell glamour is for shit. You smell like you been in a nursing home for four hundred years," the man called.

There were giggles in the van. Then, more eerily, some in the tall grass.

"Well, thank you for that constructive criticism. We have humans and a golem."

Meili looked at Matt. "A golem?"

The naked man shouted, "And?"

Matt cupped his hand and whispered. Lena and Meili couldn't hear any of it over the idling of the van, not even the hisses that hinted at whispers, so it looked like a lunatic was preparing to shout out the window but wasn't making any sound.

"Well I'll be," the naked man said. "Why in the hell not, do you think?"

Matt cupped his hands around his mouth and whispered some more.

"Well, okay, I guess. Doesn't make much sense to me, but that's above my paygrade. Okay, follow me. I'll lead you in. But don't drive too fast. You run me over, I'll kill you. You try to drive by me without permission, they'll kill you." He pointed into the grass at people Meili could not see, but she no longer doubted the naked man's sanity. Her own, on the other hand, was coming into question once again.

The naked man walked out between the headlights into the middle of the road, fell forward onto his knees, planted his palms in the mud, and began to change.

Meili began to hyperventilate.

"Calm down, dear," Matt said. "You've met stranger people than this guy."

She turned and looked hard at her boss. "I. Have.

Never. Seen. Anything. Like. This."

"True. But you've seen me make magical bubbles. So that's something, eh?"

"With all due respect, sir," Meili said, closing her eyes and squeezing her hands in her lap between her thighs, her knees bonking together to a staccato rhythm, "this is not that."

"Would it make you feel better if I told you there's an eight foot tall gender non-conforming person made of clay in Lena's backpack?"

The wolf in the high beams looked back, twitched its tail, and began to trot forward.

Meili dropped the van into drive roughly. "I'm getting a raise, aren't I?" It was barely a question.

Matt smiled. "One-time hazard pay?"

"A raise. For as long as the sight of that white guy's ass turning into his tail stays in my brain."

"Deal. And maybe don't look out the side windows."

Meili kept her eyes forward, but Lena looked into the darkness. They were far enough north and far enough into summer that even late in the night, the edge of the sky was still a light blue, and she could clearly see the shapes moving through the grass. The wolves' heads would turn towards them and catch enough light from the van's beams to glow. She lost count at twenty pairs of eyes.

At the edge of the woods, Lena read a sign that said, "Camp Bigfoot" with a cartoon drawing of a yellow blobby monster on even bigger blob feet wandering out of the picture and into the woods. The tall grass ended under the trees. The image of the dozens of wolves darting into the open space beneath reminded her of the army of werewolves who had confronted her at Kings Cross Station the year before. She found she was more anxious to see the lighted cabins and know Bel was close. How close? Had Bel heard the news of Lena's arrival yet? Lena squirmed like an excited teenager about to be escorted from the concert seats to the special backstage meeting with her favorite K-Pop band.

The wolf trotted up onto the steps of the main lodge and stopped, pointing its snout towards a small parking area where a few trucks and jeeps sat under melancholy lamps. Meili drove very slowly, terrified she'd run over a wolf in the darkness.

They all stepped out of the van in their own way: Matt with a flourish; Lena with more pep in her step than usual; Long with a happy, stumbling gait; and Meili looking like she really, really needed to pee.

The wolves from the field circled at a distance, eyeing them, some sitting and letting their tongues loll, others more wary. And they just kept coming. Lena couldn't tell if they were streaming out of the woods or the cabins. But all were in wolf form. And all were watching them. She felt dizzy, turning and seeing so many glowing eyes and teeth. Then her pirouette brought her around to the front steps again, and she blinked and looked down at the ground. The guide was a man again, stark naked and up two wooden steps so his junk was right at her eye level.

He followed her gaze, then chuckled. "Tell you all what: I'll go get your friends and some clothes, okay? You just stay where you are, and if they don't want to see you, I'll whistle and we'll tear you apart. Sound good?"

Then he turned and gave them a generous view of his full moon while sauntering through the double doors into the mess hall.

Lena did not have supernatural hearing. That perfectly matched her lack of supernatural anything. But even with her basic, unimpressive human hearing, she was able to pick up the sound of a glass shattering on a linoleum floor. And then the double doors were banging open and a blur moved through them and stopped on the top step.

Lena looked up at Bel. Bell's hair was a little longer than when she'd last seen it, the sides still shaved short but the fauxhawk standing a bit higher, now white with pink tips. She still wore the same leather jacket, now open over a The Clash t-shirt, but she'd abandoned her black leather pants for tight bluejeans. It had been a year. A year since Lena had seen the vampire, patted her on the arm in a bro-y way, and walked away down the streets of Paris, bawling her eyes out. How many women had Bel made love to in the last year? How many of them had she killed? How could Lena even consider acting on the feeling welling up from her stomach, through a tight space just behind her sternum, through her clenching throat? How could she be so crazy?

"Hey, um, I just came to say I like your new hair. And I'm still alive. And I love you."

"This above all: to thine own self be true; And it must follow, as the night the day; Thou canst not then be false to any man."

-William Shakespeare
Hamlet

Chapter 12

Cassius hated Zoom meetings. His reasons weren't the common, human reasons. While humans chafed at the physical distance, Cassius appreciated that aspect. He respected the way humans had produced this technology allowing him to see his interlocutor across the continent, though the respect was given grudgingly. He detested the way the employment of human technology made him so similar to a human. His hearing was reduced to the quality of the speakers and the quantity of audio information transmitted on the human fiber optic cables.

He could see little more than any human in the pixels on his computer's screen. And he couldn't smell the creature through the screen. Though the smell would have been unpleasant, there were distinct advantages in a negotiation produced by the ability to smell fear, enthusiasm, and boredom.

This is precisely why the necromancer was right, Cassius thought. *The humans cannot be eliminated entirely, but we have to reduce their technological progress. Yes, we benefit from their tools and weapons, but we are fast approaching the point where their technology will make them our equals. And this cannot be allowed.*

To Cassius, it was the distance that mattered. Not the physical distance, the 2,322 miles between his office and the cavern on the other side of the conversation, but the distance between both monsters and their human food. He thought about every tool the humans had created in his lifetime. Guns couldn't kill vampires, but they made the humans more dangerous to one another. The first automobiles had barely been faster than horses, but slowly, model year after model year, the humans got closer to the speeds at which vampires could run. It was so rare humans managed to kill vampires intentionally, but the vampires in Hiroshima, having retired to their seemingly safe darkness for the day, had been vaporized by the light of the first atomic bomb. That was the kind of equality the humans offered, and not only in the form of nuclear war. For their most powerful weapon wasn't some missile in a submarine or a silo hidden in the Rocky or Ural Mountains. The humans had made their whole civilization into a giant, very slow time bomb that could eventually be used to destroy all life on the planet's surface. The fact the humans didn't see this as a weapon they were unleashing upon themselves was no comfort at all. The fate of vampires and the rest of monsterdom couldn't be left in the hands of a species so stupid they would accidentally eliminate themselves. Cassius was a vampire and a leader, and both roles demanded someone who could take decisive action quickly to solve problems. He was already impatient with his current plan. He'd spent years on this project now, developing his relationship with the necromancer Nigel Marion, connecting him to the werewolf Apocalumus, staying one step ahead of the Archduke, and working with the King of Trolls to whip the right number of votes to pass Marion's New Business Item 9 at the last Annual Meeting of The Convention. Marion's defeat and death in Paris had been a setback, but it was the loss of the book itself that had been the biggest blow to the plan. Cassius wished he had Jezebel's help with this whole mess. It was a hell of a time for Bel to go through whatever existential crisis was keeping her out of the game. If he'd been able to send her to Costa Rica, he'd have the book by now. Probably. He couldn't trust her, when it came to that particular human, and it was becoming very irritating. Almost as irritating as his current appointment.

"Is it on?" the voice from his speakers said. "Yeah, you gotta unmute, you little pustule. Unmute!"

Cassius watched the red line appear over the microphone. He tried not to move any of the muscles in his face except those responsible for a very slow blink.

The image came to life. The King's figure moved slightly, revealing someone was holding the camera. The giant troll was clearly shouting at someone off camera, but Cassius couldn't hear him.

"You're still muted, Your Highness," Cassius said.

The King reached down out of the screen's view and picked something up. When his hand reappeared, he was holding a small troll, palming the little beast's head like an NBA player holding a basketball. Then, less like an NBA player and more like an amateur golfer upset with his clubs, he hurled the small troll, not quite at the camera but at something beneath it. The image of the King flew upwards on Cassius' screen as the camera fell forward, and then Cassius' screen was dark once again.

The sound of the King's bellowing exploded in Cassius' office. (A human would have started. Cassius controlled himself by focusing on seeing if he could blink even more slowly this time.) "Unmute, I said, you little shit-splatters! Unmute! Now pick that thing up. I need to see this deceased fuckwad, look him right in his soulless, beady little eyes."

"I can hear you clearly, Your Highness," Cassius said.

"I know, you pale-ass cum bubble. You think I would waste my breath insulting you behind your back?"

Cassius allowed himself a tiny smile. "Yes, I do."

"You're right, you arrogant ball of mucus, but it's just

out of habit. I can't eat your anger, you worthless, shriveled up thousand year old prick. But I enjoy insulting people whenever I can." The King of Troll's camera tilted upwards, so he floated down Cassius' screen just as he made an exaggerated shrugging gesture. Cassius noticed the way the King's eyes moved upwards, tracking as the camera rose, and that was when Cassius realized the King's entire monitor had fallen and was being lifted back into place.

"You know, you could get a tripod for the camera. Or a desk for the monitor. If only to stabilize the picture."

"Who would that humiliate?"

"Well, no one, but-"

"Oh, you think my troll's shitty workmanship is embarrassing to me, and you think I give a goat's left testicle. You don't spend much time in the comments section online, do you, Cassius? One of the keys to being a really great troll..." He turned to someone off camera and said, "You should write this down." Then back to Cassius. "One of the keys to being a really great troll is..." Something distracted him again. "No, don't go looking for paper and pencil. It's just an expression, you halfwit! Just store it away in the moldy dish sponge you keep between your ears." Then back to Cassius: "One of the keys to being a really great troll is being completely shameless. Do you know how pissed off you can make a human by humiliating yourself just to humiliate others? It's delicious, let me tell you! They can't help but try to appeal to your common humanity. The rage as they slowly realize you don't have any is like a fine wine. I guess. I don't know. I couldn't give two shits about wine."

"It's been a long time since I've been interested in wine," Cassius said. "A long time."

"Ah, so I'm wasting your precious eternity?" The King placed his hands on the arms of his throne, straightened his enormous arms, and lifted those ridiculously short legs up onto the seat. Then he turned around, yanked his loincloth to one side with his left hand, grabbed his right butt cheek to gape as much as possible, and aimed right at the screen. "Am I being an asshole, fang-face? Is that what you're saying?"

Cassius could hear the trolls off screen giggling, and then the image itself started to shake as the trolls holding the monitor heaved in time to their cackles.

Cassius allowed himself the eyeroll he'd been controlling. "My apologies, Your Highness. I-"

"Which of us is the asshole now, fang face? Say it!"

Cassius looked directly into the King's puckered cloaca and said, "I'm the asshole."

The King flipped around with surprising grace and crossed his legs, his elbow on the highest knee, his chin on one oversized fist. "That was fun for me, but we do have important business. You go first."

"I sent some of my best men to Costa Rica to get the writer. I haven't heard back from them."

"You mean the writer you told me you had in custody."

Cassius pursed his lips. "That was premature. An error on my part. I apologize. I'm the asshole."

The King of Trolls was unamused. "It's worse than that, leech-turd. If you don't have the human, that means those plants you gave me were not grown under her bed."

"No. We acquired the correct kinds of plants, but we couldn't germinate them in quite the way the spell required."

"How close did you get?"

"I tried to replicate it as best I could. We found a writer, someone no one has ever heard of, like the woman we're looking for. I sent one of my vampires to seduce him, and they had a one-night stand with the seeds in bowls under his bed. And they both started growing, so we knew it had worked. We even left the writer alive just like the spell demanded. Those were the flowers we delivered, which-"

"Which I gave to Tisina. Dammit, Cassius, if she figures out those weren't exactly what she was promised, it could be a real problem. She's dangerous."

"We're monsters, Your Highness. We're all dangerous."

Now it was the King's turn to roll his eyes. "Don't flatter yourself, spooge-on-a-stick. You've got, what, some incompetent blood-suckers who can only work halftime and who can't find one human writer in Costa Rica? It's Costa Fucking Rica, not the Australian outback. It's less than 20 thousand square miles. And I doubt she's hiding in the jungle. Know how much area Tisina controls, quarter loaf? Most of the fucking planet!"

"Well, it's not exactly an apples to apples comparison-" Cassius tried.

"You're right, the size of your incompetence doesn't matter, Cassius. What matters is, do you know what Tisina will do to you if she finds out you screwed her?"

"No, I-"

"I don't either! That's the fucking point, diarrhea-for-brains. No one knows. Because she's batshit crazy. You know how close-to-the-vest she holds her cards, Cassius? This is her big secret: Even she doesn't understand her own schemes. She's got something big in the works, and I don't think she has any clue how it's going to go, and she's just crazy enough to do it anyway. Think about that, Cassius. That sound like someone you want to fuck around with?"

Cassius tried to figure out how he could escape this tongue lashing without making his situation worse, and his phone rescued him. Pretending to look down out of shame, he looked at the glowing face under the table and recognized the number.

"Your Highness, if you'll hold on for just a second, I may have some good news for both of us."

He swiped and lifted the phone to his ear.

It was difficult to hear the caller over the sound of the King's bellowing. "Oh, I was the one wasting your time, and now you're taking a fucking phone call? You little bat-humping piece of-"

Cassius muted the Zoom call.

"Sorry, what did you say? … Canada? Really? That is not what I expected. … No, no one has to die if you do this right. … No, I don't want that, either. … I understand. … Just the book now. … No, no flowers anymore. No bowls under beds. Forget all that. Just the book. Call me when you have it, and I'll arrange a pick-up."

Cassius looked up at his screen. The King was standing on the seat of the throne again, his loincloth pulled to the side again, but this time he was facing forward, twisting his body back and forth so his penis and lolling tongue swung from side to side in rhythm. Cassius made an apologetic gesture, reached across his desk, and turned off the monitor.

"Sorry. Got distracted. What was that? … Like I said: No one gets hurt. No violations of The Convention. And everyone at the camp is free and clear and safe. … Yes. All debts paid. That's the deal. … Good. Call me when you have it."

He hung up and then, though he knew he was still visible to the King, he took a slow, deep breath before turning on his monitor.

When the image blinked to life, Cassius was assaulted by the image of not one but seven trolls. Trios of little trolls stood on each other's shoulders on either side of the king, all holding their loincloths to the side, all mimicking their ruler's dance, long tongues and short penises wagging from side to side, none of them quite in rhythm with the others, a silent cacophony of little pricks.

Cassius unmuted and let himself chuckle while the sound of the trolls' chorus of shouted, open-mouthed "ah" sounds filled the office. "Okay, you got me."

The King plopped down into his seat, then shoved the six little trolls off to either side in one massive thrust of one huge arm. Cassius could hear their yelps and screeches as they flew, followed by the deep thumps as they landed, then the scuttling sounds as they scrambled back to whatever they'd been doing before the King had organized the little routine. "Where were we, Cassius?"

"You were telling me about the size of my incompetence before showing me the size of your dick."

"Thus demonstrating that size doesn't matter. I shocked you with what little I've got. Now you'd better wow me with what you just got."

"I got the book."

"Really? Your boys in Costa Rica found her?"

"No, she must have given them the slip. Doesn't matter because I've got someone inside who's going to get me the book."

"So you don't have it yet."

"I'll get the book this time."

"Not the writer?"

"Maybe later. If I have the book, I don't need her. What's she going to do, write another book that brings people back to life? The dead can't read."

"Fine. Get the book. Complete the necromancer's

NBI."

Cassius shook his head. "Even if I can get my hands on it tomorrow, I can't proceed with Marion's work. It's too late. A new business item is only good for a year. It's going to take some time to get the book published and distributed. I'm going to need to go before The Convention and get another NBI passed. Do you think you can arrange a passing vote?"

The King nodded. "I don't like it. It's another pinch point, another possible fuck-up. The Archduke will be keeping a better eye out this time, and we don't have Apocalmus to rally the werewolves like last year. I hear there are werewolves going missing. Lots of chatter online about a place they call '*El Norte*' or 'The Camp.' Know anything about where that might be? Maybe the wolves are in one of those concentration camps for immigrants?"

Cassius pursed his lips. "I know where they are, but I can't say just yet. I promised to keep it a secret in exchange for the safety of my spy among the werewolves. She's keeping me updated on things in the new pack. She can make sure they don't interfere at The Convention. One less loose end."

"Good. No Apo, but no organized werewolf contingent to worry about." The King of Trolls nodded thoughtfully. "Still, the gremlins just like to be contrarian, so if they voted for it last time, they may vote against it this time just to be difficult. You may need to make a better argument than Marion did, and he put on quite a show."

Cassius leaned back. "You're right. I can't make a speech like that. But what if I could make a very dramatic demonstration? You said you could get me in touch with a certain warlock?"

"I said I'd do that when you got me the plants I wanted. And you gave me counterfeit. If Tisina finds out, I will be giving her your home address, you Roman-" The King stopped suddenly. "Are you Roman? It would help to know so I can insult you properly."

"Byzantine," Cassius said.

"Same fuckin' thing. But worse, of course. And funnier. Maze jokes and bureaucracy jokes. But I digress. If I have to tell Tisina you fucked her over, she will come at you like a missile, and I will be the one spreading your cheeks and pointing the laser sight right into your bleached asshole."

Cassius leaned back. "I'm fairly certain, in that particular analogy, you'd be standing a little close to ground zero, your highness."

"Don't fuck with me. You need me a hell of a lot more than I need you. So far, you've given me the wrong plants and a lot of promises that you might get a book. Know what those get you at The Convention, Cassius?" The King reached back and yanked, held up something tiny and curly and purple, and then blew it dramatically out of his hand. "Nothing. You're as useful as some of my ass hairs in the wind. Find the book before The Convention, and then we'll talk. Try and trick me and I'll Brazilian you, scab-licker."

The King of Trolls ended the meeting, but Cassius reached forward slowly and closed the window just to be certain before saying, "I think you mean 'again.' 'Trick me ... *again*.' Stupid troll." But his smugness was dampened by his genuine need for the advertised warlock in order to get the book. He decided he needed to do something he hadn't done in a few hundred years. It hadn't worked perfectly that time, and probably wouldn't this time, either, but he was desperate enough for a half-success.

Without getting up, he kicked away from his desk and slid his rolling chair across the room to a decorative cabinet the size and shape of a bedroom dresser, adorned with a lamp he never turned on, two crystal glasses he never drank from, and a decanter of Scotch he'd wasted by removing it from its bottle. It was all a needless and expensive hiding place for something very valuable no one would recognize or think to steal. Inside the dresser, he'd even placed a large safe full of cash, just so a thief would be distracted from the dresser's other occupant. In the other half of the cabinet, leaning on its side, stood a smooth slab of stone shaped like a cutting board. Which is basically what it was.

Cassius picked up the glasses and carafe of Scotch, one at a time, and set them to one side of the cabinet's top. Then he placed the slab of stone in the middle. He swiveled in his chair and looked at his desk. There was no letter opener in the pen holder on top because there was no pen holder on the pristine desk. He tried to remember if he had a letter opener inside the top drawer. Who even sent letters that needed to be opened with a letter opener? And why would a vampire be worried about papercuts?

"Curse it," he muttered. He hadn't perfected swearing in English in the 21st century quite yet. But he did know if you had to have one unpleasant meeting in a night, you might as well have two.

Cassius stuck out his pinky finger of his right hand, looked at it, raised an eyebrow, and then put the finger into his mouth. He bit down with his human teeth and applied increasing pressure until he heard the bone between his palm and the large knuckle snap in half. Then he yanked sideways and pulled the whole thing off his hand. He spit the digit into the palm of his left hand and dropped it into the middle of the stone tablet. Then he dribbled blood from his pinky stump around the pinky in a circle like he was salting his food with a shaker.

Nothing happened. Impatient, he placed the end of his left index finger in the blood and swirled it around the circle and wreathed the sacrifice. When the droplets all connected into a ring, the space inside lit up with a dull orange glow, like a burner inside a glass top stove. When the orange got bright enough it was almost white light, though it had no cooking effect on the finger, the light melted the stone's surface, and the finger fell inside the hole. Some air whooshed in after it, as though the cavity was a puncture in the hull of an airplane or submarine, a gateway to a place with less pressure. Which was sort of true, but not really.

There was a popping sound, low and bouncy and humorous rather than sharp and startling. Cassius had heard the sound before.

"Apraxis. It's a delight to see you."

"I'm delighted as well. You've never looked better, Cassius," the imp said. He floated just above the stone slab for a moment. Only about ten inches tall, his spindly legs shouldn't have been able to support his squat, pony-keg shaped torso and head even if it had been standing. Two long, pointy ears stuck up out of that single cylindrical head and body, and two small horns poked out of his forehead. His arms were thin like his legs, but his hands were oversized, and he waved one over-large hand at Cassius like a cute child. His tail was coiled like a spring and tapped at the vacuum below him uncomfortably. His flesh was leather, a dark burgundy color, and obviously on fire. When he opened his mouth, it was like the top third of his body was on a hinge and bent to expose a huge row of short, sharp, even teeth. "Why don't I move somewhere more comfortable, and we can get down to business."

"The way you said that makes me uncomfortable," Cassius tried to joke, but the imp vanished with another pop, then appeared over Cassius' desk.

Cassius kicked off and rolled back to his spot.

"So, I'm very curious to hear what you're interested

in, Cassius," Apraxis said.

"Ah. So you already know, then?"

Apraxis smiled. "Or maybe I'm not curious. Better tell me anyway, huh?"

Cassius sighed. "Fine. I understand you've had some dealings with a golem who hangs around with a woman who … has something I want."

"Yes, I've gone a little mano-a-mano with that golem from Vienna," Apraxis said. Josef was from Prague, so that counted as a lie. The implication he'd entered into hand-to-hand combat with the golem was also a lie, but the imp wished that was true, so that lie wasn't as satisfying.

"Okay, well, if I ask you if you are capable of killing him, and you say you are, that means you aren't, but if you say you aren't, that means you are, so I'm not really sure how to proceed."

"The golem prefers they/them pronouns," Apraxis lied.

Cassius frowned. "Got it, I think. You're telling me to proceed. Fine. So I need him removed from the equation, and I need it done fast. Ideally, I'd like him brought back to me and left under my control, but if you can only kill him or turn him to dust or freeze him like a statue, that's fine."

"Yes, I can see why bringing them back here and leaving them in your control is the best option for you," Apraxis said. "And how do you propose to compensate me for this outcome?"

Cassius shrugged. "I've learned not to lie to people like you, Apraxis. The King of the Trolls showed me the error of my ways, you might say. But I don't know what might be of value to you, so how about you tell me what you want in exchange for the Golem, and I will tell you if I can provide it. I have considerable means, but I don't have everything, of course." He held up his right hand and wiggled his remaining fingers to call attention to the missing pinky. It had healed over already and started to grow back, but he felt it would still make the point.

Apraxis tilted his head contemplatively. Because his head and torso were one mass, he just leaned sideways in a way that defied gravity. Then he straightened. "I'll tell you what, Cassius. I will take care of your golem problem, and you'll owe me a favor. I predict you're going to have considerably more power after this next Convention, and I think that could really come in handy."

Cassius tried to figure out which part of that was a lie, but he couldn't imagine any of it not coming true. And since his political rise couldn't possibly be the lie, he deduced the imp would never ask for anything in return. That seemed strange, but Cassius concluded it must have had other purposes for confronting the golem. That was fine with Cassius.

"That's fine with me," Cassius said truthfully. Which was stupid. He should have known better.

"...the person that had took a bull by the tail once had learnt sixty or seventy times as much as a person that hadn't..."

-Mark Twain
Tom Sawyer Abroad

Chapter 13

Tisina floated down the hallway towards her royal bedchamber, her handmaid Devochka swimming along behind her. Devochka was a mermaid, a voluptuous redhead from the waist up, a green, blue, and silver scaled fish from the waist down. She had to swim horizontally, with her eyes on the floor, while Tisina, with her jellyfish-skirted and octopus-tentacled lower half, and her gorgon tentacle hair, moved upright, and that was just the way Tisina liked it. She too kept her eyes downcast, but because of her orientation, as they passed the mermen lined up in the hallway, Tisina could feel all their eyes on her and none on the servant swimming behind her, and that gave her a little thrill.

At the doorway to her bedchamber, she was met by a tall, old merman with a beard of tentacles which writhed slowly across his still broad chest.

"General?" she said.

"My queen." He gave a stiff bow. "Some news if you have a moment."

"Please keep it brief, General Nevazhnyy. As you can see, I have matters of state to attend to." She motioned to the line of mermen behind her.

"Of course, my queen." If he felt any judgment or jealousy, he masked it, and she couldn't detect any sarcasm in his voice. "Using the suits you provided by your deal with the vampire, we were able to attack a larger island in the South China Sea and eliminate its human population. All the corpses were successfully removed, and our intelligence assures us the humans have no idea what occurred, so we are not in violation of The Convention. The island will make an excellent staging area for an attack on Hong Kong when you give the order to begin the war."

"How many more of the suits will we need to be able to mount an invasion force of the necessary size?"

"These preliminary attacks have been very successful, so it might incline a lesser general to believe we can accomplish your stated objectives with a force of only ten or twenty thousand men," the general said. "But we need to prepare for the possibility their defense forces could be alerted or could mobilize faster than we expect, so I would request five hundred thousand from your majesty to be certain of victory."

"How are you progressing on making our own suits?"

"We have been working on reverse engineering them, my queen, and we believe we can acquire all the necessary materials without entering into the air breathers' space." He caught himself. "I mean, of course, our rightful territory which the humans have occupied. However, we've found we run into difficulties when we manufacture the suits under high pressure, so they need to be made closer to the surface which, of course, means the facilities are more likely to be discovered. We are a bit behind schedule-"

"You will get back on schedule," Tisina said.

"Of course, my queen."

He didn't leave immediately, so she understood he had other news, but she didn't want to make him too comfortable by prompting him, so she stood there staring at him, the tentacles on her head writhing slowly, expectantly.

He gave in. "There is only one other thing," he said, sounding as sheepish as a general could. "There was a mission which went awry. An attack on a Russian cargo ship. We had intelligence about a potential enemy. It was our intention to attack and sink the ship, thus preventing any report of a violation of The Convention from reaching the authorities. But we did not know there were heavily armed guards on the ship, and once that was discovered, we called for a retreat. We aren't sure if the target was ever alerted, so it's possible this will not result in anything of consequence, but I wanted you to be aware of it in case it becomes a diplomatic incident."

Tisina wasn't sure if the general's lack of concern was genuine or if he was covering for something that might be more significant later, but she had more pressing concerns.

"I'm disappointed. See to it this does not happen again. If we need better intelligence, perhaps you should be consulting with some other members of The Convention. Witches, warlocks, clairvoyants of different kinds. Once we breach The Convention and they become our enemies, we will not be able to access their services, so I suggest you make use of all the information they can offer in the meantime."

The general nodded curtly. Merpeople couldn't click their heels because they didn't have any, and he couldn't slap his hands against his sides because the action would have propelled him into the ceiling, so this gesture served to announce the completion of his report.

Tisina didn't say goodbye. She dismissed him by turning her head and floating into her room. Devochka nodded to the general deferentially as she passed him, following her mistress into the royal bedchamber.

The room, absurdly spacious to convey power, had most of the furniture near the door, lest the occupant have to waste too much time crossing the vast space. A chair stood near the door for Devochka to occupy while the queen slept. Nearby, a desk with a large mirror served as a space where the queen could apply make-up or work while it was applied for her. Her hair did not require any kind of care since it wasn't hair at all. Tentacles could untangle themselves, but they could be painted, as could the scales of her bodice and the bell of her seeming-skirt. Tisina communicated she had no interest in this kind of decoration by floating past the desk towards the bed. It was a huge four poster bed in the center of the room, positioned directly beneath an ornate chandelier. The lights didn't hang from a chain like an air-breather's chandelier. Instead, the ribs of the huge room curved down and fixed it in place, serving to pull the eye up to the ceiling and then focus all attention on the bed, the exact purpose of the design.

"Devochka, I think this day may prove quite instructive for you. Were you listening carefully to my conversation with the general?"

"Yes, my queen. Not to eavesdrop, of course, but only to serve you."

Tisina's hands were clasped comfortably in front of her. She waved away this distinction with a gentle flip of her tentacles. "Did you notice how little I said to him? Men are fools, Devochka. The dumbest ones will hear a woman's silence and presume she knows nothing, and that makes them underestimate us. The smartest will presume they know what she is thinking, and that makes them likely to miscalculate. Not that I want the general to miscalculate. I want him to follow my orders and predict my desires. But everyone in this building, in this city, everyone in the world feels they could benefit from my death. That's the burden of royalty, Devochka. If I am eliminated, everyone feels this provides them an opportunity for advancement. So I keep everyone uncertain about my plans through silence. No one knows what I am going to do except me. That way, though they want me dead, they also want me alive because my plans may prove to be opportunities for even greater advancement than my death. I survive because of their greedy hopes. Does that make sense, Devochka?"

"Yes, my queen," Devochka lied.

"Today my plans will advance significantly. Are the gifts acquired from the King of Trolls in place?"

"Yes, both are under the bed as you ordered."

The flowers were in special glass jars that would preserve them underwater for only so long.

"Good. Bring in the first candidate." Tisina turned and floated toward the center of the room.

Devochka nodded and swam to the door. She opened it, leaned her head out, and beckoned the first merman in the line.

The corporal was tall, thin, and muscular with pale green scales above the waist and a dark green fin on his head matching his dark green tail. He swam slowly in order to maintain a proud, upright orientation as he came into the room. His eyes widened when he saw the queen already in bed, propped up on an elbow, a simple sheet pulled up over the jellyfish bell. She beckoned him with a finger. Excited, he allowed himself to lean forward, almost a dive, and flip his strong tail, shooting him across the room near the floor, pulling up just beneath the bed, rising up next to his queen.

"My queen," he said, "thank you for this opportunity to audition. I live to serve you, and-"

"Yes, you'll do just fine, I expect," Tisina said, looking him up and down. "Come here and lie down. Don't be too nervous."

"Yes, of course, my queen. I mean, no, I won't be too nervous. I will do whatever you ask of me-"

"A consort should not speak so much," Tisina said. Then she moved over in the bed, making room for him.

He lay down next to her.

Tisina ran a hand over his chest. She leaned close caressing his face with the tentacles on her head. He leaned forward to kiss her, but she dodged. One of her tentacles wrapped around his chin and pushed his head up. She kissed his neck. Then she moved down his body, kissing his chest, the tentacles on her head stroking the fin on his, others caressing his cheeks, his neck, one twisting gently around the corner of one of his pecs where a human man's nipple would have been.

The corporal placed his hands gently, hesitantly, on the queen's shoulders, then slid down to her breasts. These, too, were nippleless, mechanisms to deceive humans, not to feed their young who ate meat as soon as they hatched, but both their sexually sensitive areas matched humans' for the purposes of seduction, and the corporal's instincts compelled him to reach for her chest just as he would have with a human woman. When he applied the slightest pressure, the larger tentacles hidding underneath her skirts snaked out from beneath the sheet, and they gently wrapped around his wrists. He thought she might be encouraging him, so he squeezed her breasts more tightly. She firmly pulled his hands away and pressed his arms against the surface of the bed, pulling them apart so he was stretched on the surface of the mattress. He hadn't noticed, but she'd wrapped tentacles around the end of his tail as well, just above the fan, and now he was completely immobilized beneath her.

Tisina sat up on top of him. The bell flowed over him. She pressed one hand down on his chest, her fingers splayed and massaging the scales. With her other hand, she reached under her skirt amongst her tentacles. He felt her finger dance along the slit below his waist. It didn't take much coaxing and he'd sprung free. She wrapped her hand around him, squeezed slightly, then gave a couple mechanical tugs. She didn't seem particularly concerned with his pleasure, but he didn't require much encouragement. Then she raised herself slightly on her tentacles, inserted him, and pulled herself back down upon him, the tentacles sliding between his back and the mattress so she could pull him into herself.

Tisina began rocking back and forth. She closed her eyes. She forgot his face. The corporal stared up at her, entranced by her beauty, overwhelmed by the sensation.

She moved more quickly. The tentacles on her head began to dance. And then they were pointing up, stretching, grasping. The corporal realized they were seeking something specific. They found their way to the chandelier, their tips testing it, finding holds, avoiding the hot lights but wrapping around the cooler places, pulling taut.

Through it all, Tisina made no sound. Her lips were as closed as her eyes. When she climaxed, her spine spasmed, she squeezed him tightly, her head tilted back slightly, and a small smile curled the corners of her mouth, but those were the only signs.

And then she was rocking back and forth more

quickly, impatiently. He thought she was enjoying it even more, trying to bring him to a climax, and he obeyed his queen. He threw his head back and groaned, closing his eyes, so he didn't notice she opened hers and shot him an annoyed glance just as he finished. She felt the warmth, the gentle impact, and knew he was done.

Devochka, sitting in her chair by the door, kept her eyes downcast throughout, but at the sound of the corporals' grunting, she snuck a peek in the couple's direction. A thin, milky cloud emanated from beneath the queen's skirts and disappeared as quickly.

Tisina leaned forward and rested her face on the corporal's chest without disengaging.

"Thank you, my queen," he said, just a bit too loudly. "That was amazing. I love you. I love you, my queen-"

The tip of a tentacle pressed against his lips.

"Shhh," she whispered. "Give it a second."

They lay in silence for a moment. Then Tisina startled him by sitting up suddenly. She pressed her hands to her stomach. At that point the corporal discovered the tentacle on his lips was not one of the ones from her head. It was the thin tip of one of her larger tentacles, and it was wrapped gently around his neck. He glanced to each side quickly. The others were still wrapped around his wrists and tail, not squeezing, but holding them in place like weights. He didn't struggle against them, honoring the queen's desire not to be touched.

Tisina looked quizzically to one side, then turned her head towards Devochka and flashed a quick smile. "Fast," was all she said.

Devochka nodded eagerly.

Tisina looked down at the corporal. "You've done well," she said.

He tried to reply, but she kept that tip of a tentacle over his lips, so he just mumbled some "m" sounds.

"Now, I may need you to do it again," she said.

The corporal couldn't move much, but he nodded eagerly.

Tisina carefully groped under the bed with two of the longest tentacles she kept under her skirt. They found the oddly shaped glass jars holding the plants. Wrapping around the bases of each, she carefully lifted them, one around each side, sliding them out wide around the mattress and then raising them up next to her shoulders. Using the tentacles on her head, she unscrewed them. Bubbles sprang out, but most of the air stayed in the glass bells. She lifted these, exposing the beautiful orchid and the hideous spatulate-leaved sundew to the salt water. Though the plants started dying immediately, they retained their gorgeous and horrible appearances as they began to sway.

Daintily, Tisina took a blossom from the cymbidium orchid. Each looked like a white bird taking flight and trailing the green stalk. The wings of each bird were still outstretched, their feather-like fringes holding onto tiny bubbles, and now their flight looked all the more desperate, like they were trying to rocket back to the air. Plucking one bird of petals off, Tisina stuck it in her mouth. The corporal only caught the briefest glimpse of her white, sharp teeth. Then she closed her lips over the petals and chewed. They were tasteless and fibrous, and she had some difficulty in mashing them into something she could swallow, but she managed.

Then Tisina reached for the bloom of the napanthes. Devochka gasped, an odd sound to hear in the ocean, one mermaids had mastered as part of their seduction of sailors. But this was no gasp of pleasure.

Tisina looked at her handmaid. "Yes?"

"I just … I'm not sure if … the King of Trolls said you weren't supposed to eat that one and … I am not trying to interfere, but I don't want m'lady to poison herself."

"Noted," Tisina said. And then, irked, she made a demonstration of her decisiveness by skipping the step of plucking the flower with her human-like hands. Instead, she grabbed the stalk of one of the so-called monkey-cup blooms with one of the tentacles growing on her head, yanked it towards her face, lunged toward it, and bit through the red and pale green flesh of the monkey cup, then twisted her head to tear the bite away. Again the skin was fibrous, but this time it tasted revolting, the carnivorous plant's diet of flies infecting the taste of the flower. Tisina grimaced and chewed anyway, then forced herself to gulp it down.

The effect was nearly immediate. Her abdominal muscles clenched violently, and she dropped the plants. They didn't crash to the floor, just tumbled lazily through the water, the dirt in the pots streaming as the plants descended. Tisina even released her grip on the corporal's wrists, tail, and throat for a moment. Devochka shot toward the bed like a dolphin, but before she could cover the distance, Tisina held up a hand in her direction.

"My queen?" the corporal said from beneath her. "Are

you alright?"

She'd forgotten him. She placed her hands on her belly again, feeling the ache there, then a kind of vibration, a thrumming so deep only she was aware of it. Or perhaps he felt it inside of her, since they were still locked together. She looked at the corporal's face to see if he'd registered the movement but found only a sickening concern for her health in his eyes.

He started to twist away from her. "I can call a doctor," he said. He looked at Devochka. "Should we call a doctor or the royal guard or-"

"No," Tisina said. Then she turned to Devochka. "No. Say nothing."

While the queen looked at Devochka, her tentacles rediscovered the corporal's wrists and tail, this time holding more firmly. A fifth slid around his throat far more slowly while the tip caressed his cheek. And he could feel her excitement elsewhere as well. He suspected they were going to have sex again, and she could feel him becoming convinced.

Tisina smiled at Devochka, revealing her small, sharp teeth in a way that was highly out of character. "So fast," she said.

The corporal and the handmaid interpreted her words very differently.

Then Tisina looked down at the corporal, effectively dismissing Devochka who returned to her seat. Tisina ran her hands along the corporal's chest, a gesture more intimate than any part of the sex they'd had. "You've done well," she repeated. "So well." As she spoke, the tentacles on her head began to rise up again, touching and tapping and tracing their way back to their holds on the chandelier, and he was certain she would begin again.

"I will need more from you, corporal," she said.

He tried to voice his assent, but the tentacle which had only pressed against the center of his lips was now wrapped lengthwise across them, its coils looped under his chin and pressing his head away from her. He nodded as best he could. And he felt a pain in his shoulders, at once sharp and lingering, no, magnifying. And in his lower spine as well, from his waistline down to the tip of his tail.

Tisina pulled with the tentacles looped in the chandelier. Her body rose up above the bed, and the tentacles beneath the corporal pulled him up with her. But this wasn't sexual anymore. He felt a slight tug as she pulled away from him, releasing him, leaving him hanging limply until he withdrew into that nearly invisible slit on the front of his tail. But he imagined it yanked back in because it felt like all his organs were out of place. His trachea was straining in his throat even though she wasn't crushing it. The ligaments in his shoulders were sending burning pain down his arms. His stomach seemed to be yanked a few inches too low in his body cavity. Even his brain felt off, foggy, like his spine was tugging at it to get his attention. And then the corporal realized what was happening.

Now floating a few feet above the bed, Tisina's tight smile returned, the same mere curling at the corners of her tightly closed lips which she'd displayed at the moment of orgasm. And when that smile appeared, she exerted an extra burst of force.

A quartering is a difficult procedure. Thanks to the tentacles carefully managing the corporal's torso, Tisina tore both the corporal's arms and his head off at precisely the same time, but she had to give a few extra yanks to rip his tail off, and even then the spine, disappearing from his exposed neck, did not slide all the way through his body cavity. But it was enough.

A cloud of red bloomed at each point of rupture, though not nearly as much as a human would have produced. White flakes of fish flesh danced in those red clouds. And then Tisina released the large portions of the corporal, except for his head, and began to use her lower tentacles to carefully pluck those bits out of the water. Finding and pinching these smallest pieces, the tentacles would deliver them under her ribcage skirt to the much larger mouth she concealed there. Each bit of meat was carefully plucked out of the water and deposited into that mouth. Tentacles worked in tandem once the smallest bits were gone, twisting larger pieces off the stumps of the corporal's arms, shoulders, and torn-open middle. In minutes, his scales were mostly emptied and waggling as the tentacles dug deeper for the flesh beneath. Meanwhile, Tisina still hung suspended from the chandelier, her eyes closed, a serene look of concentration on her face. She passed his head from a tentacle to her hands, and she rested it against her stomach. The corporal's dark eyes were wide open, his expression one of shock, but she leaned his forehead affectionately against the womb where his children grew.

Devochka started when Tisina opened her eyes and stared at her handmaid. "Do you see now?" Tisina asked her.

"What, m'lady?"

"What silence can accomplish?" She patted the head against her firm stomach. There was an audible gurgle from inside. "I find I am contented in a way that makes me want to have sex again. And also quite hungry." She tossed the corporal's head off to one side of the bed. It floated slowly to the floor and bounced. "Clean this all up. Save the plants as keepsakes, but dispose of the inedible parts of the corporal. I will rest until you're finished, and then you can send in the next consort candidate."

"Yes, m'lady," Devochka said. Quick as a sailfish, she darted around the bed, grabbing the pieces of the corporal and slapping them to her chest like a makeshift bundle of kindling. And at that distance, as she picked up the remains of the orchid and the spatulate-leaved sundew, she could hear the rumble in the queen's womb.

It sounded like a muffled roar.

"I have learned that every man lives not through care of himself, but by love."

-Leo Tolstoy
Anna Karenina

Chapter 14

Bel looked down at Lena from the porch, and the two had a conversation with the crinkles of their eyes and their dimples, but the silence made everyone else uncomfortable. It was a discomfort all of them preferred to the tension of new arrivals among a pack of distrustful werewolves. In fact, the discomfort they felt may be among the most heartwarming of all social awkwardness. Finally Nando rescued them. "Well, Lena, I've missed you, too. C'mon on inside, everyone. Let's welcome our guests." He looked at a couple of the wolves off to his right, at the edge of the circle. Their posture told him they were the two most suspicious of these newcomers. "Levi and Nicole, will you go and see if we have some rooms ready for our guests in Cabin C?" He hoped the task would convince them the newcomers really were welcome, but at least the removal of their anxiety would calm the rest of the pack.

Matt liked Nando immediately. Despite the jeans and red-checked flannel shirt, the man spoke with authority and confidence in American-inflected English that barely hid his thick Spanish accent, and Matt interpreted this as refined and dignified and admirable precisely because he saw these characteristics as similarities to himself, his measure of quality. Matt liked people if they reminded him of himself. "My sincere thanks, Mr. DeCastille. I do not like imposing on anyone's hospitality, but there aren't any nearby hotels, so I am in your debt. If your pack ever requires my assistance, I would be honored to return the favor." He spoke as he walked confidently up the four steps onto the porch, and then he turned and placed a hand on Bel's naked forearm. "And as for you, Ms. Shipwright…" He cast a meaningful glance down at Lena, then looked back at Bel and smiled a smile that was almost a wink. "…You're welcome."

Bel registered something off about the sensation of Matt's fingers on her arms and recognized the same strange smell the werewolf scout had identified when the van had rolled across the camp's border, and she might have pulled her arm away, but she hadn't fully recovered from her shock and elation at Lena's arrival.

The scout, Steve, had sauntered into the kitchen completely naked. That was frowned upon at the camp, even in a community very comfortable with nudity. It wasn't because of sanitation, exactly. The werewolves could eat a tick-infested, sick deer raw and not even experience slight indigestion. Bel suspected the rule came from the tension of the werewolves' dual identities. A kitchen felt like a very human place, and in those spaces the werewolves wanted to feel they could fully inhabit their human selves. And that meant clothes. So when Steve walked in, dick swinging in the breeze, they knew something strange was going on, though Steve's body language told them it wasn't a threat. "Hey, so, there are some visitors. Weird group in a van. Monsters and humans. They say they know you. They said to say one of them is Magdalena Walla-"

Bel had taken off so fast, her foot cracked one of the ceramic tiles in the kitchen floor, and though she hadn't meant to harm the doors, her speed pulled one hinge halfway out, so the doors wouldn't meet correctly until that had been repaired. Bel didn't consider this metaphor of needed repair while listening to Lena announce her love. Instead, she clapped her hands over her mouth in a very human expression of surprise, then caught herself, lowered her hands, and looked sideways at Nando and Lucia, embarrassed they'd seen the gesture and even more self-conscious at their obvious delight in her joy.

The new guy's creepy touch on her arm, and his leering implication he'd brought Lena as a gift should have dampened her mood, but she just stared down at Lena, agog. For centuries, lovers had come into her life, and for centuries she'd kept them at arm's length. If they were vampires, she didn't want to be stuck in a commitment for hundreds of years or worried about bumping into an ex in a millennium. If they were human, she didn't want to watch them grow old and die, and she didn't want someone she truly loved to see her walk out the door and know she was leaving because they'd grown some wrinkles. She stuck to brief, casual affairs with humans, fun and flirty and not so serious she'd feel guilty if she decided to kill them later. And then she'd met Lena, and she'd found herself unsure about what she might want. And then Lena had left her, and that's when she'd felt the tectonic shift, an opening of a chasm within herself, a need she hadn't had before, a Lena-shaped hole.

Nando cleared his throat unnecessarily. "You have me at a disadvantage, sir. Your name?"

"Oh, my apologies," Matt said, though he'd chosen to wait to be asked for his name very intentionally. "I'm Matteo Bernasconi when I'm in Italy, Matteo Bern in Switzerland, and Matt Bern when I visit North or South America. Though," he looked around dramatically, "I admit I've never been to Canada, so I'm not sure what I'll be called in this particular part of North America."

Lena walked up the stairs. "You'll be called Matt. Because that's what I'm calling you, and we're in

Canada, so that's what you're called in Canada." She turned to Nando. "Yes, he is always this dramatic."

Nando held his arms out slightly, diagonals rather than a wide gesture, unsure. "I've missed you, Lena."

Lena fell against him and hugged him. "I've missed you, too. I know it's weird. We only knew each other for a few weeks…"

"It was only days that felt like weeks," he corrected. "But the last year apart has felt like many years. You are a very special human, to have so many of us caring about you. Which reminds me, where is Josef? Josef," he called, knowing by smell the golem was nearby, "do you do hugs, my friend?"

Dust flowed out of Lena's backpack, swirled on the ground at the foot of the stairs to acquire some new material, and then Josef appeared. The giant stepped up the stairs in a bound, wrapped its arms around Nando, and hugged him. When it released the werewolf, Nando patted the golem on the chest. "I am glad to see you. And glad you are a gentle hugger, my friend. I half expected you to crush me, and I was surprisingly comfortable with that." Then he felt the eyes of the pack still upon him, watching this exchange. The werewolves were calmed by the obvious friendliness, but they were also curious and a bit disconcerted to see their alpha hugging a human and a golem. "But where are my manners? Come inside, all of you, and we'll make our introductions while we get you something to drink, maybe get a fire going if you'd like. Welcome to Camp Bigfoot. Maybe you all can help us decide on a better name. It has been a subject of much debate among us."

When Lena stepped inside the cafeteria, she was struck by the room's size, larger than it appeared from the front, a long room with eight rectangular tables, taxidermied deer heads lining the walls, a round fireplace in the center, and only one occupant. The girl sat on top of a table, her legs crossed, hunched over her phone, her face slightly illuminated by the screen's glow within the cowl of her long, straight, black hair. She was the primary user of the camp's satellite internet and wifi service, a hefty expense for such a remote location, but no one wanted to imagine how contagious her misery would become if she lacked constant online access. She didn't look up when she spoke. "The vamp broke the door." Then she sniffed. "Are we going to eat the human?"

Lucia laughed, the first sound Lena had heard her make. It was a pretty, full, more crystalline sound than she'd expected. She'd expected the woman's voice to be more ... husky. Lena frowned at herself when she caught her own pun, scolding herself for the hack writing of her own thoughts.

"No, Tina, we are not going to eat her," Lucia said. "But if we were, you would have just ruined the trap, don't you think?"

The girl just shrugged, still not looking up from her phone. "Maybe I wanted to chase her. Did you think of that?"

Nando gestured to the girl. "Lena, this is Tina. She is not going to eat you. She's a teenager and an exceptionally rude one."

Tina flipped him off without looking up. Then she sniffed again. "Is that …?" And now she did look up for the first time. "A golem! Now that's cool!"

Josef ducked into the doorway. Tina sprang to her feet, then surprised Lena by leaping straight up like a startled cat, her Doc Martins thumping like a bass drum. But the girl clearly wasn't scared. As soon as she landed, she strode down the long table toward them. Lena couldn't make out Tina's age. She was tall, though that was hard to judge when she was walking on the table. Lena guessed she was six feet. She was thin hipped and flat chested, but those were unreliable clues for her age. A tall 13 year-old or a skinny 19 year-old? Tina had distinctly Asian features but an accent that didn't seem to match, though Lena couldn't place it. Spanish inflected valley girl? Was she from L.A.?

"Don't walk on the table, Tina," Lucia said gently. "People eat there. It's impolite."

"Whatever," Tina said under her breath. Then she looked at Lena. "What's his name?"

"Its name is Josef. It prefers gender neutral pronouns. It/its."

"Fucking badass," Tina breathed. Then she sniffed again. "And the Chinese guy is some kind of-"

"His name is Long," Matt interrupted, "and he goes by he/him pronouns. He's more of a private sort, and we respect that." Lena didn't see the expression he shot at Tina, and Tina took the hint without noticing Matt's fingers twiddling at his side, preparing a spell should she fail to catch on quickly enough.

"Fine," Tina said. She jumped down off the table. She walked up to stand in front of Josef but spoke to Lena over her shoulder. "Does it shake hands?"

"Josef does whatever it wants. It's not a puppet or a pet. It's my friend. Although, come to think of it, it's never given *me* a hug, so how do you rate, Nando?"

Josef reached into its chest and pulled out its notepad and pen. As usual, the pen was standard sized and looked ridiculously small in the golem's huge fingers. Josef scribbled and then held the notepad out towards Lena. "You never asked," it said. Then it pushed the notepad back into its chest and held a huge palm out to Tina. She wrapped both her small hands around it and pumped excitedly.

"She's young for a werewolf, isn't she?" Lena asked Nando. Her volume was conspiratorial, though she knew Tina could hear her clearly.

"She's 17, and she wasn't turned, if that's what you're worried about. She was born a werewolf. We can't breed with humans, but two werewolves can have children. We have people of all ages in our community, though a higher proportion of adults than a human community." He cocked his head to the side. "I guess it's like a human community where the population is increased by adult immigrants. I should do more research into how that changes a human city's allocation of resources to social programs. But we have more children than most werewolf communities because Camp Bigfoot is a good place to raise kids. It creates unusual demographic bulges." He frowned. "I wonder…"

Lucia smiled and Lena. "You have his utopian brain cycling up already. He loves this kind of thing, the planning and organizing to build the perfect werewolf community. It's his passion project."

Nando snapped back into the moment. "Oh, I am so sorry, Lucia. I didn't introduce you! Lena, this is my most important passion project, my girlfriend, Lucia."

They shook hands. "That's wonderful," Lena said. "How did you two meet?"

The two exchanged a glance and smiles that were almost laughter. "It's a little embarrassing to explain to a human, but … "

"Oh, I'm sorry," Lena said. "Please, if it's personal, just tell me it's none of my beeswax."

Nando laughed. "Nothing like that. It was a estupid dating app."

"Oh, pfft." Lena put a hand on her hip. "That's not embarrassing at all. That's perfectly normal now."

"For humans looking to date, yes. But we were both on there looking to meet humans to eat. We just happened to find one another. We both were expecting the usual seduce-and-chase-and-feed dates, and when we showed up and smelled one another, we laughed so hard!"

Lena looked from one to the other. Silence fell heavily.

"So." Lucia looked at the floor. "Yeah, awkward to explain to a human."

"Yes, it's the grossest meet-cute I've ever heard, and I'm happy for you both." She turned, looking for a rescue, and saw Bel was standing on the other side of Matt, greeting Meili and Long as they came in through the now-broken double doors. "Bel?" she said, perhaps more quietly than she meant to.

Bel seemed to disappear and reappear right in front of her. Lena caught a scream and turned it into a squeak.

"Sorry," Bel said. "Didn't mean to sprint like that." She ran the backs of the fingers of her right hand over her right eyebrow, a habit she'd acquired for pushing her hair out of her eyes back when she'd been human and a peasant girl in a village in a land that would later become Wales, back when she'd had long hair she couldn't pin up, before she could cut and shave and dye it into its modern form. The muscle memory of teenage social awkwardness hid there for centuries, waiting to become that gesture. She barely registered it, just enough to think *Dumb. No bangs in your eyes. Dumb. What are you doing?*

But Lena caught it, caught all of it, centuries of it, and loved Bel even more in that moment. *In England, I had a crush on a vampire who had all the answers. And now I've fallen in love with a woman who gets nervous enough around me to become the teenager she was before she was a vampire. I don't know what that means, but it feels right.*

Tina, still standing by Josef, tore her eyes away from her new object of interest to shoot some side-eye at Bel and Lena. "Vamp. Human. Get a room. I can smell you soaking your undies. You're like Nando and Lucia. It's gross."

"Tina!" Lucia shouted.

"What?"

"Behave."

"Hey, I'm just trying to help 'em out." Tina looked at Nando. "What? It's really the nicer thing to do, if you think about it."

"Tina," Lucia scolded.

"Fine. Whatever." She slowly rolled her eyes over to Lena and Bel. "You two are cute, by the way. For a human and a vampire."

"Thanks," they said in unison, accidentally, then smiled at one another.

"Barf," Tina said.

"So, what can I get everyone to drink?" Nando asked. "And would you like me to start the fire?"

"Ice water would be fine," Meili said. "And no fire for me, but thank you. I'm a bit hot, actually. It's been … The last few minutes have been … jarring."

"Please, have a seat," Nando said, pulling out a chair for her at one of the long tables. "Everyone, make yourselves comfortable. This is the longhouse. The kitchen is in the back. Your cabins are being prepared. It's not a five star hotel or anything, but we've done a lot of work on the place in just a few months. You should have seen it when we moved in. It was very run down. I'm so proud of everyone's efforts." He smiled. "Even Tina's."

She flipped him off again.

"So, drinks. Ice water for Ms. Emory. Mr. Bern, what can I get for you?"

"Water would be fine, but if you have some whiskey, I feel like that might be appropriate for the longitude. Or some mead, here in a longhouse. I love the room. I feel like a cross between a fur trader and a Viking."

"I'll see if we have mead. There's certainly whiskey. And you, Mr. Long?"

Long flashed a toothy, almost guilty grin. "Vodka, saki, whiskey, bourbon, rum?"

"Preference?"

Long shrugged. "All of them."

Nando clapped gently. "Um, Bel and Lena and Lucia, want to come help me get the drinks?"

They nodded and followed him.

Josef gently tapped Tina on the shoulder to excuse himself and followed the four back toward the kitchen, just to stay close to Lena, and then stood outside the door while they went in to get the drinks.

The kitchen was as wide as the cafeteria space and square, large enough for a whole crew of cooks to work without bumping into one another too much. While Nando pulled the glasses from a cupboard, he spoke over his shoulder in a low voice. "Is the book safe?"

Lena patted the strap of her backpack. "It stays with

me. I stay with Josef. That's as safe as I can get."

"And where have you two been staying?" Bel asked. "I wanted to find you, but I also didn't want to give away your location, and I didn't know if you wanted me to find you, so I've just been …" She almost said she'd been keeping tabs through Cassius, but caught herself. "… hoping."

"I bought a house in Costa Rica. Had it built, actually. Designed to keep the book safe. If anyone goes looking … they're in for a surprise. And that might cover my tracks for a while, too. But Matt is pretty good at covering tracks."

"How did you find him?"

"He found me. He said some monsters were going to kidnap me and take the book, but he could get me to you." She took Bel's hand. "And I was ready, I guess. To see if you would take me back."

Bel squeezed her hand, a silent "We'll talk about this later" and, more importantly, "Yes."

"Also," Lena admitted, "keeping the book away from my kidnappers saves the world, and I guess that matters to me now." She squeezed Bel's hand back.

"Well, I'm glad to hear that, because the world matters to me now, too," Nando said. "Even the human world. We're building something here, something really great, and I can't have the human world completely fall apart. Not yet, anyway."

Lena raised an eyebrow. "Still need us for food?"

"Less than you'd think. Lots of game up here, not

many humans. But I need the building supplies. We are not self-sufficient yet." He looked at Lucia. "We need that C.A., right?"

"'C.A.'?" Lena asked.

"Amazon dot C A.," Lucia explained. "We joke you can find everything you need on Amazon. But it's kind of true."

"Speaking of everything," Nando said, and he opened a series of cupboards, revealing more diverse bottles than Lena had ever seen in any bar. "I think there is some mead in here somewhere."

A few minutes later, they brought the drinks back to the rest of the people in the cafeteria. Lucia set a Dr. Pepper down in front of Tina, still in the can. "I almost brought you a diet as punishment for walking on the table."

"I would have been pissed," Tina said. "You're a bitch, but not that much of a bitch."

Lucia looked at the guests. "She has very strong feelings about diet soda."

"It's fucking battery acid and ass juice is what it is. I hate it." She punctuated her malice with a carefully timed opening of her can of liquid sugar and a dramatic guzzling.

"I apologize for getting the diet water," Meili said.

Can still in the air, Tina flapped a hand in Meili's direction, then set the half-empty can down. "Water doesn't count. That's fine. It's the diet aftertaste. Tastes like a deer's colon. If the deer had been eating nothing but pennies. It's gross."

Meili found herself feeling more comfortable with this seemingly normal teen despite her suspicion Tina probably knew what a deer's colon tasted like, and she was almost completely calmed down, so of course at that exact moment a gray wolf walked through the longhouse' still-open double doors, sat down, and transformed into an old woman. Meili choked on her water and looked around for a napkin, to no avail.

The woman leaned forward with a groan and rose to her feet. Her hair was gray and wiry and not quite long enough to cover her breasts, and nothing else was left to the imagination, either. "Fernando, I'm sorry to interrupt, but I think you'll agree this is important." She had a warm smile for Nando and a twinkle in her eye that said they were both in-the-know in some way.

Nando gave another of those soft claps. "Oh, that's great, Rita!"

"Shouldn't Rita put on a mumu or something first?" Tina asked. "I get shit about walking on tables, and this old hag is buck naked."

Rita grabbed one of her breasts and shook it. "You're just jealous because I have tits."

"Who wants tits that drag on the floor?" Tina asked.

Lena leaned over to Bel and whispered as quietly as she could. "Ohmygod I'm so uncomfortable."

Matt leaned towards Lena. "Yeah you are. It's delicious."

Lena shook her head. "Aaaaand you just made it

worse." She explained to Bel, "Matt feeds on human emotions. Stronger the better. And my discomfort right now? Off the charts."

"You could at least grow your hair out to cover those things!" Tina was shouting. "And maybe shave your gray bush. Goddamn! It's like lichen."

"Some men seem to like it just fine," Rita said.

"Gross!"

Nando stood up, but not too quickly. His voice dropped. "That's enough."

Lena was surprised to see how fast both women looked down and fell quiet.

"Rita, call them in. Everyone, you're in for a treat. This is a big day. Who is the special one today, Rita?"

"Tobias."

"That's great." Then there was an almost imperceptible change in his voice, not in volume, but in direction. He spoke to the open door. "Wait outside until your teacher calls you."

Rita's voice carried her smile. "Okay, children. Come show Nando."

Lena rose slightly in her seat to get a clearer view of the doorway. Fourteen puppies, some gangly, big-pawed small dogs and other still little balls of bouncing fur, came tromping and bouncing and galloping into the longhouse.

"Ohmygodohmygodohmygod," Lena said. "They are the cutest things ever!" She rose from her seat and started walking towards them. All of them eyed her, and a few cocked their heads at the sight of the new person. One of the youngest tilted her head so far to the side she fell over, then scrambled back to her feet, looking to see who'd pushed her.

As Lena approached, some sat, opened their mouths, and panted, their little tongues lolling. She slowed as she got closer, noticing the dark fur of the wolves caught the light in a strange way as she moved. They were wet. But the water on their fur reflected the light coming through the doors with an odd sheen. Some cell deep in her brain stem screamed, "That's not water!" in a tiny voice, but she couldn't hear it over the voices in her frontal cortex saying, "Want more dopamine? How about some endorphins? See if you can pet them!"

She got near the closest wolf pup, one of the larger ones, black and sniffing at her outstretched hand. And then a series of things happened very quickly. Her brain said, "That's not a normal wet dog nose. This puppy is covered in blood." She pulled her hand back fast. The wolf, startled by the quick motion, took a step back and growled. All thirteen of the other wolf pups rose, the hair on their back spiking in blood-clotted prickles as they joined in the growling. And then Josef was standing beside her, and the eyes of the wolves snapped to the new threat, a yellow-white glow flashing in all of them as they flicked, and that was when Lena heard herself yelp. But before she knew she'd screamed, Bel's arms were around her shoulders. And then Nando was standing between her and the puppies.

"Sit."

He almost whispered the word.

All the dogs sat down, their growling disappearing, and one even whimpered.

"Children, this is Lena. She is my friend. These people are all our guests. Please be nice to them." Then he smiled and did another of those gentle claps. "Now, please form up so we can honor Tobias. Come on. Get to your places." He turned back to Lena. "Sorry they startled you. They're learning."

Eyes wide, Lena breathed, "Learning what?"

Now Nando allowed himself his broadest grin, one that Lena, reputedly the best writer in the world, could only have described as "wolfish." "They're learning to pretend to be civilized before they kill." And then he winked at her.

Bel smacked his shoulder. "Knock it off, Nando."

Nando looked at Lena. "Sorry," he lied. And she felt a warmth because sometimes a lie truly means "I love you." Then he motioned her towards her seat. "Why don't you watch from over there."

Bel guided Lena over to her chair at the long table where she received a consoling stare from Meili who was clearly equally shaken. Lena reached across the table and took the other woman's hands in her own. "Still got both my hands. I'm okay."

Meili could only reply with a series of nervous nods.

The children had formed a half circle around Nando with an opening at the door. Rita came and stood next to

Nando, and Lucia had slipped silently to his side. "Okay, Tobias," Rita said to the doorway, "come show Nando."

Bel knew what to expect, and Long didn't seem to care much, but Matt, Meili, and Lena stared eagerly. They heard a scraping sound, then some bumps and a growl as the pup tugged something up the stairs. And then the little wolf, dark gray and among the largest in the class, came through the doors dragging the head of a large buck by the antlers. The head made a small, winding creek of blood as it splotched along in the length of the pup's heaves. When Tobias dragged it to the center of the circle, he let go of the antlers and curled back behind his trophy, then sat proudly, staring up at Nando.

Nando walked slowly forward, inspecting the buck's head and antlers, circling one and a half times. Then he rested a hand on Tobias' head and wrinkled the flesh on the back of his neck. "You've done very well, Tobias. Your first kill is an excellent specimen. Now, human form."

Tobias stood on all fours, then shook a bit as he changed into a little boy, perhaps eight years old. Nando put his palm on the boy's head, tousling his long hair. "You did well. Did you share the meat with the others?"

"Yes, Nando." Tobias looked at Rita. "Miss Rita made me."

"And did you want to share at first?"

Tobias looked down at the ground. "No. I wanted it all for myself. Miss Rita had to growl at me."

"That's okay, Tobias. But how did you feel when you

let the others feed?"

"It felt good. I felt like a big wolf."

"You are becoming a big wolf, Tobias. Only a big, strong wolf can share. Children, please say thank you to Tobias."

Some of the children stood up, shook, and turned into their human forms. These seemed to range in age from three to around Tobias' own eight. But the youngest pups, those who still looked like balls of fuzz, also stood. The children in human form sing-songed, "Thank you, Tobias." The youngest stumbled forward on their huge paws, rubbed their heads against his knees and shins, and licked his palms. Lena was surprised to note he didn't recoil from the licking, just opened his hands at his sides, palms down and fingers stiff, and let the dogs express their gratitude.

"Good," Nando said. "Now, as you can see, Tobias, we have guests tonight, so there will be even more people at your special party." He wheeled on all the other children. "And you know what Tobias' victory means, right?"

"Sugared cereal!" the ones in human form cried, and the tinier pups jumped up and down like excited goats.

"That's right. Sugared cereal for dinner! But, because we have guests, you all need to go back to your cabins, wash off the blood from Tobias' *biiiig* kill, and put on your human clothes."

The children in human form groaned, and the pups whimpered.

"I know, I know. Okay, go get your human clothes on."

A couple of the children sulked, and two of the puppies dared to growl. Nando stood up just a little straighter and dropped his voice to that near-whisper Lena was coming to recognize. "Now."

The puppies all stopped growling. A couple even yelped, and one flopped onto his side before righting himself and skittering towards the door. The human-shaped children leapt to their feet like the longhouse floor had become a hot grill, and they raced out, too.

Lena turned to Bel. "How does he do that? Is it magic?"

Bel shook her head. "No. Maybe? Sort of? Nando is an alpha. A true alpha. That's what Apocalumus saw in him that made Apo so scared, and why he kicked Nando out of his pack. See, wolves know something human leaders often forget, and which Apo never mastered: Barking is a sign of losing control. Real alphas don't have to bark."

Chapter 15

And, it turned out, real vampires knew how to bite with their human teeth instead of their fangs when they wanted to.

There was a very loud dinner in the longhouse filled with many toasts in Tobias' honor. To Lena's surprise, the different werewolves had a tradition of shouting closing words in reference to the human cultures from which they came, so a werewolf would stand up, raise her glass, shout something like, "To Tobias. May he long provide for the pack, may he defend us from anyone who encroaches on our territory, may he always do his homework and not watch too much YouTube, and may he always listen to Miss Rita!" There would be some laughter and shouts of agreement, but no one would drink. And then the werewolf would yell, "*Kanpai!*" at the absolute top of her lungs, and everyone else would shout a different word. The hall rang with shouts of "*Prost!*" and "*Şerefe!*" and "*Skål!*" and "*L'Chayim.*" Lucia and Matt both shouted "*Cin cin!*" in Italian. Lena noted her guess about Tina's accent had been correct when both she and Nando clinked their glasses and shouted, "*Salúd!*" at one another with all their might. Rita shouted, "За здоровье!" which Lena couldn't identify. Meili shouted, "*Wǒ jìng nǐ yībēi*, Tobias!" and took a gulp of her drink, but Long shouted, "*Gānbēi!*" and then drained his and poured another.

Lena wasn't sure what to shout. At first, English sounded like a lame choice, and she considered adopting her Argentinian grandmother's, "*Salúd!*" There didn't seem to be anyone choosing English. Even Bel shouted, "*lloniannau!*" which, she explained, was Welsh. Lena tried to remember if her father or anyone on the Black side of her family had used a special foreign word. She could remember some of her father's toasts. Things like, "May our children have wealthy parents," and "May your beautiful lips never blister!" and he liked to quote Shakespeare's, "I will, myself, admit that appreciation of my work is much improved by drink" when razzing someone about their work or joking about his own. At weddings he also liked to quote Shakespeare:

'My bounty is as boundless as the sea,
My love as deep; the more I give to thee,
The more I have, for both are infinite.'

He was a lit major after all. But he always ended with a simple, "Cheers," not shouted, almost an apology as he sat down. Her mother, on the other hand, would make everyone laugh, and then end her toast by joining in, a wordless cackle before drinking and then another when she realized she forgot to give everyone permission to drink with her. God, how Lena missed them both. She took so little comfort in the knowledge they'd been allowed to believe her dead for their own safety. Just imagining their grief broke her heart. And so, in their honor, she decided to shout, "Cheers!" in good ol' Oregonian English, and the louder she shouted, the more those wounds in her heart were stitched. And soon she was quite drunk.

Then Lucia and Nando were shooing her off to bed, and she was laughing and blushing and holding onto Bel's arm to keep herself steady. A brief bit of cool night air didn't sober her much at all, and then she was kissing Bel in a white-walled room without any decorations, plywood over the one window, and a desk so small it was clearly designed for a child to use to write home to Mom and Dad between hiking and archery and learning to make lanyard keychains that would never be attached to any keys. The couple stood next to the little twin bed for a bit, and Lena couldn't measure time through the alcohol, but then her clothes started coming off, and then

Bel's clothes were coming off, and then she was staring at a slightly spinning ceiling while her boots were being unlaced, and she briefly considered the possibility she'd had too much to drink, and then Bel was no longer working on her boots and she discovered she could sober up very quickly under the right ministrations. Then, just before she climaxed, Bel picked her up from her position sideways on the bed and laid her down lengthwise. Bel propped herself up on one arm over Lena and, while finishing her task, she kissed Lena, first on the lips, then on her cheek, then on one ear, and then, at just the right time, she bit Lena's earlobe. It wasn't hard, just a nibble, but being nibbled by a vampire is frightening enough to cause a gasp and tightening and chill which, when timed correctly, produced a sound Lena had never made before.

While Lena caught her breath, Bel rolled to one side of her and stared down at her, beaming, her head propped on an elbow.

Lena rolled towards Bel, flopping an arm around her waist. "Ready for your turn?"

Bel ran her fingertips along Lena's shoulder, raising goosebumps. She stared into Lena's eyes. "No, you're exhausted. I want you to sleep first. Right here, close to me, while I rub your back ..." she traced her fingers up Lena's arm, around her angel wing, and ran her nails gently down Lena's spine. "... and I'll just stare at you in a way that isn't creepy at all and keep reminding myself that this is real, okay?"

Lena pulled Bel closer, squeezed, and pressed her face

against Bel's lower shoulder. "Okay." She thought about not saying it and then whispered, "I love you."

Bel placed her cheek on Lena's forehead and whispered, "I love you, too. Sleep."

Lena whispered, "Tell me a story. A happy story. Please."

"Fiction or nonfiction?" Bel asked.

"Fiction. It's less sticky."

Bel shrugged. "Okay. You're the writer, not me. But I can tell you a story somebody else made up. I saw a French film one time about this human. He joined the French army and was sent off to fight in Vietnam. He saved a friend's life and became a hero, meeting the Prime Minister. Oh, no, wait, he didn't meet the Prime Minister because of his heroism in battle. He was injured saving his friend, and while he was recovering, he got really good at ping-pong, and he became part of the French Olympic team, and he won a gold medal. And then he met the Prime Minister. But when he came home, the love of his life was involved with another man. And she was kind of a mess. So he went on this cross-country run, back and forth across France over and over to clear his mind and heal his soul, and that didn't work. So he became a fisherman, joining the crew of some of his fellow army veterans, and they fished off the coast of France until his former lieutenant had this kind of baptismal scene and was healed of his anger about the war. And this inspired the protagonist to go back home to his small village outside Paris and find his lost love. And when he arrived, she was dying from a disease, but they made love, and she got pregnant and had a child before she died. And she left the man with his son. Or was it a daughter? I don't remember the movie that well, but I remember it was a hit because it made humans feel like their particular era of history was really important even though, between you and me, the history of humans is far less interesting than humans make it out to be, and every era is about as dramatic as the next. But the acting was good, and there were some fine shots. Especially the baptism scene off the side of the boat. That moved me more than the love story. I guess I had some anger to let go of, too. So that's the story. A stupid man had a bunch of things happen to him, and a stupid friend of his let go of his anger, and a stupid vampire in the audience let go of some anger of her own. Fiction and nonfiction, I guess."

Lena mumbled, "Um, Bel, that wasn't a French movie."

"It wasn't?"

"That was *Forrest Gump*. It was an American movie. Tom Hanks. Steven Spielberg."

"Oh. I knew it was one of the countries where white people went to fight in Vietnam."

"And Forrest Gump met JFK and Richard Nixon and a whole bunch of other American icons like Elvis Presley, not Charles de Gaulle. How could you think that was a French movie?"

"Sorry. I get human things mixed up sometimes. But does it matter whether they were French or American? I turned it into a happy story, didn't I? Because, now that

I think about it, it was kind of a sad story. But I made it happy. Oh, and you're right. They were speaking English the whole time."

Lena rolled over and propped her head up on her elbow. "Yes, they were speaking English! And yes, you did make it a happy story. I noticed you made yourself a star in it." She kissed Bel on her cheek. "I approve of that literary decision. I like it better with you in it."

"Everything is better with vampires, Lena."

Lena lay back down and looked at the ceiling. "We may have to agree to disagree on that. I can think of some stories that would not be improved by adding vampires. Except you. You can be added to all the stories now. Let's put you in *Citizen Kane* and *Ben Hur* and shit, and see how that changes the movies."

Bel was wistful. "Imagine if *Casablanca* ended with Ingrid Bergman being seduced and whisked away to America by a lesbian vampire, and the movie ended with Humphrey Bogart and Paul Heinreid standing there holding their dicks on the tarmac."

Lena smiled. "Beginning of a beautiful friendship? Okay, but which of the characters would you have eaten?"

Bel didn't hesitate. "Madeleine Lebeau."

"Wow, you pulled that name fast. Who was she?"

"Yvonne, Rick's discarded mistress. Remember when the French nationals in the bar drown out the Germans who are singing '*Die Wacht am Rheim*' by singing '*La Marsaillaise*' at the top of their lungs, and then Rick's ex-girlfriend shouts '*Vive la France! Vive la démocratie!*' with genuine tears in her eyes? She was really French, and the movie was made when France had fallen to the Nazis."

"You're sure?" Lena teased. "Not French like *Forrest Gump*?"

"No, I didn't have a crush on that actor, so I don't remember him, but I had a crush on Madeleine Lebeau."

Lena shook her head slowly. "Tom Hanks. His name is Tom Hanks. He's one of the most famous movie stars ever."

"Human man. Not my type."

"Goddamn I love you, Bel. You remember an actress from some movie from 1945, but you don't know who Tom Hanks is."

Bel shrugged. "It was 1941. Have you ever been to Casablanca? Beautiful city. I'll take you there sometime. The *Café Americain* in the movie isn't real, but they've built a place called 'Rick's Café' there. Started by a former diplomat named Kathy Kriger. They call her 'Madame Rick.' I met her. Fascinating woman. And wait until you see the place. Of course, I can't comment on the quality of the food, but the humans seemed to like it. And the piano player isn't Sam, but his name is Issam. American tourists say, 'Play it again, Sam,' and he says, 'My name is Issam.' He should also say, 'And that line is never in the movie. But I will play it for you once. For old time's sake.' That was really the line. 'Play it once, Sam, for old time's sake.' Such a great movie. And yes, I know who was American and who was French and who was German in the movie. I saw that one the first time in a theater in Sacramento in 1942. I'm not sure where I saw that *Forrest Gump*. Come to think of it, I may have been in Japan and saw it dubbed. Maybe that's why the English didn't click. Should I watch it again in English? Does it hold up?"

Bel's vampire senses, particularly attuned to the speed of blood moving through veins, recognized the change in Lena's heartbeat through the soft skin of Lena's forehead and Lena's wrist against her hip. Lena was asleep. And, she noted, very soundly so. Her cheek mooshed against Bel's shoulder in a way that pressed her lips to the side and made them flutter as she exhaled. And Bel watched that quaver and felt a flood of mixed emotions.

"I met a man at the bar at Rick's Café, led him to believe we were going to go back to his hotel room, and then I pretended like I wanted to fuck him in an alley off the *Rue El Haddada*, and I sucked him dry and left him in a dumpster. And I'll bet the police rounded up the usual suspects. That always made me chuckle a little. Fuck. How are we possibly going to make this work, Lena? I wasn't sure I'd ever see you again. It makes me so happy I ..."

Lena started to almost snore, not in her nose, but by making tiny little "puh" sounds when she exhaled. Bel relished each one.

She listened to Lena for more than two hours, feeling the warmth of her, the pressure of her skin against Bel's shoulder, their legs entwined, bodies pressed close enough to feel each other breathe. And in those hours, Bel was pleased to find her mind didn't wander far.

Mostly she thought about Lena, about her own happiness, about her desire to keep Lena safe and near her. She didn't worry too much about Lena's distant future, though it was less distant than Bel's own, and not worrying made her happy, too. Maybe, this time, she could just let herself love until love became loss, and with Lena, that would be worth it. But that was a thought for another time, and she was relieved to find she didn't fear putting it off. *After all, the book might make it all moot, anyway.*

And it was in remembering the book she became curious. Lena had worn her backpack all evening, had brought the school bookbag back to the room with them, and Bel had removed it just like all the rest of her clothing. But she'd noted its weight. Even in that moment, when she'd had other things on her mind, she'd wondered how Lena could carry so much on such frail, human shoulders.

Carefully listening to Lena's heartbeat and feeling each pulse through her skin, Bel lifted Lena's arm and leg without waking her and slowly extricated herself from Lena's embrace. Then, with a silence no human could manage, she made her way off the little bed, easily spotted Lena's backpack in the darkness, opened it, and pulled out the two reams of typed paper.

Two. Yes, there were two books. Bel sat down in the child's chair next to the small desk. She set the books down without the thump the stack should have made. Though she didn't strictly need to, she decided to turn on the little desk lamp. When it clicked, she heard the change in Lena's breathing, even heard her pulse shift, but Lena didn't wake. Bel began to read. After each page, she quietly lifted it, hearing the sibilant scrape of smooth, bleached wood pulp against the next page as she lifted, turned it, and set it carefully, face down, on the previous.

Bel could read faster than most humans, but not freakishly so. She knew human reading speed was something of a parlor trick; fast readers aren't necessarily better readers, just as early readers aren't necessarily smarter than late ones. Bel's muscles could move faster than any human's; she could make her bones flash from one place to another faster than a human could twitch the muscles of their eyes. It didn't make her invisible in the sense of being transparent, but not-visible in that she could move faster than human eyes could track. She could move the muscles of her own eyes proportionately more quickly, so she could scan a page faster than a human. But to truly read is to understand, and, much as she was loath to admit it, a vampire's mind doesn't work proportionately faster than a human's. Fast enough to control a body moving more quickly, yes, but Bel's mind took almost as long to contemplate and process abstractions. The supernatural, it seemed, also ran into the limits of electrical impulses passing from cell to cell, even if those cells could live forever or regrow if destroyed. She healed and persisted like a vampire, but she thought like a human, and reading is the purest kind of thinking.

Reading is one of the oldest and most powerful magical abilities, the conversion of mystical runes to deep meaning, and humans had been doing it since before some of the supernatural creatures on earth split off from their evolutionary branch. That thought was a bit humbling for Bel who generally thought of the humans as lesser, as food, related to vampires, certainly, but related in the same way humans are related to cows and sheep. But humans rarely fell into romantic love with cattle, so she had to reevaluate her estimation of humans or be forced to think of herself an analogous to a human engaging in bestiality, and she wasn't comfortable with that. Clearly Lena was not some lesser being. Not only was she worthy of Bel's love, and much of love is respect, but here was the proof Lena possessed a kind of magic, a human magic, equivalent to any supernatural monster in The Convention. The first book was a single, elaborate spell in the form of a novel. It told a story, certainly, but one that could not be extricated from the purpose of the spell itself, to bewitch the reader into truly feeling his own mortality. Yes, "his." As Bel read, she realized the novel's limit, the careful and subtle strand of DNA spiraling through the story. It was male. It was white. It was, if not explicitly Christian, then Western European. In fact, she wasn't sure if the book would have been able to have its deadly effect if it had been translated from English into anything other than a European language. The novel was designed to teach mortality to the people who had the power to postpone contemplating their own limits. For those limited by the structure of their civilization, the book would have been devastating, a story so tragic and personal they would have to feel the possible pointlessness of their own existence. But they'd survive that. They had learned to. For those left unprepared, the experience would have been fatal. As Bel neared the end, she discovered the cold of the tears on her face as though the chilled streaks had always been there and she'd never noticed them before.

But the book didn't kill her. It was about human frailty, so that pain was hammered and sharpened into a blade which could not pierce her. Instead, she imagined the sensation of it driving into Lena's heart. Often empathy isn't sharing the exact same feeling of another; it's taking on the pain and peppering it with the guilt of knowing it's not quite right. Bel wished she knew what it had been like for Lena to read the book, but she also suspected that was impossible. If she really felt it, it might have killed her.

She set the last page of the first book down, then turned to the next, the first page of the second book. There were only three words typed in the center of the page. "You Were Warned."

For a fleeting moment, she wondered if this was a warning which might apply to her. Was she invading Lena's privacy by reading this second book? Should she wait and ask for permission in the morning? She calculated the book was completed, since Lena was carrying it in the same way she lugged the first about, so Bel wouldn't be reading an unfinished draft. And, she decided, they had become intimate enough to circumnavigate secrets. Lovers often didn't say things, but they didn't prevent their partners from knowing those things with silence. That was how the intimacy grew: secrets dissolving even when unspoken. So, if Lena loved her, and if love meant giving someone permission to learn to read the other's mind over time, surely this allowed Bel to begin by reading a completed draft of a manuscript. That's what she told herself as she lifted the first page, set it gently on the last page of the previous book, and began to read again.

Miracles take different forms, and love is the most common, so ubiquitous humans rarely identify it correctly as miraculous. As Lena slept, she felt the chill of Bel's absence. It made her leg twitch, and then she felt the space where Bel's leg should have been. Her heart rate changed, and that should have alerted Bel, but as Lena rose from unconsciousness, Bel remained unaware. Lena blinked in the darkness. She patted the bed, remembered the night before, and sat up. The glow of the little desk lamp made a stark silhouette of Bel's shoulders, neck, and ears, and cast rosy light through her pink hair.

"Bel?" Lena asked the shape. She didn't know she'd decided on a pet name until it came out of her mouth. "Love?" She'd never called anyone that before. Bel didn't move. *Is it the wrong name?* Lena wondered. *Too soon?*

Then she saw movement as Bel reached onto the desk and silently placed a hand there. Lena heard the hiss of the page, saw the flitting reflection of the lamp's light change against the far wall, then saw the paper come down on its face on top of the pile. The pile. The too-tall pile.

"No!" she screamed, kicking off the sheets wrapped around her legs, swinging out of the bed, and nearly leaping across the room. Bel still didn't move as Lena grabbed the whole unread pile of pages from the desk and pulled them into her chest. She thought of flinging them across the room like they were on fire, but she didn't want Bel to catch even a single word on a floating page. "Bel!" she shouted. "Bel, wake up!"

"But, where ...?" Bel said. She shook her head, looked at the blank wall in front of her, then back at the empty space on the desk. "Where is the ... ? I need the-" And then her lower jaw dropped and stretched in the way Lena had witnessed once before, in the hotel in Ireland. Though Lena stood behind her, she could catch the line of Bel's jaw in the low light, that supernatural, grotesque transformation, and she could imagine the teeth, those rows upon inhumanly circular rows, each one a thin needle, each curved back to pull and hollowed to suck, and then Bel hissed, not snakelike but gurgling, a frothy anger. Every muscle in Lena's body locked. She could not have run or fought or even pissed herself. Everything was pulled in, her abdomen a steel anchor, the remaining pages of the book a stone slab pressed against her chest. And then Bel's jaw slid back into place, and when it was back to its human length, she spoke again, and Lena knew the teeth had retreated. There was even a sardonic smile in Bel's voice, confused but amused. "Where the fuck did the book go?" She sounded like an absent minded professor laughing at her own forgetfulness. "It was just ..."

And then she turned in the chair and saw Lena. "Oh my god, Love, what's wrong? You're pale as a sheet."

That woke Lena up. "Really?"

"Well, of course not. Just an expression. What happened to you?"

"To me? What happened to *me*? You were reading the book, Bel. Completely entranced. And when I took it, your teeth popped out, and you went all Exorcist girl and hissed like a ..."

"Like a monster?" Bel said. She didn't sound offended, though.

"Yeah, sorry. But you did. And I thought you were going to kill me. For a second."

"Oh, Love, I'm so sorry," Bel said as she rose from the chair. She could see Lena flinch in the darkness, see her catch it and control it, and Bel decided to reach out anyway. She put a hand on Lena's cheek and was relieved when Lena leaned into her palm. "I didn't mean to scare you. I honestly don't remember doing it. I guess I ... What was I doing?"

"The book, Bel! The *second* book. Did you read the first one?"

"Yes. I remember that." She sounded dreamy, confused. "It was sad. So, so sad. I cried. And I didn't even know I was crying. I remember now. I remember crying and then finishing the book and realizing I'd been crying."

"And then you started reading the second book," Lena said. It was not a question.

"Yes. I thought about asking permission, but I thought it would be okay. I thought … I thought … Should I not have read it?"

"No-you-shouldn't-have-read-it!" The sentence came out as a single long word that sounded surprisingly like "Stupid bitch!" something Lena never would have shouted at anyone. "It could have killed you! In fact, if I hadn't stopped you, it *would* have killed you."

"Aw, Lena, Love, it wouldn't have killed me. I'm immortal."

Lena looked down over the edge of the book pressed against her chest, staring at the dark floor, ashamed. "I know, Bel. That's exactly how the second book works."

"Unless man is committed to the belief that all mankind are his brothers, then he labors in vain and hypocritically in the vineyards of equality."

-Adam Clayton Powell Jr.
Black Power: A Form of Godly Power

Chapter 16

Lena explained the purpose of the second book to Bel, and then the partners agreed on some time apart. Bel needed to sleep during the day to recharge from the experience of reading even the small portion of the book she'd consumed, but Lena suspected Bel also needed time to reconsider whether she wanted to associate herself so closely with the book's author. Bel suspected Lena needed time to recover from the trauma of seeing her with all her teeth out. Both were mostly wrong about why the other needed the space, but right to be scared.

Lena left Bel's room and found her own in a different cabin. The room was the same size as Bel's, with identical furniture and bare walls, but the window wasn't covered in plywood, and the glow of dawn, late because of the latitude and gentler than the blazing sun of Costa Rica, comforted Lena's hung-over eyes.

"Josef?" she asked quietly.

A swirl of dust spiraled up from nowhere. Lena rested a hand on the golem's forearm, grateful for her friend's presence.

"Can you do me a favor?" she asked.

It nodded.

"Can you just stay here with the books? I just had a little scare. I'll feel a lot more comfortable knowing you're keeping them safe. I'm sorry to ask you to do something so boring, but..."

Josef placed its hand on Lena's shoulder. She was always surprised by how gentle it could be, the sandstone texture of its skin touching the skin around the strap of her tank top like flower petals rather than sandpaper. It nodded again, plucked the strap of the offered backpack from her hand, and set the bag down on the little desk. Then it stepped into the middle of the little room, crossed its arms over its massive chest, and posed like a statue.

Lena smiled halfway to a laugh. "Thank you, Josef. I'm going to go find myself some breakfast, maybe catch up with Nando if I can find him. But I'll come back soon."

It said nothing, of course, and she interpreted this to mean she could take her time.

Lena smoked two cigarettes, then made her way to the camp's main hall. It had been cleaned after the previous evening's festivities, the tables straightened, the chairs stacked and ready to be moved back into place for the next big group meal. Lena didn't know if everyone would get together for lunch or dinner, but it seemed breakfast was not a joint affair. Even Tina, the sullen teen permanently fixated on her phone, hadn't taken up her usual position. Lena knew she shouldn't be surprised by a teenager sleeping in, but she'd decided that seat was where Tina lived and couldn't imagine her anywhere else.

In the kitchen, she found some boxes of cereal in a cupboard and gallons of milk in the walk-in fridge. She chose a sugared cereal she would have been embarrassed to buy before her experience in Europe and her year in Costa Rica. It was hard for her to care too much about her health anymore. The book hadn't made her an aesthete, exactly, but there was a sweet immediacy to her nihilism.

When Nando and his girlfriend Lucia came into the room, they didn't start upon finding her, and she realized their slightly odd greeting was caused by the way they had identified her by smell, and perhaps by sound, before entering the room.

"How did you sleep?" Nando asked. His eyes

twinkled just a bit at that.

Lucia slapped his arm.

"Would you like the grand tour of the camp?" Nando said.

"Sure." She set her bowl in the sink, ran some tap water into it, and made a mental note to wash it later.

Nando led her through the back of the kitchen. The main hall stood at the keystone of a half-circle of cabins, all built to look rustic on the outside and college-dormitory-utilitarian on the inside. In the middle of the semi-circle, there was a covered area with some picnic benches where generations of Canadian children had made lanyard keychains for parents to throw away or pretend to treasure. Beyond the benches, Nando hooked a thumb toward a blank area.

"Firepit."

And beyond that, a thin strip of beach, and then the lake, a perfect mirror of the mottled clouds and peeking bits of blue that winked above. All around the lake, pine forests stood guard, the flat plains of central Canada an ocean of green stretching to the horizon.

Lena thought of the view from the deck of Matt's yacht, looking out to the west over the Pacific.

"It's amazing how beautiful emptiness can be, isn't it." She didn't inflect her non-question. Then she remembered she had left Costa Rica-Lena behind and needed to be her more social self, even if it felt like an act. She started walking around the lake, inviting Nando and Lucia with her gait and a shoulder.

"So, what is it you've been up to, Nando? Last time we

were together you did not give off a camp-counselor vibe."

He threw his arms out and spun as he walked. Even when his back was to her, she could hear the smile in his voice. "Scaling up the tribe."

"You mean growing the pack?"

"Uh-oh," Lucia said. "Fair warning. If you let him explain this, he will be very happy." But she was smiling, too.

"Okay, so the first thing to make clear is that we misunderstand one of the most fundamental things about our own existence. And we've evolved to misunderstand it. And this misunderstanding causes a lot of our problems."

The bit of beach came to an end, and Lena had to pick her way through the squelching mud on the banks of the lake, finding sticks and high, dry patches of dirt for more solid steps. "Okay, what's the big misunderstanding?" she asked.

Nando had no trouble with the terrain, so he could devote all his attention to his monologue. "We think our bodies exist to carry around our brains. We spend our time thinking about poetry and architecture and love, and it seems to us that our bodies are just vehicles to make these higher things possible. But that's estupid. Our brains exist for the benefit of our bodies. The brain is just an advanced computer for keeping us alive and balanced and happy and reproducing. The poetry is there for your body to feel it. The architecture is to keep your body warm, and we want the buildings to be beautiful because even that beauty balances chemicals in our bodies. Even love is for the body. That sounds unromantic, but it's not. Why do you mourn when a girlfriend leaves you? You think it's lost love. But it's deeper than that. Sure, some of it is sex, but having her there with you when you slept regulated your breathing. Having her there to ask you about your day helped regulate your rhythms." He reached over and wrapped his hand around Lucia's waist. "I hope this does not sound unromantic to you. I am not saying I don't love you or that love is not real. I am saying I love you because you help every single cell of my body to be healthier. You improve all of me."

Lucia looked at Lena. "He has given this lecture enough times that it helps regulate my circadian rhythms." Then she looked into Nando's eyes, sprang up onto her toes and kissed him on his nose, and then said, "And I do find it romantic. You make my body love you, too."

Nando leaned into the crook of her neck and growled. "Oh, that body." Then he remembered his place in the lecture and looked back at Lena.

"Sorry. She distracts me. So, once we see that our brains exist for our bodies, we see the problem with our social estructure. We have designed a whole society around the idea that individuals should sacrifice their bodies for this higher thing, civilization, when it should be the opposite. Society is lower than architecture, lower than love, lower than poetry. It should exist to protect the bodies of the people in it, to keep them safe from murder and war, sure, but also to provide the caring and food, and to nurture the bodies of all the people. And when you start to see that society needs to serve bodies, you'll see we have built it backwards, from the leaders down and not from the workers up."

Lena nodded. She pulled her pack of cigarettes out of her pocket. "Mind if I…?"

"Not at all," sharp-nosed Nando lied.

After lighting it, Lena realized Nando was waiting on her. She made a small cartwheel gesture with the two fingers holding the lit cigarette.

Nando leapt at the encouragement. "Scaling up the tribe isn't the same thing as growing the pack. In fact, in an important way, it's the opposite. Scaling up the tribe is about remembering what is important and building a society around that. Growing the pack is often the problem. We forget what's important to our own survival and happiness. And then, when we realize that it's unsustainable or makes us unhappy, we think we can fix society by just blowing it up and estarting over. But that's absolutely wrong. You see this with the humans, too. Their society gets broken, and they are unhappy with the injustice of it, or they see that it's literally going to kill them, whether through suicides or drug addiction or mass incarceration or global warming, and some percentage of them say, 'Tear it all down. Blow it up. Destroy it. And then I'll be better off.' They get into zombie TV shows or they estart prepping for the apocalypse or they worship religious leaders who tell them the end is nigh. And then some leader steps forward and says, 'Know how we should blow it up? By dividing the tribe. Let's blame them. We'll kick them out. Or kill them.' Always the people who don't have enough of some kind of power to fight back. Maybe they have the 'wrong' skin color, whatever that is in the human's country. Or maybe the 'wrong' religion. Or they are new immigrants."

Nando slowed, scratched behind one ear in a very canine way, and then continued. "In some cases, I admit, people with political leanings similar to mine did this very same thing by blaming the rich. And you might think, 'But that's not attacking the powerless.' But in countries with very few rich people, the rich have resources but not the numbers. They seem strong, but they can become targets of demagogues, too. And the demagogue might be playing into racism or anti-immigrant sentiment or hatred of the capitalists who have been abusing the workers, but at a deeper level, he's leveraging dissatisfaction with society itself and exploiting a desire to have a much smaller tribe. But that's because humans and werewolves misdiagnose the problem. It's not that society got too big. It's that, while it was getting big, it forgot *why* it got big. A big society is good. A society that forgot why it got big is bad."

"Okay, I'll bite," Lena said. "What makes a big society good and a forgetful society bad?"

"So think in terms of needs and an individual's ability to satisfy those needs. Start with the individual alone in the wild. I know what that's like. I have been a wolf without a pack. If I dropped you here, in the middle of

Canada, with no other people, what would you need?"

"Food, shelter, warmth, clean water. The basics."

"Right. I mean, you got the order wrong, but you're close. You'd need the water first. And to not be eaten by bears. And the warmth. So you'd need a source of water and a fire which would double as protection from predators. How much would water and fire be worth to you that first day?"

"I mean, everything, I guess."

"Exactly. You'd trade all your money for water and fire the first day, if you could. Hell, you'd literally burn your cash to survive. Okay, now scale up the tribe to three people. One of you can bring water, one can look for food, and one can keep the fire going and maybe start working on building a shelter of some kind. Would you kick anyone out of that tribe for having the wrong skin color or religion or anything?"

"I see. The water and food and warmth are more important."

"Okay, so scale it up again. Now you have thirty people. Some are finding food and maybe even growing it. Some are just hunters. Someone still needs to keep the fire going. And maybe there are children or old people who can't do those things. Someone has to care for them. How much is it worth to the group to have someone care for the children?"

"Well, if that doesn't get done, the tribe will die out, so that's just as important as the food and water in the long run."

"Right! Now scale it up again. There are three

hundred people. Some people just build homes. Some just farm. Some are hunters. Some care for children. And the group is big enough and successful enough that it has an abundance. Abundance means there's enough to be stolen. So some people have to protect the tribe from other tribes. And some people have to keep members of the tribe from estealing from each other. How important are those police and soldiers?"

Lena had good reason to be skeptical of police, but she had to concede this point. "All the other stuff is meaningless if they get overrun or start destroying themselves from within."

"Right. But now we have people with a new kind of power. People who can punish or even kill. So we need some system of leadership, some rules. Maybe a military general or a judge of disputes. Or both. Those people get food and housing and water, too. The tribe has a chief who doesn't do the same work as everybody else. But she organizes them."

Finished with her smoke, Lena mashed-potatoed the butt with her toe, burying it in the mud serving as the lake's beach. "I like that you made her female."

Nando gave her a little bow. "You're welcome." Then he kept walking around the lake's shore. "So scale it up again. Now we have people who help settle disputes by appealing to the judge. We have people who deal in information, whether as military scouts or gossips or truth-tellers to the chief. Reporters and lawyers. And figuring out how to compensate all those people who don't provide food or fire or water is getting tricky. We need currency. We make up money. It has no intrinsic meaning. It's a measure of our confidence in it, a made-up thing like race or language or the human soul."

Lena stopped walking and raised her eyebrows, smiling wickedly. "You came in hot there at the end, Nando. I like that."

He returned the smile and shrugged. "I'm just saying. And if you want evidence, notice the very people who always want money connected to gold are also the ones who believe in souls. They are deeply uncomfortable with the truth that these are made-up things, so they want to connect money to gold and souls to gods, heedless of the fact gold and gods also have no intrinsic value beyond what people give them by believing in them. People get money all wrong. They think money is this mechanism invented to make it easier to trade things. It does, but that's not why it was invented. We could just trade the estuff. Money makes it easier to pay people for their actions. Sometimes that's labor. Sometimes that's debt. Really, it's a ledger for remembering power. We have our power dynamic established, so we can create that ledger system when we need it. As Felix Salmon once said, 'It's a lot easier to turn power into money than it is to turn money into power.' Money is just confidence expressed in numbers. We have the confidence of our community already. We'll make up money when the time comes. But I digress."

Lucia nodded. "He digresses."

Nando didn't miss a beat. "So, once people are buying and selling, we need people to take care of that. So now we have lawyers and journalists and bankers. And who is going to have the most influence over determining the value of labor? The banker isn't going to admit his work is less important to the survival of the tribe than the person who builds houses or takes care of children. The banker will say his work is the most important. And as long as he says the journalist's job is important, she will spread the word the banker's job is important. And as long as the banker says the lawyer's job and the chief's job are more important, they will make rules saying the banker's job is more important. And the soldiers and police will enforce those rules as long as their jobs make more than the person who makes the fire or builds the homes or grows the food. The bigger the pack, the more abundance, and the more room for these ... " He looked at Lucia. "... shenanigans."

Lucia explained to Lena: "He knows I like it when he says 'shenanigans' with a Spanish accent. It's both cute and sexy."

Lena nodded. "Stipulated." She looked to Nando. "So you're trying to scale up a tribe without money, right?"

"No. I guess I'm more of a neo-Marxist. Old age and reality, maybe. I understand we will need currency to manage the exchange of goods at some point, and we will need a more efficient way of compensating people for their work. When we get big enough, they won't just do it out of love for their neighbor because there will be too many neighbors, and people have trouble loving people they don't know."

"So, what, no bankers? No lawyers? No journalists?"

She cocked her head to the side. "You'd better not tell a writer you're going to build a society without writers."

He laughed. "Of course not. No, we just need to keep coming back to the idea money is made up and reminding ourselves we made it up to satisfy our basic needs, so the people who help satisfy the most basic needs are worth more. The person who grows the food is more important than the police officer. The police officer is more important than the lawyer. The lawyer is more important than the chief. If people choose to take on a role that is less essential to the survival of everyone, they give up pay. Some will do it anyway. People have different motives than money. Some people like power. Some people like art. Some people like excitement. They can choose roles that offer more of those other things. But when they do, at every step, they sacrifice money rather than getting paid more to do something less useful." Nando slowed. "Want to head back? There's nothing more on the other side of the lake except more woods and more lakes and eventually the North Pole."

"Yeah, I don't have the shoes for that," Lena agreed. They turned back towards the camp. "So, a farmer makes more than the chief?"

"Yes. And the childcare worker makes more than the lawyer and banker. Because, if we really put the good of society first, the child care worker does more important work." Nando looked to Lucia, and she smiled at this.

"But who decides what's more useful?" Lena asked. "That's what's always been the downfall of command economies. Even if you are this perfect paragon of virtue, this philosopher-king willing to be an ascetic in exchange for being the chief, power corrupts. The people who decide will favor themselves."

"True," Nando said. "But it's not that power corrupts. Frank Herbert was right: Power attracts the corruptible, and absolute power attracts the absolutely corruptible. Command economies seem more susceptible to corruption than capitalist ones, except..."

"Except?"

"Except they aren't really. The difference is, in a command economy, the corruption is in the hands of people at the top, and it's intentional. It's conscious. In capitalism, it's unconscious and inevitable and much more pernicious. The corrupt party official in some communist dictatorship spent his childhood learning about fairness and equality, and he knows he's cheating and self-dealing. The billionaire in a capitalist economy learned all about winning at business. He believes he's done nothing wrong even if he hurts many more people than the party official ever could. Capitalism, on a small scale, is the best system. It's a bunch of people haggling in a little farmer's market. It's kind of beautiful. But it only leads to growing inequality and increasing inefficiency the bigger it gets. It not only leads to monopolistic practices, but it skews the values of the goods and labor themselves. The solution is a free market of goods but a command of wages."

Lena shook her head. "I still think that leads back to the same problem. The people deciding the wages."

"Yes, you're right. And that's why that only works

with two other elements in place: Radical transparency and radical accountability."

"Okay. Explain."

"First, you have to have radical freedom of the press and freedom of speech and public education so that everyone has access to the information, the means to comprehend it, and the ability to discern truth from falsehood. That needs to be seen as one of the most important functions of education: preparing the public to determine whether or not their leaders are corrupt. Then, radical accountability. When a person chooses to take on a lower paying job with more power, they also take on a higher amount of accountability. Equal protection under the law has never been equal. So let's acknowledge that and be intentional about it so we can flip it. Look at the civilizations with supposed equal protection. Who always faces the harshest consequences? The people with the least power. But one of the bedrock principles of the society needs to be that the more power a person has, the more severe the consequences. Those journalists will be vigorously reporting on whether or not the rules are being enforced that way, and the educated public will be able to judge. If the chief's buddy who has some high-powered job like banker or lawyer betrayed the public trust and harmed a million people, the chief must enforce clearly identified and predetermined consequences that are much harsher than they would have been if a farmer cheated someone out of a little bit of wheat. And if the chief doesn't, the people must be informed enough to exact the most severe punishments on the chief herself."

"Like what?"

Lucia cringed. "You probably won't like this part."

Nando shrugged. "They should chew the chief to pieces."

Lena stopped walking again. "Wait, what?"

"Or maybe exile, if they are feeling nice. But when the leader loses the public trust, not because of a bad crop or a foreign invasion or something else outside of her control, but because she misused her authority for her own gain rather than the tribe's, she must be destroyed or eliminated to make sure the inversion of the hierarchy is maintained."

"Holy shit, Nando. That's brutal. I can't imagine that ever catching on."

"Ah, that's because you're human. But I'm not making a human society. I'm building a tribe of werewolves. This part of my plan is the least controversial part for us. We've always had this understanding in our packs. When the alpha cannot maintain leadership, he or she is often destroyed by the other wolves. I'm making that far more humane. In our tribe, that won't be the consequence of aging or any failure. In a healthy society, the leader can make mistakes, can own them and learn from them, and can continue to lead or retire. She should be able to be unseated by a democratic process at any time like in many parliamentary systems without bloodshed. But if the chief is corrupt, she should face the most extreme punishment in order to make sure she enforces the rules that prevent corruption by those beneath her. Imagine if, in your human society, a judge knew if she didn't severely punish a crooked cop, she would face a harsher punishment than the cop deserved, and the person above her would face even worse if she didn't punish her, and so on?"

"It sounds like a recipe for a very strict, bloody, brutal society, Nando."

"Maybe," Nando said. He looked down at the ground, forlorn, and Lena was struck by just how canine his emotional expressions could be.

Lucia shook her head. "Maybe it would be for humans, Lena, but not for us. Or maybe I'm a naive optimist, and so is Nando, and I love that about him. Because we believe that kind of corruption will be rare. We don't think, in a society where people's basic needs are met, you're really going to have a lot of people trying to screw each other over to get ahead. Get ahead how? Why? So they can become more powerful and face more risk? People won't be desperate to test the boundaries the way they are in human society, I don't think, because in our society, the person's needs are met, and I believe that is really the motivation for most human transgressions. I'm not saying people are inherently good or inherently evil, inherently giving or inherently selfish. I think those binaries are oversimplifications. But I do believe most of the time, when people hurt one another, it's because they are hurting in some way and can't come up with a better solution. People who are warm and well-fed and loved just don't harm each other as much. So, in Nando's vision, I really don't think there will be a lot of punishment because I don't think there will be a lot of corruption as long as people enter into the society committed to the idea that providing for the most basic needs of their neighbors is the most valuable thing they can do."

They'd walked nearly back to camp, and the first of the cabins was just off to their right. "And that's my cue to get back to work," Lucia said. "Rita and I are going on a grocery store run." She leaned towards Lena. "Rita doesn't have to go. Her job with the children is more than enough. But she likes to go looking for men in her off hours. Dealing with the kids is stressful, and that's how she blows off steam. Shopping for human men. If I didn't go with her, she'd probably seduce and kill every old man in all the little towns around here."

Lena had been preparing to laugh at the story of a horny old lady, and when the laugh came out, it was shocked and louder and unsure in a way that sounded like her teenage self's reaction to a horror movie, and she didn't like it one bit.

Lucia seemed not to notice or was polite enough to pretend, and she headed off to the jeep parked on the other side of the longhouse. Nando recognized Lena's discomfort and smiled sadly as he led her inside. "I'm sorry," he said. "I know it must be hard for you to be a human here."

"You all seem so civilized most of the time," Lena said. "I mean, really better than people …" She corrected herself. "… human people, most of the time. And then, when I'm reminded you all kill human people, it's just …

shocking."

Nando and Lena walked around the exterior of the cabins, and he pointed out some details that showed why using an old summer camp was a particularly clever place to build a community of werewolves. Trails made by fast paws were carved into the tall grass between the buildings, but they dissipated as the wolves spread out into the woods each night. A summer camp was supposed to be remote, so that wouldn't draw suspicion, and a camp surrounded by woods as thick with wolves as they were with trees would keep just about anyone out.

They made it around to the one road in, then entered the longhouse from its front porch. Lena noticed Tina had taken up her usual spot. She waved, but Tina didn't look up from her phone. Nando shook his head as they continued toward the kitchen. Lena could tell something was bothering him.

"What?"

"You say we seem civilized. Are you more offended by us killing humans than by humans who kill humans, because you all seem to do a lot of killing of one another, too."

Lena shook her head. "Naw. Don't do that, Nando. I'm trying not to project my human morality onto you. Don't try to justify your morality by making a false equivalence to human immorality. Most of us don't go around biting people. We may participate in systems of oppression, but most of us don't go to the grocery store and look for people to eat. I won't say you ought to be like us, but don't say we're just like you."

"Fair," Nando shrugged. "But I don't believe in some external, universal, divinely dictated morality. You believe humans killing humans is wrong because it's socially dysfunctional behavior. All the 'Thou Shalt Not Kill' on stone tablets from God is just more easily digested versions of the fact that your societies would fall apart if you went around killing each other. But monsters killing humans is what our societies are based on. It's not socially dysfunctional. It's right, in the same way it's right for a human to pluck a tomato and eat it rather than planting the seeds. What makes it ethical is doing it in a sustainable way, staying secretive, culling the human population to maintain the tribe without bringing the wrath of the humans down on the tribe. That's ethical behavior for monsters."

"Bel tried to convince me of that. Only she used the metaphor of cattle. I don't know if I like being compared to a cow more than a tomato."

She was trying to tell a wry joke, but Nando stopped and looked at her. Hard. "Bel used the metaphor of cattle because she knows you eat meat. She loves you and was trying to get you to see her as ethical in the same way you see yourself. She was trying to make a connection. I chose the metaphor of a tomato because you love Bel, but you want her to be a vegan. And I want you to see she will have to go on killing humans just as a vegan will have to continue eating vegetables. If you are going to love her, you need to decide if you can see her as ethical even though she kills humans, because killing humans is the moral thing for a monster to do. You can't be with Bel and hate she is Bel. That would undermine everything you two try to build."

Lena didn't know how to respond, so she looked away, stepped over to the sink, and found her bowl inside. Someone had filled it with water to rinse out the blue milk, then left it in the sink rather than washing it and putting it away. Lena hated when people did this; leaving the job half done. Yet she did it all the time, filling her sink with dishes until she'd find herself filling up a glass of water by tilting it sideways.

Then Lena remembered she was the one who'd left the bowl there.

Ashamed, she couldn't look back at Nando behind her. She wondered if she was being equally hypocritical about all these monsters murdering humans. If so, what was the shape of the hypocrisy? Was she making excuses for murder because she loved Bel, or was she frowning at behavior which was completely justified for them but wouldn't have been justifiable for her? She couldn't shake the feeling it could only be one or the other, and she was a hypocrite either way.

"First, it is necessary that you should understand accurately the difference between swearing and cursing, vulgarly so often confounded. They are entirely different things: the first is invoking the witness of a Spirit to an assertion you wish to make; the second is invoking the assistance of a Spirit in a mischief you wish to inflict. When ill-educated and ill-tempered people clamorously confuse the two invocations, they are not, in reality, either cursing or swearing, but merely vomiting empty words indecently."

-John Ruskin
Benediction

Chapter 17

Tina could hear Lena wash the bowl Lena had left in the sink. Tina hated the sound because the towel made a high-pitched squeaking as Lena dried. And Lena was drying the bowl for an excessive amount of time. Lena was lost in thought, but to Tina's ears, it was another grown-up being intentionally annoying.

Tina rolled her eyes, bowed her head, sighed dramatically, then flopped forward off the table and stomped out of the longhouse.

As she descended the front porch, a loud, high voice shouted, "Tina! Tina!"

Before the children could see her, they'd identified her by smell and the sound of her Doc Martins on the wood planks of the deck. She sniffed and picked their scents out, too. She loved these kids, but expressing that was not her brand.

She greeted them as they ran around the side of the building. "What's up, dingleberry butts?"

"What's a dingleberry?" Ericka asked. She had dark olive skin, freckles, and a mop of red curls, frizzy and wild, which Tina thought looked very cute when pulled up into a pair of afro-puffs, but Ericka hated anything constraining her when she turned into her wolf form, so she always yanked the bands out at the first chance (and kicked off her shoes, and only wore pants and a t-shirt grudgingly).

Tina sneered. "It's when you take a squat and shit sticks to the fur around your butthole, and then you carry that around and everybody can smell you coming."

"Oh," Ericka said. Then she twisted as much as she could and sniffed. "I don't have any, um, poop, on my butt."

"We drag our bottoms on the grass after we poop," Juanito said. His voice was soft, but he smiled, proud to share this accomplishment and thrilled by the opportunity to employ forbidden language.

"Ah, yes, but what do you do when there is no soft ground around?" Tina asked. Her voice took on the hint of the sing-song employed by Rita, the children's teacher and her personal nemesis, but she would never admit to the similarity.

Ericka looked down. "Yeah, when there are only pine needles or rocks that's not good."

"I hate pine needle pokeys in my butt," Juanito said, frowning. Then he smiled and whispered, "Butt."

Ericka looked up suddenly. "Hey, we're not dingleberries!" and she flashed a hand forward and smacked Tina's forearm.

Juanito jumped sideways and started circling Tina. "We're not dingleberries. You're a dingleberry. Butt." He made his way around her side and whispered, "You're a butt."

Tina crouched and prepared to bite their ears if they lunged at her. "Okay, okay, you've got me surrounded. What did you little monsters want, anyway?"

Juanito, distracted, stood up straight, cocked his head to the side, and looked at Ericka. "What did we want to tell her?"

"About the hunt, dingleberry butt!" Ericka shouted.

"Oh yeah," he said. Then, "butt," and a chuckle.

Ericka looked up at Tina, elbows out and fists pressed on her hips. "Juanito was the first to bite the deer!"

Tina raised an eyebrow and turned overly slowly towards Juanito. "Is that true?"

"Yep! But it wasn't my kill because I didn't make it fall down. I bit it on the ankle of its back leg, but then…"

"Then what happened?"

"It kicked him in the nose," Ericka explained, all sympathy for her friend.

"It didn't hurt until later," Juanito said. "Why is that?"

Tina raised an eyebrow. "Do you know what

adrenaline is?"

"No."

"It's a part of our magic. When you're in the middle of a hunt, you know how you feel excited?"

"Yes."

"That's adrenaline, dingle-berry butt. That makes it so you can run faster, bite harder, and things don't hurt as much. But then, after the hunt, it wears off, and you move slower, feel all noodly, and then any pain hurts even more. Does that make sense?"

"Is adrenaline just when we're wolves?"

"Nope. You get that juice in either form."

Juanito frowned. "Seems stupid to have it in these dumb human bodies. We don't hunt like this."

Tina flashed a wicked smile. "I'll tell you a secret. When you're older, you'll learn we hunt in both forms."

Ericka scrunched her face to create as many wrinkles as her kid face would allow. "Really?"

"Yep! And you'll learn to hunt more things than just deer."

"Like elk?" Ericka asked.

"And caribou?" Junatio asked.

"Yes, and more!"

Juanito widened his eyes. "Bears?"

Tina laughed. "What would you do with a bear, dingleberry butt?"

"Eat it?"

"It would kick your ass. But yes, with your pack, you could even hunt a bear in either form."

"I would hunt it as a wolf," Ericka said. "Human bodies are dumb."

"They're good for hiding in groups of humans though, right?"

"I hate hiding in humans. We have to wear shoes and can't change into wolves whenever we want. It's dumb."

Juanito nodded. "Dumb."

Tina tilted her head. "It is dumb sometimes. But it can also be fun. And there are some kinds of hunting you'll need to do that way."

"I don't want to do those kinds of hunting," Ericka said.

Tina smiled. "Okay. But you may someday, so you should learn how. Not my problem though. Rita will teach you."

Both children beamed at the mention of Rita's name. "We love Rita," Ericka said.

"She's nice," Juanito said.

Tina sneered and shrugged. "She bugs the shit out of me, but I don't like nice people."

"Why not?" Junito asked.

"Because I'm mean."

Juanito looked a little frightened. He shot a glance at Ericka, then looked at Tina. "But you're nice to us."

Tina gently placed her hands on both children's heads. "Because I'm trying to win you over to the naughty side!" She roughly rubbed their hair, then stalked off towards her room in one of the cabins across the camp.

Ericka looked at Juanito. "She's cool."

"Yeah," Juanito said. "Ass shit butt."

They giggled and ran off to play.

Chapter 18

In Lena's room, Josef stood guard. A casual observer might have concluded Josef was a mindless statue, but that would be a mistake. Josef was the creation of generations of rabbis, and, as such, it could sit quite still while its mind wheeled. Mostly it thought about the names of G-d, the meanings of Hebrew words, and the way those words described the world. Considering the parts of the world it had seen, it had a lot to work with. Josef had walked across the bottom of the Atlantic Ocean once and the English channel twice, so it had some interesting ideas about the references to the firmament, the leviathan, and the waters under the earth in the description of creation. It didn't expect to have an opportunity to sit and discuss these with a group of rabbis anytime soon, but somehow its thoughts always felt like a test prep session for just such an occasion.

But, like any student preparing for an exam, Josef's mind would wander. There were things it did not want to think about too much. Specifically, it was only in the last year, a recent occurrence for a golem, Josef had decided to broaden its programmed obligation to seek out and destroy Nazis to include whichever modern variant it found to be the new version of a genocidal fascist. At first Josef found it completely reasonable to use this justification to protect Lena, a human from a whole bunch of marginalized backgrounds who was threatened by the necromancer Nigel Marion, a racist, sexist monster who was plotting to wipe out most, if not all, of the humans on Earth. Once Josef chose to defend Lena, it also felt right to continue defending her from other monsters who wanted to steal her books to cause more genocide. But when Josef was left to its thoughts, it veered dangerously towards questioning whether Lena was the most genocidal creature of them all. At this point she'd created not one but two weapons of mass destruction. And she'd left Josef to guard them. It could have considered the possibility the most Nazi-punching course of action would be to destroy both books and their author. But Josef truly loved Lena, its best friend, so this strategy was one it forced out of its mind.

Instead, Josef chose to contemplate music. It

remembered the sound made by a young violinist, a Jewish man from Warsaw who passed through Prague on his way to New York. The man played at a cafe near enough to the synagogue Josef could hear the sound from the attic. The sound was also heard by a young Jewish woman from the Hungarian side of the Austro-Hungarian Empire. She heard the music from around the corner and came to find the source, watched the man play, fell in love with him, and joined him on his journey to New York where they had their first daughter, then to Los Angeles where they had their second, then to Oakland where their third daughter was born, and where they both lived the rest of their lives.[1,2] Josef did not know any of this, of course, but it would not have been surprised. It remembered the sound of the instrument more than a hundred years later, and it tried to capture the sound in words because it loved words, and things worthy of love find one another just like the player and his future bride. The music, Josef decided, was "small," "fragile," "innocent," "open," "vulnerable," and "brave." Josef spent four hours contemplating these six words in five languages, considering their slightly different connotations in each, and ultimately changed his mind. Not "brave." "Valorous."

---

[1] By pure coincidence, the apartment where the Jewish woman lived at the end of her life was on the very same street and only two city blocks away from the house where Lena's father grew up.
[2] By absolutely no coincidence whatsoever, the violinist and his wife were the great-grandparents of the author of this novel. Thanks for their story, Grandma!

It was about the time Josef settled on "valorous," when it heard the small pop. Perhaps, if it had been thinking about the names of G-d, not צבאות which it found most interesting, but אל שדי which it found the most straightforward, Josef might have moved more quickly, but the internal linguistic debate distracted it just enough it scanned too slowly when seeking the origin of the sound. This gave Apraxis, who had appeared directly above Josef's head, the opportunity to cast his spell.

Apraxis, by means of some hastily whispered words and silent hand gestures, called forth the word אמת from Josef's soul, the spiritual DNA with which the rabbis had breathed life into their homunculus. If Apraxis had wanted to kill Josef in the moment, he could have, and he had considered it. By removing the א with a quick strike, Apraxis would have changed "truth" to "death," and Josef would have turned to dust and never returned. Such a maneuver could even be made by quick human hands; this was the rabbis' failsafe should their monster get out of control in Prague. But Apraxis was not limited to human speed. He had decided to take the risk and attempt to rewrite the word. With nimble claws on fingers flashing faster than any human's, Apraxis curved the lines in the clay on Josef's forehead until they said עֶבֶד, Hebrew for "slave." Then, as quickly as he could, Apraxis teleported. He appeared on top of the backpack on the desk, tense and ready to teleport again, and looked at the golem. But Josef had frozen with one arm in the air, halfway to swatting the imp at his previous location.

Apraxis spoke slowly and carefully. "When I tell you

to leave this room … not yet, but when I tell you to… go to Las Vegas, Nevada, in the United States. Find the vampire Cassius in the penthouse of the Venetian Resort. Pretend you are his slave. Tell him he is your new master, and you are his slave, and do everything he asks. But when I come to you, remember you are *my* slave, and you do my bidding until the end of time. Now, I order you to go."

Apraxis didn't have to wait to see if his ploy had succeeded. The moment he said, "Go," Josef turned into a cloud of sand and dust, then turned invisible, then flew out of the room so fast Apraxis could see the fibers of the carpet pulled towards the gap under the doorway.

The imp was so relieved, it sat down heavily on the backpack, leaned back, and sighed a luxuriating "Phew!" And then it popped back to some other dimension where the air pressure was lower and the pressure to cause as much pain and suffering as possible was much, much higher.

A golem in flight can move very quickly. Josef, when highly motivated, had once moved fast enough to break the sound barrier. But Josef could not move faster than the signal from a satellite phone, so Cassius had not yet met his new servant when his phone rang.

He didn't waste time, either. "Tell me you have it."

"I have it," she said. "I can deliver it now."

Cassius contained his relief. "Good. Get it to the rendezvous point as soon as possible. Oh, and was the golem a problem?"

"No, he wasn't there when I got the bag."

"Excellent."

"So," she said, "We have a deal, right? You will leave everyone here alone if I hand this over to you. Forever. And I'll never hear from you again?"

"I won't reach out again, but if you ever need anything, you know how to reach me."

"Fair. The package is on its way."

The phone clicked. Cassius leaned back in his chair but didn't echo the imp's sigh. This was a step, he reminded himself. Just a step along the way.

Moments later, Lena returned to her room. The door was closed. Because the cabins were built to house children, the doorknobs had no locks. As the door swung open, her mind registered the abject wrong-ness inside before she could even see more than a few inches through the gap. No Josef. No Josef meant no book. No book meant Bel had come for it, taken it, was reading it at that very moment, and would die. Lena deduced all of this before she stepped into the doorway, looked at the empty desktop, and stopped breathing. She wanted to breathe. She wanted to scream. But her feet were taking her back down the hallway in an all-out sprint before she could scream, and then she needed the air to run.

She leapt over the two stairs as she left the building, landed on one foot, and kept going. Werewolves, in even their human form, react to someone running like their canine cousins. As this human ran across their camp, heads snapped in her direction, and then they were giving chase without knowing why. Lena ran into Bel's cabin, her shoulder bouncing against the wall as she made the turn down the central hall, her other shoulder crashing into Bel's door as she turned the handle.

Bel's room was empty, too.

In the kind of panic she hadn't felt since her escape through Europe the year before, Lena screamed Bel's name. Then she ran for the longhouse. When she came bolting out of the cabin, three adults and two children were waiting by the door. She jumped through the middle of the happy, panting group. They took off after her, unsure if they should join her for the run or tackle her and tear her to shreds.

Meanwhile, in the longhouse, everyone except Meili, the lone human, heard the sound of Lena's first scream, and they were running to the front door when Meili heard the second. "What the-?" Meili started, and the whole group came to a halt just as Lena breached the doorframe to the sound of Meili's expletive.

The werewolves were fast, but Bel was faster. She wrapped Lena in her arms in the doorway, comforting her and defending her from the threat which she assumed was coming from the five smiling people running up the stairs behind her. "What's wrong, honey? You're okay." Bel put out a hand to warn the chasers to take a few steps back, and she noticed the grins on their faces. "They're just running because you were running, Lena. You're safe. Shh. You're safe."

Lena pressed her face into the side of Bel's neck, her tears set free from one eye to run down Bel's skin, still holding fast in the other, obscuring her vision. "No," she said, then hitched and coughed. "No." She sniffed a nostril of snot. "The books are gone and Josef is gone and I thought you were dead. But you're alive. You're alive."

"Yeah, I'm fine. Wait, what? The books are what?" Then Bel felt the burning and heard the sizzling. She was standing in the last rays of the setting sun. "Come inside, Lena. Tell me what's going on."

She led Lena into the center of the great hall. Most of the pack was already inside, preparing for dinner, and it seemed everyone else had been alerted by Lena's shouts and running. The room felt dangerously crowded, and Lena could sense every eye aimed at her. "Should we talk about this here?" she whispered.

Nando placed a large, gentle hand on Lena's shoulder. "Everyone heard you, Lena. And we all have a right to know. You said 'books'? Like, two books?"

Lena aimed her face into the crook of Bel's neck and tried to press the shame away. She succeeded in seeing stars.

Bel looked over the top of Lena's head. "It's a long story. Let's get her some water and space, and we can all figure out what's going on here."

"So, Josef took the books somewhere?" Bel asked.

Lena shook her head. "No way. It was guarding them. It didn't steal them."

Tina scowled. "Could someone have killed the golem? I like the golem."

Nando shook his head. "I wouldn't even know how to kill Josef. But we did see it defeated and captured once. In Edinburgh. By a warlock."

Lots of eyes homed in on Matt.

Matt raised his hands defensively. "It wasn't me. That wouldn't make any sense. I'm the one who brought Lena and Josef here safely."

Nando looked at Bel, his voice soft er than usual. "She said there are two books? You said it's a long story."

Bel turned her head and pressed her cheek to Lena's forehead. "Let's talk about that another time, Nando. I don't want to cause a panic."

Meili leaned over to Matt and whispered, "Everyone is whispering. I have no idea what the fuck is going on, Matt."

Everyone but Lena heard her.

And it was at exactly that moment, when they were all thinking about whispers and panics, when their ears were as cocked as werewolves' ears can be in their human forms, the rat-tat-tat of a triple burst of machine gun fire rang out from the woods.

Nando's eyes flashed around the room.

"Where are the pups?"

"How clearly I have always seen my condition and acted like a child nevertheless, and how clearly I still see now, and still with no sign of a cure."

-Johann Wolfgang von Goethe
The Sorrows of Young Werther

Chapter 19

Bel, the fastest among them, remained wrapped protectively around Lena, but every parent followed Nando at top speed towards the door. As soon as Nando's foot stepped across the threshold onto the porch, another three-round burst rang out, and pieces of wood from the roof just above the porch splintered and fell at his feet.

"Halt," a voice commanded. The sound was magnified through a megaphone from somewhere in the woods. Nando probably could have identified the source by smell, but he didn't have time.

"Step back into the building," the voice ordered. "We have a hostage. We didn't have to miss you, and we won't miss when we shoot the old woman."

More than one of the pack members muttered Rita's name.

"We want to talk," the man's voice said. He didn't sound angry or frightened, but his voice was clearly forceful, perhaps even more so because of some restrained quality picked up by the speaker. "We're coming toward the building with the hostage. Move inside the building and back away from the door."

The whole community looked at Nando. He walked backwards while slowly raising his hands. The other werewolves did the same. When they got to the tables and chairs, they simply pushed them back towards the kitchens with their butts. The sound of the legs scraping and skipping on the waxed linoleum would have been comical in other circumstances, but in the moment, it just made everyone more frightened.

And then came the red dots. The beams came through the pair of windows in the front of the building, through the first pair on the sides, and even through the next pair behind the crowd, though no one could see those on their backs. The lights danced and bobbed in a way that revealed they were directed by human hands, but Nando didn't take much comfort in this when they found foreheads and chests and then held very still. These were humans, but they were soldiers, and there was not enough room in the longhouse for everyone to dodge, and not enough time for everyone to shift. If anyone made a move, it would be a bloodbath.

"No one has to die today," the voice on the megaphone said. It was much closer now, out of the tree line and just out of sight near the front of the building. "We're here to make a trade. One for one. Then we will leave you all alone. But please know that's a choice we are making. Every one of my soldiers is fully loaded with silver bullets. We know what you are and how to kill you. All of you. Even the vampire. We can do it. We're good at it. But we don't want to. Not tonight. Tonight is a talk and a trade and that's it."

There was an audible clomping as two pairs of heavy boots traversed the hollow deck beyond the door, but still no one came into sight in the doorway. Then two dark barrels leaned into the dimming rays of the sunset, leveled, and tilted inside. The two soldiers holding those guns stepped just far enough into the room that their shoulders and a single eye were visible, each aiming across at the crowd on the opposite side of the room. The movements were so perfectly choreographed and menacing, there might as well have been a badass techno score. And then a figure slowly climbed the steps between them. He set the megaphone down on the edge of the porch while he climbed the stairs, then walked straight in with empty hands. The last bit of sunset made him a silhouette. He walked six feet into the room, just enough to make some of the werewolves take a cautious step back behind Nando. The room's light overmatched the light in the doorway, and when Esau was revealed, Matt whispered, "Oh, shit," so quietly only the werewolves could hear him.

Before Esau spoke, a dozen of his soldiers, led by the two at the doorway, came in behind him in an organized formation, one at a time through the door but every other into a semicircle around and ahead of him. Bel noted most of them had their guns pointed 45 degrees towards the ground, and with their fingers outside the trigger guards in what the field manuals called an "Alert Carry." This wasn't the way they would enter for an assault. Bel found that comforting. Then Torreblanca came in last and stood next to Esau. She held her rifle higher than the others and with her finger on the trigger in a "Ready Carry" which "is employed when contact with the enemy is imminent." Bel knew she could still move faster than Torreblanca could raise the gun all the way up, aim, and pull the trigger, but not by much, and certainly not fast enough to grab Lena and pull her out of the way without risking snapping her neck. She watched the end of Torreblanca's barrel carefully, ready to try to place her forearm and skull between Lena and the gun to deflect a bullet. It would hurt, especially with silver bullets, and if it lodged in her skull it could possibly kill her if not removed in time, but she might survive and protect Lena. She really hoped Torreblanca would aim at her instead, though.

Esau looked directly at Nando. "Our thermal scans say you have three humans in this room. That's why you're alive right now. I kill your kind, but I don't kill mine. I am willing to make exceptions today. One exception would be the previously mentioned trade. I will give you back the old woman, and I will take one monster, and everyone else lives. The other exception is you reject that offer, and then there's a lot more bloodshed. The old woman will die. The humans in this room will die. I expect some of my soldiers will die. And some of you monsters will die. As you can see, I have taken a significant risk coming into your home. I'm hoping you care enough about your people to respect the risk I've taken and choose to keep your monsters alive. What do you say?"

Nando sniffed and didn't speak immediately, but he also didn't break eye contact. "Our community doesn't just let someone come in and take some of us away."

Esau nodded very slowly. "And I can respect that. Luckily, I am not here for a member of your community. As I said, by temperature, it looks like you have three humans in here. But you don't. You have two. I want the monster who looks the most human, even to a thermometer, but is the worst monster in this room. And he's not a member of your community. Give him to me, and everyone else lives."

Lena had to do some quick math. She didn't see Long in the room, so she deduced Esau was talking about her and Meili, leaving Matt as his non-human target. She wasn't the only one who came up with that answer; a handful of others shot glances at Matt. Matt watched Nando. Bel didn't take her eyes off Torreblanca's gun. Nando didn't break his stare with Esau, but he bit down as he thought, his jaw muscle flexing to the rhythm of his contemplation.

The silence stretched just long enough a few other soldiers raised their rifles to the height of Torreblanca's and put their fingers into the trigger guards.

When the radio crackled, everyone tensed, but luckily not enough to put more than five and a half pounds of pressure on any of the triggers in the room. It was Thomas, the guy Torreblanca was sleeping with. She was just starting to wonder if she considered it dating yet. But now she heard something new in his voice. She'd never heard him sound so high pitched and shaky.

"Movement! I've got movement out here. Oh, fuck, they're all around me. I need some backup. Fuck!"

The sound of a burst of gunfire came through the walkie talkie and the doorway at almost the same time, one clean and distant, the other close and marred with sandpaper static, but the sound of a puppy's sharp whimper of pain only came through via radio waves. Regardless, the yelp was the sound galvanizing everyone. That particular sound plucks at the taut strings of DNA in humans and werewolves alike.

Nando took a dangerous stride towards Esau, undaunted by the fact Esau was drawing a nickel plated Ruger out of the holster on his right leg. The pistol's barrel was a little longer than a standard issue Glock. Esau's thigh holster was low enough he could draw it quickly, but not nearly as quickly as Nando could move. And Esau knew it. And Nando knew Esau knew. So Nando didn't leap, and Esau didn't fire. Nando stopped, and Esau pointed the gun in his face, but both knew Nando had chosen the scenario.

"Our situation has just changed. If one of the pups is dead, you will not walk out of this room alive."

"If my man is dead, you won't."

"Esau," Matt said, "please, you don't have to do this." He shouldered through the crowd of werewolves. "Can we please just talk?"

"We can talk after you walk out of this room with me, and then I'll find out if Thomas is alright, and if he is, I'll let the old woman go, and we'll leave. But if Thomas is dead, I'm going to light this place up like Hanukkah and Kwanzaa and the Fourth of July rolled into one. So walk out that door behind me right now."

Matt held up his hands. "Hold on, Esau. I didn't say I was-"

"And you," Esau gestured at Nando's face with the pistol without losing his aim by thrusting it forward slightly. "You'd better get your little monsters back here before they do something to my soldier. Whistle or something."

Nando growled. He looked like a man, but it was not a sound any human could make.

Matt put out his hands and stepped almost between the pistol and werewolf. "Whoa. There has got to be some other way we can-"

"No!" Esau shouted. Everyone suddenly felt confused as much as frightened, because the sound of Esau's voice, the unusual calm and control, had vanished.

His own soldiers looked away from their targets to their leader, their confidence shaken.

"No, Matteo! There is no other way." Esau's throat was constricting, pinching his words, as he fought off tears. "You don't get to decide this time."

There were audible gasps when Esau swung his arm in Matt's direction, pointing the gun at Matt's forehead, and walked towards him.

"I loved you, Matteo. And you dumped me on a boat, thousands of miles from anything. You broke my heart, Matt." Esau was letting the tears stream down his face now. "You broke me."

Torreblanca lowered her rifle, and she made a show of removing her finger from the trigger. Bel wasn't the only one who noticed. Some of the other soldiers lowered theirs as well.

Matt mumbled, "Technically, it's a ship."

"Shut-up-Matt-god damn!" Lena's voice cut through the room's. She started to walk towards Nando.

Bel's hand shot out in front of her. "Lena, please-"

Lena shook her arm off more violently than she intended. "No, Bel, this is stupid." She looked right at Torreblanca. "Look, you all need to listen to me for a second, okay? We just learned a full-on weapon of mass destruction has fallen into the wrong hands. It can wipe out the human race..." She turned back to the assemblage of werewolves. "...and all the monsters in the world, too. All of everybody. So, clearly we have some dramatic shit going on right here." She pointed at Esau and Matt. "And there's some more important shit going down in the woods. But the only people who can save all of humanity ..." She turned back to the werewolves. "And monster-manity." Then back to Torreblanca. "The only ones who can save everybody are right here in this room. And if we kill each other, everyone you love who is outside this room is going to die. So you all need to put your guns down ... " She mimed pressing something to the floor, and, much to the surprise of everyone in the room except Lena, including the soldiers themselves, they followed her orders. "And then you need to take a deep breath, maybe get a cup of coffee and do some yoga or something, and then take a seat so we can talk this through and figure out what we're going to do."

Lucia walked past Lena, placed a hand gently on top of Torreblanca's lowered rifle, and said, "Please, can you tell your men to send Rita, your hostage, in? I think that will help everyone calm down."

"What about Thomas, our man in the woods?"

Lucia's hand above the rifle stiffened imperceptibly, and her voice fell nearly to a whisper. "I'm sorry. He didn't make it. One of the children is crying, but she will live."

"You can hear that?"

"Yes."

"But not Thomas?"

"No. The other children are..." She almost said "feeding" but caught herself. "Thomas is gone. I'm sorry." She hesitated again, reading the emotions on Torreblanca's face as the woman processed anger and resignation and more anger. "Please," Lucia said. "Listen to Lena. We have to handle the larger situation first. Then we can grieve."

"We weren't that close," Torreblanca said.

Lucia could tell Torreblanca was talking to herself, and Lucia wisely chose to nod and place a hand on her shoulder. She squeezed gently, gave Torreblanca a moment to breathe, and then said, "Please."

That woke Torreblanca up. "Oh, yeah." She clicked the mic of her earphone. "Stand down. Bring in the hostage. Do not hurt her under any circumstances. And everyone come inside. Everyone, including the snipers. The situation has changed. There are still monsters in the woods, but we're safe in here. Get in here quickly."

"Um, yes, but please tell them not to run," Lucia said. "They will be safer if they just walk quickly."

Torreblanca tapped the mic again. "Don't run. Walk fast, but no running."

The soldiers had enough experience with the unexplainable to refrain from questioning that, but someone said, "Where's Esau, Ma'am?"

"He's …" Torreblanca stared at her boss and mentor. He was still pointing the gun at Matt's forehead, and he was still crying, but he'd taken his finger out of the trigger guard, and something about the position of his shoulders told her he wouldn't fire. "He's … He's fine. Just get in here. And don't call me 'ma'am.' I'm twenty-eight for shit's sake."

"Yessir."

Torreblanca decided it wasn't the time to address that. She clicked off her mic and spoke to Lucia. "We need to get our bearings a little, here."

"Yes, and we need to tend to the children, but after your people are inside. Trying to keep things deescalated here."

"Agreed. So what's this weapon of mass destruction? Like, chemical or biological or nuclear or …"

"Worse," Matt said over Esau's shoulder. And then he looked back down the barrel of the gun. "Much worse. It's magic. And Esau, we're going to need your help."

Chapter 20

The Archduke slouched as he came into his office. As he sat down in his leather wingback chair, he gave a great sigh like an old human man. Behind him, Jeeves entered the room standing ramrod straight, his spine and the bottom of his bushy mustache at perfect 90-degree angles.

"Well, I think we can all agree this will be unpleasant," the Archduke said over his shoulder.

"As you say, sir," Jeeves intoned, "both of us agree on

that."

"Not much point in putting it off, though. The chores must be done. Unpalatable characters must be dealt with."

"Right you are, sir."

"Jeeves, can I bother you to turn on this blasted device? I swear I touch modern technology and it's like I'm cursed or something. Of course that's preposterous, but … " He ran his fingers through his hair, tugging slightly to accentuate the wavy mop. " … really, it's like I've been bloody … jujued or something."

"As you say, sir," Jeeves said. His straight hair was oiled and plastered to his head in such a way it didn't move at all as he leaned over his employer and tapped on the keys, moved the mouse a bit, clicked on some buttons, and brought up the Zoom call. Then he stepped briskly behind the large chair and stood at attention over the Archduke's shoulder while the call connected.

In the window, the Archduke saw the King of Trolls sitting on his stone throne. A much smaller troll stood on one of the arms, his chest puffed out, eyes looking slightly up and away, and his hands pointed down like a caricature of a soldier at Buckingham Palace. Except he was completely naked. And a troll.

The King of Trolls was already speaking, or perhaps yelling based on the spittle flying from his mouth, but no sound came from the computer.

"Jeeves," the Archduke said, "could you…?"

Jeeves stepped forward.

The Archduke's hand shot out and wrapped around Jeeves wrist, too fast for any human and far too fast for the old man character he was playing. "No, on second thought," he said, "let's just allow him to wear himself out a bit."

"Right you are, sir."

The Archduke let go of his butler's wrist, and Jeeves stood up straight but waited by the computer. They both watched as The King of Trolls continued to shout. Finally the giant troll stopped, frowned, and then flipped them off.

"Yes, now I think you'd better-" the Archduke said.

"Of course, sir," Jeeves said, and then clicked "Connect computer audio."

Still silence.

Then the smaller troll on the chair's arm started to laugh, and the King of Trolls elbowed him into thin air. Jeeves and the Archduke heard the thud, then watched as the small troll clambered back up to his post and made a show of snapping back to attention.

"I got myself a Jeeves just for our meeting, fecal faces. This is Egg. Say hi to the bloodsuckers, Egg."

Egg continued to stare away into the distance. "Hello, limp-dick corpses. Your spiney-fang faces look like puckered buttholes in need of a good waxing."

"Well, so far this is as boring as usual," the Archduke said. "Wouldn't you agree, Jeeves."

"Tedious, sir."

The Archduke leaned forward. "But you didn't ask to

speak with me, your Highness. You asked to speak with Jeeves. That was unusual. You know I'm available if you need to talk."

The King of Trolls looked down, pursed his lips, and harrumphed through his nose. "Yeah, I needed to get your attention about something … delicate." He caught himself. "As delicate as you two fragile fucks. So here's the thing: I know about your little game where you switch places every few decades. Whatever. I don't give a flaming fart about your weird roleplay games. But it's no fun if that gets out, right?"

The Archduke turned and looked back at Jeeves. "You don't need to threaten me to get my help, King. You can just ask."

"Yeah, well, in this case, I want to know which one of you I should be talking to."

"I am the Archduke. Isn't that right, Jeeves."

"Absolutely, sir."

The King of Trolls tilted his head to make a show of looking at the corner of his screen, no small feat when dealing with a Zoom call. "Then Jeeves, who would be the Archduke if the guy in the chair got killed? Because your little game could cause some problems in the line of succession soon."

Jeeves and the Archduke shared a glance. The Archduke spoke. "We would both like to avoid those kinds of headaches."

"Well, your headache has a name. It's Cassius. And, no offense, but I had no problem with his grand plan to knock you off and take over the vampires. It's no hair off my back. But Cassius fucked up. He betrayed Tisina. And he did it in such a way it will look like I fucked over Tisina. And she worries me. She worries me because she doesn't worry Cassius enough. See, his plan is to continue Nigel Marion's plan to kill ten percent of the humans. I enabled that last time around, and I know you were opposed. I'm aware you intervened to prevent his success. Your people did a good job with the clean-up, but when that many werewolves disappear, their absence is noted. And who else could have done it so cleanly? Not Cassius, apparently. He's been making messes. Quite a bright one down in Central America, I hear. And not Tisina. She's been making messes around the Pacific, I hear. And if you took out the werewolves, I'm guessing you took out Marion, too."

The Archduke carefully dodged the accusation.

"His plan would have killed far more than ten percent of the human population. He was a necromancer. If, say, 90% of the humans had died, he would have been fine. Personally, I like an abundant food supply. I expect you do, as well."

"Yeah, I think I made a mistake at last year's convention," the King of Trolls said.

Egg turned and stared at him, surprised.

"Fuck off, Egg. I get to make mistakes and learn from them. That's what being the king means." Then he knocked Egg off the arm of the throne again, but he did so halfheartedly, and Egg clambered up the King's leg and back to his position with an adoring, appreciative smile on his face.

The Archduke dared a glance back at Jeeves, then turned back to the screen. "Do you have any plan regarding resolving this situation with Cassius?"

"'Course I do, you lazy asswipe. Here's my brilliant plan. I tell you you have a fox in your henhouse. Then I fuck right off to deal with my own shit. You take care of the fox."

The Archduke cocked his head. "It's not an altogether bad plan, but…"

"Yes, it does seem to overlook some things, Sir," Jeeves said.

The King of Trolls leaned forward. "Oh, really, butt-butler? What have I missed?"

Jeeves looked at the Archduke. The Archduke said, "If I may, Jeeves."

"Of course, Sir."

The Archduke turned back to the screen. "Here are a few concerns with that plan. For one thing, Cassius is already on the agenda to present his new business item at The Convention. Were he to have some dramatic and fatal accident in the next week, it would look very suspicious. If he simply didn't show up to make his proposal, at the very least it would be noted by all the attendees at The Convention. Maybe that's worth doing anyway, considering the damage he might do, but we should be thoughtful about it, right Jeeves?"

"Of course, Sir."

"Jeeves is always telling me to slow down and-"

"I don't care about your sex stuff," the King sighed.

"Right-o," said the Archduke, unfazed, "but you ought to care about the fact that a noticeable disappearance by Cassius would lead an angry Tisina in your direction, not mine."

"Flaming-hot Cheeto farts!" the King of Trolls barked. "Did you hear that, Egg? The little scab licker makes a very good point. So, Arch Support Insoles, what do you recommend?"

"I suspect Cassius already has a floor strategy for the convention all worked out. He's expecting your support, I'm sure. I suggest we address the issue of Cassius after the convention. Let him pass his little NBI. It's been passed before. He will be more likely to include you in the execution of the plan if he believes you remain supportive. I will mount only the most tepid opposition so I can remain a target for him without tipping him off I suspect him. Meanwhile, you and I can try to figure out a way to aim Tisina's ire squarely at Cassius. Perhaps a tip from a third party that Cassius has betrayed her?"

"Carefully timed," Jeeves said.

"Yes, yes, excellent point Mr. Jeeves. Timed to complicate both their plans by turning them against each other just when they ought to be focused on other things."

"I like it," the King of Trolls said. "Hey, Half-Duke, tell your butler I like the way his brain works."

The Archduke started to turn awkwardly in his chair.

"Er, His Royal Highness says-"

"And Butler, tell your boyfriend I still think he's a drooling moron who only gets hard for goats."

Jeeves rolled his eyes upwards and sounded exhausted as he intoned, "His royal highness wishes to communicate more unpleasantness."

"Nah, I'm just busting your dried out old walnuts. When you see me at the convention, pretend you hate me."

The Archduke scratched his head. "But I do. Doesn't everyone hate trolls, Your Highness?"

"Great pretending! And I'll pretend I respect your authoritative position among the fangtooth fish and don't think you're a ridiculous joke of a monster. See you there, ya' pair of shit stains!"

Chapter 21

The room looked like a pretty standard office suite. A small waiting room sat in front of a receptionist's desk, and, behind that, a decorative fake wall separated the reception area from a room with fairly standard office equipment. A large printer/copier/scanner/fax machine dominated the second half of this space, and an island table provided a place to arrange printouts while storing paper inside. A large paper cutter sat on this island, but it was otherwise empty. Paper slicers are by far the most exciting and menacing of office supplies. The little, red, plastic latch on the side of the slicer held the blade in place, warning employees that, with a flick, this ancient non-electric machine could spring to life and decide to assist in important but menial office tasks or swiftly remove a thumb and make this an exceptionally memorable day at work.

The golem in the room was similar.

Josef stood with its back to the fake wall in the middle of the large room, out of the line of sight of anyone who might come into the waiting room. It stood guard in the empty space just as it had at Camp Bigfoot, motionless, held in place like that slicer's arm, waiting. But at the camp in Canada, it had been able to hear the birds singing outside, the cautious hooves of unwise deer, the galumphing of oversized wolf cub paws, the occasional yip or premature howl as they played. All this had been excellent background music for Josef's contemplations of the names of G-d. Here, on the other hand, the sounds beyond this particular room were well masked. Hotels, at least ones this expensive, went out of their way to block sound. Casinos don't like their suites to be used as office space, but they make special exceptions when certain guests have the right kind of pull. Cassius had it in spades. The fact that the receptionist, on Cassius' order, could kill the casino's entire security force unless agents of CimBim could stop her was reason enough to let Cassius do as he pleased, though the casino owners were not privy to that danger. They knew he had a nearly infinite supply of money and, more importantly, the political connections to make them money, and that was their real motive to allow him an office near the top floor of their hotel/amusement park/gaming establishment. It really was no bother. The office didn't advertise, had very few guests wandering in and out, and served as a standard room since Cassius, the receptionist, and the golem remained inside day and night. The rotating team of security guards, always two outside in the hall, barely raised eyebrows.

The receptionist, Mildred, looked like she was in her early twenties. She wore her blond hair in a ponytail just as she had when her family had decided to travel from Oklahoma to California in 1936. None of them made it, and none were missed. At the time, Cassius had been building his empire, and he recognized the Great Depression as an opportunity to buy low. He invested in the kinds of industrial enterprises that could be easily turned into weapons manufacturing when the humans got tired of all the starving and got back to their killing. He invested in political connections which could position him well when the killing slowed back down. And he invested in human capital, or, to be more precise, the conversion of human capital into a larger vampire organization. He wasn't vampire royalty like the oldest of their kind, but he was ambitious enough to see being merely one or two thousand years younger didn't need to be a barrier to entry into that exclusive club. What did all those dukes and duchesses, countesses and earls have that he didn't? Titles the humans didn't even know about? The loyalty of monsters who would drink their own mothers dry? Big deal. He could have more wealth, a larger army, more pull, and eventually supplant them.

Mildred had been part of his growing army. When her family had been neatly dispatched on the side of a highway in Nevada, she'd been taken to one of Cassius' growing number of underground facilities to learn how to live as a vampire and serve him. She'd turned out to be only adequate as a fighter and hunter. The stringy arms he'd mistaken for the products of starvation turned out to be enduring even after her transformation, and she didn't compensate with speed or any particular fighting skill. Just a run-of-the-mill vampire, completely capable of seducing and killing enough humans to keep herself going, but not fit to be a foot soldier in an army battling other vampires or working for CIMBIM and keeping the other monsters in check. So, Cassius had done what armies do when they have a loyal soldier they don't want to put on the front lines: Desk duty. And her loyalty was beyond reproach. For more than half a century, she'd served as his personal secretary, arranging his schedule, greeting his guests, acquiring humans who wouldn't be missed when he needed a snack during a stressful night of work.

And, of course, her loyalty had been tested. Rival vampires plied her for information and attempted to enlist her in plots. She faithfully informed Cassius of all these efforts, played double-agent effectively when he told her to, and allowed him to see the pace of his progress. He measured his effectiveness in his enemies. Low-level gang leaders had been replaced by real royals, and those royals had transitioned from mild curiosity to attempted theft to plots to murder him. Cassius knew he was getting somewhere.

He also had to be very careful. Consequently, when

the FedEx delivery person showed up, she had to get past the two guards outside the door, and then they followed her into the reception area in front of Mildred's desk.

"May I help you?" Mildred said, her voice perfectly pleasant.

"Yeah, I got a package here for a Mr. Cassius at this room number. I was going to leave it at the front, but they said to bring it up, so…"

The two guards stood silently on either side of the door, presuming the delivery driver to be a fake and almost bored by their expectation they would be killing her soon.

Cassius ran out of his office so fast, only the other vampires and Josef were aware his door had opened and closed, but he made a point to stop and compose himself before stepping around the partition.

"Ah, yes, I've been looking forward to this delivery. Thank you, Ma'am." He held out some bills, folded in half, pinched between his index and middle finger, so the delivery person wouldn't know he was giving her five hundred and five dollars until she stepped out into the hallway.

"Oh, no, sir, thank you, but we aren't allowed to accept tips."

"Yes, but you also aren't allowed to upset your customers by refusing, so if I demand you take it, what, three times? Is that the magic number? Then you have to, right?"

"Well…"

"Take it-take it-take it-take it," he said, a pleasant, if a bit syrupy laugh in his voice, as he stepped towards her and pushed the bills into her hand. "Just don't tell anyone you had to come all the way up here or that I came out to get it personally."

"Sure," she said.

As the door closed behind her, one of the guards said, "Want us to go make sure she doesn't tell?"

Cassius was looking down at the cardboard box in his arms. "No, I want her to tell. But I figure the tip and strange conversation will delay things enough. She won't mention it at work, probably, but now she'll tell someone at home. And it will be within earshot of a cellphone. Word will get back to some of my enemies through a phone company or the NSA, but it will take a few days. That's my hope. Not relying on it, but it's likely."

"Good call, boss," the other guard said. He wasn't as dumb as he sounded. He was just leaning into the goon role.

Cassius waved them back to their places outside the room, then turned to Mildred and beckoned her into the office behind the wall. He barely noticed his newest acquisition. He wasn't sure about the monster's intelligence, just that it obeyed him, so he treated Josef like Alexa. "Golem, move over there," he said, pointing to a space further in the corner so he and Mildred could more easily move around the island.

"You are excited, aren't you? What's in the box?" Mildred *Se7en*-ed.

Cassius caught the reference. "Worse. So much worse. And it was such a monumental pain in the ass to get this.

Lost three good men over it down in Costa Rica. Well, at least one was good. Satisfactory. Useful. Then, it turned out to be in Canada after all. Had to do some tedious wheeling and dealing and schmoozing and…" He rolled his eyes. "So much drama. Boring. Anyway, I finally have it. I'm like a kid at Christmas.

Mildred leaned over the island, propping herself on a thin arm bent slightly backward under her weight. "So? Are you going to tell me what it is?"

"It's a book." He said it as though the Mormon Tabernacle Choir would provide backup.

Mildred was a good enough employee to know the silence which followed might make her boss uncomfortable. "What's it about?"

"I don't know. Not important. What matters is what it does. It's a magic book. The writer was chosen by three witches, then forced to write it while under an enchantment. It kills humans. They tested it out, very scientifically, in Ireland. Made humans read it. They all went insane. Killed other humans. Killed themselves. Went catatonic."

"So what are we going to do with it?"

"Exactly what The Convention decided to do last year and then failed to accomplish. New Business Items, according to the bylaws of The Convention, are only good for a year, so we'll have to go back and get another vote to extend it, and that would have been impossible without the book itself. The representatives will need to know why last year's NBI wasn't completed. But now, with the book, I can get the necessary permission to complete Nigel Marion's plan."

Mildred frowned. "The necromancer? I heard he died. Which seems weird, since not dying is kind of what they're all about."

"Yes, they are good at staying alive. Their food supply is as ubiquitous as ours, and they get more years out of a single human than we do. But necromancers, though tough, are not nearly as tough as we are."

"Who killed him?"

"I'm not quite sure, but I suspect it was vampires."

Mildred balked. "Us?"

"If the Archduke wasn't behind it, he certainly participated in covering it up. And he was the one behind killing the werewolves in London. That was just before Marion was killed, and that can't be a coincidence."

Josef noted it felt no compulsion to reveal the creature who had killed Nigel Marion was none other than Josef itself. It had to obey the imp, and thus it had to follow the command to pretend to obey Cassius, but it did not have to communicate information which was not requested of it. Josef filed this information away.

"But why would the Archduke go against The Convention?" Mildred asked Cassius.

"He opposed Marion's plan from the beginning. Thought it might cause too much food scarcity, I suspect. And in a way, he's right. It will cause a period of significant instability, and that's bad for the powers-that-be. If I was in his seat, I'd be equally conservative."

"So why are you pushing this?"

Cassius smiled. "Because I'm not in his seat."

"Ah. Gotcha." Mildred looked at the book, then around the little room. "Okay, how can I help?"

"I need copies. We can't have a snafu like last year, with just one copy available. Separate copies in different locations, enough to give out free samples to influential voters on the floor. Let's start with… thirty. Too many would be a security problem. Wouldn't want to give the milk away for free."

"I can get it done today, sir."

"Thank you, Mildred. I'll start organizing the security and arranging the transportation."

Cassius zipped back into his office, closing the door behind him quietly despite his speed.

Mildred lifted the heavy box off the counter like it was weightless, set it on the island, and punctured the tape with one of her inhumanly hard and sharp nails. She'd have to repaint it, but she enjoyed the Zen of the regimen, so she actively sought out office tasks that might damage her nails. And, when hunting, she favored her nails as weapons for the same reason. She didn't enjoy seduction-style hunting. She preferred more direct violence, baiting a victim into a fight in an alley rather than picking one up at a bar. But mostly so she could chip the paint on her nails.

When the threads of plastic made their satisfying little pops, and the lid peeled up, she glanced at her nail. The scratch in the surface was minuscule, probably invisible to human eyes, but she could see it. Outwardly, she only let the corner of her mouth curl, but inside she pumped her fist and hissed a victorious, "Yes!"

She pulled the stack of paper out of the box. Two reams. Long book, she noted, but then, it ought to be. Too much for the auto-feeder on the copier. It would require some collating. Still boring. She'd be stuck at the speed of the copier machine. She took a ballpoint pen from an open box in one of the top drawers and began numbering the pages, scribbling in the bottom corner of each page so fast her hand was a blur, but cognizant very important monsters would be seeing her handwriting. Her mind couldn't read the text on each page as fast as she flipped through them, but it picked up the occasional word, capitalization, repetition, and spacing, snagging her attention enough to identify some character names. It made her curious.

Once the pages were numbered, she isolated the first forty and set the copier to work making thirty copies. While the machine worked, she prepared the island by moving the original manuscript back to the counter next to the copier and disposing of the box. Then she laid out the thirty copies in stacks, face down, on the island, and started the next batch of forty pages.

Josef watched all of this, its eye-less face as unmoving as its body, inscrutability hiding its hyper-vigilance. It knew about the second book, knew what it could do, so it wrestled with its obligations. If Josef truly was a servant of Cassius, the decision would have been more straightforward. It would have been obligated to warn its master its new colleague was playing with fire. But Josef served the imp who had commanded it to pretend to serve Cassius. So, did it have to warn Cassius to maintain the facade and obey that order? It couldn't decide. And indecision took the form of immobility. Instead, it contemplated G-d. That was a habit. But now it thought of the Israelites in Babylon. While they tried to maintain their allegiance to Him during that diaspora, did they curse Him? Daniel, Shadrach, Meshach, and Abednego all served the evil king Nebuchadnezzar. And the scriptures called Nebuchadnezzar G-d's servant because he enacted G-d's wrath against the unfaithful Israelites. Josef had listened while the rabbis discussed this, and, at least early on, some had made the argument that Hitler's Nazis were similarly part of G-d's plan. Josef was made to fight the evils that plagued The Chosen who lived in Prague. It had only recently come to the conclusion it owned the responsibility to identify the targets of its murderous purpose. Now, in the thrall of the imp, it couldn't understand itself. Was the imp its Nebachadnezzer, or was Josef acquiescing to a new Hitler by serving this new master? Josef caught itself. Any analogy involving Hitler was always broken and required deeper thinking. Only Hitler was Hitler. And only Nebuchadnezzar was Nebuchadnezzar. Well, except Nebachadnezzer II was not Nebuchadnezzar I. And Nebuchadnezzar the Great was not great. Josef chuckled at this, a soundless bouncing of the shoulders which caught Mildred's attention.

"What?" she asked.

Josef shrugged dramatically, then waved the subject away.

Mildred shrugged back. She had no choice. Once the

stacks of the first forty pages were laid out, she took the original and set it, also face down, next to the large stack that was the original manuscript. Then she stared at the back of the last page of the short stack, tempted. *Why not?* she thought. *It kills humans, not vampires.* It was her turn to chuckle. The thought a book could kill a vampire was so absurd, it illustrated how fragile humans were. *What could possibly be written on those pages which would cause a human to go mad?* The more she wondered, the more she had to know.

Her eyes flicked to the copier. It was hard at work on the next batch. She could easily finish the first pages before the next batch were ready to collate. *What could be the harm?*

After a furtive look at Cassius' closed office door, Mildred grabbed the stack and turned it over. "Don't Read This Book," the first page told her. But she would not be dissuaded.

Over the next five hours, Mildred read the first book. Josef watched her reaction carefully. It had witnessed Lena's. It remembered the days afterwards. She didn't eat, didn't bathe, fell asleep crying, woke up crying, and mostly stared out at the Pacific horizon. A week passed before she got back to eating meals, and even then they were picked at. Then she took up the project of employing the Archduke's money to hide the book. That had become all-consuming for a time. The money had to be laundered so the Archduke himself wouldn't know her whereabouts. Then she had the house built on a bomb. Not easy. Lena explained to Josef the pool wasn't really for her, just an excuse for the excavation and all the cement around the foundation, but once it was filled, she discovered time spent floating in the pool occupied her just like her walks on the beach or her prolonged smoking binges. Eventually she reacquired the ability to read to pass the time. And then to write.

But her writing was not the same. Before Ireland, she'd written out of an artist's compulsion to create. Then, in Ireland, she made her masterpiece under the enchantment of a warlock. Only Lena and Josef knew it was a book she'd conceived long before. That was her most shameful secret, and she entrusted it to Josef one night in a long monologue, explaining she needed to tell Josef not because Josef couldn't speak, but because it was her closest friend, the only one who could possibly understand, her therapist, her emotional protector as much as her physical one. And when she'd finished, she rose from her lawn chair, crossed the dark patio in the glow of the blue light of the pool, and hugged Josef, weeping. It worried she would scratch her face on its sandstone chest, so it made its exterior a fine dust, and as that mixed with Lena's tears, it became a mud running in lines down the outsides of her cheeks and next to her nose. Josef wanted so badly to brush the mud away with one of its enormous thumbs, but it knew it could not. It would only scrape her soft skin or leave more dirt. There are things therapists simply can't do.

By the end of her reading, Mildred cried as well, but not too much. She turned to Josef. "The first half is sad … for humans. But it also makes me happy, in a way. It makes me happier to be a monster because I'm glad I'm not one of them."

Josef nodded at this. There certainly were advantages to not being human. Josef knew it valued different advantages than Mildred. And maybe that was why it let her turn the page and continue reading.

After she'd arranged the last stacks of *Don't Read This Book* and collated the first stacks of *You Were Warned* on top of them, she began reading the original manuscript. If Cassius had been listening carefully, he might have noticed the prolonged silence. When the copier completed the second stack of *You Were Warned*, Mildred picked up the original pages and continued reading, but she didn't start the next batch copying. Josef noticed her movements as she acquired those pages. She had her normal vampire's grace and speed, but there was something hazy, dreamy, in her steps, like she was drunk and wandering through a field rather than standing in a too-clean office illegally located in a casino's hotel suite. She read standing up, but when she'd been reading the first, she'd leaned her butt on the island and crossed her legs in front of her. Now she faced the counter, her angled head almost touching the cupboard in front of her, her own shadow falling across the book, the low light ignored, both her feet planted shoulder-width apart, her heels pressing down heavily on her stilettos. Everything about her posture was uncomfortable, and all her discomforts were a million miles away because she'd been teleported into the universe of the novel.

Josef didn't know much about the book's contents. It

hadn't read the first, and Lena hadn't told Josef if the second contained the same characters, or even if it was in the same universe. But the novel clearly was not in Mildred's. She was elsewhere.

She turned the last page face down with that same dreamy motion. Now the tears which ran from her eyes after the first volume were replaced by a different kind. The first were sad, streaming down smooth cheeks, but now her eyes squinched so the tears were forced out the sides. She turned sideways so Josef could see the tightness in her face, sorrow turning to anger, bitterness, rage. The muscles of her jaw worked, first like a human holding something in, then breaking free, a vampire opening her mouth to feed, that extended jaw growing, those rows and rows of wriggling, curved syringe teeth grasping. She inhaled to scream, an audible sucking sound which so obviously preceded a piercing volume even Josef, who had no fragile human eardrums, winced in preparation. Josef was a huge tympanic membrane and would feel every decibel.

But she did not scream. To Josef's surprise, she closed her mouth. Even that was done wrongly. He could hear the teeth, all those teeth, grinding against the flesh inside her head. She was biting her own gums, chewing into them on purpose. And then, even more suddenly, she burst into a run at her inhuman vampire speed.

Josef could track the blur which would have been invisible to a human, and then her form coalesced when she smashed her shoulder into the full length window behind the heavy black-out curtains. Her force ripped the curtain rod right out of the wall, the four little screws that protected her from the Vegas sun went pinging and skittering as the bar fell comically on her head. She didn't even notice. When she'd hit the window, a special plexiglas made for the high altitude rooms and high roller guests, strong enough to weather earthquakes and stop bullets and prevent liability, the impact had jarred her mouth open. Josef realized it must have been completely full of blood because the quantity which ran down her chin and into her shirt was almost enough to seem like she was vomiting. She didn't react at all. She also didn't quail at the sunlight blasting through the now uncovered window, searing her flesh so fast it sizzled like meat in a pan. Unfazed, she examined the spiderweb of cracks in the window, calculating while smoke began to rise off her skin.

Cassius appeared in his doorway, then instantly ducked back into the shadow when the light hit him. From the recess of shadow and a thin crack, he had time to say, "Mildred? What's-?"

She took three large strides backwards, then simply toppled forwards, like she planned to face plant, but when she was so low Josef couldn't see her beyond the island, she launched herself into another vampire sprint, aimed, and smashed her shoulder into the exact same spot.

The window exploded, and Mildred arced straight out of the suite into her parabola towards the Vegas strip.

Clive just happened to be standing on the sidewalk, aiming his phone across the street at the Venetian at that very instant. He'd come to Las Vegas reluctantly. He would have enjoyed a trip with only his wife or with some buddies from back home in Modesto, California, but having the kids along changed the trip just as he knew it would. He'd been dreading the whole experience, and Julie and the kids could feel his tension. Clive's surly attitude (accompanied by his firm belief in the spare-the-rod school of child rearing) made the girls more likely to snap at one another, made his son more sullen, and made his wife more irritable and anxious, but Clive didn't take responsibility for any of that. He just got more annoyed by all of them. Finally, while they swam at The Flamingo's pool, he excused himself to go play some slot machines. He decided the pretty cocktail waitress must have found him attractive because she brought him three free Long Island iced teas while he played, so his mood was considerably better despite his gambling losses when he took a stumbling walk down the strip. He thought he'd take a quick video for his friends, mostly to brag but also to amuse them with his vaunted wit, and he was just getting to his punchline about how the Venetian, Belagio, Tuscany, and Caesar's Palace proved the Italian Mafia ran the place when

Mildred made her dramatic exit.

The microphone mostly captured the sound of a couple other tourists shouting in horror, but it did pick up Clive's muttered, "The fuck?"

Mildred's modest mass, 135 pounds of monster and professional attire, and the 36 stories of the casino's height, combined to grant her a little under six seconds to fall. It was not enough time for her to die, but it was enough time for her body to fully catch fire in the Las Vegas sunlight. Her blond hair, modest blouse, tasteful skirt, and most of her skin burned away almost simultaneously, so the shape of the flaming meteor was hard to make out from the street, but Clive's new phone caught the shape of one melting high-heeled shoe in the tail of the comet. The sound of the crunch defied easy identification, a mix of wet meat and burning charcoal the tourists couldn't quite compute. The wooden knock of the second shoe falling shortly behind would have been comical in other circumstances. Despite the way it caught and fluttered during its descent, it still managed to get up enough speed to bounce ten feet into the air before coming to rest in two pieces.

Mildred was still alive there on the ground, and Clive's video would have been even more horrifying if she'd been screaming and flailing as she burned to ash. But she didn't move or make a sound.

Why would she? She'd read the second book. There was no point in crying out. There was no point in anything.

Chapter 22

"First things first," Nando said. "We need to find the book. Once we know where it is, then we can figure out how to esteal it back."

Nando paced while he thought, and his pacing looked remarkably like stalking. Lucia sat staring at the table, nodding and watching him. Lena was next to her, but she eyed Bel. Matt and Esau were at opposite heads of the long table, intentionally not looking at one another. Tina sat on a nearby table's top, staring down at her laptop screen, the glow making a cathedral in her long black hair. Long was across the room in the opposite direction, idly poking the embers in the fire … with his finger. Meili and Torreblanca, also at the main table, both noticed Long's behavior and shared a frown.

Meili leaned toward Matt. "Boss, did you see that?"

"Don't worry about him. Of all the people in this room, he's the least likely to eat you."

"Um, what?" Lena said.

Before Matt had to explain, Torreblanca leaned forward and let her head fall into her hands. "Jilted lover. Fuck me. I never would have guessed that. Who wins the bet now? What the fuck am I even doing here?"

Nando didn't understand her reference to the bet, and he decided he didn't care. "We're trying to save the world. Everything else? After." Then he turned back to others. "I don't have the contacts I once did out there," he said. "Lots of my ears and noses have moved here to our community. Bel, how about you? Anyone in CimBim you can still call for some intel?"

Bel shook her head. "Cassius isn't too pleased I dropped off the face of the Earth. I'd rather he didn't know where I am. My other friends in CimBim would probably let him know as soon as they heard from me."

"What's CimBim?" Meili asked Matt.

"It's The Convention Inquisition of Major Breaches and Minor Infractions. It should be the C-I-M-B-M-I, but everybody calls it CimBim because that's easier to say. It's the group in charge of making sure the existence of monsters stays off humans' radar. Mostly that involves bribing or killing the right humans, but occasionally it involves policing the monsters who act out. Bel and

Nando here used to do that work. If a monster decided to do something a little too public, Nando would kick its door down and Bel would cut its head off. An effective deterrent against a first infraction, exceeded only by its effectiveness in preventing a second." He nodded at Bel respectfully.

"What about you, Matt?" Bel said. "You have a lot of resources. Any contacts you can call to find out the whereabouts of the book? Or spells? Like a homing spell of some kind?"

Matt nodded. "I can make some calls. Meili, I'll need you to free up some funds. I expect this will get expensive quickly. But, unlike humans, I understand an existential crisis is worth any financial investment since the money won't be worth anything if civilization falls apart, so I'm willing to spend whatever we require." His eyes flicked from Bel to Lena and back. "Doesn't make much sense to win the battle and lose the war, right? As for spells, I'll have to give it some thought. I don't think I could locate the book, but maybe I could locate someone who read the book, or someone who was killed by the book." He paused, contemplating. "I might be able to call forth the witches. They would know where the book will be in the future. Or a demon. They know lots of things but always make you pay a heavy price. Risky, but, again, existential crisis…"

"We're going about this wrong," Esau said, directing his voice clearly at Nando. "What's your security situation here, Mr. DeCastille? Do you think someone just snuck into your camp and took the book? I know my men are just human, but they're the best humans have to offer, and they couldn't sneak in without getting sniffed out. So unless you think someone did a lot better job, then it seems obvious to me someone here took the book. Find the traitor, and that's where we start to figure out where the book has gone."

"I trust my people," Nando said. "And the book went missing after your people arrived, so you might want to check in your own henhouse."

Torreblanca lifted her head. "We didn't know about the book," Then she flopped her head down again. "We didn't know about any of this, really."

"I think you all know what we came here for," Esau added. But he looked down at the table, embarrassed.

"What if someone in your group did know about the book? Has anyone left the camp? Gone missing?"

"The only one of us not accounted for is the one you werewolves ripped to shreds," Torreblanca said. "Think his corpse took your book?"

Nando frowned, then sniffed. "No. No necromancers here. And I can still smell the body."

"Fuck you," Torreblanca said.

Nando shook his head slowly. "Humans attacked a pack of werewolves, at night, in the woods, and you blame me because one of yours went down in the process? You are all lucky to be alive, you know."

"We could have killed everyone who was here in this room, and you know it," she snapped.

"And yet you were unaware of a pack of pups on your flank, oh military genius. How do you think that would have gone?"

Torreblanca sneered. "They're just kids."

Lucia shook her head. "A three-year-old human shouldn't scare you. A three-year-old wolf should. I'm sorry you lost your friend, but respect him by understanding that."

Torreblanca looked down, then nodded, still averting her gaze.

"I agree with Esau," Matt announced. "Find the traitor first. And I have my suspicions."

Nando looked at Lena, suddenly unsure of this new friend of hers.

"Go on," Lena said.

"Um, guys," Tina muttered.

Everyone ignored her.

"Process of elimination. Who knew about the book's existence?" Matt asked.

"It was an NBI at The Convention," Bel said. "All monsters know about it."

Matt shook his head. "No. All monsters know it was commissioned, and rumors have spread far and wide that Nigel Marion is dead. So maybe he made it first, and maybe he didn't. But who knows he did? Esau and his little Monster Squad may have heard rumors, but they couldn't be sure. Would they attack a whole community of werewolves to get a book which might not exist? Unlikely. I believe their stated motives.

"And Mr. DeCastille here knew. But what would he want to book for? Insurance, perhaps. But he'd have to call attention to his community in order to broadcast he has possession of a weapon of mass destruction, and that seems like a bigger gamble than he'd like to take. He cares too much about his people's safety for that.

"And my people brought the book here. If I wanted the book, why would I go to the trouble? I could have taken it in Costa Rica."

Lena rolled her eyes.

"Oh, not at your house, of course. Boom."

Lena's eyes widened.

"Yes, I knew about the explosive house you built. Money will buy a lot of information, Ms. Wallace. But I could have taken it on the docks or at sea. You trusted me not to, and you were right. I don't want the book. I really was telling you the truth about reuniting you with the woman you love to show you the world is worth saving."

He looked at Esau. "Which brings me to the author herself. She's the one who informed us about the second book, and she's the one who told us it's gone missing. So it could be her, right? Only she lived on a bomb for a year to keep it from falling into the wrong hands. So the only reason she would hide the book from everyone here is if she felt it wasn't safe here, which means she isn't the traitor but might suspect someone here is."

He took a deep breath, ready for his crescendo, and then caught himself. "Oh, and it wasn't Meili because she doesn't know much of anything about monsters. No offense, Meili. And it wasn't Long because … " He snorted and chuckled. Everyone looked over at the old man pushing at the burning coals with his fingertips. "Well, we all know it wasn't Long."

Long didn't look away from the fire. "That's not how it's pronounced."

"Lung?" Matt asked.

"Still no."

"Sorry." Matt looked back down the table towards Esau. "So," he said, and rolled his head dramatically towards Nando and Lucia, "if it wasn't a werewolf," and then he looked at Lucia and Nando and rolled his head toward Esau and Torreblanca, "and it wasn't The Monster Squad," and then he looked back at Esau and tilted his head quickly towards Meili, "and it wasn't me or my people, then who knows about the book, isn't a werewolf, was here before we got here, and had the opportunity to take it from the author?"

He looked directly at Bel. "Who may even have made the author nervous enough to hide it?" He stared at Lena. "I guess the question is really for you, Lena. Did you hide the book from Bel, or did she steal it from you?"

Lena looked at Bel, so everyone else did, too.

Bel slowly raised her hands from her lap and set them on the surface of the table. "I. Did. Not. Take. The Book. And you are on very thin ice right now, old man."

"First," Matt said, "killing me now wouldn't help your case much. And second, I'm a lot harder to kill than you think. Just ask Esau. He's killed a lot of your kind over the years while trying to kill me, I suspect. How many warlocks? Zero. Of that I'm certain. So maybe think about it before making your next move, old woman."

Lena raised her hand, not like a child in school, but like a board member at a meeting, holding it there at face height while she spoke. "I believe Bel. I have to. She's the reason I'm here."

"Guys?" Tina said.

Matt shook his head. "A human seduced by a vampire. Look, you know I wanted to believe in your true love. I did. But just because your love is real doesn't mean hers is. Lots of relationships turn out to be more one-sided than they appear. Just ask Esau."

"Fuck you, Matt," Esau said. Then to Lena, "But he's right."

"I am not going to sit here while you all tell the woman I love that my love for her isn't real," Bel said. She reached over and took Lena's hand and squeezed.

Lena squeezed back. Briefly. Equivocally.

Bel looked at Lena. "I did not take the books. I promise."

Matt rolled his head around in the most dramatic eyeroll he could manage. "Again, I apologize, Lena. Just as I apologize to Esau here. I acknowledge your pain right now. But monsters just don't love humans in the way you all expect us to. We pretend to. Because you are our food. We love you like you love a super-sized order of French fries."

"Wow," Meili whispered. "Worst apology ever."

"Right?" Lucia whispered back.

"Guys, seriously-" Tina said.

"First, I am not a guy," Bel said. "That's fucking sexist, and generally I let it slide, but you caught me at the wrong time, and I know you're a woman too, Tina, but women can be sexist and I'm in no mood for that shit right now. So knock it off. Second, I didn't take the goddamned book." She looked at Lena. "I fought fomorians to get you out of Ireland. I fought a warlock to get you out of Scotland. I fought werewolves in London.

I fought an army of skeletons in Paris. And you dumped me. You left me there. If I wanted the book, would I have let you walk away?"

"If you loved her, would you have let her walk away?" Matt said. He looked at Torreblanca. "How many vampires have you killed, Ms. Torreblanca? In all the time Esau had you tricked into believing you were slaying monsters to make the world a better place, did you ever come across any vampire who lived in the suburbs with a human, their average two point five children and a Golden Retriever? Werewolves are pack animals. They family up. But not with humans. Vampires don't love anyone. They're just alcoholics for blood. And junkies always lie."

Torreblanca looked across the table at Bel. "I don't care about the soap opera, Bel. Just tell us where the book is."

"I don't have the book."

Torreblanca raised her gun from under the table but didn't aim it. "That isn't what I asked you, bitch."

"Again with the sexism," Bel said.

"Bitch, I will be as sexist as I want when I unload in your blood sucking face if you don't tell me where the book is."

"You know you won't even pull the trigger before I kill you, right?"

"I know you're not faster than everyone in this room, and I might aim for the writer first."

"Wait, estop right there," Nando said.

"What? Far as I'm concerned, if I can't get the vamp who took the book, I can be the one who takes out her supplier who made a fucking weapon of mass destruction that can wipe out the human race."

"Hey, that wasn't her fault," Bel said. "She was enchanted."

"No, it's fair," Lena said. "I'm half the problem here. Matt, you said so yourself."

"Honey, no, I am not letting anyone kill you. Especially not Lt. Lapdog here."

"Why do you have to insult dogs?" Lucia said.

"Sorry," Bel mumbled.

"And 'bitch' is more than just sexist," Lucia said to Torreblanca. "It's also-"

"Bitch, I will put all of you monsters down!"

"Hold on," Nando said. "Bullets are not going to solve this. Bel, if you tell us where the book is-"

"Nando! You know me better than that! I have no idea where the book is. I didn't take it. How could you even think that?"

"I'm sorry, Bel, but if it wasn't you-"

"Goddamn it, Nando!"

"Esau," Matt said, "I suggest you get ready to Buffy." Then he slid his chair back but did not stand up.

"Fuck you, Matt. When the bullets start flying, I'm aiming for you."

Matt looked down at his lap, as though ashamed. In truth, he wanted to change the angle of his head. He hoped looking down would make the movement of his lips appear to be the quivering of a man about to cry. The spell he was casting was so complicated, it was easier if he could mouth some of the words just to make sure he got them right. In fact, it was three spells. One of them created the perfect illusion of his body remaining in the chair. The other made his real body invisible. The third was the constant spell he had to maintain to keep his now invisible body strong and mobile like a body many centuries younger. It was a lot to hold in his mind all at the same time, and the room was full of distractions, but he'd had plenty of time to master this kind of magic, and he really didn't want to be sitting at that table much longer.

"Guys, listen to me!" Tina shouted.

"Get your pistol out of my face, now!" Bel shouted at Torreblanca.

"Torreblanca, whatever you do, do not lower that weapon," Esau said, and he cocked his own pistol under the table.

"Everyone, no fighting," Nando said. "We can figure this out. Lucia, get out of here."

"I'm not leaving without you," Lucia said.

No one noticed Long walking over to the table except Matt who was completely invisible and standing in the old man's path when Long changed course to walk around him, then stepped up next to Torreblanca. He caught the lieutenant's eye so she would see his movement coming and not accidentally shoot Bel. He held out his hand towards her as though offering her something inside. When she looked, quick as a cat, he flipped his hand over and smashed it down on the tabletop. The glowing coal he's been holding exploded into cinders which should have shot out in every direction, but instead they flew upwards like sparks from a bonfire, dancing as they drifted up and disappearing in the rafters.

"What the fuck was that all about?" Lena said. In the midst of the chaos, she was remarkably calm. If Bel had stolen the book, she had no particular interest in surviving a firefight.

"I suggest you all listen to the girl," Long said. Then he turned and walked back towards the firepit.

"Guys," Tina said, then glanced at Bel, "and gals. Folks? I found the book."

Lucia smiled. "Why didn't you say so?"

Tina swallowed a scream of exasperation. "If you can all just put your dicks back in your pants for five seconds, I'll explain, but I'm not coming over there until you put the guns away."

"Young lady," Nando said. "Such language." He was obviously very pleased.

Tina shook her head as she hopped off the table. "I'm telling you, Nando, these fucking people. What a bunch of assholes. No one listens to me. They can all kill each other for all I care. The only ones that are halfway decent are some of the humans, and I'd rather have them for dinner. And the old guy, whatever he is. Smells all fucked up."

She set her laptop on the table, tapped on the mousepad, and turned the screen in a circle. No one could see the video it played long enough to get a clear idea of what they were seeing, but they heard some humans screaming and a deep voice mutter, "The fuck?"

"Your books are in Las Vegas. I even know what hotel. I even figured out what room they are in."

"How? Where?" Bel said.

"CimBim keeps tabs on some human monster-obsessed websites. Humans who collect rumors of monsters but aren't taken seriously. Helpful for CimBim. So I hacked into the intelligence arm and found their chatter, went to a couple sites, and found this video. Vampire just jumped out a window of the top floor of the Venetian in Las Vegas. Well, second from the top. Thirty-sixth floor. One of the fancy high roller suites. Rented to a Mark Cassius."

"Fucking Cassius!" Bel said. "He took the book." She looked at Nando. "Betting he's making a play to replace the Archduke."

"Oh, you bet, do you?" Matt said. It was not easy to make it sound like his voice came from his seat, but Bel wasn't listening closely enough to identify the deceit.

"Shut up, Matt. It doesn't matter if you all think I took it. When we take it back and Lena has it in her possession, you'll believe me. Or you won't. I don't care." She took Lena's hand. "As long as you believe me, that's all that matters. So I'm going to get you the book."

"No."

"What?"

"We need to get the book, but I don't want you to touch it. Not even touch it." She looked at Esau. "You need to get me in there. No one else can touch the books. No humans. No monsters. You saw what happens." She looked at Matt, or at least where she thought Matt sat. "You said Bel was a junkie. Anyone could succumb to the temptation to check it out. Just a little bit. Just a page or two. And then they're fucked. Forever. Wrecked, like me. Broken inside. At best. I don't want that for any of you.

So get me in there. I'll get the book. And all the rest of you, keep one another from killing me to get it. Then, once we all get safely out of there, we should destroy the books and any copies they've made, and then you all should kill me."

"That's not going to happen," Bel said.

Esau put his hand out. "We're getting ahead of ourselves. Let's get the book back to Lena, and then we can figure out what to do next."

"No," Bel said. "We need to agree, right here and now, that we're not going to kill her."

Now Lena did squeeze Bel's hand. Hard. Sustained. Unequivocal. But then she shrugged. "We're not all going to agree on that. So let's get the book."

"I hate this plan," Bel said.

"It's not a plan yet," Esau said. "But we do need a plan."

"I have some ideas," Matt said. "Risky ideas." He looked at Long. "But maybe we'll be lucky."

"If you want to make peace with your enemy, you have to work with your enemy. Then he becomes your partner."

-Nelson Mandela

Chapter 23

Linda had seen a lot of weird people in her line of work. Back when she'd worked at the New York-New York Hotel and Casino, she'd seen every kind of person come through the hotel's surprisingly small and unimpressive little lobby before heading off to their rooms or the truly fantastic gaming floor. Now that she'd hopped to this new gig at The Venetian, she got to work in a far more impressive space. The check-in desks were situated at the end of a long room with a three story ceiling painted with replicas of classical works just like some renaissance palace in Venice. But, much to Linda's surprise, at least once a year, the people were even weirder. She'd never connected the timing of the strange people to the annual Colorectal Obstruction Federation convention, but now, working at The Venetian, she couldn't escape it. The doctors and ... whoever these other people were attending a convention for proctologists, were hands-down the strangest people she'd ever met. She greeted all of them with the same charm she'd used back at New York-New York (the charm which had won her some memorable nights with a spikey haired woman named Bel once, and which had almost worked on an American named Lena she met on a vacation to Costa Rica), but some of these people made her want to run screaming, often for reasons she couldn't quite identify.

The strangest tonight were a group of four men who came into the hotel together. Three were tall and thin with long arms and strange potbellies, and the fourth was short and had enormously broad shoulders. All had the same pallid white skin, like they never got out into the sun, and all four were balding but kept their remaining, almost identical brown hair in the most unflattering comb-overs. Before any of them spoke, the strangest thing about them was the way they moved. The short one walked right past the desk into the middle of the lobby and headed toward the gaming floor. Despite his seemingly normal legs, he waddled in a comic way, his knees barely bending, his huge shoulders tiktocking back and forth. And he was the most normal one. The other three walked with their strange potbellies gyrating like they were trying to operate invisible hula hoops as they moved. Their heads stayed level and centered, but their torsos were all over the place. One of the three swung and shimmied up to the desk, and when he reached it, he fell forward and landed hard on his elbows, but he didn't react to the pain.

Linda winced for him.

"Welcome to the Venetian Hotel and Casino, sir. How may I help you today," Linda said, more robotically than normal because she was so taken aback.

"Hey toots!" the man barked. "Your thighs are too fat and your chest is too flat, so I guess you can just get us our rooms."

Linda pursed her lips and closed her eyes. Some disgusting verbal abuse was a part of the job, but this was over the top. Still, it seemed easier to give him his room than to make a scene. She communicated her distaste by the way she got to work on the computer and muttered, "O-kay."

She let him stand there a little longer than necessary, but not quite long enough to encourage any more comments, before she said, "Do you have a reservation?"

"Yep. The name is Cuddlemee. Haywood U. Cuddlemee."

Linda did her best not to react. She didn't bother searching for the name in the computer. "Alright, sir, I'll need to see your ID and a credit card for incidentals."

Mr. Cuddlemee reached back for his wallet, and that's when Linda was struck by how short his arms were. He slapped at his back pocket three times, and she was positive she heard a rumble from the man's stomach. Then he found his wallet, pulled out three cards, and slapped them down on the counter. One was a credit card, the next his license, and the third a business card.

To Linda's surprise, both had Mr. Cuddlemee's full name. So if he was stealing it from that old *Simpsons* episode, he was very committed to the bit. Only he was *Doctor* Cuddlemee. Dr. Haywood Unis Cuddleme, MD, Proctology. From West Virginia. Linda didn't meet many guests from West Virginia, but people came to Vegas from all over the world, and she'd never before met a guest from West Virginia she didn't like. Until now.

"'Unis' is a family name," Dr. Cuddleme said. "Kind of embarrassing, eh? But not as embarrassing as being named 'cute' in Spanish when you're at best a 4, right Linda?"

She refused to be baited. "You must be here for the medical conference?"

"Yep. Asshole fingerers, all of us. We get together to sniff each other's hands." He leaned even further forward. "For fun!"

"Alright, well you've got four rooms all booked for your party. Would you like one key each, or two?"

The short one suddenly stopped his waddling, turned, and shouted back down the long room in a voice so loud Linda thought the plaster might crack and ruin the frescoes above them. "What?"

Dr. Cuddlemee looked back over his shoulder. "Sorry, Dr. Highness. I just-"

"You think I'm made of money? Four rooms? You all can share one. Hell, you can sleep in my closet, I don't give a fuck. Hey, hotel human person, can you do me two favors? Can you cancel three of the rooms, and can you slap Dr. Cuddlemee in the face as hard as you can?"

Linda didn't miss a beat. "I'm sorry, sir. We're prohibited from slapping guests. But I can cancel those three rooms and refund Dr. Cuddlemee's card. There will be a hold on those funds, but they should come back in two to three weeks."

"Thank you, sweet-cheeks. I'll stick a finger up your ass any time you want, on the house."

Linda's finger hovered over the ENTER key, and then she hit ESC. *Poop,* she thought. *Guess I just forgot to process the refund. Doctors Asshole and Asshole can take it up with customer service when they get back to West Virginia.*

The King of Trolls was nearly to the other side of the long room when two figures approached from the gaming floor. The one in front was hunched over and wore a rumpled gray suit. His necktie was slightly askew, and a lock of his hair was hanging out of place over his forehead. The man behind him stood ramrod straight, making him look taller than his companion. He had a bushy mustache, neatly trimmed, and wore a tuxedo.

"Dr. Highness," the Archduke said.

"Dr. Duke. Dr. Duke's Dr. Butler," the King of Trolls said. "What are you two doing here? Why can't we meet in your room or in mine? This glamour is itchy as shit. And I mean that literally. Like when you don't wipe your ass, and the shit is itchy. I feel like an itchy ass crack all over."

"Ah, but yours is so convincing," the Archduke said. "All seven of you with four perfectly matching haircuts. No one would ever think that's strange."

"Fuck off," the Kind of Trolls said to the Archduke. Then, "Fuck off" to the six trolls approaching behind him. The six of them, or at least the three serving as the legs for the compatriots on their shoulders, took him literally enough to skedaddle, and perhaps literally enough to complete the order once they'd reached Dr. Cuddleme's room.

The King of Trolls watched them go, their cartoonish failure to imitate humans irritating him more than it amused him. He aimed his ire at the Archduke. "Why are we talking in public, slime licker?"

"Three reasons. First, since we're in Las Vegas and there are eyes everywhere anyway, I thought it might be best if we just had it out in public. I don't care who knows we are on opposite sides of this particular issue. In fact. I'd rather them know."

"Fine," The King of Trolls said. He wiped his nose with a knuckle to show he got it, but his voice retained his irritation. "What are the other two reasons?"

"Second, I don't want you in my room. And third, I don't want to go into your room."

"Walked into that one."

"I'm pretty proud of it," the Archduke admitted.

"An excellent joke, sir," Jeeves intoned.

"You can both go give yourselves thorough self examinations with rusty, oversized tools, doctors!" The King of Trolls shouted. He would have said the same thing in private. Only the volume was theater.

"Fine. I didn't expect we would see eye to eye on this. And if there is a floor strategy, I will not expect your support as parliamentarian."

"How dare you imply I would favor any one side in my official capacity, sphincter face! I hold myself to the highest ethical standards of anyone at the C.O.F. conference. Of course you won't have my support in your nefarious shenanigans."

The Archduke leaned forward and spoke softly. "'Nefarious shenanigans'? Such uncouth language, Dr. Highness."

"Fuck off. I said I'm itchy all over. It messes with my game." He went back to yelling before the Archduke could pull his ear away. "So no, you can take your scheming and shove it straight up your rectum, take a hard left at your sigmoid colon, and keep on going to your splenic flexure, Doctor, because I'm going to run this conference by Robert's Rules, and rule one is: Don't fuck with the parlamentarian! Good day, sir!" And he waddled off, trying not to rub against the glamour which encased him.

"I say good day to you as well!" the Archduke shouted at his back.

"I think that went as well as could be expected, sir," Jeeves said.

The Archduke shook his head sadly. "Yes, I fear I may just be coming to respect Dr. Highness a little bit. Oh, dammit. I feel like he tricked me into saying 'cumming,' Jeeves. He's infectious."

"Highly amusing, sir."

Chapter 24

After discussing the details of Matt's plan late into the night, the community of Camp Bigfoot retired to their cabins, and Esau's soldiers headed back to their nearby basecamp. When Lena and Bel stepped into Bel's room, Bel turned quickly, closed the door, and whispered to Lena, "Okay, can I just say this plan is batshit bonkers?"

"Yeah, I don't like it, either."

"No one likes it. Why did we all just agree to it?"

Lena shrugged. "Matt made a very compelling case."

"Sure, but …" She motioned with her hand out just beyond her hip, measuring a height. "But the little … ?" Then she raised her hand to her own height. "And the rest … ? I just can't believe they said yes."

"He's right though," Lena said. "I mean, maybe not about the plan itself. Probably not. It probably won't work. But when the stakes are this high, anything, really anything at all that improves the chances of it working even a little bit becomes worth trying. Because if it doesn't work, everybody dies."

"But-" Bel tried.

"Every. Body," Lena said sternly. "Remember, you only started reading the second one, and you went full-on fugue state. If I hadn't saved your ass, you'd be dead now. You know it works. Imagine millions of copies in millions of hands. And you know how humans are. We say, 'You'd better get this vaccine or you might die,' and half the people say, 'I would have, but because you told me to, I won't." And monsters are even worse. You tell them, 'Don't do this or bad things will happen,' and they say, "Gimme some of this, whatever it is.' You know they would read it. Enough would, anyway. And then total societal collapse, humans and monsters alike. No one here would be safe from that. And we can't run away. Start some little underground city in Greenland or something. Because you need humans to eat. And so do the werewolves here. Pretty soon you'd be eating me, Bel."

Now Bel looked stern. "I would never, ever feed on

you, Lena. I would starve and die first."

"That's nice of you, but don't forget who you're talking to. You think I love life so much I'd let you die to give myself a few more years? I wrote both those books, Bel."

They were silent for a moment.

"So you think this plan might work?" Bel said.

"I doubt it."

"You don't seem nearly as upset about that as I am, and I'm the one most likely to run out of there in one piece."

Lena sat down on the edge of the bed, bowed her head, clasped her hands between her knees, then looked up and held her hands open, palms up. "I have a different relationship with death than anyone here, Bel. Even you. Especially you. The humans want to live out every possible moment of their short lives without thinking about death. You want to go on forever. I … I just go on. Until tomorrow. And the day after. I go on knowing when I die, everything that comes after is irrelevant to me. The world ends, I won't know about it. And everything before that moment is also meaningless because of it. I lived a full, happy life? I wrote two books that ended the world? Doesn't matter. I'll be gone, the joy will be gone, the pain will be gone. Nothing matters."

Bel sat down next to Lena. "Are you, like, in a technical sense, suicidal?"

"No. I'm not even fully nihilistic. At least not in my actions. A hypocritical nihilist, maybe? I am living." She reached out and took Bel's hand. It felt warm and soft and dryer than Lena thought it should have been considering Bel's agitation. "I am loving," Lena said, and she allowed herself to smile even though it made her face flush. She looked down, embarrassed. "And I'm going to do this thing. Fight this fight. Try to fix the shitshow I've created. If I were a good nihilist, I wouldn't care. But I do care." She squeezed Bel's hand, just once quick squeeze. "I do. I feel what I feel. The love. The sense of justice and the desire to correct injustice. It's just I see those feelings like a veil. They color the world, but I can also see the fabric itself. I can take it off and examine it and know the feelings are just my feelings. The veil isn't the world. The world beyond the veil is a stone, no, a landscape of stones. Moving the rocks around really does affect the world. Reality beyond the veil does exist. But it doesn't care. When I'm dead, it won't matter that the stones are in different places because of my actions. Which means my actions now don't matter, either."

Bel shook her head. "That sounds … terrible. Terribly painful and isolating and … I don't know, just empty, I guess."

Lena nodded. "It took a lot to get me to come find you, Bel, and that's not because I don't love you. It's because I don't trust any of my own motivations. Why should I get to find you? Why should I get to be happy with you or sad without you? Why not do nothing? I did nothing for a long time. Just nothing. I tried to feel nothing. And it was impossible. I felt pain and loneliness and despair.

I couldn't escape feelings. And then Matteo showed up and told me he could bring me to you. And I thought, 'If I have to feel, I will feel love.' Well, I didn't know if you'd love me back. I didn't know if you'd even remember me. But I thought, 'I will feel this love and that loss and that pain even though I can't hide from my knowledge none of it matters. I may be the only human who has ever stared into the void until it was inside me, but I'm still human, Bel. I still feel. I still act. I can't stop breathing. Wallowing in Costa Rica was still a choice, still action, so since I couldn't escape that, the immutable fact of action, I decided to love and maybe suffer knowing it would not ever save me from what I have become because of the first book."

She stood and stretched, then turned back to Bel. "So all of that is a long-winded way of saying I can do this, play my part in this terrible plan, probably die the day after tomorrow, and I can care about it while also knowing my caring doesn't matter, my actions don't matter, my death doesn't matter. So no, I'm not suicidal. I won't try to die. I will try to succeed. But I can see the veil. I know I am behaving like a person acting on a heroic impulse while also not believing in heroes. And while also believing all impulses are, at root, vanity and capriciousness. I'm not sure I'm explaining this well. Does that make sense?"

Bell, still sitting, reached forward and took Lena's hands. She pulled Lena to her, so Lena stood between her knees. "It doesn't make sense to me. Not really. But that's not your fault. Like you said, humans choose not to understand the world the way you do, and vampires can't even if we wanted to. We have no veil to see. I don't distract myself with desires to feed and love and fight injustice and build monuments to avoid thinking about my own death because I really won't die. Not for millenia, at least. Maybe not ever. The heat death of the universe, I suppose. But I'm not hiding from the thought of that. I'm feeding and loving and doing whatever else I want because I just exist and enjoy existing. I guess, if you are a nihilist, I am just a hedonist. It sounds really shallow, but it's as simple a philosophy as yours, right? Do you think less of me for being simple, Lena? I do what feels good. Is that bad?"

"You're asking the wrong human, Bel," Lena said. "I don't know what 'bad' means anymore."

"What about 'naughty'?" She flashed a grin. "Because if Matt's plan is as bad as I think it is, this may be the last time you and I have together in private."

"You know that's the most fucked up pick-up line ever, right?"

"It's the hedonist's line," Bel said. She released one of Lena's hands and ran the nail of her middle finger down Lena's jeans to her knee, then slowly up her inner thigh. "'Eat." She traced the seam of Lena's jeans so gently Lena could barely feel it. Then kept going up Lena's stomach. "Drink," she said, pressing slightly harder on the bottom of Lena's breast, then up to her nipple, then past the collar of her shirt, scratching against the exposed skin. "And be merry, right?" she asked, her hand now sliding around to the back of Lena's neck and pulling her down into a kiss.

Lena stopped when they were nose to nose. "I can't believe you can make such a cheesy line work."

Bel laughed, a full, deep, dangerous laugh. "Oh, just wait."

Neither waited long.

When Lena awoke the next morning, she had to grope in the dark for her phone because the room's only window was boarded up and there was no light for her eyes to adjust to. She found the device on the edge of the bedside table but knocked it on the floor.

"Want me to get it?" Bel said. She sounded completely awake.

"No, you sleep," Lena said. "I don't even know what time it is."

"10:14," Bel said. "I can tell by the amount of light coming through the plywood."

"I can't even see any light coming through at all," Lena said.

"There's always some," Bel said. Then her voice changed. "Plus, I'm wearing a watch."

Lena smacked Bel's naked hip. "You got me." She sat

up, patted the thin carpet based on where she heard the phone bump on the floor, and eventually found it. She woke it up, then swiped down to find the flashlight.

Bel hissed and dropped her voice into a deep, Transylvanian accent. "Thee light! It burns!"

Lena laughed. "Shut up. Go to sleep."

She found fresh clothes in the phone's beam, dressed, and opened the door only as wide as her body, then slipped into the cabin's hall. As she tapped off the flashlight, she thought about the anachronistic name for the device in her hand, made all the more ridiculous when she was this close to the Arctic without any cell service. The little pocket computer was so many things; her flashlight, her music player, her handy notepad when she had an idea for a novel or short story. When she had service, it was a portal to news and social media, though she didn't post anything to her own anonymized accounts because she was hiding from the various monsters searching for her books. Before she'd gone into hiding, it had been her means to text with friends and coworkers. The phone function was one of the least used features of her "phone." This half-an-insight observation reminded her of Andy Rooney, the guy who used to do those "back in my day" rants on a news show she would watch from her father's lap when she was a little girl. Lena had never wanted children of her own. She wanted dolls and liked babies, but even before she saw a picture of a penis for the first time, when she was given a brief but clinical description of the necessary steps required to get pregnant, she was immediately overwhelmed by revulsion. By the time she learned about the options of artificial insemination and adoption, she was already firmly set in her sense she would never be a mother. She didn't regret that now, but she did wish she could live long enough to someday tell her grand-nieces and nephews the story of the etymology of "phones," even if it would make her sound like the old white man who did observational stand-up for other old white people at the end of a news program.

People were milling around the camp with a palpable anxiety; there wasn't anything for them to do yet because Matt and Meili were still arranging the transportation to Las Vegas. Esau's soldiers had remained at their own camp to reduce the likelihood they'd be attacked by monsters (or Esau would decide to shoot Matt). The youngest children ran about the camp, some in their wolf forms, others in various states of nakedness. Lena noticed more of the parents standing around watching them. The adults' faces were complicated masks, hiding feelings but also expressing them as much as the ancient Greek megaphone faces, so much worry and love and sadness, but often displayed one in place of the other. A mother would shout at her child angrily because she was worried. Another would sound sad because she loved. A father would look loving through his worry. Each anxious face was an honest betrayal.

Lena made her way into the big hall, then back to the kitchen. She planned on scrounging for a bowl and some cereal, but when she pushed through the saloon-style doors, she discovered Lucia there sitting at the small table, a blank notebook and pen in hand, just staring. Lucia didn't look up at Lena, and Lena realized Lucia had identified her approach by smell. Only this disinterest lasted longer than normal.

"Um, hey?" Lena tried.

Lucia flipped the book closed and stood suddenly. "Want to come on a shopping run with me? C'mon. Let's go into town and get some groceries."

"Uh," Lena hesitated.

Lucia shook her head. "Human food, not humans. We've got more people to feed than normal." She looked away, barely speaking to Lena. "People still need to eat. Yes, we'll go to the grocery store. C'mon."

Lena motioned towards the cupboard with the bowls. "I was just going to … But, yeah, I guess I could grab a Danish or something."

Lucia ignored the indecision. "Good. Let's go."

In minutes they were in the camp's jeep, driving down the gravel road toward the highway. Lucia drove in silence.

"So," Lena said, "what do you think of Matt's plan?"

"Not yet," Lucia said.

"Not yet?"

"A little further."

They continued, Lucia's eyes straight ahead, Lena watching the wild grass in the valley wave toward the forest of pines which decorated the low hills of the plains.

The morning sun bleached the landscape like a hangover.

Lucia didn't slow enough as they made the turn onto the highway, shoving Lena into the jeep's door. Lena winced and weighed her words against Lucia's warning to silence, and she'd almost decided whether to let Lucia have it or to express concern when Lucia looked over at her.

"Okay, we're out of earshot."

Lena was taken aback. "I was just making conversation. What do you think of Matteo's-"

"Here's the thing," Lucia said. She held the wheel with one hand, but she needed the other free to speak Italian English. She karate chopped the air. "I can keep a secret, okay?"

"Okay?" Lena said.

Lucia ignored her. "But I need someone to talk to. Like, I can keep things to myself when I need to, but I have to tell someone. And normally. Normally. That's Nando, right? He's the one I can talk to about anything. Like, anything. Sometimes nothing. Sometimes I just ramble about nothing, and he listens, and then I listen when he has his big ideas, and it's perfect. We're perfect in that way."

"Mmm-hmm," Lena said, confused.

"But now, when I can't tell him something, I don't know what to do. And you are, like, the last person I should confess this to. Like, you're very sweet and I like you and I've known you for like five minutes and now you're going to hate me more than anyone else. And that's fair, and I deserve it. But I can handle you hating me because you're a human, you know?" She looked away from the road briefly. "I'm not going to eat you." Then her eyes snapped back ahead of her and she fell silent.

Lena spoke softly and carefully. "I appreciate that."

"Right, but I have to tell somebody, so why not you, right? Like, rip the Band-Aid. And maybe that's what I should do. Maybe I should just tell him. Just blurt it out. And he'll never trust me again. But I need him to know I wasn't trying to betray him. I was doing it for him. For his vision, the community he wants to build, you know? And it may not be enough. Good intentions, you know? He may hate me anyway. But I did it for him. That should count for something, right?"

"Lucia," Lena said, "what did you do?"

"The books. I stole the books. I didn't know what they were. And the vampire said they would leave us alone if he had the books. More than leave us alone. Protect us from The Convention. Keep us a secret from the rest of Apo's pack and the other monsters who are looking for Nando. And if I didn't get him the books, he'd do the opposite. Tell them all where we were. We'd be overrun. We need time to get bigger. Stronger. Until we can protect ourselves. I thought I was buying us time."

"Oh shit," Lena breathed.

"Yeah, and that's not even fully true. If I'm going to tell him, I have to tell the whole truth, you know? I did know. I mean, Nando had told me the story about you and Ireland and Paris. When you came, I knew I had to call Cassius. And he said to get the book and not read it. So I did, and I drove it into town and gave it to some vampire." She looked at Lena again. "I'm so sorry." Then away. "I'm so, so sorry. He's never going to forgive me."

"Lucia, I don't mean to be insensitive, but your relationship issues with Nando are ... People are probably going to die tomorrow."

"I know."

Lena thought of something. "And Josef! Did you-?"

"No, Cassius said he had that part taken care of, and when I got to your room, the golem was already gone. I had nothing to do with Josef."

"But if you'd said something!"

Lucia pounded on the wheel. "I know!" Her eyes filled with tears, and one spilled down her cheek to her jaw, then another along her nose. In an effort to keep her nose from running, Lucia snorted the second tear. "Fuck. I'm so sorry, Lena."

They didn't speak for a moment, so the volume of the tires on the pavement and the sniffles in the car increased. Lena resented each successive sniff, but she let Lucia cry for a few miles. When Lucia's tears and snot seemed to be drying out, Lena decided Lucia hadn't cried enough. "I don't know how you make this right, Lucia, but you need to do something. And telling Nando is step one. Not today, though. Not tomorrow. Let's get through this, get the books back, and then you can come clean, but we don't have time to distract everybody with a trial or a burning at the stake or whatever your community does when somebody fucks everyone else over."

Lucia nodded vigorously, eyes fixed on the road ahead, tears flowing again. She chose to sit with Lena's words, with the image of Nando sitting in judgment, the community tying her to a pole on top of a pile of kindling and setting her on fire. Sure, it was historical witch imagery, not a current or ancient werewolf custom, but she felt like she deserved that kind of punishment. She imagined herself shouting about how she'd meant well. If some member of the community lost their child in the attempt to recover the books, how hollow would her cries of positive intent sound in their ears as they stared up at her and felt the heat of those flames? No, she already deserved some kind of punishment, even if it weren't so barbaric and dramatic. Exile, probably. Public shaming at least. Lucia acknowledged Lena was right, both about the need to confess, and about the timing.

"You're right. I'll tell him. Do you think he'll be able to forgive me, Lena? Will you ever be able to forgive me?"

Lena clasped her hands in her lap and frowned for a moment, then gave Lucia a look that could do more than move stones; her stare could shatter them. "It will depend on how many people die tomorrow."

Chapter 25

As the call connected, Cassius steeled himself. He had to appear strong and confident, but, in truth, he felt stressed and exhausted. After the discovery of the second book, his plans had kicked into overdrive, and he no longer had Mildred to help, so the whole burden fell on him. He pushed away feelings of resentment towards Mildred. It wasn't her fault, he thought. But her timing was terrible.

A picture of the royal seal of Tisina, Queen of the Sirens, Lord over all the Merfolk, Rider of the Leviathan,

Ruler of the Depths and Heights of the Sea flashed briefly, and then she turned on her camera. Cassius caught his breath before he could gasp audibly. Cassius had always thought of pregnancy as binary. Either one was pregnant or one was not. Now, he reassessed. He'd heard the phrase "very pregnant" applied to people (mostly humans) who were far along in their term, but Tisina was so very pregnant, every other pregnant person he'd ever seen, even the most "very pregnant," looked "partly pregnant" by comparison. Her frame was normally thin beneath her ribcage where her true mouth hid, then belled out where a human would have hips so her lack of legs could deceive a human victim into believing she wore a large skirt. Now the "skirt" began just under her breasts like an empire waist. And the skirt that was really more like a jellyfish's bell was now enormous, as wide as she had been tall, but longer now, too, extending below the camera's frame even though she floated some distance back. The bell, now more of a balloon, made the human-looking portion of her body a ridiculous appendage. Most disturbing, the balloon was stretching as something wriggled beneath it, and as the lumps appeared and moved, the skin of her lower half, now her lower two thirds, became semi-transparent, revealing hints of the dark, shadowy creature inside her beneath a lace veil of blue veins.

"Um, it seems congratulations are in order, your Highness."

She smiled and rubbed her belly, then nodded, but

she didn't reply.

"I hadn't heard your good news, so the reason for my call might seem like a trifle given your current circumstances. All things being relative, this is less important than the birth of a child. And not just any child. The future heir of all the seas. Again, my most heartfelt congratulations, and my deepest apologies for bothering you with this at such a time."

Another slow nod, and then she said, "Go ahead, Cassius."

"Well, as you know, tomorrow is the first day of The Convention. I plan to propose my … er, repropose Nigel Marion's new business item. I have the book in my possession as I told you before, so I suspect the representatives will support the measure, but I want to be certain I have the votes. You never can tell how the gremlins will go. Or the imps and other demons. Of course I have some of the vampires and some of the werewolves, and the werewolves lost some of their voting share because of the kerfuffle in London and some internal divisions. Still, I don't want to underestimate the Archduke. Who knows what support he may have garnered. I've added language to my NBI giving me absolute authority to carry out Nigel Marion's plan with any resources at The Convention's disposal, and that will give me power over the Archduke, so it's a direct threat to him. He has to fight me somehow. And he won't be caught with his pants down like last year. So, in light of our mutual arrangement which seems to have worked out beautifully for you, I'm hoping you'll offer me your support and the support of all your delegates' weighted votes. That should put me over the top regardless of the Archduke's schemes. You're the queen of all the seas, after all. That's two thirds of the whole planet."

He paused to give her a chance to reply.

"Yes," she said.

"Yes. Um, yes to which part?"

"All of it. Yes, I do rule two thirds of the planet. Yes, I expect the Archduke of the vampires will fight you as best he can. And yes, you will have my full support."

"Oh, thank you, Your Highness."

"But."

"But?"

"I need an assurance from you."

"Whatever I can offer."

"I don't think you fully understand what you've given me, Cassius."

"The flowers?"

"Yes. You see, I'd been cursed. These things happen to royalty. It comes with the territory. A political rival cursed me so I would not be able to bear children. But there was a carve out. An exception. If I could find those two ingredients and place them under my bed, I would conceive. I'd get to make a choice. If I chose to place the rarest, purest, most beautiful flower in the world under my bed, I'd give birth to the greatest hero the merfolk would ever know, the savior of my people. He would make peace with the inhabitants of the land and the sky, and he would rule the sea for a thousand years." She looked down at her belly. "If I chose to use both, I'd give birth to twins. A hero and a monster. The monster would wreak unimaginable terror, but ultimately its brother would defeat it and rule the sea and the land for the rest of time." She looked up at Cassius. "Obviously, I chose both. A thousand years of ruling the sea is good. But making peace with the humans? Unacceptable. My son must rule them for all time. And first, my other child will secure the revenge my people have desired for generations."

Tisina shrugged. "The math was easy for me. And now I will require your assurance. Your amended new business item will give you power to direct the actions of the entirety of The Convention. They won't realize it at first, but I do. You could say anything is in service of Nigel Marion's plan. You could direct CimBim to treat the ascension of my children to the lands of the humans as a violation of The Convention and direct every monster in the world to fight them. Or you could decide the arrival of my children is just a part of Nigel's plan to attack the humans. I know that interpretation will be … controversial. The fundamental principle of The Convention is it keeps the existence of monsters a secret from the human world. My children will be violating that when they conquer. But, I would argue, we are also violating that principle when we distribute the necromancer's book. We are interfering in their world in a way monsters never have, not culling the herd but slaughtering much of it outright. So, when my children do the same, will you guarantee me you will order CimBim to cooperate with them, or at least stand down while they do their work in concert with yours?"

"That seems entirely reasonable to me."

"Yes."

Silence.

"Yes?" Cassius asked.

"Yes, it is reasonable. But that's not a promise, Cassius. I want more than your assessment of the logic of my request. I want your word. And I want you to know that my children will be guided by me. So if you try to double-cross me, if you change your mind about my very reasonable request, I will order them to start their assault on the land dwellers by destroying you. Personally. You will have my support tomorrow if you make me this promise knowing your life hangs in the balance should you fail me."

"I promise. I will use all the power at my disposal to support your children or keep The Convention from interfering with them, and if I go back on my word, may your children strike me down."

"Good." Tisina said. "It's done. You can rest easy, now, Cassius. No matter what happens on the convention floor tomorrow, you will have all my delegates' votes, and those will be enough to overcome the Archduke's efforts. You've won. Now you get to enjoy it."

"Thank you, Your Highness. I won't keep you any

longer." And he clicked "Leave Meeting."

"Fuck," he said aloud. Now he could rule the vampires with more authority than the Archduke, but soon enough they would all be subjects of the Merfolk. He'd achieved his goal just in time to find out he'd created a ceiling for his ambition in the process. "Fuck," he repeated.

He didn't even consider the consequences of his choice to give Tisina the wrong plants. What did it matter? They'd obviously worked.

Tisina felt far more sanguine about the call. She'd won as much as she hoped to achieve. She turned away from the camera. Before she'd been able to move with such grace, but now even that small movement cost a lot of effort and made her feel embarrassed about her bulk as she scooped water sideways with both her webbed hands, then waited as her belly twisted after her. Finally she faced her handmaid.

"Thoughts, Devochka?"

"I expect he will betray you eventually. He does not seem like the kind of person who will one day accept your son's rule."

"Agreed. But I have bought time for my children. Not that they need it. The lifting of the curse makes everything in its wake an inevitability. But there are spaces in the prophecy. Question marks. How long will it take my monstrous child to ravage the surface world? What obstacles will he face? And how difficult will it be for my son to defeat his brother? Will they cooperate at first, one riding the other into battle, then have a falling out later on? Or will they always be opposed to one another? I do not know. But if they don't have to deal with the meddling of CimBim until after their initial invasion, it may help. Cassius will be occupied with his project at first. I expect he will not betray me until after the monster is defeated and my son takes both thrones. And that will make it much easier on him. We know he will rule for eternity, but we may have just made the beginning of his rule a time of consolidation of power rather than a war with the monsters of the land, and then Cassius will be easier to defeat later on. At least, that's what I hope. Ultimately, it doesn't matter. Everything has gone exactly as the breaking of the curse dictates. There is little I can offer the child who will have it all. But I am giving the little I have."

"Meetings are an addictive, highly self-indulgent activity that corporations and other large organizations habitually engage in only because they cannot actually masturbate."

-Dave Barry
The World According to Dave Barry

Chapter 26

"Positions?" Nando said. "Sorry. That sounded a little order-y. Where is everyone?"

"For fuck's sake. Positions?" Esau barked.

The comms were in everyone's ears. Well, almost everyone. Their positions had changed dramatically in the last few days.

Thanks to Matt's financial resources and Esau's connections to … whoever he worked for, the group had been able to hire a large, long range chopper which picked them up at Camp Bigfoot more quickly than they could have traveled by road to the nearest airport. A private aircraft, not one of those little jets for the ultra-rich but a military-style transport, took them to a private airfield in the desert outside of Las Vegas. When they arrived there, a bunch of vehicles which had been rented from a number of different places (to avoid ringing any alarms) were already waiting for them.

There are a lot of places willing to rent unusual vehicles in Las Vegas. They'd wrangled five vehicles: a silver seven passenger Infiniti QX60 luxury SUV; a shiny, black Hummer; a nondescript white Nissan Rogue; and a tall, squat tour bus bearing a banner that said "Comedy On Deck Tours" with a sign in the front advertising its destination as the Hoover Dam, and…

"Dibs on the Ferrari!" Tina shouted.

It was, in fact, a bright, metallic red Ferrari 812 GTS Competizione. The other cars sat and waited. The Ferrarri crouched, anxious to pounce.

"No way you're driving that thing," Rita, her teacher and constant nemesis, said firmly.

"Actually, she will be driving it. And very fast. And not safely. That's part of the plan." Matt shrugged.

Tina sneered at Rita and raised a fist, then slowly articulated her middle finger. "Boom."

Matt winked at Tina.

"Don't wink at me, Old Man. I'm sixteen. You're like a couple thousand or whatever. It's gross."

He mimicked her slow flip-off.

Rita smiled in approval, though of which it was not clear.

While cars were assigned, Esau walked over near Lena. He kept his eyes on the cars, seeming to assess the inventory, but when he was close, he stepped sideways and leaned towards her. Then he whispered so quietly Lena didn't know if she was hearing him or reading his lips. Esau couldn't be certain, but he hoped his voice was smothered by the sounds of the engines and wouldn't carry to vampire ears.

"I need you to do me a favor," he mostly mouthed. "Well, both of us a favor."

"Um, okay? Maybe?" Lena scowled but listened.

"This guy, Cassius, has been in this business a long time. Longer than you or I could ever fully understand."

"And?"

"And he keeps very good records. He took your books. It seems only fair that when you take those back, you take his books, too." He held up a flash drive. "You won't need any passwords or anything. Just plug this into his computer. It will copy everything, and then we'll crack it all after we get back."

"And you want this information so you can what?"

"I want to track down his business associates. Save a lot of human lives by killing the right monsters. That's my business. I know it's not yours." He didn't aim this as a jab, and he rolled on before she could decide it was a veiled one. "But I thought you might want the information, too. After all, he's been your girlfriend's boss for centuries. It would be good to know, right? Not to pry. Just to know without forcing her to relive it all. You get me his records, I'll tell you only as much as you want."

Lena reached for the drive, hesitated, then grabbed it and shoved it into the key pocket of her jeans. "I'll think about it."

"Thank you. You'll help save a lot of lives."

"And cause a lot of deaths."

"Undead, mostly. Less like murder and more like pulling the plug a few hundred years too late. But that's neither here nor there. You'll find out what Cassius has made Bel do. If you want to know it. He's not going to tell you. And you don't want to make her tell you. So just … think about it."

Lena gave him a tight nod, and then they walked away from one another.

The group climbed into their different vehicles and took off through the desert towards the city. Once there, they waved off valet parking and made their way into the 14 story parking structure southwest of the hotel itself. Parking a Hummer in a parking lot is difficult. Nando managed, but there wasn't enough room for the people in the back to get out without dinging the doors of the cars on either side. They dinged them. Hard and unapologetically. And left no notes. Because they are monsters.

Tina could turn the Ferrari on a dime, but she hadn't quite got the hang of the sensitivity of the gas and brake pedals, so she stopped four feet into the space, then tapped the gas and bumped into the concrete wall in front of her, cracking the front of the $410,516 car. When she climbed out (dinging the door of the car next to her as well), she looked at Matt, pursed her lips, and almost shrugged.

He winked aggressively.

The parking lot of the Venetian is not conveniently placed under nor attached to the hotel for three reasons. For one, there is no way to make a parking garage fit the aesthetic of The Venetian, so it's designed to look like some separate thing, a brutalist monstrosity the hotel is not responsible for. Second, the designers wanted guests of the hotel to see as much as possible of the gaming options on the way to their rooms. And third, they wanted those guests to remember the slog with their bags as an added disincentive to leave and spend their money anywhere else while visiting. Everything in a casino is ingeniously designed to keep the occupants there and losing money for as long as possible. This was a problem for a group planning on getting in and out of the hotel quickly without calling attention to themselves. The hotel's designers had not been thinking about preventing heists, especially not of world-ending books kept in penthouse suites converted to vampires' offices, but they would not have changed their designs to make theft more convenient.

Tina, Nando, Lucia, Steve (the scout from Camp Bigfoot who Lena would forever think of as Naked

Steve), Lt. Torreblanca, and a few of Esau's other soldiers stayed back with the vehicles. The rest split into groups and made their way into the hotel.

The earpieces they wore were designed for soldiers wandering around in urban environments, mostly metropolises in the Middle East, so they were good at activating when the wearer spoke and blocking out most of the background noise, but when Esau muttered "For fuck's sake," the device had a hard time distinguishing between his voice and all the convoluted noises of the casino's gaming floor. It also picked up the digital chimes of the slot machines around him and sounded like someone was doing a half-assed job of censoring him. It resolved into his authoritative voice when he said, "Positions?"

"Torreblanca at Vehicle 4 but ready to hat up and un-ass at your word, sir."

Esau knew Torreblanca did not like much about this plan. He knew why. He was counting on her to react quickly when he changed it, but he couldn't reveal that yet. "Hold your position, Lieutenant. Everybody else? Positions?"

"Tina is in a mother fuckin' Ferrari, bitches!"

"No, she's not," Nando said. "Tina is estanding in a parking garage, leaning on a Ferrari, vaping. I can see you from here, Tina. Get in the car and be ready."

"Born ready, boss."

"Don't dick around, Tina," Lucia said. "I know it's boring now, but seconds will matter here."

Tina exhaled smoke loudly enough for the system to think she was speaking. Then she said, "Fine," and sauntered around the car.

"Nando and I are in Vehicle 1, ready to go."

"Fire Team One is in the elevator," Rita said. Then she spoke in a slight sing-song. "Do you hear that? That's us. Fire Team One!"

The mic didn't clearly pick up the responses from the rest of Fire Team One, but it sounded like distant cheers.

"Fire Team Two is spread out around the gaming floor," Bel said. "Positions? You're right, Nando, that does sound order-y."

They could almost hear Esau's eyeroll. "I'm sitting at a machine on your nine, twenty feet from you."

"Long?" Bel asked.

Silence.

"Long?"

"Sorry," Long said. "I was distracted when the woman next to me screamed. She won five thousand dollars at the roulette table."

"I told you to stay by the machines," Matt said.

"I know. I was just trying to saunter so I'd look inconspicuous, but the machines and the tables are all mixed together. I'm moving to the hallway closest to the convention room."

"Good," Matt said. "Camouflage Team is on the 36th floor. In position down the hall and out of sight. Ready to trip Esau's spell when you say the word."

"Wait, Camouflage Team? I thought we were Fire

Team Three," Lena said. "Don't change things now."

"I wanted to be Insertion Team One," Long said. "It's funnier."

"I agree with the weird guy," Tina said. "It is funnier."

"The team led by the most lesbian of all of us was not going to be Insertion Team," Bel said.

"What makes you think you're the most lesbian?" Lena said. "And I'm now on 'Camoflauge Team'? I do *not* like being on Team In-The-Closet, Matt."

"Believe it or not," Matt said, "Maintaining multiple glamours at the same time takes a great deal of concentration. All your chatter is distracting, and calling ourselves Camouflage Team helps me focus on what I am trying to do right this very instant while you all talk and bother me."

"Sorry," Bel said. "Fire Team Two, let's make our way into the convention room. Matt, I'll call it as Esau crosses the threshold." She stood from the slot machine's chair and started towards the hallway outside the convention rooms. Esau, on her left, did not look at her as she passed, but he stood up so he would be a safe distance behind her. Long did look at her as she passed him in the hallway, but he didn't make any obvious sign. He just pushed off the wall where he'd been leaning and fell in behind her.

As she neared the doors to the convention room, Bel passed some tables giving out buttons for the candidates who would be up for election tomorrow, and one selling t-shirts and hats bearing slogans like, "I got my fill at the

Colorectal Obstruction Federation convention!" and "I packed a lot of fun in at the Colorectal Obstruction Federation convention!" The gremlins' fake name was a stand-in, so their shirts really read "The Convention of Fiends convention." It was like "ATM machine" or "PIN number" or "LCD display," and those always made Bel cringe. The two short men giggling on the other side of the table were obviously gremlins in elaborate glamours. The gremlins got the biggest kick out of their joke. The slogans irritated Bel, not because they were puerile, but because of the redundancy of the fake acronym. She already hated that the term "The Convention of Fiends" was the name for the documentation which made all the monsters a part of the same group, the name of the group itself, and the name for the annual gathering of the group. One could be a signatory to The Convention, a member of The Convention, and a representative or guest at The Convention. Of course, the gremlins loved that their little dirty joke was extra cringe-inducing. If Bel had been human, the gremlins would have fed on her irritation, but they irritated their fellow monsters out of habit.

Past the merch table, Bel queued up in the ID badge line. Behind that desk sat a creature wearing a very cheap glamor which made him look like a pasty, mustachioed, balding man with a comb-over. Bel guessed he was a troll. Behind him, a pretty, olive skinned, very silent woman flipped through long, skinny boxes, finding the passes as the man called them out. She, Bel realized, was really a siren. She wasn't allowed to use her true voice on any monster. It was one of the stipulations of the sirens' admittance to The Convention (the document, the group, and the annual gathering). If she needed to speak, she'd type into her phone, and a digital voice would read it out, but she'd picked a job where she could remain silent instead.

Bel reached the front of the line.

"Name?" the pallid man said.

"I'm not a rep. We're with CimBim. I need three passes for the observer section."

"ID?"

Bel pulled her thin wallet out of her back pocket. It was aluminum, only slightly larger than a credit card, and only had a few cards inside, and one was her CimBim ID. (The other four were fake drivers' licenses and credit cards with ridiculous credit limits. Compound interest plus a very long life plus a complete disregard for human rules about theft had made Bel wealthy enough to never need cash.) The man took the card, examined it, and handed it back to her.

This was one of the first places where the plan could have fallen apart. If he'd asked for Long and Esau's CimBim IDs, they would have had to scramble; they hadn't had time to make fake ones. Bel held her breath. To her horror, Long stepped forward, reached past her, and placed his hand on the desk.

The man looked up at Long, then behind them at Esau, then back at Long. Then he turned and spoke to the woman behind him. "Hear that, sweet tits? Three guest passes for these fucking gumshoes here."

Yep, Bel thought. A troll. And he was trying to be nice to appear more human. This was as close as he could get.

The siren passed him three pieces of plastic on three black shoelace lanyards that had "C.O.F. Convention" printed on them in white letters over and over.

The troll handed them all to Bel. "Attach them yourselves, fuckwits. Welcome to the con."

"You're a delight," Bel said.

"Piss off."

The three figuratively pissed off to the main room's entrance. Another line was caused by the bottleneck of ID checks, but it moved smoothly. Bel watched the people in front of her to get the timing just right. The change wasn't exactly at the threshold of the room, as she'd expected, but a few feet inside. The woman two spots in front of her flashed her ID, the door monitor nodded, and she stepped inside the room. Two steps in, her pinned-up curls and pillbox hat disappeared, and the nest of snakes holding position above her head flopped down in relief and then began swaying and tasting the air around her neck and shoulders with flickering tongues.

The man immediately in front of Bel wore a white lab coat and walked with two forearm crutches, his feet firmly pressed together as he hop/stepped. He didn't take either of his hands out of his canes to show his badge. He just stepped up to the monitor and the badge swung from his neck in her direction. She caught it deftly, examined it, released it to swing back to his chest, and motioned him in. Again, he made it two steps before the glamour disappeared, revealing he was a naga, a serpent-shaped creature with no arms or legs. It had been moving within the glamour by coiling itself into a chunk for the torso, then two long loops forming the arms and crutches, then back into the lower torso coil, then down to the third point which had looked like human feet, and then back up into that main trunk body. Once relieved of the glamour, it flopped into a coil on the ground, only its head still raised up out of the pile of green scales. The whole mass swelled slightly and released a bit of the green smoke. Back home in Cambodia, it would turn into this green smoke to pass through and among the roots of trees when hunting humans lost in the woods. Here, it exhaled a relieved sigh and slithered off towards the rows of tables where delegates sat facing the main stage.

Bel came in next, flashed her badge, and walked in. She didn't feel the location where glamours fell away because she looked human except when feeding. "Ready for my mark?" she said into her earpiece.

"Ready," Matt replied.

Esau came next. The woman checking the badges nodded at him and raised her eyebrows, impressed at the quality of his glamour which even made him smell human. He nodded in return and walked past her into the room. Two steps in, Bel said, "Now."

Forty floors away, Matt scowled and balled his fists as

he cast a particularly difficult spell while maintaining his others.

Esau's shoulders rose as though he felt a pinch in his neck. Then his right shoulder bulged, then his left, like two balloons unevenly attached to the same tank of helium. Next, his head lolled forward, and then it began to inflate as it rose. His forehead distended, two lumps behind and above each eye, and these grew until they clearly formed wide, curved, pointed horns. His nostrils flared, then stretched forward and pulled his upper jaw along with them, then the lower. The whites of his eyes filled with black liquid. He blinked, and his irises vanished.

He looked down at his massive hands, then tried to look back at his own horns. "I'm a cow, aren't I?"

"A minotaur. Half bull," Lena said.

"I hate you, Matt," Esau said.

Through the earpiece (normal sized and in a normal human ear, concealed inside the glamour), Matt replied, "It seemed fitting. I know you think I'm the bad guy, but I'm not the only one who has only been half-honest, Esau."

Behind them, Long waved his badge at the woman checking IDs. Neither Lena nor Esau could see her eyes widen, and Long only shrugged in reply, then stepped into the room. Like Lena, his appearance didn't change.

"C'mon," Bel hissed. "We don't have time for this ..." She found herself at such a loss for words she stopped walking.

"If you say 'lover's quarrel'..." Esau started.

Matt came onto the mic again. "Or 'dick measuring contest.' I hate that one, too. Like men can't have a legitimate disagreement."

"I was going to say 'bullshit,' but..."

"Oh," Matt said. "No, that would have been fine. That's funny."

Esau shook his giant, horned head. "No. Bad. Embarrassing to everyone. Glad you caught yourself."

A new voice came over the earpiece. "Hey, um, Ms. Shipwright? Jezebel?" Torreblanca asked. "If it wouldn't distract from the mission, and you have a second, could you take a picture of Esau for me?"

"Radio silence, Torreblanca," Esau said.

"Yessir," Torreblanca said. "Sorry, sir. And I will pay a thousand dollars for the picture, Jezebel."

"Two thousand," Bel said.

"Done. Out."

"Don't worry," Bel said to the massive bull head hiding Esau's. "There's no time. They're coming back into session. Let's get our seats."

The three made their way over to the rows in the back set aside for observers who did not have the credentials to get onto the floor. Long walked down the little aisle first and sat next to a cyclops. Both gave each other polite nods ending in soft blinks, one blink more dramatic than the other two. Then the cyclops goggled at the minotaur coming to sit between the small Chinese man and the woman with the dyed hair. Esau didn't know why his appearance would be surprising to a cyclops, or even if the cyclops was truly surprised, but his eye did look exceptionally open.

Bel scanned ahead of her. The scene looked similar to the previous year's convention which she'd witnessed from almost the exact same spot. Delegates sat on one side of rows of long tables arranged facing the stage. There, behind a lectern, stood the current president of The Convention, a vampire who looked like a young man wearing a gray suit, unnecessary wire-rimmed glasses, and gray dye in the corners of his jet black hair to create the calculated appearance of an intelligent, humble, put-upon bureaucrat rather than a millenia old vicious killing machine. To his right, the vice president of The Convention, a harpie in a carefully tailored black blazer, used a clawed talon to lift a glass of water to her lips because she had no hands. To the president's left sat the secretary, a fetch who looked like a translucent ghost because she hadn't chosen a human's image to copy in order to trick them and feed on them. Beyond the fetch sat the parliamentarian, the King of Trolls, wearing his silver crown and matching silver nose ring, his scaly purple shoulders glinting on the spotlights, the sickly green of the rest of his flesh somehow consuming the light, but not enough to hide the view under the table of his completely naked … everything. His enormous arms rested on the table as though he was sitting, but Bel could see he had to stand on his chair because his legs (and everything else below the table) were so small. His disproportionate frame was an affront as much as his dangling penis, and Bel knew a troll enjoyed any revulsion he caused.

The regional vice presidents were mostly the same, too. Africa was still represented by a hochigan who looked like a tall, thin, Saan man from Botswana with pronounced cheekbones, short gray hair, a long beard, and friendly dark eyes. South America was still represented by a paryton, a half-deer and half-bird. With a coat of shiny black fur, black and gray wings, and his enormous black antlers, he mostly blended into the dark curtain behind the stage. His eyes, bright red and made of fire, leaked little tongues of flame out of their corners, but Bel didn't know what emotion, if any, that revealed. Oceania was still represented by a nasnas, a creature from Borneo which looked like half of a human cut down the middle. It had half a head with no face, half a body with a human face in its chest, one arm, and one leg (which it could hop on), two large bat wings keeping it from falling over as it hopped, and a sheep's tail. The face on its chest watched the president speaking, occasionally frowning by moving its one shoulder down to scrunch the space above its eyes and furrow its brow. Europe was still represented by a banshee from Ireland. She looked like a very handsome older woman with long black hair hanging straight down on either side of her face. Like the sirens, the banshees were not permitted to speak at all during the meeting, since their wail could kill monsters as well as humans. Since the banshees' speech was even more dangerous than the sirens who could only seduce and not kill outright, banshees had to wear a gag. She wore hers with as much dignity as a gagged person can, and sat typing on her phone, probably preparing to use the speech-to-text technology to participate in the discussion.

Two of the regional vice presidents were new. Asia was now represented by a baku, a seemingly shy chimera with an elephant's trunk, rhinoceros' eyes, an ox's tail, and a tiger's paws, who ate human dreams. Bel couldn't read the baku's mood, either, but its trunk was manipulating some papers on the table in front of it, so it wasn't giving the president its full attention. North America's representative had been Apocalmus, the head of the werewolf pack who had exiled Nando. She'd watched Nando rip Apo's throat out with his teeth when both were in their human forms in the middle of King's Cross Station in London the previous summer. Unlike vampires, werewolves couldn't do much when dead except decompose, so the North American delegation had been forced to choose a new regional vice president. The werewolves had been in too much disarray to promote a viable candidate, and Bel hadn't heard who'd won the election, but now she saw it was a mogollon monster, a relative of the bigfoots and wendigos, but from Arizona. The different bigfoot clans tended to keep to themselves and avoid politics, but Bel suspected they must have formed some kind of coalition to manage to elect a candidate of their own to such a high office in The

Convention. This mogollon had gray fur on the top of her head, shoulders, and giant feet, so Bel guessed she was an elder. Despite the serene look on her hairy face, her eyes kept scanning the crowd, and Bel suspected the mogollon felt a lot of anxiety in such a crowded room.

The president raised his ornate and oversized gavel and tapped it on the piece of marble on the lectern. "Well, Not-So-Gentlemonsters, I'm pleased to announce we're now to the end of the changes to the bylaws, so we're to the part you've all been waiting for, the new business items. Our first comes to us from the North America region. Would the maker like to speak to his motion?"

Cassius rose from one of the long tables, slipped behind the other vampires in his delegation and out into the aisle, and then walked toward one of the microphones positioned at intervals down the long hall. He wore his usual pinstripe suit, and he carried a briefcase.

Bel said, "He's starting."

"We read you," Lena said. "Camouflage Team is in position."

"Fire Team One is moving in," Rita said. "C'mon, kids."

"Stay safe, Lena," Bel said.

"You, too. You're in a lot more dangerous place than I am," Lena said.

"Oh, they'll be fine. Trust me," Matt said.

Esau's minotaur teeth ground visibly, and he growled through them, "Everyone stay focused, god dammit."

Cassius cleared his throat, a dry and affected sound meant to quiet the most rambunctious of the monsters (mostly the gremlins who were always making noise and throwing things). This didn't silence the gremlins, but it made Cassius sound pretentious, and Bel suspected that was intentional, too. "Fellow monsters," he said, "last year you saw an elaborate presentation from the necromancer Nigel Marion. He had an ambitious plan to eliminate ten percent of the human population, cast them back to a more primitive time, and reduce the danger they pose to our constant food supply. We passed his NBI handily, so I'm not going to waste all your time with a long, dramatic presentation. The short version is this: As you all know, a new business item is only good for year, and it seemed Mr. Marion's plan was a failure because, though he did manage to acquire the book he planned to use to kill ten percent of the humans, he then lost it, and then he was killed. Killed by a vampire, if the rumors are to be believed. So, a dead NBI, right?"

He turned as much as he could away from the stage, looking back over his shoulder at most of the delegates while still speaking into the microphone. "Wrong! I'm here to announce I acquired the book." He dropped his voice a bit, as though the next details were unimportant, but he made sure the mic picked up his voice. "And the sequel to the book which can even kill monsters." The delegates started to whisper among themselves because of his carefully articulated aside. He raised his voice again. "But that's neither here nor there. What's important is this." He set the briefcase down on the delegates' table next to the microphone. It banged loudly enough to be picked up by the mic. At the sound, the room fell silent again. Cassius clicked the latches, opened the case slowly, almost reverentially, and pulled out a large stack of papers.

"Oh shit," Bel whispered. "He's got a copy of the book down here. We're going to need to go to Plan B." She waited. "Plan B. Do you read me?"

Cassius lifted a stack of papers over his head in one hand. "Fellow monsters, this is the manuscript Nigel Marion made for all of you. I ask you to vote yes on NBI Number One so we can complete the plan we made together last year. Thank you for your time."

"We need to move," Esau said.

Bel nodded quickly, a yeah-yeah-yeah. "Camouflage Team, do you read? Going to Plan B. We have a problem here."

"Yes, um, we have a bit of a problem up here, too," Matt said. "Go to Plan B and do it now." He was obviously straining, his voice knotted like he was lifting something heavy. "Fuck. Do it now. Now!"

"Never work with children or animals."

-W.C. Fields

Chapter 27

The plan went the way plans do; perfectly, then feasibly, then dubiously, then so disastrously it would have been better to have no plan at all.

While Lena and Matt waited at one end of the long hall, around a bend and out of sight in an alcove by an ice machine, Rita and her team approached the floor in a different elevator.

"Okay, children," the teacher said in her usual sing-song voice, "You know your job, right?"

The ten children packed in the elevator ranged in ages

from Tobias who was almost nine to Ericka and Juanito, both five. They managed to look believably like a single class of students on a field trip from some posh private academy largely because of the school uniforms Matt had Meili purchase and overnight to the airport in Vegas. The children all wore mustard yellow polo shirts, navy knee length shorts or skirts, and blue berets with a gold seal advertising "St. Matthew's Academy" followed by the Latin motto, *"monstra vertere in terribiliora monstra"* (turning monsters into more terrifying monsters) and then "Since 1876" (the year of Matt's birth). Matt had tickled himself when designing the seal, but Rita had to admit the kids looked very cute.

The chime announced the group had reached the floor, and the car came to a stomach-bouncing stop, so the children all pushed toward the door. It didn't open immediately, causing a slight traffic jam, some growling and elbowing, and then a stumbling flood of skinny limbs pouring into the hotel's somber hallway, like the blood in Kubrick's *The Shining*, only adorable.

Rita instinctively held out an arm to block the door and waited while the children lined up in the hall, then stepped out of the elevator herself. "Alright, this way everyone." She pressed the headphone into her ear, unmuted herself on her phone, and said, "We're in the hall and in motion. Thirty seconds, Matt."

Matt was ready. "Give me a 'Now' when you need their backs turned."

Roberto and Augustus had started working for Cassius back in Italy after the fall of the Empire but before the reign of Charlamagne. He'd chosen them because of their dependability and lack of ambition. Career military men, they didn't want to take his place. They liked the satisfaction of successfully following an order or completing a mission, and they didn't complain when the mission was to stand guard. This meant, in over a thousand years, they'd done a lot of watching. Cassius could not have predicted their reactions to modern forms of watching, but when the television came onto the scene, he wasn't entirely surprised the men chose to spend their downtime essentially sitting guard, viewing the world through the small screen, waiting to be told what to look at next. It wasn't a problem when they were on duty. Both men were vigilant and held one another accountable as guards should, a habit less essential for vampires who barely needed to sleep, especially if frequently fed. But Bob's newest viewing habits were becoming a problem. He'd shifted from television to YouTube.

Bob was a tall man by modern standards. At 6'3", he was an absolute giant by early medieval ones. He was thin, white, with thick dark eyebrows and an unusually square jaw and a flat, high forehead, like a black and white movie version of Frankenstein's monster. Augy stood at a medieval average height of 5'4", strong and blocky, his voice rough and deep like the keel of a ship running aground. Bob's voice was also deep, but soft and hollow, always conspiratorial unless responding in the affirmative to a direct order. Because of his combination of height and soft voice (and his constant companionship with the much shorter Augy), he'd developed the habit of leaning to the side to speak close to any interlocutor.

He leaned. "I saw this interesting video."

"Yeah?" Augy asked.

"I mean, I know there's a lot out there that's not accurate, but this one got me thinking."

"What was this one about?"

"Birds."

Augy risked a short look up at Bob. "What about 'em?"

"They aren't real."

"What do you mean?"

"They used to be real. There were birds. No one disputes that. But then, at some point, the government replaced them all with drones. Now they can watch us all the time."

"The fuck?" Augy asked.

Bob nodded. "I mean, it might not be true, but it makes you think. Maybe there are no birds."

"Makes you think, huh?"

"Yeah," Bob said.

"Bob, you know that's bullshit, right? We're fucking vampires. We can see better than the humans. We can hear better. Hell, we can fucking smell the birds. Have you ever seen a bird and smelled a drone? Heard any little whirring and clicking gears?"

"No, but that's part of what the video said. They are really advanced technology. Indistinguishable from the real thing."

"Why would the government have to make them so indistinguishable vampires can't even tell the difference, Bob? Did the video explain that?"

"Well, the maker was human. Probably doesn't even know we exist."

"Right. We've talked about this, Bob. You are already a part of a conspiracy. You know you don't have to fear 'The Government' because you know The Convention already has their tendrils …" Augy wriggled his fingers like he was feeling around in mud for hidden worms or reading the guts of a pigeon to see the future. "… all throughout the humans' governments to keep us a secret. So we know what they know. And they don't know half as much as humans think they do. Not just about us. They don't even know as much about humans as, say, Facebook and Google and, hell, your precious YouTube know about humans. If we can keep them all from knowing about us, don't you think we'd know if they had replaced all the birds in the world?"

"Maybe The Convention is in on it."

"In on what?"

"Maybe The Convention knows they replaced all the birds to watch the humans, and we let them because it just gives us a better way to watch the humans, too."

Augy frowned. "Okay, sure, but like, all the birds, Bob?"

"I don't know. Maybe. Or maybe most. Probly most."

"Why so many? Like why do they need to watch all the humans all the time from power lines and shit?"

"They gotta be listening all the time to hear when people start seeing through the bullshit."

"Is this back to the world being flat, Bob? Or the moon landing being faked? Or the Holocaust not being real?"

Bob shrugged. "A lot of stuff is lies, man."

"Goddamit, Bob," Augy grumbled. "You've traveled around the world lots of times. And you know the Holocaust was real. We were fucking there."

"You know my opinion on the world being round. Maybe it is. Or maybe we've just traveled around the edge of the flat disk. I've never flown over Antarctica. And sure, we saw a lot of what the Nazis did with our own eyes. But not all of it. And have you ever gone to the moon, Augy? I'm just saying, it's good to be skeptical."

"Why?"

"Huh?"

"Seriously, why? What's the point of believing maybe the world is flat and the Holocaust and moon landing didn't happen and there are no more fucking birds, Bob? Like, what does that get you?"

"So you don't get tricked by the government. You see

through their lies."

"But you are a vampire, Bob. You think the government is trying to trick you?"

"They're trying to trick everybody."

"Why?"

"So we won't know who is really in control."

"Yeah, but Bob, we know who is really in control. The conspiracy is us, man. We don't need to trick ourselves into thinking the world is round just so we can travel all over the globe run by monsters. What does any of it explain that helps you at all, Bob?"

Bob nodded for a while. "I guess it's the thing you said," he admitted.

"That it makes you feel smarter than other people?"

Bob slumped a little. "Yeah, it's probly that a little bit."

"But Bob, you are smarter already. You know about The Convention. You're a goddamned vampire, Bob. The humans don't know we exist. You don't need to know human bullshit conspiracy theories. You are the smart one."

"Yeah." Bob sounded unsatisfied.

The two men stood in silence for a moment.

"Somebody should make a YouTube video about how The Convention is secretly controlling everything," Bob said.

"No," Augy said, shaking his head. "No, they shouldn't."

"Why not?"

"Because then we'd have to kill them and anyone who watched their video, Bob. We're the ones keeping the secret, remember?"

"Oh, that's a good point."

Augy looked at Bob. "YouTube is rotting your brain, man."

"It's the algorithm."

"The what?"

"It's a conspiracy by the government to hide the videos that tell the truth and keep us docile."

"That's not the government, Bob. That's us. Mostly the trolls, but also CimBim keeping the truth from the humans. It's our conspiracy, Bob. You're falling for lies we tell to keep the humans from knowing what we don't want them to know. You're like, I don't know, like a spider stuck in its own web or some shit. Like getting high on your own supply. I don't know what the right metaphor is."

"Like Copernicus?"

Augy frowned. "Huh?"

"Like he knew the world was round, but he pretended he didn't know because he wasn't allowed to say it was round. Only the opposite?"

"No, Bob, the world isn't flat."

"But, like, as a metaphor."

"How so?"

"Like we're in the conspiracy but shouldn't believe the conspiracy we're telling the humans to believe."

"So, we're like the Church?"

Bob leaned over Augy. "I'm just saying, beavers aren't fish."

"What the fuck are you talking about?"

"The Catholic church says beavers are fish. Look it up. People wanted to be able to eat meat during Lent. Not allowed to eat meat. But you could eat fish. So when people asked if they could eat beavers, the Church said, 'They swim in rivers like fish. Guess they're fish.' But beavers aren't fish. So, like, believing our own conspiracy is like making Copernicus say the world is flat when we know it's round."

"Yeah, but they really did think it was flat. And you think it's flat."

"Because I want to eat meat during Lent, man. That's the metaphor."

"Now I'm confused," Augy said.

"They want you to be confused."

"Okay, but who is the 'they' in this metaphor?"

"We are the 'they.'"

"So we want to confuse ourselves?"

"Maybe. Makes you think, doesn't it? When was the last time you smelled a bird?"

Both men sniffed.

"You smell that?" Augy asked.

"Wolves."

"And kids." Bob sniffed again. "And confusion. Irritated confusion sweat."

"That's me," Augy said. "But the wolves and kids are that way." He pointed down the hall.

"And stinky old man. And a woman with lavender oil in her hair who uses Secret antiperspirant."

"Yeah, they're that way." Bob hooked a thumb in his direction. "Funny that the Secret isn't really a secret. Makes you think."

"No, it doesn't," Augy said.

The pair watched as Rita and the kids turned into their part of the hall and walked towards them.

"Kid werewolves," Augy grumbled. "The Convention is fuckin' weird. Who brings kids to The Convention?"

"School field trip," Bob said. "Gotta admit, they're cute for werewolves. In their little uniforms."

"Now children," Rita said to the silent children, "be sure to keep your voices down in the halls. People might be sleeping."

"Hey, can you guys help me?"

Bob and Augy snapped around to find a man had snuck up on them. They hadn't smelled, heard, or seen him approaching, and that surprised them both. He looked like a human in his late twenties or early thirties, handsome but a bit discombobulated, in the part of a drunken stupor where walking straight becomes challenging. Only he didn't smell drunk. Or human. Or smell at all.

"I think I had too much to drink at the bar," he said, "and I need to find my room key." He started fishing roughly in the pocket of his jeans. "And I went outside. And I don't know why because my room is here." He motioned to the hall generally by flicking his wrist in an uncertain circle. "But then, like, the sun was so bright. And then it fell out of the sky onto the sidewalk. So that was weird. And I picked it up and put it in my pocket with my room key. So, like, what should I do with this?"

He pulled his hand out of his pocket, then turned it and opened his fist. And there, resting on his palm, was an orb about eight inches in diameter, something which couldn't possibly have fit in his hand or pocket. It glowed as brightly as a 60 watt bulb, then a 100 watt bulb, the light increasing exponentially until Bob and Augy couldn't see the man, the hallway, anything at all except the pocket star the drunk man claimed to have found on the sidewalk.

The vampires couldn't feel any heat, but they reacted instinctually, yanking their suit coats around and over their face with one hand and pushing out their other to try to block the rays of the little sun as much as possible, perhaps hoping to smack the orb out of the man's hand. Even through the fabric of their coats, the light was still blinding, and neither managed to make contact with the source with their other flailing, scratching hands.

Nothing else mattered. Not the strange sounds of fabric rustling and rubber tennis shoes plopping behind them. Not the tiny thumps of soft pads on carpet. Only the danger of the sun mattered. Then both men were knocked forward from behind. Augy and Bob had expected pain. And the pain was in the right places: their backs, their arms, their legs. It was not the sizzling heat they'd expected, but in the moment, they couldn't contemplate why this particular sun ripped at their skin instead of burning it. And the sound was all wrong. The hissing of cooking meat was a growling and crunching. The sun was tearing their ligaments and breaking their bones, chewing into their insides rather than searing their outsides. Instinct still ruled, but now their bodies wanted to fight, to throw punches at the light, to kick at it, to carve through it with their sharp nails, to bite it with their true teeth. Yet they held their eyes as tightly shut as possible and could only wriggle a shoulder, a single knee, because the light was pulling at their wrists and ankles, chewing beneath their chins, tilting their teeth away from their bodies towards that horrible light, that awful, stupid drunk who accidentally brought the sun up the elevator in his pocket. It had all happened so fast, and then…

It stopped. A wolf barked, loud and sharp and fast. Then another couple barked responses, other orders. The crunching sounds came to an end. The light on the other side of their eyelids disappeared. Bob and Augy blinked. Bob found he was face down on the hotel's thin carpet, but he could look out of one eye and see Augy next to him. Augy was still alive, too, though he was facing the wall and couldn't turn his head to see his tall friend. Bob couldn't feel enough of his own body to take stock of his situation, but by looking at Augy, he had a pretty good sense of where he stood. Or lay. On the hallway floor. Without his arms or legs attached. He could hear an older woman's voice pinched into a sing-song lilt.

"Good job, children. See? The vampires will live because we didn't take their heads off completely, but you did an excellent job of cutting tendons so they can't move, and it will take them a long time to grow their arms and legs back again. It's against the law to kill another monster who is a party to The Convention. But this is … well, it's probably still illegal but it's forgivable. Just bending the rules. Extreme circumstances. I'm sure these gentlemen understand. Gentlemen, we apologize for the inconvenience. Children, tell the gentlemen you're sorry for ripping their arms and legs off."

A few children said, "Sorry," and others intoned, "Sorry for ripping your arms and legs off," and some even sounded genuinely apologetic while others sounded like they were apologizing through broad, bloody smiles. They were little monsters, after all.

Bob didn't respond to the apology. He did find he could choke out a few words, despite missing many of the muscles in his cheeks and much of the soft tissue of his throat. "Augy," he said. It came out as a gurgled whisper, and then he coughed up some blood and some tissue that certainly belonged on the inside. "Hey, Augy," he tried again. "See? The sun isn't real, either."

Augy did not respond. By choice.

Ann had been hired as a temp that very day. She was young for a vampire, turned during her valley girl days in the nineties in L.A. when she was in her early twenties. She'd wanted to find a job in acting, but she'd ended up working as a production assistant at a studio, then getting other secretarial work, then attracting the eye of a low level bureaucrat vampire, Jonathan, who thought she'd make a good permanent secretary for his office. He'd seemed nice enough at first. He didn't try and get her to make a porn video at her interview, and for Hollywood, that was decent. Then he'd killed her and turned her. That asshole was probably a delegate downstairs, she thought now, but she'd left his employment and bopped around for a decade on her own before finding her way to temp work. Now she aspired to rise up in the ranks of the vampires and someday be Jonathan's boss. It would take a while, but he'd given her time.

When she'd received the call from Cassius about the gig, she'd jumped at it. Cassius was an up-and-comer, and vampires knew it. But when she'd arrived, he'd explained the job was pretty menial. She had to make photocopies of a couple books without reading them. Easy. She didn't like reading anyway. She set one of the books aside (not sure which was which) and started on the other, dividing it up into stacks to copy, carefully keeping the pages face down.

She'd also been directed to guard the books with her life. Only there was this big giant golem guy in the office and two guards just out the door, so guarding seemed pretty unnecessary.

The golem annoyed her. He didn't help at all, just stood there in the workroom with his arms crossed. The guards seemed like good possible connections for the future, but she didn't get much of a chance to talk with them before they were on shift. Cassius left for his big presentation, and she stood over the copier, swiping through TikTok, bored.

When she heard the commotion outside the office door, she almost mistook it for background noise in the video she was watching.

"Did you hear that?" she asked the golem.

It nodded.

"What do we do?"

The golem shrugged, then walked around the partition and stood in front of the reception desk.

She remembered what Cassius had said about protecting the books. He'd been unequivocal about the nature of the job and the consequences of failure. Also, he'd said something about a locker of weapons, just in case.

"Hey," she shout-whispered to the golem, "where does Cassius keep the guns?"

Josef did not reply.

"Worthless," she muttered. "This job sucks."

"The guards are down," Rita said into her earpiece, then looked down the hall to see Matt and Lena jogging in their direction. Matt was back to his prim, coiffed self, though Rita and the children hadn't seen the drunken version with the sun in his pocket. That enchantment had been for Augy and Bob's eyes only. From the perspective of the children, the two vampires had suddenly turned to a blank space in the hall and then, just as suddenly, tried to wrap their heads in their coats and flailed around blindly while the children leapt out of their clothing, transformed, pounced on them, and delimbed them.

A few of the young wolves growled at the figures approaching their "kills," instinctively defending the meat from intruders who were not in their pack, but Rita, quickly but casually pulling her coat over her naked body, made a very human shushing sound, and the children quieted.

"Holy fuck," Lena moaned at the carnage in the hall. The separated arms and legs had been yanked off violently enough to toss the blood onto the ceiling, and splashes arced all over the vertical stripes of eggshell and white wallpaper. The curves of splatter and the pooling blood clashed with the brown, blue, and cream renaissance-era design printed on the carpet. This would not clean up easily. The puppies sat patiently or padded around softly in the blood, guarding their victims' bodies and showing off their success. "You all did so well," Lena told the young wolves. "And you look so damned cute." Half to herself she muttered. "It's really disconcerting." Then, to the children, "You are such good, good … children."

They wagged their tails. More blood flicked onto the walls.

"Yes, nicely done," Matt assented. "Okay, next step. What's inside, Rita?"

The teacher, who looked like a fit woman in her late sixties and was easily two hundred years old, plopped down onto her knees, her long costume coat flapping up onto her lower back, revealing a human butt Lena didn't want to see but couldn't help but admit was in good shape for a "woman" of her "age." Rita stuck her nose against the bottom of the door and inhaled slowly, then sniffed a few more times quickly, frowned, then sniffed again. "We have a problem."

"Problem?" Lena said.

"Problems." Rita stood. "There's another vampire inside. And your friend. The golem. Or another golem who smells the same. Or they have a pillar of sand and dirt in the middle of the room that smells like it has its arms crossed."

"You can smell that?"

Rita nodded. "Angry and dirt. But not furious. Just stern."

"Oh, well that's nice. But what is Josef doing here?"

Matt frowned. "They captured him. Golems can be enslaved. He's going to fight us if they tell him to."

"Can you free him?" Lena asked.

"I doubt it," Matt said. "Remember when we first met in Costa Rica? I would have captured Josef then, if I could have, just so we could have had a conversation without the danger of me getting killed. And I had time to plan that all out. But golems are not easily captured. I'll bet Cassius had help. Which means Josef might not be easily controlled when Cassius is downstairs. It might be ordered to guard the book, but it might not be ordered to kill us, specifically. Do you think you can get through to it? Make it find a loophole?"

Lena shrugged. "It *is* pretty legalistic."

Rita stood. "They know we're here. The vampire is listening to us right now." She sniffed again. "And she has-" And then Rita leapt forward down the hall, tackling Lena and Matt. They heard the signature chick-chick while they were still in the air, and they'd just hit the ground when the shotgun blast punched a hole in the door and the hallway wall where Rita had been standing.

Rita rolled off the human and warlock and bounced into a crouch. She motioned with one hand, and the children ran away down the hall, then stopped twenty feet away and waited.

Matt watched Rita's gestures and decided to try his own. He sat up and leaned his back on the wall, hoping to make a less likely target. He pointed to Rita, then motioned to his leg and kicked the air, then pointed to the door. Then he pointed to himself and whispered loudly, "I'll throw a grenade." He held up his empty hand. Then something flashed inside. It was an MK2, an American grenade from 1918, fondly referred to as a "pineapple hand grenade." Matt had chosen that one because it was the most obvious design he could think of. The grenade disappeared again.

Rita nodded. She pivoted on the balls of her feet, then crawled carefully under the hole in the door. On the other side, she reared back and kicked at the base of the door with one bare foot. To Lena's surprise, the door swung open easily. Rita rolled away as a second burst from the shotgun blasted the bottom of the doorframe nearest her position. She didn't escape completely. Buckshot and splinters of wood caught her hip, shredding her long coat, and Lena could see the little blooms as blood soaked through the heavy canvas fabric.

Lena could also see Matt remaining next to her, his back against the wall. She could not see the version of Matt who leapt across the doorway and threw the grenade inside, but she heard another clap of thunder as the shotgun sprayed the empty space in the middle of the doorway, right in the chest of the apparition she couldn't see.

Luckily for the crew in the hallway, Ann didn't focus on the effects of her perfect shot on the man who leapt across the doorway. If she had, she surely would have noticed he didn't seem affected by a chest full of buckshot. Instead, she watched the grenade bounce across the floor of the little anteroom and come to rest right in front of the golem's left foot. Josef didn't move or react at all. Ann decided it was not her job to save the golem. She leapt behind the partition separating the reception area from the workroom, knowing her minimalist desk and the false wall wouldn't offer much protection, then considered herself lucky when the grenade did not explode immediately and she had time to scramble behind the work table.

The grenade did go off. Or, at least, it made the sound of a grenade going off, and it produced a flash of superheated air filled with tiny fragments of metal which did not exist. Josef was not bothered by any of this. It had no eyes or ears. Its perception of the world was more elemental, perhaps spiritual or magnetic or based on the plucking of the one dimensional strings at the quantum level. The distinctions get a bit blurry and metaphysical, but essentially Josef was aware of the material world existing around it, not the illusions Matt could toss about within the space, since those weren't made up of the particles resonating as potential material for its own golem body. From Josef's perspective, Ann fired into the empty doorway, then leapt into the workroom for no reason. And that was fine with Josef. It didn't really care how any of this went down. It didn't even want to be there.

Josef did feel a small pang of regret when ten wolf cubs ran into the room. It didn't want to kill children or animals, and these were both.

The wolves made a semicircle around Josef but didn't charge. They growled, but the children were uncertain what they were supposed to do. Rita's signals had directed them to attack the golem, but their noses told them he was both a friend from camp and an inanimate object. They had not been trained to hunt seven-foot-tall statues in the forests of Camp Biugfoot.

Then Rita, in her full wolf form, bolted into the room just beyond the ring of children and ran as fast as she could for the right opening into the workroom. That got Josef moving. He'd been ordered to guard the books, and she was heading in that direction. When Josef moved, the wolves all leapt at its back, giving Rita a chance to pass it. As she did so, she began to shift, forming into her half-wolf, half-human form to fight the vampire.

Ann was waiting. Confronted by an elongated, enormous half-wolf creature, Ann was startled into firing a little more quickly than she should have, and the buckshot ripped off a chunk of Rita's shoulder and ribs instead of her head. Then the huge clawed half-hand, half-paw swatted the rifle out of the vampire's hands. Rita lunged at her with her teeth, and Ann stuck a forearm in Rita's mouth, then punched her in the head before the wolf could bite her arm off. The blow knocked Rita back and half onto the worktable in the middle of the room. Rita tried to push herself back up, but her huge hand swam on the stacks of copied pages, then slid them off the table. Meanwhile, Ann, moving at vampire speed, leapt at her, fingernails pointed forward like speartips, and jabbed punctures into Rita's stomach and chest. Mostly to guard her exposed torso, Rita bent inwards and struck out at Ann's face as an afterthought, her claws slashing the young woman's cheek so deeply she revealed the vampire's cheekbone and a swath of her skull above her ear. This barely bled and began to heal immediately, as did Rita's abdominal wounds. Ann took a step back and circled, and Rita rolled off the table and made the same arc, keeping the island between them.

Ann raised her hands like a boxer, but with each flat like a blade, her bloody nails pointed slightly in. "You're too old for this, you know?" she said. Then she jabbed three times before ducking under one swing of Rita's claws. The punches left three new bleeding wounds. "I can do this forever. Like, literally forever." She jabbed three more times. Rita's blood splattered on the remaining sheets of paper on the work island. Rita lunged with her teeth, but she had to dodge back and ended up with a sliced ear for the attempt.

They circled.

"How much blood you got left in those old bones, bitch?" Ann asked, smirking. "Let's find out, shall we?"

Josef flung the snapping wolves off its back with barely a thought. The cubs hit the walls with wet thuds and even more sickening yelps. Josef had been careful not to kill them, but it wanted them stunned so it could get back into the office and fulfill its order unimpeded. It rounded the corner and saw the werewolf and vampire circling the office island, and it was about to attack when it heard Lena's voice.

"Josef?"

Her voice was tentative, hesitant, but enough. Josef stopped and turned to see her standing in the blasted doorway.

"Josef?" she repeated.

It couldn't decide what to do.

"Don't kill me, please," she said. Her statement was only half a joke, and the other half broke Josef's heart. Yet it had no choice. It had to follow the imp's orders. Only the imp had told it to pretend to serve Cassius. And Cassius hadn't told it to kill Lena. But it had to maintain the ruse; that was obligatory.

Josef was a monster made of dust and rock and sand, but, more fundamentally, of rage. It was rage made patient, rage which could sit in an attic in the synagogue of Prague for centuries, could march along the bottom of the Atlantic ocean for decades, rage that could be sustained from pogrom to pogrom so whenever the debts got too high and the Gentiles decided to forget they'd demanded a banking sector in their economy, remembered their prohibition against usury, and slaughtered the Jews as a bloody form of medieval debt relief, Josef could be there to get revenge for the last time and the time before that. It could take all that anger and hold it in, use it to sustain its form with nothing more than the particles dancing in the rays of sunlight coming through the attic's tiny windows. Josef was those motes made into murder. And now it couldn't decide where to aim all that wrath.

Dustmotes, when indecisive, swirl.

Josef turned into a cloud, and then it began to spin. The larger pieces of sand gathered the force of hail, then sandpaper, then nettles, working their way towards bullets. The cubs shrank back, some slipping out the door between Lena's legs, others hiding behind the two chairs in the foyer's corners, whimpering. Lena held her place in the doorway by grasping the frame with both hands. The wind pulled at her curly hair, dust trapped inside, and granules of sand hit her cheek and the side of her neck and her exposed arm like slaps.

"Josef!" she cried. "You are my friend! You are good! You punch Nazis! Let me take the books! Don't let the Nazis get the books!"

But how could Josef do otherwise and fulfill its obligation to pretend to serve Cassius? Cassius had given orders. If it let Lena get the books, Cassius would know. And it had to maintain the pretense. It had no choice. It belonged to the imp now.

Standing in the hall behind Lena, Matt worked on the spell. He muttered words, gestured with his hands like he was poking at some invisible machinery in front of him. Slowly, far too slowly, those gestures smoothed until his hands were forming a sphere, molding it, turning it, and then he stepped past Lena into the maelstrom. While the sand had only been stinging her, at his new distance it pelted his face with such force his glamour was stretched off his skin, and the real skin beneath, that frail, ancient parchment paper flesh, was punctured by tiny pins of fast flying sand. Then Matt pushed the spell forward, and suddenly the golem was contained. All the particles outside his sphere dropped to the ground. The wolves behind the couches scurried out the doorway into the hall. Lena stood aside, gesturing them to safety.

Matt began to shrink the swirling ball of dust. "Got him," he said.

"It," Lena corrected Matt's pronoun automatically.

"Got it."

The sphere was ten feet in diameter, then seven, then five, then three, now clearly floating above the ground. When it was down to two, Matt continued to gesture in the direction of the sphere with one hand, but he touched his earpiece with the other, just a quick tap to unmute. And in that brief moment, the sphere distended as though it had been punched, and it began to grow again.

And then the roar of a shotgun blast came from the workroom. Drywall and splinters of the stud in the partition wall's upper corner sprayed down into the room.

Lena could hear Bel's voice in her ear: "Camouflage Team, do you read? Going to Plan B. We have a problem here."

"Yes, um, we have a bit of a problem here, too," Matt said. "Go to Plan B and do it now." He crouched, worrying about the next discharge of the shotgun but straining to hold Josef in place as the sphere grew, shrank, and grew again. "Fuck. Do it now. Now!"

"There is only the fight to recover what has been lost / And found and lost again and again: and now, under conditions / That seem unpropitious. But perhaps neither gain nor loss. / For us, there is only the trying. The rest is not our business."

-T.S. Eliot

Chapter 28

Esau watched the scene ahead of him but kept turning to look at the cyclops. Now the creature's one eye was narrowed in a kind of curious skepticism, then a bit of distaste. Esau resisted the temptation to say it aloud, but he couldn't help thinking it: *He's giving me the stink eye.*

"Plan B," Bel hissed and thwapped him in the thigh hard enough to raise a welt.

"I heard. But when?"

And then the cyclops' eye flew as wide as it would go,

wider than it had been when they'd arrived, and the monster raised a shaky hand and pointed at Esau. It made a bellowed ululation that may have been in another language or may have just been a surprised attempt to find a word. Esau looked at his hands and knew his glamour was gone. He jumped up and began walking down the main aisle, past the plastic chains cordoning off the visitor's area, past the two volunteers checking ID badges for delegate certification (a snake woman who "stood" on her coiled tail at human height and flicked her tongue as he passed by, and a wizened old gremlin standing on a high stool holding a number clicker in one hand and a clipboard in the other who only had time to shout, "Hey!"), past the first few rows of long tables where delegates pointed and gawked and then began to lick their lips and crawl over the tops of their tables in his direction.

Well, Esau thought, *this is a 100% inescapable death scenario. But it will be a dramatic way to go.* Without stopping, he pulled his Ruger out of the holster, pointed it ahead of him at Cassius, and shouted, "Hey, vampire, if you give me the book and let me walk out of here with it right now, I won't shoot you in the face. You have five seconds to decide."

It was a ridiculous amount of time in a room full of creatures who could run faster than the human eye. They were counting on the monsters' morbid curiosity.

"Five!" Esau shouted, still striding forward.

Bel took off from her seat at her fastest sprint. Esau

couldn't see her pass him, just register a blur in his peripheral vision and feel a gust of air whoosh through the sweaty armpit of the arm holding up the gun.

"Four!" he shouted.

Bel appeared in front of Cassius, her back to him, her arms wide. "Master, I'll save you!" she yelled theatrically.

"Three!"

To prove vampires can not only move but can sometimes speak faster than they can think, Cassius said, "Bel? I really don't need you to… And why didn't you…?"

Then Esau shouted "Two!" and pulled the trigger.

They'd rehearsed this part sixteen times so she could get the timing just right, though never with Esau's special silver hollow-point bullets with liquid silver cores. And that was lucky because, during those practice sessions, when she moved too soon it was obvious, and when she moved too late, she got shot, and that still hurt even a vampire. This time, he fired on Two as planned, and she waited just long enough (muscle memory, no time for contemplation) and ducked. Cassius easily could have ducked as well, but because he couldn't see through her head, he didn't know which direction to go. Esau was too far away and in motion, and it was a pistol after all, not built for long range accuracy, so despite all his practice, even the luckiest shot would have been off. And this was the luckiest shot. It passed through the space where Bel's head had been and caught Cassius just below the right cheekbone. The casing ripped off when it smashed through his molars, and some of the liquid silver inside the bullet was left in his head while most of the expanding metal took a chunk about the size and shape of a can of soda out of the back of his skull, to the right of his spine.

Meanwhile, Bel twisted on the balls of her feet, pistoned back and upwards, and grabbed the stack of copied pages out of Cassius' hands. Every time she'd practiced, she said the same word at this point as she mimed the motion, so she said it now with the real prop in hand. "Yoink!"

Next was the hardest part of all. She had to get back to Esau, grab him, and get out before thirty or forty vampires landed on him. He knew the speed of her impact would break his ribs, and he was ready for it, but the thought made him clench his stomach muscles, so all his subsequent shots were a little bit off the mark. Still, he turned and started firing at all the monsters on either side of him as quickly as he could. He knew he needed to create a ring. As monsters dove backwards to avoid being shot, the ones behind them would have a moving wall of bodies to climb over before they could get to him. He needed that wall to be as wide and round as possible, with only Bel's entrance available.

And even with this plan in place, it would not have been possible. The curious onlookers, watching the drama unfold, had spilled into the aisle all the way at the back of the room. Bel could see, even when she reached

Esau, she'd have nowhere to go. Some monsters were running for the exit, some were diving under tables, but others were jumping up onto those same tables and galloping towards them, vampires bounding gracefully, some pulling guns or swords, werewolves in their half-wolf forms scrabbling over and around other frightened monsters, claws already bloody, saliva hanging from their retracted lips. A minotaur (a real one) was grabbing tables and throwing them back over his head to make a straight path for himself. All the monsters were converging on the lone human firing into their midst. In many cases, the bullets didn't even slow them down. His pistol only had sixteen bullets, and then he would have to swap, and she knew he didn't have the time.

They'd discussed Plan C. He would keep shooting until he couldn't anymore, then keep swinging. She would run for the door without him and hope the smell of human blood would distract the monsters enough to let her get out the door. Bel was of the opinion a plan which relied on one of the participants dying horribly was a shitty plan, even if the participant was a human, and Esau had agreed even though he was the one who had come up with Plan C. Long hadn't voiced an opinion about Plan C at the time, but Bel noticed he'd frowned at it and then shaken his head slightly.

She hoped Long had started for the door just as she'd started running, but she doubted the old man could have made it. What she needed now was fire, something to destroy the manuscript before both she and Esau were killed. She didn't know if Esau brought anything explosive. They hadn't discussed a Plan D, but she hoped so.

Instead of grabbing Esau on her shoulder and continuing, she came to a halt right behind him, back to back. He was so startled, he tried to turn to fire on her, but she followed his movement, keeping her back against his, until he realized who she was. "Got any white phosphorus?" she shouted. "Burn the book!" She jabbed at a nearby gremlin, hitting it in the throat with her fingernails and removing its head entirely. *Well*, she thought, *that's a clear violation of the Convention. That's that. I'm donezo.*

Esau shot a monster.

"Nope," he called over his shoulder. "Do you know the best thing about dying?"

He shot another.

"We won't care what these fuckers do once we're gone."

In the room above, Matt ducked down to avoid another round from the shotgun. The sphere of pulsing energy wasn't holding. It throbbed like a beating heart as Josef tried to break free. Matt felt each punch like a weight pushing him down towards the floor. His peripheral vision darkened, and he knew he was going to pass out. He stumbled a bit to one side, falling onto one knee. From there, he could see back into the workroom. He couldn't see the vampire with the shotgun, but he saw something more important: The window. The shattered window had been replaced by a sheet of plywood and another sheet of some darkened plexiglass, probably bulletproof, probably harder than stone. That gave Matt an idea.

From his prone position near the ground, he swung the ball of energy away from himself and away from the nearby entrance to the workroom, all the way to his left. It smashed into the drywall so hard it broke the pine two-by-fours and made it all the way into the next suite. He didn't wait to see if that room was occupied; if the people inside hadn't run from the shotgun, they deserved to be hit by a trapped golem. Instead, he froze the ball there in the middle of the neighboring room. To his great relief, the jostling had startled the trapped monster. Josef stopped pushing on the walls of the sphere momentarily, probably trying to identify its new surroundings. Matt could feel the weight lift off his shoulders like a physical release. His strength came back in a surge. Gripping the air in front of him as though holding something physical, he swung the ball back into the room, intentionally bashing into the side of the hole between rooms again, shaking the monster. This time Josef recovered more quickly, sensing it was once again near its captor. It started to push.

"Oh, no you don't," Matt said. This time, with a little more room to ramp up the motion, he flung the ball of swirling dust the other direction. It hit the edge of the partition between rooms and took out a third of it, but that barely slowed it, and it smashed into the wall in the workroom, not hitting the window, with its bulletproof glass, but aimed at the space in the wall right next to it. Matt expected more resistance than the interior wall, but he was relieved to find there wasn't much. The wall wasn't load bearing, he'd hit a spot between the steel girders (expecting they framed the window and therefore similarly framed the space next to it), and the stone exterior wall of the casino was fake because, well, it's in Las Vegas, and everything there is fake.

The ball punched a rough hole in the wall and flew out over the strip. Matt closed his eyes and maintained his concentration.

"Is he…?" Lena asked.

"Not yet," Matt said, cutting her off with a rude hand in her face. He pinched his eyes shut and focused. He didn't need to direct the ball, just imagine where he wanted it to go. He didn't even know if it had to head north or south or east or west. It just had to go to a place close enough he could hold on until it got there, but far enough Josef couldn't come right back.

He pictured it.

He held on.

Josef kept flying.

Somewhere to the west, a young couple on their

honeymoon and the pilot of their helicopter tour had a very close encounter with a UFO over Lake Mead. Had it hit them, Josef probably would have been freed. But Matt didn't know his Nevada and Arizona geography well. Otherwise, he would have aimed for Lake Mead itself. Instead, he held on longer, the ball accelerating every second, now flying faster than any military aircraft, and then, just as Matt pictured it in his mind, the ball slowed, made a steep arc, and descended into the Grand Canyon, more than 6000 feet from its flying height, into the Colorado River.

And then Matt let go.

The magic sphere disappeared. Josef was a swirling bubble of dust and air at the bottom of a churning river. The air escaped upwards. The dirt turned under. Josef could not fulfill its duty to deceive Cassius, so it couldn't obey the imp. It flowed away down the river between the federal land of the Grand Canyon-Parashant National Monument and the Hualapai Indian Reservation, in the shadow of the canyon. As it dissipated, Josef felt relieved to be nothing more than silt traveling to Mexico.

Back in the office, the gun which had gone off had been caught sideways in Rita's jaws. Ann had risked lunging for it and had given Rita just enough time to leap over the island at her, but Ann had swung around and protected herself from the werewolf with the gun's barrel. Acting on instinct, the wolf had tried to yank the gun out of Ann's hands, swinging her huge head from side to side, pulling Ann off the floor. In the jostling, it had gone off, blowing a hole in the partition. But Ann held on to the gun, bracing herself by widening her legs between the island and the photocopier which still hummed and churned out pages covered in neat rows of deadly words. Rita swung her so hard to one side, she bashed her head against the cabinet above the copier, then so hard the other way, she slammed into the top of the island, but she held.

"You're getting tired," Ann almost sang, laughing to hide the pain of the blows even from herself. In truth, she felt trapped, too. If she removed either hand from the gun to jab at the wolf, she'd lose her grip. If she kicked, she'd come flying out of her space. But dogs, she remembered, are stupid. They will yank and swing at a toy until they exhaust themselves.

There was nothing else Rita could do but swing and yank. If she let go of the gun, it would be pointed in her face and fired faster than she could move. And she was getting tired. So, so tired.

Then Matt's flying ball-of-Josef crashed through the partition and made a hole in the wall. A dog might not have calculated the opportunity. Ann didn't. But Rita had time to decide what she was going to do and even contemplate a quip she might employ as she did it. She swung again, smashing Ann into the cabinet, and since it was now splinters of pressboard, the wood lacerated her badly. Yet the vampire was healing by the time Rita smashed her down into the island again.

Ann came up laughing. Sure, it hurt, but it hadn't

accomplished anything. *The old wolf is just wearing herself out,* she thought. *Right?*

Then Rita charged forward. Ann's pinned legs lost their purchase on the island and copier machine, and her feet couldn't touch the ground. She didn't think to let go of the shotgun until it was too late. Rita leapt, and both monsters sailed through the new hole in the wall.

The sunlight caught Ann full force in the face, though Rita's body provided some shade for her torso. Her arms caught fire almost as quickly as her hair and the exposed skin of her face and neck, and the burning flesh stuck to the barrel of the shotgun. Meanwhile, still acting on instinct, Rita clawed at Ann's legs and torso with her hind legs.

And then both were tumbling and burning and bleeding as they fell and fell and fell.

Clive couldn't imagine things possibly getting any worse. He stumbled down the strip, a Hurricane in a large plastic cup in one hand. The cup said Harrah's, but he couldn't remember going there to buy the drink. He could vaguely remember he'd told his wife they were about to be very, very rich. He'd told her twice, once in the hotel room at the Flamingo. Susan hadn't believed him, and he'd called her some pretty awful names. She'd taken the kids back to Modesto. Then he called home to apologize, and when she still didn't believe him, he threatened to keep all the money for himself. He'd spent the whole next day (days? a week?) calling every major news outlet he could think of off the top of his head (TV stations), then the ones he remembered (radio stations), then the ones he had to look up (newspapers). No one had believed him. No one even wanted to look at the video, let alone give him gobs of money for it. And since Susan hadn't believed him first, now he felt fairly certain it was all her fault.

He didn't realize he'd made his way back to the street in front of The Venetian when he called her back, but as the phone rang, he looked around. Most people seemed to be walking with intention at this stretch, since there wasn't a giant fountain or pirate show to see down this way. *Or is it up this way*, he wondered. *I'm all turned around. But isn't this where…?*

Susan picked up. "What is it, Clive?"

"It's your fault, is what it is."

"What are you talking about?"

"No one will believe me. Because you didn't believe me." Clive considered this and decided it still tracked after he'd said it out loud.

"Believe you about what?"

"The video! The woman on fire who fell out the window of the hotel. I got it on video. It's like, really dramatic and pretty much the greatest video ever."

"So put it up on TikTok or YouTube or something."

"No, Susan, you stupid … You don't get it. It's worth money. Like, people will pay to see this."

"Have they paid?"

"No, but they haven't seen it yet."

"Why not?"

"They don't want to see it."

"Maybe because it sounds gross," Susan speculated.

"No, people love gross stuff."

"Clive, are you drunk?"

"No. Yes. I mean, so what? It's Vegas, and I have this video, and no one will believe me."

"Clive, what's going on with you?"

"What do you mean? I have this video!"

"You've been acting really weird. Are you cheating on me?"

Clive hit his forehead with the heel of his hand. It hurt, but he kept doing it as he tried to force the thoughts from his brain. "No, I'm not crazy and I'm not drunk and I'm not even cheating this time."

"This time?" she screamed.

Her voice poked his eardrum so hard he pulled the phone away from his head, then held it in front of his mouth and shouted back, "Goddammit! You aren't listening to me, either! I saw a woman on fire fall out of a forty story window and no one will believe me!"

"Well, Clive, maybe no one will believe you because you're a cheating liar. You want to see something on fire? Come back home quick enough and all your shit will be piled up in the front yard, and maybe it won't all have burned to ashes by the time you get here." And she hung up.

"Fuck!"

And then he heard the first loud bang from inside the casino. From his distance, he couldn't make out exactly what had happened, but it looked like there was a hole punched in the wall on the fortieth floor.

He squinted. "That's about where…"

And then something leapt out of the hole. And caught fire. Again.

"Goddammit!" he shouted, but he felt a little better than he had moments before. He tapped on his phone's face, trying to pull up the camera. He took a selfie of the top of his head, then one of himself yelling at the screen, then a picture of the cement in front of him, and then got the video rolling.

"Did you all just see that?" he shouted. He looked from side to side. A few people were stopping and looking in the direction he was pointing his phone.

"What?" a man asked.

"Someone just fell out of the window and caught on fire. Maybe two people this time. It was one person the last time. Ladies. All ladies. On fire and jumping out windows. Three, I think."

"Bro, you're drunk," the man said.

Someone else laughed.

Clive shot the couple a glance. A young Black couple, probably newlyweds Clive assumed. He was wrong. Both were wearing shirts with the Greek letters of their fraternity and sorority, and they were there for the annual meeting, but Clive didn't know what fraternities and sororities were, let alone how to read the Greek alphabet.

"Yeah, I'm drunk, but that doesn't make you see people on fire falling out of windows. And I got it on video. Think my drunk ass made that just be on my phone, 'bro'?"

The man shook his head. "I did not like that 'bro,' bro."

His wife shook her head. "Nope. Not even a little bit."

"Nobody will believe me! I'm not a fucking racist."

"Um, that's a thing racists say," the woman said.

"Will you just look? There! Up near the top floor. There's a hole in the wall. That's where they fell out of. And last time it was the window right next to it."

"You're drunk," the man said.

The woman placed her hand on her husband's forearm. She squinted up at the hotel. "There is something there. That window is a different color. And there's a smudge on the wall, or…"

"It's a hole!"

The man stepped next to Clive. "Can your phone zoom in?"

Clive, excited by even this much credence, gasped, "Yeah, yeah! Look!" He put his fingers on the screen and pulled them apart, then took a moment to find the window. "Look! There's someone moving around in there! That's no smudge."

"I don't know," the woman said.

"Maybe?" the man started.

Then both clearly saw a Black woman in a white tee-shirt step in front of the hole, look down, and then duck back into the room.

"Oh shit!" the man shouted.

"I saw her, too!"

"Yep!" Clive said proudly. "Just watch. Bet she falls out and catches on fire."

He looked over to see the couple eying him quizzically. "Seriously! That's where they keep falling out of!"

Clive's phone was zoomed in on the window of falling women, and that's why he missed it when the roof of the casino's north wing exploded.

"You can no more win a war than you can win an earthquake."

-Jeannette Rankin

Chapter 29

"We won't care what these fuckers do once we're gone," Esau said, then shot another of those fuckers. (It happened to be Jonathan, the vampire delegate who had turned Ann. But that's just coincidence.)

"You want that on your tombstone?" Bel asked.

Esau shrugged. "Sounds about right."

Bel heard a voice she recognized, though it was garbled. "Kill them!" She looked back down the aisle. Cassius was rising unsteadily to his feet, his elbow poked out because he was pressing the palm of his hand to the side of his face so he could speak. He still sounded like someone dying of tuberculosis, and Bel guessed bubbles came out of the back of his head when he shouted. The silver was in his system. He'd heal eventually, probably, but he was in no shape to fight. Still, the monsters in his employ and those who wanted to curry favor took his order seriously. Not that they needed much motivation. Many were just excited by the smell of a human in the room. Bel had hoped Esau's presence would distract them from Long so the old man could escape. She looked back over her other shoulder but couldn't find him in the surging crowd of oncoming monsters. So that was lucky.

Esau shot another monster. "That was my last one. Been nice knowing you."

Bel shook her head. "Oh, Lena," she muttered. There was no time to unpack that. She just felt, very purely, her longing for Lena and desire not to leave her behind. "I'm sorry."

She looked at the minotaur who was throwing tables over his head to get to them. The other monsters, mostly vampires and werewolves, had slowed and formed a rough perimeter, and most were shooting glances in the minotaur's direction, some excited to see the creature attack, others leery and wanting to stay out of his way. Then the minotaur looked back over his own shoulder, and Bel heard a sound she'd never come across in almost a thousand years. It started as a surprised moo, then turned into a high pitched scream. She couldn't see what the Minotaur was screaming about until the jaws opened above the huge monster's horns and came down around him, devouring him in a single bite. And then she was looking directly into the eyes of a charging dragon.

Esau wet his pants.

The dragon's head was more human than reptilian, but with an elongated snout. The scales were a dark green, and it had what Bel could only describe as a thin mustache and a long, thin goatee, only made of bright yellow tentacles flowing in some unseen wind. These matched the ones growing above its eyes where a human would have eyebrows, and these matched the ridge of bright yellow tentacles running down the monster's back. The rest of the body, which Bel could see because it zigzagged as the head approached directly towards them, was a lizard's, with those same rough, dark green scales on top and a pale yellow set of flat scales on its belly. Its four pistoning legs each ended in talons six feet high when slammed into the floor, five when they pierced the concrete under the rug and yanked the creature along. It had no wings, but it didn't need them. It rushed up on Bel and Esau so fast, they only had time to crouch and clench and close their eyes. Then it turned sharply to one side and began to flow around them, flinging the last tables in every direction, swatting away any monster daring to come too close, snapping at a few more (though none were quite as unfortunate as the minotaur), and then, when it seemed the dragon's face would slam into its own body, the head lifted into the air, and the whole body followed, swirling above its own back, those enormous legs pinwheeling in air, touching nothing but running nonetheless. The hurricane of scales climbed, a third layer on top of the second, a fourth. Bel grabbed the shoulder of Esau's shirt and pulled him away as the rear left leg entered the circle of dragon flesh, and then she knew what she had to do.

As the dragon's tail thinned, she could see through the space in between the swirling dragon and the floor. She hauled Esau up onto her shoulder like a soldier rescuing a wounded comrade, the manuscript tucked under her other arm, and she ran. Just as the dragon was far enough above the ground for her to slip beneath, she was out and charging for the door. Without setting down Esau, she raised the arm holding the manuscript and tapped the headphone in her ear.

"Fire Team Two here. Or Insertion Team. Whatever. We're on our way to the cars and coming fast. Have those engines ready. Camouflage Team, you on your way?"

Upstairs, Lena stepped back from the hole in the wall. There was a small pile of something below, but nothing distinguishable as Rita or the vampire she'd fought, just a burning puddle. She scanned the room behind her, then unmuted her earpiece. "Yeah, um, just a sec."

"Not a lot of secs. We're in a hurry."

There was some giggling on the coms.

Lena ignored all that. She went to the copy machine. There she found both manuscripts sitting on the loader, pages of the first book disappearing into the machine, copies coming out the other side. "Bel, did you get a copy of the book? The first one?"

"Yep. Safe and sound. You got the second?"

Matt came into the workroom, but Lena turned and shouted, "Not yet! Keep everyone out of here."

"Ouch," Torreblanca said. "Try not to shout into the mics."

"Amen," Nando said.

"Sorry. I've just got to … " Lena trailed off as she flipped through the pages of the manuscripts in the copier. All from the first book. Mildred had divided both books up into piles to copy them, but Ann had left the whole second book together on a counter to start later, so it hadn't been scattered in the fight.

Lucky.

Lena found the second book and hugged it to her stomach. "Okay, Matt, I need to find some way to burn the rest of this."

"I can do that. Fire is pretty easy. Not my specialty, but simple enough."

"Okay. I just need to make sure I get everything from the office, too."

"I'll check the bedroom."

"Okay, but don't read anything."

Matt wanted to joke about how he wouldn't be able to identify the book without reading, but he knew there was no time. He ran into the bedroom, grabbed the comforters and sheets off the two queen beds, and brought them out to the island in the workroom, where he tossed them in a pile.

Lena looked out from the office. "What are you doing?"

"Quick way to make sure nothing is hidden. Don't go through the files. Throw them all on the blankets. Everything can be burned."

"There aren't many printed files." Lena shouted.

"Grab the computer. Let's hope there aren't cloud backups of the book."

Lena pulled Esau's thumb drive out of her jeans pocket and plugged it into Cassius' computer. A single light blinked, then a row of lights ascended quickly, like the little plastic device was sucking the light out of the computer itself. Lena didn't know if it had finished its work, but there was no time to find out. She yanked out the drive, pocketed it, and then grabbed the tower. She pulled it hard enough to unplug it, then lugged the tower into the workroom and dropped it on the pile of sheets and blankets.

Matt came back from the bedroom. "Clean. And I doubt he had time to scan the books. Looks like he was just making hard copies. Probably wouldn't have trusted it to the cloud anyway." He put out a hand and gently pushed her back towards the reception area. She stayed close, watching to see he did it thoroughly. "Here goes," Matt said. He did a little twist of the wrist, and a flame appeared in his hand, not much larger than a candle's flame. Then he spoke some words to it, and it grew. "Step back," he said. "You're going to lose your eyebrows."

Lena didn't move.

Matt shrugged. "Okay." Then he stepped forward and blew hard on the flame in his hand. The gout which shot forward looked more like a large glass of liquid tossed as an insult at a party gone wrong. Only when the glowing orange liquid hit the blankets, it rolled down them like a fog descending mountains, dripping onto the pages on the floor, and then, with a loud Whooomp! it sucked the air from behind them and erupted in flames. Lena did feel the heat singe her hair as she ducked away into the foyer, but she was glad to be certain. She ran out into the hall and found the children had put their clothes back on.

"Where's Teacher Rita?" one of the little girls asked.

"She …" Lena started. "She didn't make it."

"Wait, what?" Tina's voice came through Lena's earpiece.

Matt tried to explain briefly as they shooed the children towards the elevator. "Rita took out the vampire in the office, but, they both …"

"Died?" Juanito said.

"No!" Ericka said, stamping a foot and instantly bursting into tears.

"Lena, give your earpiece to Ericka," Tina said.

"No, we don't have time for this," Torreblanca said. "Get down here."

The group upstairs climbed onto the elevator. "Ericka?" Lena asked.

Ericka nodded.

"Here." She handed her earpiece to the little girl.

"Ericka, this is Tina."

"Tina, the human lady says Rita is …"

"I know, honey. I'm with you, okay. I'm with you. Just come down here fast, okay. We'll get out of here and figure it out when we get together. Okay?"

Ericka nodded and sniffled, handing the earpiece back to Lena who said, "We're good. We're on our way."

Outside, Clive swung his camera to the sound of the explosion. There was no fire, no smoke, but the pieces of the roof launched as though something enormous had burst through. And then, on his zoomed-in camera, he caught sight of something.

"It's ..." Clive muttered.

"What?" the woman asked.

Her husband was flicking his gaze back and forth, looking at the roof, then the drunk white guy's camera. "I don't see anything."

"He's ... flying. It's Superman," Clive said.

The couple shared a glance. "Explosion, yes," the woman said. "I saw that. And a hole in the wall. Yes. Very weird. But I didn't see any flying man or women on fire."

Her husband shook his head. "Me neither."

Clive took a few stumbling steps away from the couple, raising the camera to catch the last glimpse. "I got Superman on video," he muttered. The man flew away behind the hotel, and Clive slowly lowered the camera, staring at it, frowning, as though it might tell him something. "I got Superman on video," he repeated. "I'm going to be fucking rich. And you know what's the weirdest part?"

"What?" the couple chorused.

"I'm pretty sure he was Asian."

The couple looked at one another, and then the man said, "Really? *That* was the weirdest part?"

"I gotta go put this on YouTube!" He took a couple shuffling steps towards Harrod's, broke into a jog, then turned back to the couple and shouted, "Fuck Susan!"

The last stage seemed like cake compared to what had gone before. The groups made their way to the cars in the back while Tina peeled out ahead of them, turned onto Sands Avenue north of the casino, then turned left onto Las Vegas Boulevard, the strip, then left into the valet parking turn-around in front of the hotel. While the groups made their way through the tunnel to the parking garage, Matt sent a glamour of Lena walking back beyond them holding the manuscripts of both books tightly in her arms and scanning the crowds furtively. She moved just fast enough to draw a lot of attention while half-jogging through the gaming floor towards the front entrance.

"Ma'am?" a couple dealers and security guards called after her, then took to their radios.

The monsters were collecting themselves, putting their glamours back on and reentering the hotel. Cassius and his employees monitored the security channels. "That's her," Cassius shouted. "Get her!"

The vampires, because they didn't need glamours, were first out of the chaos of the convention floor. They ran at top speed after "Lena." They'd slow to a human walking pace when rounding a corner, seeming to appear, walk casually, and then disappear again on the security cameras. All of this would be a nightmare for CimBim, Cassius knew, but this had to be handled first. They'd deal with the humans later. But he couldn't leave the main convention hall with half his face missing. He'd have to trust his soldiers.

"She's got to be one of us, Boss," a voice told him. "She moves faster than we do."

"They must have turned her. Get some people up to the office now. Find out what is going on up there. No one is responding. The rest of you, get to the front exit, now."

He paced until he heard another voice on the walkie. "Sorry, Boss. Just when we got to the front, she was jumping into a Ferrari."

"Get after it. Motorcycles. Vans. Everything. Get that Ferrari!"

A new voice: "Sir, the office is on fire. Torched. Total loss."

"Fuck!"

So, while all of Cassius' operatives chased Tina's Ferrari through the suburbs, the rest of the surviving crew got into the cars waiting in the garage and headed back to the rendezvous point at the airport.

They had the books, but they did not celebrate. Missing Rita, Long, and Josef, the thieves traveled in silence.

"Stab the body and it heals, but injure the heart and the wound lasts a lifetime."

-Mineko Iwasaki

Chapter 30

They milled about in the hangar while the sun set and the flight crews prepped two planes, one for the monsters returning to Camp Bigfoot, the other for Esau's troops heading to a destination he would not disclose. Nando, Lucia, and the parents did their best to console the children while they waited. Lena and Bel sat in fold out chairs, holding hands, grateful to be reunited and trying not to show off their joy in front of so much sadness.

"So, Long was a dragon?" Lena asked Matt.

"Still is, I'm sure. He's probably halfway back to the

Himalayas by now. Or maybe he wanted to visit the Andes. Where does a three hundred foot long dragon go for fun?"

"Wherever he wants," both women intoned.

Matt nodded.

Bel squeezed Lena's hand and nodded towards Nando and Lucia. "They seem okay."

"We got the books back. She didn't know. No harm, no foul, I guess. She'll blame herself for Rita, though."

They were not, in fact, okay.

Nando looked towards Lena and Bel's direction. Lucia looked at the ground.

"Fuck," Lena said.

"They can hear everything," Bel said.

"Dammit."

"Oh, quit your moping, everybody!" a loud voice called from the far end of the hangar. "And somebody get this old bitch some human clothes."

"It's Rita!" Ericka shouted.

"And Tina!" Juanito echoed.

All the children ran to the dark end of the hangar and came back into the dim light surrounding two women, one young and dressed and half carrying an older, limping, naked woman.

"My God, how did you survive the fall?" Lena asked. "I looked for you and didn't even see you down there."

"I limped off right after I landed. Instinct." She looked at the children. "You don't just lie there out in the open when you're injured, do you children?"

"Nope. Find a safe place to heal," Juanito said.

Ericka wrinkled her nose. "You found a stinky place."

Rita shrugged. "Storm drain. But near Trump Casino. They have sewage problems there due to shoddy construction. Place always smells like shit. Easy to find when your eyeballs are half burned out, and it hides the smell of burnt fur pretty well." She looked at Matt. "Is there a bathroom in here where I can clean up before you all have to ride with me on an airplane?" She looked at Ericka. "I am stinky, aren't I?"

"But I love you, Stinky!" Ericka said and threw her arms around her teacher's waist once again. Juanito took this as permission to do the same, his face pressed into Rita's lower back.

Tina pulled Rita towards her with a strong one-armed hug and bounced her there a few times. "I guess I love you too, Stinky."

"Thank you for finding me, Tina. It would have been a long run home from here."

"You would have made it. You're annoyingly indestructible."

"Did you find her in the Ferrari?" Lena asked.

"No, I had to dump the Ferrari on the side of the road in the desert to lose the vamps. Wolfed out and ran back, but I had to pass through the city anyway, so I thought I'd take a sniff around and see if I could find her." She looked at Ericka. "Not because I wanted to. Because I promised you I would. Got it?"

Ericka nodded dramatically. "Got it. Thanks, dingleberry butt."

Everyone laughed, including Tina. Juanito whispered, "Butt."

Matt left to confer with the crew outside. A moment

later, the sound of one of the two planes' engines started.

"So what's the plan now?" Tina asked Nando.

"Home. Then pack. Then move. If Cassius can find us and Esau can find us, we're too easy to find. And we aren't ready to fight off the whole Convention if we're harboring fugitives."

"None of you broke The Convention," Bel said. "Just me and, well, I guess Long ate a minotaur. That's pretty cut and dry."

"I killed the vampire in the office," Rita said. "She's super-dead."

Bel said, "I'll bet no one can prove that. Or would even want to. As long as I'm not at Camp Bigfoot, and as long as they know I'm not there, I think you all should be fine."

Nando and Lucia shared a crestfallen glance, then nodded.

"Don't worry about it. It was time for me to head out anyway. I want to show Lena a lot more of the world. And I'll call and email and stuff. If they tap the lines, the more I'm in touch, the safer you all will be."

Lucia nodded. "We'll miss you both. Where will you go?"

Bel raised an eyebrow at Lena. "Ever been to Cambodia? Want to see Angkor Wat? Or Egypt? See the pyramids?"

"Okay, those sound good," Lena said. "Not too sunny for you?"

"I'll be fine. They're both more comfortable to tour at night, anyway. Hot countries. Maybe Matt can take us right away, once we get these folx home and say our goodbyes."

On cue, Matt came back into the hangar. He clapped his hands. "So, who gets the first jet?"

Esau stood slowly. "That would be us. But we have two more items on the checklist before we go." Without raising his hand, he snapped his fingers. His soldiers pointed their weapons at preselected targets. Red dots appeared on each of the children.

"I don't like killing kids," he said. "But I'm more comfortable killing monster kids than you are losing them. So here's what I need. Lena, you walk over here really slowly and bring me both those books. They are safer with me than with a bunch of monsters, and you know it."

"What are you going to do with them?"

"The human one I'll burn. The monster one I'll deploy. I'm a monster hunter. I kill monsters. And you have the ultimate monster killing weapon right there. How did you think this was going to end? It's us or them. They're monsters. I know you love some of them, but they're still monsters."

Lena hadn't moved. "So, you're taking the books. Those are your two items?"

"No, I didn't come for the books in the first place." Esau held the hand he'd used to snap his fingers at his side.

Lena noticed those fingers rubbing against one another now nervously. Esau was not normally a nervous man. She started to rise from her chair. "Wait. I'll give you the books."

A lot of people moved at once. Matt stepped between

her and Esau. "No, you can't do that, Lena."

Bel was on her feet, an arm barring Lena's way. "He's right."

The parents, Nando, Lucia, and Tina inched between the soldiers and the children.

"Halt!" Esau bellowed. "Stop right there. Freeze. Don't make us open fire on all of you. I said I didn't want to kill the kids, but I will. And anyone in the way. You might get some of us before we get all of you, but we will get all of you. It doesn't have to go that way, though. The books. And Matt. Now."

Matt turned towards Esau and started towards him. "You can have me, Esau, but let them go."

"That's what I said. So stop right there."

But Matt didn't stop. "Esau, I'm sorry, but you have to let this go. I know I hurt you. I'm prepared to own the consequences, whatever they may be-"

"Whatever they may be?" Esau shouted. "Whatever they may ..." His voice cracked. He pulled out his reloaded Ruger. "You have no idea. You made me this. Every monster I've killed, you want to own those? Fuck you, Matt. You don't get to own the consequences anymore. You missed that boat. Now you just get vengeance."

"Wait," Matt said, not shouting but in a calming, warm tone with a tinge of panic hidden underneath.

Esau pulled the trigger.

The bullet passed through the illusion of Matt.

The bullet passed through the manuscripts of both books.

The bullet lodged in Lena's chest.

"I'm not sure, I understand only a little, I can hardly see, / but it seems to me that its singing has the color of damp violets, / of violets that are at home in the earth, / because the face of death is green, / and the look death gives is green, / with the penetrating dampness of a violet leaf / and the somber color of embittered winter."

-Pablo Neruda
"Nothing But Death"
(Translated by Robert Bly)

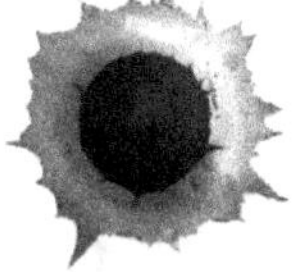

Chapter 31

Lena looked down at the books she'd held pressed against her chest. There really were sooty singe marks around the hole though the first page, but no smoke like in the movies. Her blood stained the last pages, and some had squirted through the hole onto the other side. She briefly considered turning it around in her arms to examine the front. It would look dramatic, she thought. But then she was struck by a wave of lightheadedness. She sat heavily, unaware she was doing so, unaware Bel caught her inches before her backside struck the cement floor, unaware of Bel at all. Instead, her brainstem screamed, "You are dying!" But her prefrontal cortex decided not to flood her brain with adrenaline because it was oddly comfortable with the outcome. She'd been thinking about this for years, and though she wasn't completely prepared, she was perhaps the most prepared person on the planet. She wasn't suicidal. She'd decided to live a year ago when she'd come to understand the metaphysical implications of this moment. She'd known what this meant. And she kept living. She didn't regret that now. She didn't think about it.

She thought about her work. Though her right arm was losing sensation fast and flopped down to her side, her left clung to the books. She pulled them back to her chest again. They were heavy, but once her arm locked them in place, she couldn't feel the weight. The weight of paper and words. Did any of them matter now? Could it be she'd committed her life to writing fiction to ward off this moment, because fiction was the place where death can be set aside? Was the essence of being human learning to love stories, listen to stories, tell stories not just as a mechanism to share lessons, but to satisfy a deeper urge to enter worlds where people could die and come back, or where their stories would connect to others so those lives had meaning? Because Lena understood the finality of the moment. The bullet had passed through the center of her sternum, and she had no doubt it had punctured her heart. She could feel a great deal of pain, but it seemed to be somewhere else, a brightly lit billboard on the side of the highway advertising her approaching end, but receding over the horizon in the rearview mirror. She didn't need the pain to tell her. It blazed, but she ignored it. And was she breathing? She moved her mouth like a beached fish, but she wasn't sure if any air passed through her throat.

Instead of her own life flashing before her eyes, she thought of the stories where characters died and came back. Even this didn't feel important, just a comforting reminder she could call them up, like patting her pocket and knowing the grocery list was there as she walked into the store. Most were heroes. Theseus. Heracles. Odysseus. Aeneas. She'd always felt a kinship with Orpheus because he was a bard. And Psyche because she was the only woman on the list. But she was a demi-god, so if Lena counted her, she was halfway to counting Persephone, so maybe two women. Oh, and Ishtar. And Lemminkäinen's mother. Still, mostly a male journey. Hunahpu and Ixbalanque did it. Gilgamesh did it. Thor went for Baldur but came back empty handed. Izanagi went for his wife Izanami but ran back screaming once he saw what she looked like. Jesus, of course, came back. And Lazarus. Odin was nailed to a tree. Did he die, officially? she wondered. She couldn't remember. Lena patted this list of names. But she also patted the flash drive in her pocket. She wanted Bel to know it was there, but she couldn't remember why.

Bel saw the fingertips of Lena's right hand tapping her thigh and could only wonder if it meant something. Not enough for code. Just three little taps. All of this had happened in seconds, but Bel could take in more, notice more. Her thoughts didn't move much faster than a human's, but her eyes could. She'd trained her brain to notice her environment more quickly than humans so she could get her superhuman limbs where she wanted them as quickly as possible, and now her hyper-sensitivity mocked her, recording every detail. The wide eyes of the rest of the group. Esau lowering the pistol. She hadn't bothered to wait and see if the battle was over. He could have shot her. She wouldn't have cared. She'd caught Lena, fallen to her knees, and now cradled her as best she could. And she watched. It was all she could do.

Lena let the list go. The heroes come back, but only in stories. All her life, she'd needed the company of fictional characters, but now she thought about the non-fiction section. She saw her mother's face, but not as it looked when she'd last seen her a few years ago. Instead she saw her laughing at a Christmas dinner when Lena had been six. Laughing at one of Lena's jokes. Yes. She'd made her mother laugh. And then her father, also younger, at that same table, smiling at his wife's loud guffaw. She'd made him proud, too. And her brother's smile. And Abuelita's. She'd been alive at that dinner. And there was someone else. Someone who was also not alive but important now. Who?

Lena finally noticed Bel. Lena was human, and while humans wish they can live inside the present of love, they simply can't. Love makes humans think about the future and the past. Love stretches through time into imagination. In that way, love betrayed Lena. She didn't want to think about the scant time she'd had with Bel in the past, and she didn't want to imagine Bel's pain tomorrow and tomorrow and tomorrow. Lena knew the future was a world she couldn't visit, let alone reside in, and she knew, more deeply than any human, it should not matter. Things would happen there, and none of those events belonged to her. She would be irrelevant in that place. She shouldn't care. But love made her care despite what she'd written in her first book. Love made her worry about a world which should not have been able to hurt her. She wanted to tell Bel not to mourn. She wanted to tell her she had made peace with her death a year ago, had sought Bel out without hope, and was grateful for the time. She wanted to say Bel shouldn't mourn, or Bel could mourn if she felt like it, but it wouldn't matter to Lena so she had no expectations, no demands, no fear. She wasn't sure this was entirely true. There was no time to contemplate her new ambivalence. A dark ring of storm cloud wrapped

437

around the edges of her vision. No time. She had to say something. Words. She was a writer. She needed last words. Maybe she was at peace with all of this, and maybe not, but she had to tell Bel something quickly. Yes, maybe she was at peace.

She managed to whisper, "Maybe–"

And then she was gone.

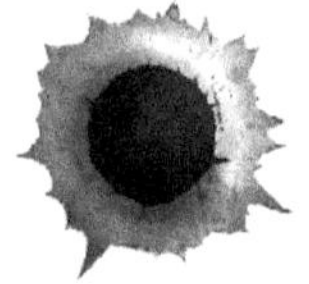

Chapter 32

"Get out," Bel ordered. "Everyone."

"Oh shit," Torreblanca said.

"I didn't mean for that to happen, but I still have two items on my list, so-"

Bel looked up at Esau and silenced him with her eyes.

Torreblanca grabbed the shoulder of Esau's shirt and hauled him backwards. "We've got to go, sir. Right fucking now." Then she called out to her men in an authoritative voice, "Everyone, back towards the door. No one fires a shot unless attacked. We're leaving." She looked at Bel. "We're leaving, okay?" There was a flint in her voice, and also an apology, and also a plea. "We're leaving."

Bel looked back down at Lena's face, and that was permission enough.

"But-?" Esau tried. His voice now sounded uncertain, even frail.

"Shut the fuck up, sir," Torreblanca hissed. "Live to fight another day."

He acquiesced, turning his back on his murder victim and her found family, slinking away with his own, into the plane Matt had left running outside.

Nando stepped forward and placed a hand on Bel's shoulder. "You don't have to ..."

She placed her hand on his and squeezed. "I do. Go. Take everyone and go now."

Nando wanted to ask if she would be okay, or if there was anything he could do, or where she would go, or when he would see her next, and every question seemed stupid and insensitive and wrong. So he took Lucia's offered hand and waved the others to follow him. He held them at the hangar door until he saw the last soldier get on the first jet, and then he led his group to the next one.

Matt wasn't on either plane, at least as far as anyone could tell. His assistant, Meili, was also gone. The werewolves' plane had two pilots on board, and Esau's plane had two of his own men in the cockpit. The pilots conferred quietly. Nando's plane took off for Camp Bigfoot. Esau's left immediately afterwards, headed in a different direction.

When Bel couldn't hear either plane's engines anymore, she picked up Lena's body like she was a sleeping toddler, loaded her corpse carefully into the back of the SUV, and drove away.

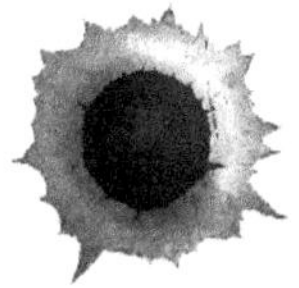

Chapter 33

When Lena regained consciousness, even before she opened her eyes, she placed her hand on her sternum and pressed her fingers against the space where the hole had been. Solid as a rock. But no book. She patted her stomach. The books were gone.

"They're safe," a voice said. "They're right here."

A low tapping. A bass drum made by soft fingertips on a stack of two reams of paper.

Lena opened her eyes and lifted her head. She was in a hotel room. It was dark. Very dark. Nighttime and all the lights off and the shades drawn. But she could see perfectly clearly. She could hear the sounds of traffic in the distance, but nearer, the neighbors in the next room, both snoring softly, and further, at the hotel's main desk, a man sat with his feet up. He was reading something. She could hear the sound of his fingers on the glossy paper. A magazine. She could hear the sound of the rubber of his shoes against the countertop. He stuck a finger in his ear and twisted. She could hear the sound. Beneath the distant road noise, the sounds of thousands of insects, somewhere a police siren, a stoplight clicking as it cycled, but underneath, the squeaking of the finger grinding earwax like a pestle in a mortar.

And closer, she could hear Bel. So silent, her heart barely beating.

And another heart beating, right there in the room, right next to her. She could feel the warmth of the man's arm even though they weren't touching. She could smell his cologne, his sweat infused with alcohol, the salt of tears. That smell came from both Bel and the man. Bel's tears were fresh. The man's were crusty and old. Like the scabs. He'd bled recently. She could smell that more strongly than anything. Pennies and cotton candy and heroin.

"What have you done?" Lena asked the ceiling.

"What I had to do."

And then a new sensation more shocking than the incredible barrage of sounds or the clarity of her vision in the darkness. She'd been hungry before. She'd been sexually aroused. She'd been jealous. But she'd never known a wanting like this, all three combined, and all so easily satisfied. Right there. The man was right there. His blood pumped through his veins, and she could feel it.

"I can't," Lena said.

"You have to."

"He's a human being."

"He was a very bad man," Bel said. "A child rapist. I found him trying to upload child porn on the internet. I posed as a kid, and he came here." She kept her story short because she knew Lena would learn to smell a lie. This story was half true. The man had been uploading something. She'd posed as someone else. He'd come to the hotel. He'd been trying to upload the videos of Mildred falling out the window of the Venetian and Long flying through the roof. Not child porn, but far worse according to CimBim. YouTube kept rejecting the videos and informing CimBim about his attempts. They'd put out their APB. Bel had some good graces to get back into. She'd posed as a reporter who would believe his story and give him a lot of money. He showed up at the door, she let him in, and then she fed. But she restrained herself. She only drank enough to heal herself from the loss of the blood she'd given Lena as part of the ritual. It had been enough to knock Clive out, too. And then she waited. For two days, she'd waited. And now, after the second sunset, it was time.

"You may hate me for a while," Bel said. "You may hate me forever. But please, if you don't want to have to kill more humans tonight, please don't scream. The lives of the other three depend on you staying quiet."

Lena knew who she meant. The two people next door. The man at the front counter.

"I don't want to kill anyone," she said.

"I know. You think you're still one of them. It takes a while. But you need to eat. So start with him."

Lena rolled onto her side and looked at the sleeping man's face. She could see it as clearly as if all the lights were on, even more clearly, down to the last follicle of stubble on his jaw and neck. "What is his name?" she asked the darkness.

"He doesn't have a name."

"Everyone has a name."

"Not for you. Not anymore. It's harder when you name your food."

Lena sobbed once. Her next words came out in a moan. "I don't want to be this, Bel."

"I know. But you can only feel disgust with what you are because you still exist. And I need you to still exist. I'm sorry."

Lena felt like she was gagging, but it wasn't the tears. Her other teeth were pushing forward, moving on their own. She tried to retract them, to swallow them back into herself, like a rising gorge, and she failed. Her lower jaw swiveled on its hinges, like she was chewing. Then something came unstuck. The bone of her jaw itself changed shape, stretching and widening like a pelvis during pregnancy, but much faster. And the teeth, the new teeth, her real teeth, pushed forward and arced out, then back in, numbered like a shark's, shaped like the teeth of a viperfish. She hated them. Even without seeing them, she could feel them, and they repulsed her. So she hid them from herself in the quickest, most effective way she could; she sank them into Clive's neck and mashed them down and down and down until she could pretend they didn't exist, and everything in the universe was the perfect taste of blood and forgetting.

Clive didn't scream, didn't kick or punch or flail. He moaned though, and the sound was not one of pleasure, more a mixture of a response to being rudely awakened followed by despondent acceptance. Lena wanted to believe it meant he felt some acquiescence, but she knew it could just as easily have been the unconscious exhalation of wind over vocal cords as he lost the energy to continue his first feeble gasp. He was losing blood faster than a gunshot or a severed limb, not just bleeding out but being sucked dry. His heart couldn't get enough blood to his brain. His brain couldn't tell his heart what to do about it.

When his heart stopped, it felt like getting a piece of strawberry stuck in the end of the straw in a milkshake. The liquid just would not move anymore. She pulled away from the man's body. Her teeth retracted, her jaw reverting to its original shape. She rubbed a rough palm across her chin, expecting to find lots of gore to wipe off. To her surprise, it was mostly clean and dry; she'd contained it all with her lips. She licked them. The taste was still there.

She stared at the man. Despite the darkness, she could take in every new detail of death; his pallid skin, now waxy, his chest unmoving, the smell of his last breath and last fart. Luckily, he hadn't wet himself or voided his bowels. She didn't know if that might still occur. Everything about him disgusted her now. "You said he was a bad person? A child rapist?"

"Don't think about him, " Bel whispered. "He was a meal. Now he's the leavings, and we'll need to clean those up. That's all."

Lena was self-aware enough to evaluate her own feelings. She could distinguish guilt from this distaste. She understood this revulsion served an evolutionary purpose, if evolution applied to their kind. At least a survival function. They hated dead bodies because they could not feed off them anymore. Human death, to them, was the end, not in a great existential sense, but in the most immediate way possible, sustenance no longer available, food denied. And the blood had become so important to her.

Lena also knew when she was manipulating herself. She could tell she was favoring this cold, materialist understanding because she preferred it to the guilt of a moralistic framework. She remembered she had speculated blood might be like a drug to Bel, producing euphoria and then horrific withdrawal when unavailable. Now she could see that theory was part of her own attempt to shove Bel into her own human moral framework, like pushing a cat into a carrier to the vet. The cat might fit, might end up inside the box, but it would let the owner know it didn't belong there, and the owner would have to keep telling herself it was for the cat's own good, that she was being a responsible pet owner, that the cat would appreciate it if only she understood. Lena had tried to believe the blood was Bel's cocaine or heroin because it would mean Bel was a victim along with the people she killed, a sufferer of the disease of addiction, and Lena was the great, suffering girlfriend loving her in spite of her illness. Lena had liked the story, and now she had to mourn its loss.

The meal did not produce some ridiculous, blinding pleasure. It was not orgasmic. It was a meal. Delicious and satisfying like pasta. The hunger before she'd fed had been this inhuman rage to kill and suck and devour, but the meal itself was a merely pleasant end to the screeching need.

She did feel the healing, though. It was a glow radiating from within, soft and thrumming. Gentle tickles rippled across her skin, mending tiny abrasions and dry patches she'd been unaware of even with her heightened senses. She could feel it tingling along her scalp, down her spine, spiraling around her thighs, playing at her calves and ankles and all the way to the dead skin between her toes. Everything was healthier and stronger and just ... right.

She rolled away from the corpse and stood. She couldn't judge accurately yet, but she suspected she'd moved more quickly than a human should, certainly more quickly than she'd ever sprung up from a bed before, not like a chipper morning waking, more like a panicked springing to vertical, yet she felt no desire to move quickly and hadn't consciously decided to do so.

"It will all take some getting used to," Bel said. "A

period of learning. Training. But you have time now. All the time you need."

Lena's glare was diamonds. "I didn't want more time, Bel."

Bel dropped her head, and Lena read this as guilt, but then Bel whispered, "You didn't want more time with me?"

"No, that's not what I meant. I just … I had decided to live one human life. It took a lot to get there, Bel. I faced my mortality in a way most people can't. And I decided to live. But not forever, Bel. A lifetime. I'd accepted a lifetime."

"You didn't get a full human lifetime," Bel said.

"I did. It was a short one, but some lives are shorter than others. A lot are much shorter than mine was. This … " She opened her mouth and fanned at her face with one hand like she'd eaten something too spicy, waving at the hidden teeth. "This is not an extended human life. This is a different life. I didn't ask for this."

"You didn't ask to die, either. A lot of choices have been made for you, Lena. And I'm sorry about that. Sorry to participate in it. But I hope, someday, you'll come to see this time a choice was made for you by someone who loves you and wants more of you, and that's still selfish on my part, I know. But maybe, maybe you'll decide it was better coming from love than from malice or disdain, even if it was wrong of me."

"Your good intentions?" Lena said with scorn.

"No, I mean … Yes, but … I know my intentions will never be a justification. I just hope someday you'll think of them as a factor when deciding whether or not to forgive me."

Lena raised an eyebrow. "So, while I'm still in the middle of realizing the consequences of your selfishness, your first concern is whether or not you will be forgiven?"

Bel opened her mouth, inhaled before her response like a goldfish on the counter seeking water to breathe, then chose to surrender. We often betray ourselves by being ourselves, and, when we do, we're lucky if we see the true cause of our failure, even when we see it last.

They sat in inhuman silence, picking out the sounds, sights, smells, and even the descending temperatures of one another's miseries from the distracting, oppressive barrage of tiny, distant inputs.

Then both women started at the impossible sounds of six feet pressing down the shag carpet and flexing the floorboards in the hallway just outside the motel room door with three very different pairs of shoes. The sounds were jarring because they hadn't approached from anywhere. Both Bel and Lena would have heard them coming from a thousand feet away. Instead, these feet simply appeared.

Knuckles rapped on the door.

Lena and Bel shared a quick glance to check whether the other understood, and each found the other's confusion. Bel stepped between Lena and the door, unlocked it, and pulled it open a few inches.

The Weird Sisters McElroy, the three women they'd met briefly in Edinburgh a year before, stood shoulder to shoulder in the hall.

"We need to talk," the eldest said. Justinia was hunched over and looked impatient with the entire situation. And that situation might have included everything.

"Sorry about our timing, but it's important," Taravissa, the middle-est, said.

Bel pulled the door wide and let the three women enter.

The youngest, Garifinia, gave Lena an elevator glance, then looked at Clive's corpse on the bed. Then she looked at Bel. "You turned her into a vampire. Well, that was super-predictable."

Taravissa shrugged. "Everything is super-predictable to us, so maybe they didn't see this coming."

Garifinia rolled her eyes, then frowned at Lena. "You should have seen it coming. She'd never let you just die."

"Well, that's a good thing," Justinia said, "because we have a warning for you. Some really bad shit is on the way. World ending shit. And you need to get ready. You have less than a year."

"Is it the books again?" Lena asked.

"No, this end-of-the-world isn't your fault for a change," Taravissa said, "So good on you."

Lena accepted that with aplomb. "Okay, what is it this time?"

Garifinia started to speak, stopped, frowned, considered, and then explained. "Well, it starts out gross, and then it gets buck-wild, and then it just gets shitty."

Justinia walked further into the room, sat down on the

bed next to the corpse, and patted the spot next to her. "Come sit down with me and Clive here, and we'll explain."

"Clive?" Lena asked.

"Yep. Your first victim was named Clive," Taravissa said.

"He was a very bad man. A child rapist," Lena said.

"Really?" Garifinia drew the word out.

"Isn't that true? He was, wasn't he?"" Lena asked Bel.

Justinia looked bored. "Sure he was. Whatever. Unimportant." With one hand, she shoved Clive's body off the bed. It bumped against the wall and landed in the gap between the wall and the bed, the thuds like a couple overlapping beats on a double bass drum. "Deal with that later. Come. Sit. We need to explain what you have to do. Then you won't be able to say you weren't warned."

"Okay?" Lena shot Bel an angry look while moving to the bed, and then she sat down next to the old woman.

Garifinia sing-songed, "I told you it would be gro-oss."

Taravisia shushed her.

Justinia took Lena's hand. "First, you are going to need to get your friend Josef back."

"Josef is still alive?" Lena shouted.

Justinia shrugged. "Eh. It's a golem. Define 'alive.' Are you alive?"

"I guess I don't really know," Lena admitted. She looked over at Bel. "Are we, technically-"

Justinia squeezed her hand. "Neither here nor there,

dear. Who cares? You'll have to find your golem. Won't be easy. But that won't be the hardest part. Next, you'll need some clues from Cassius's hard drive."

Bel looked at Lena. "I thought you torched his office."

"We did. But Esau convinced me to copy his computer's hard drive onto a flash drive. As I was dying, I tried to point to the flash drive in my pocket." She pulled the little piece of plastic out and held it up.

"You'll need that to find the luck dragon."

"Long will help us again?" Bel asked.

Garifinia squinched her face, then said. "That's complicated-"

"And you're pronouncing his name incorrectly," Taravissa said.

Justinia silenced her sisters with a waggle of her hand. Then she placed her hand on Lena's wrist. "Now, tell me..." Then Justinia paused for so long, Lena worried she'd fallen asleep mid-sentence.

"Yes?"

"What do you know about mermaids?"

"Unfortunately, the sort of individual who is programmed to ignore personal distress and keep pushing for the top is frequently programmed to disregard signs of grave and imminent danger as well."

-Jon Krakauer
Into Thin Air

Chapter 34

Tisina, Queen of the Sirens, Lord over all the Merfolk, Rider of the Leviathan, Ruler of the Depths and Heights of the Sea, famous for her reticence to speak, had no reservations about screaming during childbirth. Her cries echoed through the palace and out into the depths of the merfolk's capital city in the middle of the Pacific. Outside the city, a large school of approaching sardines heard the screams and executed, in unison, the aquatic maneuver best termed a "Nope," their silver sides flashing as they all darted away together. Even further off, three different submarines picked up the sound and recorded the anomaly but couldn't triangulate the location because one was American, another Chinese, and the third Russian. But the sailors on each noted the sound resembled a human woman screaming. The screams did sound remarkably similar, though far louder, partly because of the way the water carried them, partly because Tisina was not human, and partly because she was delivering twins.

In Tisina's bedchamber, Devochka, her favorite maidservant, watched in horror as the queen writhed above the bed. Tisina's tentacles, usually hidden under her flowing jellyfish "skirt," were now wrapped around the two posts at the bed's foot, and Tisina's hands gripped the posts at the head of the bed, stretching her out like a torture victim on a rack, except the queen's back floated three feet above the bed's surface, like she was being quartered by four straining horses. Her face was slack, perfectly serene, but her real mouth, the one normally hidden just under her ribcage, now opened surface-ward with every contraction, and the deafening screams projected from that inhuman maw towards the vaulted ceiling above.

"Your Highness, something is wrong," Devochka said, almost shouting against the volume of the screams. "It's the two plants. Using both. Shall I call a doctor? All the doctors?"

"Do ... no ... such ... thing," Tisina said with the mouth on her face, and now that she'd opened the aperture, she took gulping gillfulls of water between each word. Then she suddenly looked sideways at

Devochka and strung together an uninterrupted sentence. "I don't trust anyone."

The mermaid maidservant chose to be flattered by her unique permission to be in the room, despite Tisina's carefully selected words.

Deceiving one's self is often the worst betrayal.

The first birth was anticlimactic. The top of the head crowned. Tisina screamed with her larger mouth once again. The purple, blue, and green gorgon tentacles on her head writhed, some wrapping around her wrists, others gripping the bedposts on the head side. Two of her thicker, lower tentacles reached inside the jellyfish bell and gently but firmly gripped the head as it came out. Then the agony of the shoulders produced another, brief scream, and then the baby was free. The lower tentacles cradled the merbaby and held it up over Tisina as she presented her son to herself.

He had black hair, already long enough to wave slightly in the agitated water. His skin was a shiny, dark bronze above the waist, his tail scales the same purple, blue, and green of his mother's hair, but as reflective as metal. He began to wail as the tentacles lowered him to Tisina's chest, but once he was placed against her flesh, he calmed. His eyes, black upon black, opened and took in the dim light of the depths for the first time, finding the queen's face, and then they closed as he nestled against her neck. The tentacles of her head relaxed from their grip on the bedposts and around her arms, snaking down to caress her perfect child's head, his back, his face, his long tail. Yes, Tisina thought, this elder brother was the perfect ruler she'd been promised, her heir who would rule once the other had destroyed the world of the surface dwellers once and for all. She had outsmarted magic itself. The merfolk would finally defeat the humans (and all the other members of The Convention), and then this beautiful child would be the king of a perfect world.

As she smiled at this vision of the culmination of all her plans, the next wave of pain struck her. Her larger mouth roared, shaking her body so much, her baby was tossed slightly above her, like a trampolinist who rises to the apex of the jump and then floats there, but he only rose a few inches, then floated there in front of her face. She tried to catch him with some of the gorgon tentacles on her head, but then the next contraction hit, and the whole sea was pain.

Devochka watched as all the queen's tentacles strained, twisting around one another, barely holding onto the bedposts with her straining hands and a few strong exceptions beneath her bell. And then it was Devochka's turn to scream. Because something different was coming out of the jellyfish skirt now. It wasn't a merbaby at all. It was purple like some of its mother's hair, not shiny like its brother's tail, mottled and pitted like coral. It was shaped like the claw of a lobster or crab, but Devochka could see, when it opened, a pink mouth hid within, ringed with dull, uneven, grinding teeth. The claw was attached to a segmented, shelled arm far too long for any crustacean. Eyeless, the claw clicked, tasting the water for direction, and then it swung back towards its mother, the segments of the arm curling like a scorpion's tail. When it arced fully, it aimed toward her chest, the same place Tisina had placed its brother so lovingly. It followed that path, opening and closing with audible clicks.

It hesitated in front of Tisina's face, then rose away from her slightly.

It found the floating body of its brother. With a jolt, the claw lunged forward, gripping the baby around the waist.

And then it clipped him in half.

Devochka screamed again, and this time she couldn't stop. The rent pieces of the prince floated apart, but the claw snapped at each, the mouth inside consuming flesh while the claw cut away pieces like scissors.

Tisina did not scream. She watched this horror without expression. If she could have moved more, she might have managed a shrug. "So, it will only be destruction, then," she said aloud.

A second claw, this one blue, came out of her bell. Then a third, green one. Then a fourth. Then a fifth.

Devochka kept screaming.

The first claw, finished with the meatier parts of its brother, let the bones and shiny tail skin float away. It clicked towards Tisina's face, tasting. The new claws sounded like castanets as they approached the tentacles holding the posts at the foot of the bed. Tisina tensed, her tentacles bunching with one last exertion as she prepared for the claws to lunge.

But the second child recognized something about its mother which stopped it. And then all the claws, now 17, swung on their segmented arms, and pointed at the mermaid beyond the foot of the bed, still screaming.

New appendages came out from Tisina's bell. In addition to the claws, which continued to appear, tentacles curled out, gripping its mother's. They were thinner than Tisina's mighty but exhausted ones, barely holding her in place above her bed. She couldn't enjoy the tickle of her second child's limbs coiling around her numb ones. She barely had the energy to look down the length of her body and watch as they made their way to the bedposts at the foot of the bed. And then her second baby grabbed those posts, and she felt one final searing pain as it pulled itself free.

Devochka, through her hyperventilating screams, still managed to look around for some exit, then seek out the creature's face among the tentacles and segmented arms. But there wasn't any. It held itself above its mother, swinging slowly between only two posts. Though they were thinner, its tentacles were much longer than Tisina's, like tubeworms, but covered in veins and nodules. At first, most of these pointed out in every direction, like a spiny urchin surrounded by lobster claws, but Tisina could feel the motions in the posts as it began to swing its bulk back and forth in Devochka's direction.

"I'm sorry," Tisina said, but the words were mere social obligation with no underpinning emotion. They sounded as exhausted as their speaker.

When Devochka heard Tisina, she knew it was her last chance. Her red hair ballooned and flashed as she made a giant kick with her powerful tail and launched herself towards the bedroom door.

The creature whipped all its tentacles back and pulled itself between the posts, launching all its claws in the mermaid's direction.

She made it to the door but had to stop to turn the knob. The guards in the hallway saw the door open and a lock of red hair float in their direction. But the hair was not attached to Devochka when it fell to the floor. Confused, they looked into the room, and then both were yanked inside. Their shrieks drew more guards.

Tisina watched in silence as her child devoured Devochka and four guards in the doorway. As it fed, she could see it swell, additional claws appearing from the center of the roiling mass, new tentacles grabbing limbs as they floated apart. As the many mouths yanked the soft flesh out of armor once the mermen had been dismembered, the first claws doubled in size. Once the bodies were picked clean, the creature pulled itself through the door and down the hall.

Tisina didn't need to say anything. Silence is what allows the worst horrors to grow.

To Be Continued

About the Author

Benjamin Gorman is an award-winning former high school English teacher, political activist, author, poet, publisher at Not a Pipe Publishing, and host of the *Writers Not Writing* YouTube show/podcast. He is now an author-in-exile living in  Barcelona, Spain with his favorite wife, bibliophile and guillotine aficionado Chrys, his favorite daughter Franke, their small dogs Merry and Pippin, and their dire wolf Havoc. He is proud to be the father of his favorite son, Noah.